Dan Koboldt

SILVER QUEENDOM

ANGRY
ROBOT

ANGRY ROBOT
An imprint of Watkins Media Ltd

Unit 11, Shepperton House
89 Shepperton Road
London N1 3DF
UK

angryrobotbooks.com
twitter.com/angryrobotbooks
Everyday they're hustling...

An Angry Robot paperback original, 2022

Cover by Alice Coleman
Edited by Paul Simpson and Travis Tynan
Map by Dan Koboldt
Set in Meridien

ISBN 978 0 85766 994 0
Ebook ISBN 978 0 85766 997 1

Printed and bound in the United Kingdom by TJ Books Ltd.

9 8 7 6 5 4 3 2 1

To Christina

THYROS

VLASK
(The Jewel Empire)

RETHALTA

Chillston

Eskirk

Caron

Fairhurst

Brycewold

TAL OREA

GANAR

The
Scatters

CHAPTER ONE
Uninvited Guests

Darin Fields never got invited to elegant affairs, but that didn't stop him from showing up.

Tonight's occasion was a gala hosted by the Duchess of Eskirk to celebrate the end of harvest season. Never mind that the Rethaltan nobles in attendance had little to do with the harvest itself. No, they had people for that. They packed the ballroom of the duchess's summer palace like colorful hens. The buzz of nervous conversation filled the air and, beneath that, a heavy layer of perfume. Neither was sufficient to dispel the salty-sweet odor of fear. After all, there was always a risk that the duchess might make an appearance at her own gala.

Only the blood plague killed more nobles than Her Grace's temper.

At least the plague could be avoided; its bright red pustules were hard to miss. The duchess offered no such warning, and the guests knew it. Their terror showed in how they snapped at one another like strange cats. How they didn't eat, but drank to excess. And not just any drink, either. Darin recognized the dark-wood barrel that everyone was looking at while pretending not to.

Imperial dreamwine.

Ounce for ounce, the most precious substance in the queendom. Dreamwine was an extravagance even for those born into prosperity. There were times in Darin's life when he might have afforded a glass. Brief times. But he vowed he'd never touch the stuff no matter what it promised. The nobles drinking it sat on plush divans around the edges of the room, their eyes glazed with hallucinated euphoria. The nobles who hadn't yet indulged hid their impatience poorly.

Thus distracted, they paid no attention to Darin as he slipped through the press and relieved them of their valuables.

The first coin was the hardest. He plucked it fair and clean from the purse of a fat lordling who'd already sweated through two layers of silk. It was a good coin, too: a queenpiece. He exhaled softly as he pressed the silver into his palm. The crowded room came sharply into focus. He moved more quickly now, cutting purse-strings with an invisible blade. Cajoling the coins into his pockets. Liberating the occasional necklace or jeweled brooch. He had a fortune of purloined jewelry secreted about his person, and fewer than ten paces to reach the exit, when he stepped on someone's boot.

"Watch yourself, you oaf!" a man spat.

Darin tried to ignore it, but someone grabbed his shoulder and spun him around. That shook something loose from the stash hidden in his jacket. Felt like one of the sapphire earrings. He whispered a silent prayer, and it fell into his breeches rather than clattering to the floor.

The owner of the trodden boot, unfortunately, was not so easily swayed.

"I called you an oaf," he said.

He was a highborn noble of the worst sort, young and fat-cheeked and angry. Darin wore the plain dyed woolens of a servant. It made him an easy target.

"Apologies, m'lord." Darin kept his body still, to minimize the clinking of half a dozen purses tied to his belt. "I was just–"

"Wipe it off."

Oh, wonderful. This flabby brat actually wanted a fight. Darin took his measure while pretending to think it over. *Soft* was the word for him. No callouses marked his hands. Big surprise. Men like this didn't work for a living. "Beg pardon, m'lord?"

"You scuffed my boot. Wipe it off."

His breath carried the mingled smells of wine and spiced meat. The least-capable member of Darin's crew could gut him like a deer. *But we don't have time for that.*

Darin made his voice cheerful. "Can't say I see it, m'lord."

"It's right there!"

"Never did have the best eyes, but I'll be certain to have them checked."

A wisp of a girl in a silk and taffeta gown tittered with laughter behind a tiny hand. She looked barely of an age to be husband-shopping, but the gems encrusting her bodice could serve no other purpose. Darin's fingers itched just looking at them. Yet another highborn. So that was why he was putting on this display.

Sure enough, the man's cheeks reddened even further. "Are you mocking me?"

"Wouldn't dream of it, m'lord." Darin tried to move around him, but the man shifted over to block his path.

"You're not going anywhere."

"That's terribly flattering of you, but I'm happily spoken for."

"You insolent little–"

"I wish I could stay and chat, but I've been sent to fetch wine for my master. He's not a patient man, I'm sure you understand."

"Who is he?"

The pearl and silver necklace threatened to spill out of Darin's left sleeve, so he thought it best to head this fellow off. So he spoke the name of the most dangerous and short-tempered man in Eskirk. "Lord Peyton."

Recognition bloomed in the man's eyes. *Oh, yes.* Even the most wine-addled fool would know to be cautious here. Peyton had challenged and killed men for the smallest of insults.

Harassing one of his personal servants would undoubtedly qualify.

"You've heard of him, I take it," Darin said.

"I should hope so." The brat wore a smirk that stabbed unease straight into Darin's belly. "After all, he's my father."

Of course he was.

Being around all these nobles made Evie want to stab someone, but since her mother had raised her better than that, she'd settle for robbing them blind.

She glided between the embroidered frock-coats and opulent evening gowns, trying not to look at any of their faces. Better to consider them strangers rather than the holders of names she once learned on her mother's lap. Better not to be recognized by anyone who would understand how far she'd fallen. Her plain servant's garb rendered her practically invisible among so much finery.

But not completely invisible, as the lecherous old Count of Sunbury's unwelcome hand in her skirts reminded her. She grabbed his pinky finger and bent it backward, rewarded with a yelp and the sight of the count spilling his drink on himself. He withdrew the offending hand when she released his finger. She moved on without a backward glance.

She approached a pair of women in luxurious silk dresses, one as green as a cut emerald, the other a deeper blue than sapphire. Exotic dyes both, and that spoke to the wealth of their owners. "Drinks, my ladies?" She held forth a silver tray with seven little porcelain vessels. A few brandies, a cognac, and a small assortment of other spirits. Fine offerings by most accounts, but both women refused.

"Come back when you have dreamwine," said the one in green.

Always with the dreamwine. Evie couldn't fathom their obsession with something so expensive, yet so fleeting. She dipped her head as they expected, then brushed her fingertips against the woman's side. "What a *lovely* bodice." She slid past, plucking two emeralds free and dropping them into her sleeves. Gemstones always brought good coin. A bit harder to move, perhaps, because you couldn't melt them down. Maybe that was why Darin often went for the silver instead. *Well, that's not the* only *reason.*

She hadn't wanted to come here. Eskirk's gala was the event of the season. In the not-so-distant past, she'd pleaded for an invitation. *Begged.* But only the elite got their names inscribed in silver ink on the coveted scroll. Half a lifetime ago, that might have included her, but no more. She knew it, and so did the castellan who managed the guest list. He was deaf to her pleas, but not entirely immune to her charms. He looked her up and down and offered her a job serving drinks during the event. She'd considered it just long enough to be polite, as much as she wanted to throw the offer back in his face. Serving those who were once her peers went beyond ordinary humiliation. Yet it was good she hadn't burned that bridge. The job paid far better tonight.

Now, in the moment, she realized it was foolish to expect that anyone might recognize her. The invited guests were too self-involved and probably too inebriated to look twice at the help. Besides, she needed to be here to keep Darin out of trouble. He possessed certain talents, but marks like these had their own culture. Their own vocabulary. Understanding them required a childhood in their world, and for Evie, that was all she had. Even now, the timbre of rising voices from Darin's spot near the door told her he'd gone off script.

She wove her way through the crowd to find him squared off with a stout lordling who could only be Lord Peyton's eldest son. She *tsked* to herself at Darin's impeccable ability to find trouble of the worst sort. She slid between them to present her tray at just the right level to draw his eyes to her cleavage. "Another drink, m'lord?"

A girl in silk and taffeta to her right stared at Evie and fanned herself vigorously, the equivalent of a snarl. Well, nothing she could do about that now.

"A drink? No," said young Peyton. His eyes slid up and down her as if sizing up a hog at the market. "Is that all you have to offer?"

Evie could almost sense Darin's blood rising but gave him a curt signal to stand down and giggled, touching Peyton's arm. "At the moment, m'lord. Perhaps later..."

The girl in taffeta gave her a look that would freeze imperial dreamwine. "He'll be busy later."

Peyton's gaze shifted from Evie to the girl and then to Darin, who'd begun to edge ever-so-casually toward the door. His eyes narrowed. "Where do you think you're going?"

"I was thinking anywhere but here," Darin said.

"You're a liar," Peyton said.

"An honest mistake, that's all." Darin offered a curt bow. "My apologies. I'll be on my–"

"Who are you?"

"No one of consequence."

Men in dark blue uniforms had taken notice of the confrontation and began working their way through the crowd. Evie gave Darin a tilt of her head. They needed to break this off and get out before the audience got any bigger.

But Peyton had other ideas. "I'll have your name." He took a step forward and shoved Darin in the chest. "Or I'll have you thrown in a cell."

Silk and taffeta girl gasped. Palace guards had begun to quietly assemble in a loose circle around the two men. Darin drew a deep breath, and Evie could practically see the wheels turning. She prayed that he knew better than to try plan B. Not with Peyton here and spoiling for a fight. But even as she whispered the prayer, she knew there was little point. The gods were too deaf.

Darin sighed. "Very well." He adopted a new posture, spine

straight, shoulders back. Evie caught his eye and ran two fingers through her hair – her own panic signal. It was too late, though. He'd slipped into the new role like a man tugging on his favorite jacket. "My father is Lord Delamere. Viscount of Harradine Fields."

Silence fell over those within earshot. Faces turned toward them. And then, whispers flew across the room like wildfire. Guests elbowed one another, nodding in Darin's direction. It was all in the bearing, the diction. And the careful study of long-forgotten noble lineages.

"You're a peer," Peyton said.

It might be Evie's imagination, but some of the ruthless bravado had faded from his voice. Still, this ruse made her nervous. Granted, the Viscount of Harradine Fields hadn't appeared in public for decades. No one here had seen him or knew much of his family. The duchess's clerk might dispute Darin's claim, were the man not passed out under a table near the back. Even so, by taking this step, Darin opened himself up to new avenues of danger. Ones he wouldn't understand or see coming. The worst part was, she couldn't wave him off any longer. He'd already spoken the name. She gripped the edge of her tray to keep her hands steady. She could feel the hilts of the daggers hidden up her sleeves. The cold steel was a comfort.

"My father wished for me to keep a low profile," Darin was saying. He'd settled into the casual confidence of a man born into wealth and privilege, like someone putting on a pair of favorite gloves.

"Understandable," said Peyton, through gritted teeth.

"If you'll excuse me." Darin put his back to them and faced the ballroom door once again. The full weight of his gaze fell on the two guards in his way. They stepped aside hurriedly, murmuring apologies.

"One more thing, Delamere," Peyton said.

Darin turned right into the slap of the glove. His cheek

reddened where it struck him; Peyton had put some weight behind it.

Knew he wouldn't see it coming, Evie groused to herself.

"I demand satisfaction," Peyton said.

Satisfaction would be meeting this man in a dark alley, with a sharp dagger in each hand. Evie elected not to say so.

Darin let out another sigh, a more theatrical one. Like a queen indulging a pleading commoner. "Tomorrow, at midday. Swords."

"There's no reason to wait. As it happens, I brought mine with me."

"You brought your sword to a gala?" Darin said.

Peyton's eyes glinted victoriously. "I like to be prepared."

A hawk-nosed guardsman with two stripes on his shoulder stepped forward and coughed politely. "My lords, Her Grace the duchess has a dueling green just outside."

Evie pursed her lips. Of course she did.

CHAPTER TWO
Insubordination

Tom thought for sure this time he'd get to see some action. A fistfight. A shoving match. Hell, even a heated argument. Instead, here he stood, wearing a too-small uniform in Eskirk's colors. Babysitting a bunch of overdressed rich people as they glared at each other over some expensive drink. The closest he'd come to excitement was his interview for the temporary guard posting. As usual, the guard captain took one look at him and offered a job on the spot. Not the best pay, though. So he took Darin's advice and asked for a bout with one of the men to prove he deserved more. A broad-shouldered corporal volunteered to face him.

He called Tom a "country oaf" as they squared off.

If and when he woke up tomorrow, he'd be greeted by a sore head and a stretched-out uniform.

Just like that, Tom had done his part. Gotten a guard post in Eskirk on the important night. Now all he had to do was "look out for trouble" and make sure none of it found Darin or Evie. He almost wished someone would try something. But the guests were too gussied up to be expecting a fight. Most of them, at least. Too drunk, as well. Three different people had managed to spill a drink on him, despite the fact that he never moved.

At last, a small crowd of people began to clump up. Voices were raised. *Finally*. An excuse to stretch his legs. Hopefully something more. He shifted away from the wall and began a slow mosey across the ballroom. Most of the guests gave him one glance and hastened out of his way. A couple of fellows were too deep in their cups to move. He gave them a gentle but firm shove to the side. It was hard to tell from a distance but judging by the hum of excitement in the crowd it sounded like there might be a duel afoot. That was good. Entertainment for him, and a nice distraction for Darin and Evie to get their work done. A two-for-one deal, his favorite.

He got close enough to spot Evie in the mix. Or someone with her dark curls and exact same dress. He hesitated. It wasn't like her to put herself in the middle of attention. Not while on a job, at least. She saw him and flashed two quick signals. *Darin* and *trouble*.

Then the entire crowd moved toward the hallway that led outside, with Darin near the fore. Everyone seemed happy about where they were going. He had to hand it to Darin, he sure knew how to get out of a crowded room. He'd started to return to his post by the wall when Evie tugged his sleeve.

He bent down so she could talk in his ear.

"Darin's been challenged to a duel."

"With who?"

"Lord Peyton's son."

"Is he good?"

Evie chewed her lip. "I don't know, but he's built like an ox."

"What are they fighting with?"

"Rapiers. Peyton brought his."

Tom grunted. Darin was decent with the rapier, but he hadn't brought a familiar sword. Tom would gladly give his, but it was a stout longsword and no use against a skilled rapier swordsman – which this Peyton might be, if he carried his own. Few of the other nobles had swords with them, and these were only show-pieces. When push came to shove, Tom could think of only one source for a reliable rapier, and it happened to belong to the captain of the Eskirk guards. Also known as his boss for the evening. Guard-captain Salbas had fair hair, a ridiculously large mustache, and too many trappings on his uniform for Tom's liking. Still, he carried himself like a fighter. That made him easier to find in the corridor outside the ballroom, where he strolled along with the crowd on his way to watch the duel. Darin's duel.

Tom fell into step beside him. "Need to borrow your sword, captain."

"What for?"

Tom considered telling him the full truth, that Darin needed a real sword from someone who knew his business or he might get run through in front of the worst crowd possible. But Darin was always discouraging over-telling, so he settled on short truth. "The duel."

The captain snorted. "It won't be much of a duel. Peyton's killed three men in the past year. Looking to outdo his father, if you ask me. Besides, I'm sure he brought his sword."

"The other man didn't."

"Who is he?"

"I don't know," Tom admitted. Darin swapped names like some people changed clothes.

"You expect me to lend my sword to a stranger?"

"Keep mine as collateral."

Salbas eyed Tom's longsword with distaste. "That siege weapon? I don't think so."

They came abreast of a side hallway off the main corridor. Tom put a hand on the captain's shoulder and steered him into it. "Let's have a private word."

"Take your hand off me!"

Tom obliged but blocked the route back to the corridor behind him. "It's important, captain."

"I don't give a damn what you think's important." Salbas gripped his sword's hilt. "This belonged to my grandfather."

Tom glanced over his shoulder. Darin was already outside, as was most of the crowd. *I don't have time for this.*

"Move out of my way. We're going to miss it," Salbas said.

"You're half right."

"What–"

Tom drove his knee into the captain's stomach. He doubled over, gasping. A sharp elbow to the back of the head, and he buckled like a cheap stool. Tom caught him beneath the arms. "Sorry about that. I sneezed."

Guard-captain Salbas didn't answer. He was out cold.

Tom propped him up against the wall and collected his rapier. The corridor was empty. He hurried out the far door into a courtyard featuring a large dueling green. Guards in Eskirk's colors lined both sides. The last of the palace guests were climbing the steps to a sort of balcony that offered a better view.

Darin stood alone at one end. He looked as calm as he always did, but his eyes swiveled left and right as if searching for an escape route. Across the green, Peyton stood with lots of people in fancy clothes around him. He was big, just like Evie said. Not as big as Tom, but few men were. Still, Peyton had round shoulders and carried himself a certain way. He was comfortable on a dueling green. That alone said something. He'd doffed his jacket, revealing a tight-fitting garment of white silk beneath.

A fighting tunic. Tom gritted his teeth and walked out to greet Darin. Someone had given him an épée, but a poorly made one. It was at least half a foot shorter than a true rapier.

"Happy to act as your second tonight, sir, since you're alone," Tom said, making sure his voice carried across the green.

"How kind of you," Darin answered loudly. He lowered his voice. "Where have you *been*?"

"Had to talk to my captain."

"It's not a long-term job, you know."

"I know."

Darin nodded at the rapier. "Is that for me?"

"Thought you could use it." Tom handed it over and took

the épée. He was right about the quality. It was better suited as a child's toy.

Darin drew the blade. "It's got good balance." He swung it in a figure of eight. Good control as usual, but not perfect.

"It should be me fighting instead of you," Tom said.

"Thanks for the vote of confidence."

"Come on, Darin. Was this part of your plan?" *Please say yes.* Darin always had a plan. With a second one to back that up, and another one past that. His head must be full of them.

"Not entirely," Darin said. "I must have a knack for these things."

Tom eyed Peyton, who was still preening for his admirers on the other side of the green. "He's a bruiser. He'll throw his weight into you."

"Don't worry, Tom. I got a look at his hands. They're soft. He can't be too experienced."

"Unless he wears gloves," Tom said.

As one they looked across the green, where Peyton was pulling a pair on.

CHAPTER THREE
First Blood

Darin never fought a duel unless he could profit from it, but he couldn't see a way to avoid this one. He'd managed a brush-pass with Evie during the kerfuffle to offload some of the goods, but not nearly enough. Soft metal clinked when he moved. The magic in it beckoned him.

Guests crowded onto the balcony above to watch. They lined the rail in their peacock finery, still unaware that he'd purloined most of their coins and jewelry.

"You can still call this off," Tom said.

I wish that were true. Backing away now would only raise more questions, more sharp inquiries. Someone might think to rouse Her Grace's clerk from under the table. Darin shrugged. "I can use the exercise. You, meanwhile, should stick to the plan."

Tom nodded. "Try not to get killed."

"That's good advice, Tom." Darin put the sword away, grateful that Tom had thought to bring him a decent weapon. "Any idea when your captain will arrive to start this thing?"

Tom's brow furrowed. "Guess I'd better step in for him."

"You?"

"The captain isn't coming. Come along, then."

Darin followed, cursing Tom's constant brevity and mindful of the soft metallic clinks from his pockets. He glanced up and caught a certain flash of dark hair. Evie still worked the crowd, taking advantage of the distraction to pick off any valuables they'd missed. He admired that, even if he wished she'd use this distraction to get out.

Peyton waited on the green with a smirk on his pudgy face. He had a glass of wine in one hand, and his own sword in the other. It said something about a man when he brought his own weapon to a social function. He was taking his time, too. Savoring the last bit of wine, preening for the crowd of assembled nobles. If he took much longer, they'd grow restless. Someone might notice an empty purse or a missing necklace.

Darin thought it best to move things along. "Are you ready, m'lord? Or did you need a little snack, as well?"

Peyton snarled, and would have come for him, but Tom stepped between them. "This duel ends at first blood."

"What?" the lordling demanded.

"The duchess doesn't want to find a corpse here tomorrow. So it's first blood."

"Fine," Peyton said, but his eyes promised murder.

Tom didn't move. "I'll have your word on it."

Peyton broke off his stare long enough to look Tom up and down. "You have it."

"My word as well," Darin said. *Well done, Tom.* Maybe this wouldn't be so bad after all.

"Have at it, then." Tom moved out of the way.

Before he'd even stepped off the green, Peyton lunged with his sword.

Darin managed to parry. "Thanks for the warning."

Peyton snickered and came again, blade flashing.

Lunge.

Parry. *Riposte.*

A silence gripped the courtyard, broken only by the rasp and whisper of steel on steel. Peyton left several openings; Darin could have skewered him like a mutton roast. But that would only earn him more attention. More scrutiny. He needed a different way out. So did Evie, for that matter. He caught glimpses of her among the nobles above. She'd covered most of the balcony already.

He slapped Peyton's heavy-handed thrust aside. A diamond pendant began to work its way out of his sleeve pocket. *Damn.* They scuffled again, locked blades. Darin threw him off and circled. He muttered a soft command to the pendant, which hopped back into his sleeve.

Evie reached the end of the balcony, but one of the marks in the front row had noticed something. He patted around his belts, and the pockets of his tailored crimson jacket. Like he was missing something. He glanced over in Evie's direction. *She's blown.*

Darin bit his lip and let his guard slip too low. Peyton thrust in over it. He twisted away as the blade ripped through his tunic. The crowd uttered a collective gasp. The mark missing his purse forgot all about it. Evie blew Darin a kiss and made her exit. *About damn time.*

Judging by the smirk on his face, Peyton seemed to be savoring his imminent success. He expected to win this thing. Probably to run Darin through in front of all his admirers. His parries got sloppier with this new confidence. Darin could have ended it, but that would only complicate things. The alleged heir of Harradine Fields needed no more scrutiny.

The silver might be Darin's best way out. One of the fat coins still pressed against his skin, begging to be used. It would be so easy to cheat with it. Make Peyton stumble, or blind him, or render his sword arm immobile. Trouble was, he risked exposing himself if he reached out with metallurgy in front of such a large crowd. Hells, he wouldn't put it past the Duchess of Eskirk to keep a witch on the payroll just in case. She'd out him instantly, and then he'd never break away clean. So overt uses were out. Maybe he could try something more subtle. It had to get him out the door, no questions asked, when this ended. Inspiration struck so suddenly, so perfectly, that he smiled.

This appeared to throw Peyton into a rage. He swung a vicious slash at Darin's neck. Darin ducked just in time. He felt the breeze from the sword on his head. *So much for first blood.* He backed off, circling, to buy himself time to do what he needed. He'd never tried using metallurgy on himself before. It was not as hard as he expected, but something told him he'd pay the price later. Or maybe sooner. A red tinge began to creep in on the sides of his vision. *I need to end this.*

The next time Peyton closed, Darin closed as well. They scuffled and locked blades. Darin kept his feet too close together, leaving himself unbalanced. Inviting Peyton to hit him like a brawler. But the man stubbornly refused. Maybe he didn't want to fight dirty in front of a crowd. Darin decided he needed a nudge.

"You ready to give up yet?" he asked in a low voice.

He and Peyton circled round and round, their blades still locked.

"I'm going to put you down like a dog," Peyton said.

"Shame it's taking so long."

"Why?"

Darin put on a wicked smile. "Your father would have ended this by now."

Peyton snarled. He reared back and slammed his shoulder into Darin's middle.

Darin shouted and stumbled back, clutching one hand against his chest. "You got me!"

Peyton halted in his advance. His brow wrinkled. "What?"

"You've drawn my blood, sir."

"I did not!"

Darin lifted his shirt's collar and peered beneath. "Oh, yes. Masterfully done, m'lord."

Murmurs began in the crowd above. They sounded disappointed, a fact that was not lost on Peyton.

"What are you talking about?" he demanded.

Darin bowed. "Victory is yours."

"Let me see it!" He threw down his blade, marched over, and ripped Darin's shirt open.

Then he stared, while the color drained from his face. Dozens of bright red pustules covered Darin's torso, glistening blood-red in the torchlight.

"Blood plague," he rasped.

"It's fine." Darin coughed hoarsely to one side. "Just a little fever, that's all."

Peyton babbled incoherently. His face was white as a ghost. "Blood plague!" he shouted. He turned and fled.

The nobles on the balcony surged away from the rail. Men shouted; women screamed. They trampled one another to get back inside.

Not half a minute later, Darin stood alone in an empty green. He buttoned his shirt. He jabbed the borrowed rapier into the ground. The owner might not have the courage to claim it, but Tom would want it returned.

Metal glinted from the grass nearby. Darin strolled over and found a much finer sword in the grass. Peyton must have dropped it when he ran. Sure enough, there was an elegant *P* monogrammed in the blade near the base. No scabbard, but the emeralds in the hilt would fetch a pretty penny on their own. Now all he had to do was get out of Eskirk with the haul, when everyone thought him a walking corpse.

CHAPTER FOUR
Chance Encounters

Kat hated seeing good ale go to waste.

For two hours, she and the boys had parked their wagon outside the gate to the Eskirk's sprawling manse, trying to sell ale to anyone coming or going. She'd brewed an entire barrel for this. Four hundred pints at three coppers apiece should have brought a tidy profit. Gods knew the glittering highborns who rolled by in bright lacquered carriages could afford it. Most guests hardly gave her wagon a second glance. The thing was, they *looked* like they'd had nothing to drink all day. It was hot, too. Harvest season might be upon them, but the humid heat of summer had lingered. There was no shade but for a little wooden station across the driveway from where she'd set up. Four men and five women had been standing there since before she'd arrived. They didn't talk. They didn't move. They just waited, sweating in all of their gossamer and silk. Kat had been of half a mind to send one of the boys over to try to sell wine, but the wealthy waiters hardly gave off a friendly vibe.

Despite all of this, she'd sold exactly thirteen pints. At that rate, it would take her fifty-eight hours to empty the barrel. She doubted this gala would go on so long.

One of her boys poked his head out from the wagon canvas. "Any luck, Miss Kat?"

"Not for a while, Timmy." Kat frowned up at the manse

beyond the gate, where servants had begun to light dozens of oil lamps on the terraces as dusk fell.

"Are we going to leave soon?"

"Not sure. Why?"

"Abel's hungry."

The boy in question poked his head out and watched for her answer. Abel still didn't talk much, and never to anyone grown. They'd found him scrounging in a garbage heap in Caron, alone and ghost-thin. An orphan, just like Timmy, who'd lost his parents at sea. Kat had even less food than she did now, but couldn't bear the thought of Abel wasting away to nothing. "We'll get something to eat soon."

She had no idea how she'd keep that promise. She had thirty-nine coppers in her purse and still owed the carter forty-two. They'd have to stick it out and sell at least a few more pints, or they'd end up upside-down on this whole venture. What a gods-damned waste of time.

Darkness fell quickly. No one came to hang a lamp on the little waiting station. This seemed to upset those who were still waiting; their complaints grew louder and less restrained.

"Abel's still hungry," Timmy said.

Kat sighed. "Start packing up. We've got a long ride home tonight." *A long, hungry ride.*

A disturbance from inside the gate drew her attention away from setting the packhorse into its traces. Footsteps pounded, heading in her direction. Three people. No, four. Five. A deeper, steady sound rose behind it. Blocky shapes rushed down the driveway. *Carriages.* The first one didn't even slow at the decorative cast-iron gates but barreled through them, the two huge draft horses snorting and stamping as they did. Kat cursed and dragged her own animal's reins, pulling her wagon farther away from the opening. A good thing, too, because a stampede of carriages and horsemen charged pell-mell out the opening amid shouts and screams. The air smelled of sweat and terror.

Timmy popped out of the wagon again. "What's going on?"

"Nothing good. Get back inside, double quick!" Kat hissed. In truth, she had no idea. Something had terrified these people beyond reason. As she watched, one man staggered into the path of a speeding carriage. The driver didn't even flinch before running him down. Kat shuddered, and felt ashamed at the wave of relief she felt that the boys hadn't seen. Her own horse tossed and rolled his eyes backward, trying to see what he could hear and probably smell. If he bolted, she'd lose the barrel, the wagon, and maybe her boys.

"No, no, don't worry about that," she said, keeping her voice soft. "Look at me." She kept pulling, one step at a time, moving her wagon and precious barrel and doubly precious boys slowly away from danger. *Lady, give me a few paces.* She didn't ask for much. Ten paces later, she started to breathe again. Thirty paces from the gate, the noise began to fade. Guests still fled from the grounds, most of them on foot. Some of them appeared half-dressed, as if they'd practically ripped one another's finery off in their rush to escape. Colorful scarves and elegant cravats littered the ground. Kat was half-tempted to run back and scoop them up, but it wasn't worth getting trampled.

She was so focused on keeping her horse moving that she didn't see the man drop over the wall. He landed heavily, with a muffled curse. She spun, startled at the sound. He was unremarkable in every way – clean-shaven, average height, plainly dressed – except that when he moved, he positively *jangled*.

"Pleasant evening, isn't it?" he asked.

She eyed the sword at his belt. It had the look of a rapier, and an expensive one. "A little hot for my taste."

He laughed. "You're more right than you know."

"Well, don't let us keep you." The noise might have faded, but whatever happened up at Eskirk's gala was bound to attract unwanted attention.

"What's in the wagon?"

Kat felt a twinge of caution in her gut. "Why do you want to know?"

He smiled and spread out his hands. "I'm only making conversation."

He had an easy way about him, but that gave her pause. Anyone this kind to a stranger wanted something. "It's none of your concern."

"Well, now you're only making me curious." He walked past her, like a man out for a casual stroll. "My name's Darin, by the way."

"Get away from the wagon, Darin."

He didn't quite listen but lifted the loose end of the canvas tarp under the cover. His mouth fell open. He lifted his hands in the air and took two steps back.

Abel emerged from the shadow of the canvas, holding the crossbow with steady hands. The same crossbow Kat usually kept behind her seat and didn't think the boys even knew about.

Timmy stood up beside him. "Abel wants to know if this man's botherin' you, Miss Kat."

"Thank you, Abel. I haven't decided yet." Kat looked at Darin, who hadn't moved. "Is your curiosity satisfied?"

"Perfectly."

"I told you to get away from the wagon."

"Yes, you did."

Kat had to admit, she rather enjoyed the mixture of concern and admiration on his face. "Do you make a habit of doing other than what you're told?"

"I'm afraid so, Miss Kat. Hazard of the job, I suppose."

"What job would that be?"

"I move things from one place to another."

Kat frowned. "Sounds like a fancy way of saying you're a thief."

He laughed. "I think I like you."

"Not interested."

"But you haven't even heard my proposal yet." He pouted

in mock affront. He seemed to have forgotten the crossbow leveled at his chest. A child might be holding it, but it was no toy. If Abel so much as sneezed…

"Best speak quickly, then," Kat said.

"I'll pay you a silver queenpiece for a lift to the harbor."

She stared at him. "Why would you do that?'

"Because it beats walking."

"What if my horse doesn't like being ridden?"

"I'd prefer the wagon, actually. Where these clever lads can keep an eye on me."

She hesitated. A silver queenpiece would cover her debts and a hot meal with some to spare. Yet it seemed too easy. Too generous. *What if he wants more?*

"A ride is all I'm asking for," Darin said, as if he knew her thoughts. "You're going to the harbor anyway."

"What makes you think that?"

"A dozen little things. The salt stains on the wagon canvas. The mariner's knots on your horse's harness. A distinct smell of fish on Abel's breath. No offense," he said hastily, glancing at the boy still holding the crossbow on him. "Besides, it's the only place you can park a wagon overnight without being harassed by the city guards."

Kat should have refused him. It was foolishness to go anywhere with a man who spoke like this. Who saw things like this. Instead, she found herself saying, "Let's see the silver."

Almost before she'd finished speaking, Darin snapped his fingers and produced a silver coin. Even as he danced it across the back of his fingers, the Queen's face on the front was hard to miss. "I'm good for it."

"Snowflake," she said to Abel. That was their code word for *harmless*. Which she'd have to change now, but it was worth it. Especially when Abel pretended not to hear for a second, just to make Darin sweat a bit more. Then he lowered the crossbow.

"I live to see another morning. How wonderful," Darin said. He almost sounded like he was joking.

Kat tried to imagine the mind of someone who was amused by nearly taking a bolt to the chest. She decided it wasn't possible. And that did nothing to convince her to strike a deal with him. "Is your name really Darin?"

"The one I was born with."

"Can you prove it?"

His easy smile fell away. "Wish I could, but the two folks who gave it to me were taken from this world a long time ago."

Another orphan. He was a grown man, so it shouldn't affect Kat to hear this. But it did.

"Get in the wagon," she said. "Boys, make room. I'm betting he'll want to sit back under the canvas."

Darin paused with one boot on the wagon wheel and gave her an assessing look. "How did you guess?"

Kat gave the horse a reassuring pat and climbed back into the driver's seat. "You're dressed like a servant, but you climbed the wall with silver in your pockets and someone else's rapier."

"I can't decide if I should be impressed, or mildly offended."

"Be whatever you want," Kat said. "You're not the only one who knows how to move things."

Evie couldn't wait to get out of Eskirk, but the merchant caravan showed no signs of departing anytime soon. She waited in the shade of a canvas shelter on the edge of the village green, fighting the urge to tap her foot. A motley collection of craftsmen and vendors came here each year hoping to sell wares to the guests and their retinues. A long journey for most. And profitable, too, if even one guest in ten came down to spend their coin. Unfortunately, Darin's little stunt sent most of the would-be customers fleeing into the night.

Evie had traded her plain servant's clothes for tight breeches and a loose-fitting crimson tunic. With her hair in a tight queue down her back, and her travel bag apparently stuffed with bolts of fabric, she was the very picture of an up-and-coming cloth merchant. Granted, no legitimate vendor would carry a small fortune in stolen gems hidden in her bundle. That only became an issue if someone insisted on searching her, which didn't seem likely. Especially given the foul mood most of the merchants and vendors seemed to be sharing. No, their caravan would be a perfect cover for her to slip away without attracting attention. Darin had a berth in a ship, and Big Tom was riding out with a mercenary company. As it stood, they'd almost certainly get away clean.

It would be a good haul, too. Darin was carrying most of it, but he'd managed to pass a few pieces to her before his duel. One of those was a particular emerald pendant on a fine silver chain. An impossible pendant. She still held it – concealed in the palm of her hand, of course – and wondered if her eyes were playing tricks on her. It couldn't be the same one that her father had given her mother all those years ago. Before the hard times. Before they'd had to sell every last scrap.

"Hey," said a deep voice, jolting her from the memory. The hulking form outside her canvas tent wore a faded uniform two sizes too small for him. It could only be Big Tom.

"What are you doing here?" Evie hissed. "You were supposed to be gone by sunrise."

"Darin's in trouble."

She glanced around. None of the merchants appeared to be watching, but a man of Tom's stature wouldn't take long to attract notice. "Get in here." She dragged him into the shadows beneath the canvas. He followed obediently, which was a good thing given that he weighed three times what she did. "Explain."

"They closed off the harbor before Darin's ship got out."

"How do you know?"

"I watched him board." Tom's hand drifted to his waist, but he wasn't wearing a sword. He frowned when he noticed this. Strangely, he had a small wooden cask tucked under his left arm instead. "He didn't look good."

Evie harrumphed. "Does he ever?"

"He was pale and could barely walk."

Sick from silver, she didn't say, mostly because it would require an explanation that wasn't hers to give. "What's in the cask?"

"East Bay leaf."

"You're supposed to be riding out with a patrol, but instead you bought tobacco."

He shrugged. "It's good leaf."

"That's a filthy habit, you know."

"I know." Tom at least had the grace to blush.

"Who closed the harbor?"

"Soldiers in Eskirk's colors. They're boarding every ship."

"Darin will be well hidden. They won't find him," she said.

"What if they do?"

Then we're poor again, she thought. Then again, they'd be better off than Darin. Gods knew what a woman like Eskirk would do if she got her hands on the man who'd infiltrated her gala and robbed her guests. Evie shuddered.

"I thought so," Tom said.

"Darin would want us to stick to the plan and make our escape."

"Darin's not here."

The big man possessed a talent for understatement, Evie had to give him that. It was up to her and Tom. Should they bet on Darin talking his way out of any trouble, or should they put themselves at risk to try and help him? It wasn't an easy call. That was probably why Tom came to her. Of course, as she considered this, the merchant caravan started assembling on the edge of the square, making ready to leave. "What do you think we should do?"

"Lend a hand. Got any ideas?"

"How many ships are in the harbor?"

Tom pulled on his ear, as if it might jog his memory. "A lot."

Evie allowed herself one last glance at the assembling caravan and the escape it promised. She took his arm and led him in the other direction. "Let's take a walk, shall we? I've always wanted to see the harbor district."

"What about your caravan?"

"There will be other caravans. You didn't tell me what happened with your patrol."

"They ride slow. I wanted to make sure Darin got off."

"Do you always hang around after a job?" It was just like Tom to put others first when he was supposed to be making his own getaway.

"I worry about him."

"I see." She pressed her lips tight together.

"What?"

"You weren't worried about me?"

"Figured I'd check on you next."

"But not first," she teased.

"You're good at avoiding trouble," Tom said. "With Darin, it's like he goes looking for it."

"Too right. Let's hope we can intervene before he finds even more."

CHAPTER FIVE
Illicit Cargo

Say what you want about smugglers, but they had a flair for creativity. Darin pondered this as he crouched in a tiny compartment in the bilge of a leaky ship. The trapdoor that sealed him in this compartment lay hidden beneath a tar-soaked tangle of ropes and sheets. The oily stench carried down into the space below and assaulted his nostrils like a swarm of gnats. He was no stranger to pungent odors, but this was the first one that took up unwelcome residence inside him. His lungs burned with each shallow breath.

It was early morning, as best he could tell. The overnight was misery. Were it not for Miss Kat and her boys, he'd never have made the harbor. Given the state he was in, they could have robbed him and dumped him into a canal. Instead, Miss Kat herself helped him make the long, torturous walk to his berth.

The ship was a two-masted trader bound for Tal Orea. If she made it half that far, he'd be truly surprised. But he'd seen worse, and even *smelled* worse than this. And he would again, if the duchess's agents caught him in the harbor.

Someone slid the bar out to unlock the trapdoor overhead. Darin's fingers found the hilt of his dueling dagger. The familiar leather handle offered a whisper of comfort. Maybe he'd take one of them with him. Then again, maybe he should use that half-moment to turn it on himself. Lord and Lady only knew what cruelties the duchess's torturers had mastered in their many years of practice.

The trapdoor creaked open. Darin half-drew his blade, but it was only Burgess, the ship's pale-bearded captain. "Get up on deck," he said. "Double quick."

Darin tucked his dagger away so he wouldn't lose it in the two inches of muddy water that sloshed around his boots. "What for?" The ship had barely moved away from the dock; by his guess they were still in the palace harbor.

"We're about to be boarded for inspection."

A ball of instinctive unease formed in Darin's gut. "Better to keep me hidden, then."

"Wouldn't work." Burgess spat to one side and traced a star on his chest, a ward against the unnatural. "They've got a gods-damned witch with them."

A silver witch. Darin felt an odd mixture of unease and excitement. So the duchess *did* keep one in her employ. It was unusual to do so in a monarchy where magic was mostly reviled. But the Duchess of Eskirk was an unusual woman. If she'd revealed her metallurgist now, it meant she was deadly serious about finding the jewel thieves. Or the alleged blood fever victim, or both. "How long do I have?"

"Not much."

"Stall them as long as you can."

Burgess rolled his eyes to show what he thought of that, but disappeared from view.

Darin changed out of his rumpled servant's garb and raced up to the deck. Armed women in Eskirk's dark blue tabards swarmed over the deck like a pack of angry termites – which the ship already had aplenty, judging by what he'd seen below. The jet-black masts of two royal cutters bobbed on either side of the bow, their hulls held fast by three grappling hooks each.

Burgess's sailors were forming a ragged line along the starboard rail. Their captain was up on the wheel deck making his displeasure known to the severe-looking woman who seemed to be in charge. She kept a hand on her sword hilt as she ignored him.

Eskirk harbor basked in the unrelenting sunlight of early morning, lending an azure warmth to the deep waters that belied the chill to them. The sea lanes were busier than a soldiers' brothel on payday, hundreds of ships backed up around the piled-stone breakwater that formed the harbor. Five warships held anchor at regular intervals between shore and seawall, sterns to the sea, their oars stowed but at the ready. The ship in the middle, a three-master, dwarfed every other vessel in the bay. Long banners flew atop its masts. Darin shaded his eyes. Blue and silver. Those were Eskirk's personal colors. That made the ship *Her Grace's Wish*. If the duchess herself was aboard, no one would be leaving the harbor anytime soon.

Darin forgot all of that when another woman climbed aboard. Or more accurately, floated over the rail like a ghost. Her slate dress shimmered when she moved, like sunlight dancing on water. She was petite and dark-haired. Younger than he expected, too. His eyes wandered down the neckline of their own accord. Goosebumps prickled on his forearms. She must have some kind of enchantment about her. He'd already stared for too long, but she *pulled* at him. Big mistake. She swung her gaze about and caught him looking.

Damn.

He looked down at his boots and fidgeted. Maybe she'd think him nervous. Hell, he *was* nervous, but with luck she'd think that's all it was. Just a regular sailor, scared to death that she'd call down lightning to cook him where he stood.

She glided over the tarred ropes and other filth that covered the deck – a nice touch by Burgess to discourage lengthy inspections – and touched down lightly before the assembled crew. She made her way down the line of sailors, giving each a cursory inspection. No more than a few seconds each. She was three sailors down, then two. Darin mustered an expression of bored irritation. *Keep going, keep going...*

She halted right in front of him. He had no choice but to meet her eyes. They were old eyes, the same slate color as her dress.

"See something you like?" Her voice was soft, her words like a song.

Darin didn't trust himself to answer. He clamped his jaw shut and shook his head. She reached out suddenly and brushed his cheek with too-warm fingertips. He fought the urge to jerk away. This would end faster if she satisfied her curiosity. Then a smile flickered across her face, and Darin realized his second mistake.

He was the only clean-shaven man on deck.

She leaned close to him. "You don't look like much of a sailor."

He gave her a little smile. "You don't look like much of a witch, but here we are."

She blinked. The corners of her mouth tightened. She lowered her hand from where she'd touched his face and curled her fingers into a fist. "I don't care for that word."

The air thickened, wrapping Darin around his chest like a too-tight bandage. It got harder to breathe, but he'd be damned if he gave her the satisfaction of showing it. "That the best you can do?"

She lifted her hand up, and he felt himself heaved bodily off the deck.

His stomach lurched. She lifted him out over the rail, floating on his belly with twenty feet of empty air and then the cold sea below. *Just had to open your mouth, didn't you?* A pair of shadows detached themselves from the gloom beneath the ship's hull. Dogfish, by the look of them, with those goddamn hooked teeth that got hold of something and wouldn't let go. So they added yet another unpleasant option to the growing list of ways he might die horrifically in the near future.

"Is that good enough for you?" she called.

He closed his eyes and took a breath to regain his composure.

Which was no easy task, dangling twenty feet above infested waters. "I meant no offense."

"Oh, you didn't?"

"I only meant that you're far too young and pretty to hold that kind of power."

The hard line of her mouth didn't change. "Too young?"

There was something dangerous in her tone. He must have touched a nerve. At least she hadn't–

She flicked her wrist. He felt a wave of vertigo as he spun heels over head. Once, twice, thrice. Then she held him fast. Upside down. With coins and stolen jewelry raining from his pockets. *No, no, no...* In seconds, it was all gone. He still had a few pieces hidden about his person, and a purse squirreled away in the bilge, but he imagined he could feel the rest of that newfound wealth sinking slowly into the blue abyss.

The witch crooked a finger, and he drifted slowly back over the rail. She brought him right up to her, face to face, dangling over the deck and squarely in her power. So close, he could smell the silver in the medallion she wore around her neck.

"You're certainly the wealthiest sailor I've ever met," she said.

He tried to offer his most charming smile. "Until a minute ago, at least. It was mine, I swear."

Her hard gaze didn't soften a fraction. Gods, he'd never charm his way past this one. *I'd have better luck with the dogfish.*

Shouts from the wheel deck brought him a brief respite. The stern-faced officer pulled the brass spyglass from her belt and swung it out across the harbor. Darin twisted as best he could to look in the same direction, shoreward, where a dark pillar of black smoke rose from *Her Grace's Wish*. Smoke meant fire. That wasn't good.

"Lord and Lady be merciful," one of the sailors whispered. "Look at her colors."

Darin hadn't thought to, but now he did. The *Wish* had run up a set of flags on her signal-line. Three black squares, three green circles. A signal that every sailor learned before they went to sea, a signal that shot a cold steel bolt into the stoutest of sea-faring hearts.

Living fire.

No one knew what it was, exactly. Some said the green flames skittered across seawater like a shoal of fish. Others claimed it rose from the inky depths like a sailor's nightmare. Two things were certain. First, that it hungered for wood and canvas and flesh. Second, that nothing could stop its onslaught. Living fire only departed when there was nothing else to consume.

Burgess's sailors fell out of assembly, ignoring the witch's squawk of protest as they rushed headlong to their stations. The guard captain ordered her soldiers back to their cutters on the double time. Burgess's men began cutting loose the grappling lines, and no one raised an argument.

"What is it?" the witch demanded, to no one in particular.

Meanwhile, Darin bobbed in the air like a forgotten child's toy. *I'll let someone else tell her.*

She grabbed a passing sailor by the front of his shirt and dragged him around to face her. Not a small lad, either – she must be stronger than she looked. "What is it?"

Fear warred with caution on the young sailor's face. "Living fire," he said at last.

"God's balls." She released the man, as the color drained from her face. "Her Grace is aboard that ship."

Then she's doomed, Darin nearly said, but he bit his lip. He had no love for the Duchess of Eskirk, but even she didn't deserve that kind of death.

The guard captain stormed down from the wheel deck, her nostrils flaring. "Make ready to cast off!"

"How close can you get me?" the witch asked her.

"Depends on how much you want to die," the captain said. She glanced up and spotted Darin. "Who's he?"

"The luckiest man alive, apparently," the witch said.

The guard captain marched toward her cutter. The witch paused, staring out at the water toward the *Wish*.

"Beg pardon," Darin called. "Do you think you could–"

She made a half-hearted wave over her shoulder, and the invisible hand that held him up let go. The deck flew up to meet him. He grunted at the stabs of pain in his knees and elbows. Sun-hot tar soaked into his filthy shirt to bite his skin. Something told him the sailor he'd borrowed it from wouldn't be wanting it back. He picked himself up. "Don't go near it."

She half-turned. "What?"

"Not even your arts will work against living fire."

She scoffed at him, an impatient noise. "Not really my decision, though, is it?" She grabbed her skirts and stalked heedlessly across the filthy deck back toward the cutters. The duchess's soldiers were already casting off their lines. The witch clambered over the rail with considerably less grace than she'd shown when she arrived.

The moment the cutters broke free, Burgess spun the wheel and shouted, "Full sail!"

The ship swung to port and took them away from the mess of smoke, away from the panicking harbor, into the wide blue expanse of waiting sea. Darin ran to the stern and watched as the three Eskirk cutters put on sail and turned toward the pillar of smoke. The woman in the slate dress stood at the bow of the largest one, stiff backed and determined. *What a waste,* he thought. Then again, there was no guarantee he'd avoid a similar fate. Burgess's ship was headed practically upwind out of the harbor. If the living fire decided to head out to sea, they'd be right in its path. The sailors knew it, too. It showed in how they kept glancing astern while they worked, as if expecting to see death sneaking up on them. Darin didn't look himself. Evie and Tom would be leagues inland by now, following their own escape routes. They were safe. That was all that mattered.

CHAPTER SIX
Dangerous Roads

Tom really wished he'd thought to keep his sword.

He and Evie decided they should stick together for the long ride home from Eskirk. She said they'd already messed up their exit plans with the harbor business, so they had a clean slate to do as they chose. Her merchant caravan was long gone by that time. Tom might have caught up to his patrol group, but they were all strangers. Evie was better to talk to. Especially because she knew not to expect much talking at all.

She did enough for both of them. She told Tom about all the people she'd spotted at Eskirk's gala, who they were, where they lived, and what they were about. He didn't understand how she knew so many people in high places. It wasn't like any of them stopped by the inn to say hello. Still, Darin had told him not to ask Evie about her highfalutin days. And she seemed a different Evie when she talked about these things. More animated. Less angry about things. He liked hearing her talk even though he understood less than half. He still listened with attention, though. Sometimes she quizzed him.

They had no trouble in Eskirk. The roads were well-maintained, and strangers waved or said hello as they passed. Some even traveled alone, or in small, unarmed groups. He shook his head to himself every time they passed one. In the Scatters, where Tom grew up, people who traveled alone on the seashell-paved roads wound up in the bay with their throats cut. Eskirk was like another world. Evie seemed to like the wide country lanes with their too-friendly travelers. All they did for Tom was make him nervous.

When they crossed the border into the duchy of Fairhurst, he felt more at home. Spreadvines grew unchecked on both sides of the road, their narrow leaves reaching over it like green hands. Deep wagon ruts crisscrossed what little roadway remained. Everything went fine, until they encountered the first group of men who wanted to rob them.

It was a classic setup. The road curved downhill and into a dense thicket of cedars and scrub brush. A man with a broken-down horse cart, but no horse, waited there to stop them. He had a gaunt face and stains on his wrinkled tunic. No visible weapon, but it was probably in the wagon. When he spotted them, he at least made a show of inspecting one of the wagon wheels.

"Sorry, she broke down on me," he said.

As Tom and Evie drew close to the wagon, his eyes flickered to the road behind them.

"Where's your horse?" Evie asked.

The man shrugged. "Ran off."

Rustling and a muffled curse came from the thickets behind them to the left of the road. Their timing needed work. The men cutting off their retreat should have closed the gap the moment they entered the thicket. The wagon itself was barely large enough to bar their way, and the wheel chock was on the wrong side, right where you could see it.

"Let me give you a hand."

Tom leaned down and yanked the chock free.

"No need to–"

"It's no trouble." Tom put his shoulder to the wagon and gave it a shove. It lurched forward, forcing the man to dance out of the way.

White showed around the man's eyes. "Stop that!"

"Come on, maybe we'll find your horse," Evie said sweetly.

Everyone knew what was what. The man started cursing at them, and pushed back on the wagon. Tom already had momentum on his side, and Evie scurried up to push with him. Boots pounded as his fellows charged up behind. The trees opened up ahead, maybe twenty paces. Tom dug in and renewed his efforts. But the man reached into the cart and came up with a loaded crossbow.

Tom lurched to a stop, grabbed Evie, and pulled her down beneath the rim of the cart. He *hated* crossbows. Any fool could point one and pull the trigger. Too many had.

"That's what I thought," said the sallow-faced man. He was out of breath, but his tone had a hint of smug satisfaction. "Let's have your purses."

Tom looked at Evie. They both had show-purses tied to their belts with a few coppers in them. She shrugged. They tossed their purses into the wagon.

Scratching noises in the wagon. "This it?"

"We're traveling on foot with not much more than the clothes on our backs," Evie groused. "What do you want?"

"Your boots, for starters. And then we'll see what else you've got."

Evie had her dagger out before he even finished talking. She might give up a few coppers, but he'd have to pry her boots off her corpse. Tom knew it in his bones. And with the two men who'd close the jaws of this trap nearly in view, he had little choice.

"Get ready." He turned and gripped the bottom edge of the wagon.

The bandit started talking again, probably something about what he planned to do after he robbed them. Tom didn't catch it. He set his legs and heaved upward. The wagon edge came up to his chest. He moved his hands and shoved it all the way over. The man tried to get clear but gave a muffled shout as it brought him to the ground. Evie scampered over the wagon's floor and scooped up his crossbow from the ground. It was still drawn. She found the bolt, too, slotted it, and aimed it backward up the road.

Tom began edging his way around the wagon. There wasn't much room at the side. Evergreen branches and scrub-brush pulled at his clothes. The owner lay on his belly, pinned down at the waist. Blood streamed from his nose. He groaned and muttered something. Tom couldn't quite make it out, but Evie glanced down and delivered a sharp kick to his face. He grunted and went still. Either unconscious or wishing to be. Tom reclaimed his purse and Evie's from the ground.

The other two men charged around the bend, swords in hand. They wore the same plain, dirty woolens. No mail, no helmets. Not even a scabbard for the swords, which meant they were probably stolen.

"Another step, and I'll put a bolt in whoever's closest," Evie called.

One man spat. "You'll miss us from there."

"Maybe, maybe not." She lowered the crossbow until the bolt hovered above wagon guy's head. "But I won't miss your friend."

Right on cue, the man under the wagon groaned. His comrades held fast. Their shoulders slumped.

Evie smiled. "Who says there's no honor among thieves? Toss your swords to us."

A strange emotion flickered over their faces. They clutched their swords with white knuckles.

"Evie," Tom said.

"What?"

"Let them keep the steel."

"Are you mad?"

"It's all they've got." And Tom knew exactly what that felt like. What it did to a man.

Evie made a disgusted sound but gave in. "Toss your swords into the trees," she said.

The men complied almost gratefully.

Tom held out his hand. Evie gave him the crossbow, picked up her skirts, and stalked up the road. Tom considered it for a minute, then dropped his purse beside the man under the wagon. "Sorry. Never try to take a lady's boots."

He jogged to catch up to Evie, who hadn't slowed. On the way he snapped the trigger off the crossbow and tossed it into the bushes.

"Why did you do that?" she asked.

Tom considered her question and decided she must be asking about the purse. "They need it more than I do."

Evie snorted. "Don't be so sure. It's a long way across Fairhurst."

Darin seemed to pick up a new unpleasant odor on every leg of his journey. The bilge compartment on Burgess's ship smelled of brine and old tar. The slightly more reputable northbound trader that took him on at the next port carried the heavy musk of tobacco leaf. Tom would have loved it. Last but not least, there was the fishing vessel that carried him upriver into Caron whose pungent odor needed no florid description. By the time he made landfall, he reeked like the underside of a wharf at midsummer. It was the kind of stench where even strangers recoiled, politeness be damned. Besides, this was the Middle Queendom. People didn't take ten minutes to dance around talking about something. They told it to you straight.

He actually looked forward to what Evie and Tom would say when he met up with them. Separating after a job was good thief sense. Three individuals traveling separately drew less attention. It also gave them all time to make sure they weren't being followed, or tracked by some arcane means. Still, he hated not knowing with certainty that they'd gotten away clean. No contact. That was the protocol. They could both be chained in the dungeons beneath Eskirk – assuming that the duchess had some kind of dungeon, which seemed likely – and he wouldn't know different until he got there and saw them.

Years ago, broad evergreen forests blanketed this part of the Old Queendom. The disused dock where the fishermen had dropped him off had once been a bustling lumber port. Now only stumps remained within wagon-distance. Brambles and shrubs had taken over, but there was no money in those, so the sawyers had moved elsewhere. Farmers didn't bother planting crops in the dry, leached soil. All this land could support were grazing animals. A quarter league inland, he found a loosely tethered plow horse grazing in a field of long grass.

"Well, well. Look at you, Buttercup," he said.

The horse spared him not a glance but kept on grazing.

She was at least fourteen years old and nearly deaf, but it sure felt good to see a familiar face. Even on a burden animal. Spend enough time among strangers, and you learned to appreciate things like that. He made a quick search of the area and found an oil cloak draped across the hollow left by a wind-blown tree. Under that were the bit and tackle, saddle, and blanket. He carried these back to where the pony grazed, and made sure to get in her line of sight before he approached her. Buttercup didn't startle easily, but no sense risking a kick to the giblets.

It took another hour to get her saddled and rigged, but that still beat walking the many leagues inland. Dusk had fallen by the time he reached the tumbledown two-story inn with a faded crimson bird painted on the sign out front. Once upon a time, the inn presided over the crossroads of two major trade routes and catered to a constant stream of traveling merchants. One road ran north into Chillston to the foot of the Shrouded Mountains, whose narrow snow-capped peaks were obscured by clouds on most days, and from which hardwood timber had provided shipbuilding materials for generations. South, it wandered into the duchy of Eskirk and the neatly ordered farm fields that fed half of the queendom's citizens. The fact that the Rooster was in disputed territory – drawn within

Chillston on some maps, and in Eskirk on the others – carried a few benefits, most notably the lack of regular tax collectors. Granted, it also meant that the roads were shit and military protections virtually nonexistent. People in these parts took care of their own.

The other road ran east along the border of these two duchies to the Opal Sea, whose shipping lanes had ironically supplanted most of the land trade that once swelled traffic on those crossroads. And west it ran into Caron, the central duchy and seat of the queen. There was obviously no Duchess of Caron, so managing the day-to-day affairs of the duchy fell to the barons and her majesty's advisory council. It was rumored that the same could be said of running the entire queendom, given the queen's declining health.

Those were big problems, certainly, but, at the moment, Darin was tired and the inn a welcome sight.

As inns went, the Red Rooster had little to brag about. The structure resembled a mishmash of four unsteady buildings that leaned on one another like drunken sailors returning from shore leave. The food in the common room was unremarkable, and service notoriously slow. It was almost as if the owner had a second job that he cared more about.

Darin dismounted and led Buttercup around back, unsaddled her, and gave her fresh water. She'd sniff her way down to the grain bin when she was good and ready.

He yanked open the steel-banded door to the Red Rooster common room. Only a faint cloud of pipe-smoke drifted near the ceiling, and most of the thirteen mismatched tables bore no sign of recent use. That made it a slow night, even by Rooster standards.

A tall bar ran along the back. It served a number of purposes, not the least of which was keeping the frightening array of house weapons out of view of the customers. Seraphina stood behind it now, her bone-white hair askew, with a tilt in her posture that said she'd reached for a weapon when Darin barged into the room. She looked older than she was but could still shoot a crossbow or throw a spear like a woman forty years her junior. She straightened when she saw him. "Darin! Gods be praised."

Darin sighed, savoring all of the familiar, comfortable sights. Someone had moved two of the stools, but everything else looked in place. "Evening, Seraphina."

She wagged a finger at him. "You're two days late."

"Would've been three, if you hadn't left Buttercup for me." He moved the two stools back, then slumped in a third one against the bar.

Seraphina was already pulling a mug of ale for him, bless her heart. "Was she all right? I'd planned to send someone to get her tomorrow."

"What were you going to leave me? The stable looks empty."

She looked down and raised her eyebrows. "I'd a mind to send a goat in its place."

"What in the hell would I do with a goat?"

"I'm sure you'd think of something."

He laughed. "You really are an old bitty, you know that?"

"And you're an irreverent pup who should respect your elders."

He grinned. "I respect the hell out of you. Now, where are the others?"

"You're the first back."

A dark chill took up residence in Darin's gut. "They had a two-day lead on me."

She shrugged, clearly not willing to share his unease. "It's a long way from Eskirk. People get delayed. You certainly did."

"I was stowed in a compartment in the slowest and most rickety sailing junk in the queendom." He shook his head. "Think they got into some trouble?"

"They haven't sent a distress message."

"That doesn't mean anything." They might not have been able to, or the message simply might not have made it. Couriers and paid-to-deliver missives were hardly reliable. Not with the queendom crumbling into pieces.

"You worry too much," Seraphina said.

"That's my job." He drained the rest of the ale and slid the mug back to her. "Maybe I'll ride down to the crossroads."

"Not on my Buttercup, you won't. She's had enough riding for one day."

"Come on now, just a little nip down and back. It won't kill her."

"She's nearly as old as me, in horse years. And your time is better spent on a bath."

Darin sniffed himself. "Am I that bad?"

"You're worse than bad. You're like a rotten plum covered in horse shit."

He blinked at the colorful mental picture that drew. "You know, I'm starting to remember why we never invite you along on these things."

"It'll wash off with a good bath. And by the time you're done, I'm sure Tom and Evie will be back."

She was wrong on both counts.

CHAPTER SEVEN
The Red Rooster

In the end, he did take a bath, though under protest. It did nothing to take his mind off the rest of his crew. A wide and often-unfriendly continent stretched between Eskirk and the Red Rooster's safe bastion. Maybe they'd simply gotten held up on the road, but maybe they'd never even gotten out of the harbor. That was the disadvantage of scatter-and-flee escape plans. No contact protected them, but also meant no one came to your aid if you got caught up somewhere. Big Tom would probably be all right – it would take an entire squad of men to get hold of him. Evie was a young woman traveling alone. Sure, she could handle herself, but it was still a considerable risk. The thought of her coming to any harm twisted Darin's heart in a strange and unwelcome way.

He scrubbed off about one-third of the travel grime – the stench of stagnant seawater would take more than one soak to wash away. Then he dressed and clomped downstairs to help Seraphina clean up.

She came over right off to straighten his jacket, and brush some of the dust off the shoulders. "You smell better, but you still look like hell."

"You always know the right thing to say."

"Why don't you knock off and get some rest? I can wake you when they arrive."

"I don't mind waiting."

She *tsked* at him but gestured at the table near the bar, which held a half-loaf of bread and a wooden bowl of stew, both of them piping hot. That was one of the perks of asking her to run the Rooster while he was away. The woman always seemed to know what day he'd return and made sure there was something good simmering in the hearth kettle.

"I can still smell it on you," she said, after a while.

"Gods, woman, I spent a week in the bilge," Darin grumbled.

"I'm talking about the metallurgy, boy."

"Oh." Darin suppressed a bout of nausea. "That."

She cackled. "Used a bit more than you planned, didn't you?"

"What gave it away?"

"I can always tell. Your tolerance is shit."

"I'm well aware," Darin said.

"It wouldn't be, if you deigned to exercise your ability once in a while."

"You know how I feel about that." Metallurgy was useful in his trade; there was no denying it. Still, he hated resorting to it. Even when he had the silver, which currently wasn't the case.

"If you're going to be a fool, let's at least get some food in your belly," Seraphina said. "You look like you haven't eaten in two weeks."

Well, it couldn't hurt to eat. It'd keep him busy, too, keep his mind off how late they were. He tucked in, savoring the taste of hearty, home-cooked food. A good stew took two days to cook right, so it had been a while. "This is good."

"Better than salt tack, I'm guessing." She brushed the breadcrumbs to the floor and slid another full bowl over to replace his empty one.

He wolfed it down just as quickly and soaked up the rest of the broth with the heel of the loaf. "Really good."

"Look at you, finding your manners. Maybe now you'll have the sense to get some rest."

Not likely, he wanted to say, but the stew had pooled in his stomach like a warm, glowing ball of comforting flame. It pulled him down against the stool. It wouldn't hurt to close his eyes, just for a minute or two. He shut them and savored the lingering taste of the stew in his mouth. It had a subtle new flavor he didn't recognize. Earthy. That's what it was.

He opened his eyes again. Saw how she was watching him. "Did you change the recipe?"

"What's that, now?"

"I said, did you change the stew somehow?"

"Not really." She collected his empty bowl and carried it over to the bar for a scrub. "Of course, there was a piece of sleeproot that tumbled in before I brought it to you."

And now I'm hearing things. "I'm sorry, did you say *sleeproot*?"

"Did I forget to mention that?"

"You… you drugged me!" he sputtered. His tongue felt strangely heavy in his mouth.

"Just a little."

"You're a horrible… horrible woman." The words seemed so clear in his head, but he knew he was slurring them.

"Yes, yes," she agreed. "I can't imagine why they haven't locked me up yet."

The table rose up to greet his heavy head, and darkness fell over him.

By the time she finally spotted the roof of the Red Rooster, Evie felt the travel fatigue in her bones. She wanted nothing more than to shed her gear, find the nearest hot bath, and soak in it until she was an old woman. That wouldn't be nearly long enough to get all the road dust off. Her mother had been right about the central queendom: most of it was "ride-through country." No fewer than five separate groups had tried to rob them along the way. They'd fought off some and paid off others. Part of her couldn't believe they'd made it back. The most frightening part of all was that she didn't know if Darin got out of Eskirk harbor. She lost track of how many times she cursed the stubborn man's rules about no contact after a job. The worry became a knot of discomfort in her stomach that rode with her the long way back. Gods, it would be a relief to see him safe and sound so the knot could fade away.

Someone had parked a large wooden cart stacked with oak-stave barrels in the middle of the yard. There were traces enough for one horse, though no animal was in sight. The canvas cover looked sturdy enough, but carried more than its share of travel stains. Evie's heart beat a little bit faster when she saw it. *Darin.*

Then a stout woman strode into view, muttering to herself. She picked up one of the barrels in a bear hug and carried it around back. Three boys popped out of the cart and scampered after her, laughing and pushing one another.

"What's that about?" Evie asked.

Tom shrugged, but when she looked at him, he had his head cocked to one side.

"Tom."

"What?"

"Nothing."

Evie pressed her lips together. He knew something, but there was no getting Tom to spill when he didn't want to. His silence had Darin written all over it.

They dismounted in the yard and were leading horses around when they came face to face with a woman, presumably the owner of the barrel cart.

She saw them and grinned. "Hey there. Plenty of open stalls in the stables, if you're looking to house those two."

Evie blinked at the woman's unexpected friendliness. "We've, ah, been here before."

"You're locals, then." The woman seemed pleased by this news. "My name's Kat. Maybe you can give me the skinny on this place. Do they serve ale in the common room?"

"Not usually, no," Evie said. "It's not really the kind of place for people to just… drop by."

Without being asked, Tom stepped up beside her and loomed there. He was good at looming. Evie had found that his presence excelled at shortening unwanted conversations. Only not in this instance.

Kat looked him up and down. "You're a big one, aren't you?" She turned to Evie. "It's all right. I know it's not a regular inn. Darin invited me."

She knew Darin's name, which was something. Then again, it wasn't like Darin to invite a stranger to stop by the Rooster.

"Perhaps you're mistaken," Evie said.

"I don't think so. Unless there's another Red Rooster inn at a no-name crossroads in this part of the queendom."

"Noticed your harness out front," Tom said, breaking suddenly into the conversation. "Interesting setup."

"I know what you're going to ask, and no, it's not an accident," Kat said.

"No bit."

"I don't believe in them."

"Me neither," Tom said.

"Why torture a poor old horse that knows what it's doing?"

"I'm with you."

"Then you've got a level head on your shoulders. What's your name?"

"They call me Big Tom."

Kat barked a laugh. "Now *that* I believe."

Evie rolled her eyes. "I'm going inside."

Three weeks and two hundred leagues since leaving Eskirk and wondering if Darin was safe, she found him perfectly alive, perfectly safe, and perfectly passed out on the common room table.

She scowled. The *nerve* of the man. Probably waited all of half an hour before getting into his cups. Or worse, the silver they'd taken from the job.

Tom lumbered in the door behind her. "There he is."

"Yes," Evie said. "There he is."

"Are we sure he's not dead?"

"He's snoring, for one thing."

"Doesn't he always snore?"

"How should I know?" She shot Tom a look. "Don't even *think* of answering that."

"Wasn't going to."

"Where's the woman?"

"Kat?"

"Are there any *other* strange women hanging around?"

"She's nice. Offered to get started on our horses."

Making herself at home, isn't she? Evie wanted to hit something. And Darin made an easy target.

CHAPTER EIGHT
New Arrivals

A distant but inexorable buzzing noise pulled Darin from the deep recesses of slumber. Sometimes it was higher-pitched, sometimes lower-pitched. Always alternating back and forth between those things, never letting him drift back into the nothingness. Slowly, the buzzing resolved into voices.

"Not sure he would like that," a man was saying.

"A really *small* knife. No larger than someone's hand."

"My hand, or yours?"

"Mine, obviously."

"A knife is still a knife," the man said.

"You're no fun, you know that?" The woman's sultry voice stirred something deeper in the corners of Darin's mind. Old instincts made him snap his eyes open, which he regretted. Harsh, unforgiving sunlight streamed in through the door, which someone propped open most mornings to air out the common room.

Darin squinted to make out the shapes of the people standing over him. The dull pain in his eyes promised a blinding headache later. Sleeproot always left you sensitive to light when you woke up. Which, depending on the dose, might be an hour later, or a week.

His brief, painful glimpse outlined two forms over him, one slender and feminine, one roughly the size of a small building. Evie and Big Tom. Either they'd made it through, or he'd overdosed on sleeproot and landed in this blinding afterlife.

"You're back," he croaked.

"Hey, you're alive!" Tom said. He slapped Darin on the shoulder, a gentle tap that nearly tossed Darin off his stool. "Whoops, sorry."

"I don't know, Tom." Evie leaned in close for a look at Darin's face. "When we parted ways, Darin looked like a respectable servant. A lord in disguise, even. This here's more like a, a–"

"A half-drowned muskrat," Seraphina offered, bustling in from the kitchen with a washbasin. Knowing her, it already had clean, warm water in it.

Evie paused to incline her head. She was always carefully deferential where Seraphina was concerned. "A fitting word for it."

Evie swung her gaze back to Darin. "You'd think, after three weeks apart with no word between us, he'd at least have the decency to wait around and see if we were still alive. Instead, we find him passed out on the table with stew in his beard."

"That's a man for you," Seraphina said.

Darin tried to muster the strength to give her a dirty look, but before he could manage, she blew him a kiss and disappeared back into the kitchen. Instead, he forced himself to really look and be sure it wasn't a fever-dream, or a sleeproot illusion. But no, it was his crew, still in their riding gear and muddied boots. Several strands of coarse horse-hair littered the wool covering Tom's barrel-broad chest; obviously he'd been out to the stables already to check on the mounts. Evie's perfect oval face made his heart flip over. Somehow she came in from the road as clean as a chirurgeon's table. Her long hair was braided and tied with ribbons in a long line down her back.

He could say a number of things right then – that he'd missed them, that he'd been worried about them, that Seraphina had slipped the sleeproot into his stew – but he settled for, "What took you so long?"

"We were delayed in Eskirk harbor," Evie said.

Eskirk harbor. "Gods, the living fire," Darin whispered. The only consolation as Burgess's ship fled the thing was that Evie and Tom were safely out of the city. "You weren't supposed to be there."

"Someone decided to hang around," Evie said.

Tom. Darin shook his head. He should have expected that a man who worried about the horses during every thunderstorm would worry about his crew at break-off. "If I'd known, I'd have–"

"What, thrown yourself to its mercy?" Evie asked. "I don't think that would have worked. Even if it had been living fire."

"Was it not?" He didn't think for a second that he'd mistaken the signal on the *Wish*. It had haunted his sleep for days. *No one deserves watching fire devour their ship beneath them.*

"False alarm," Tom said.

"Who in the hell would make it seem like–" Darin began. Then he saw Evie's wicked grin, and it dawned on him. "*You?* Please, tell me you're having a jest."

She stuck out her chin, unapologetic. "It got you free of the duchess's soldiers, didn't it?"

"And her silver witch, too."

Tom made the warding gesture and spat over his shoulder.

"Tom!" Evie scolded him.

Darin waved her off. "How did you pull off that little ruse?"

Evie touched his cheek lightly and let her fingertips trail down to his chest. "I can be persuasive."

"But the smoke–"

"Full casket of dried leaf," Tom rumbled. "Good quality stuff, too."

Darin tipped an imaginary hat – he'd lost his real one gambling with the sailors – and then fought a wave of dizziness. *Damn that old woman and her sleeproot.* "I owe you one."

Strangely, he also felt relieved that the witch hadn't gone off to face real living fire. Not that he cared what happened to her in particular, but still. He'd rather enjoyed the verbal sparring until she'd hoisted him over the rail.

"You can start by telling us about the woman," Evie said.

"What woman?"

"The one unloading an endless pile of barrels out back."

"She said her name is Kat," Tom added.

It had been a long voyage home, but not so long that Darin forgot who had gotten him to Eskirk harbor. "Really?" The woman didn't waste any time, did she? Probably living out of that wagon as it were, so maybe an inn sounded pretty good. "Good. We can use her."

"What's her story?" Evie asked.

"Haven't gotten all of it from her yet."

"So you just, what, thought you'd invite a total stranger to visit our base of operations?"

The danger in Evie's tone cut through Darin's groggy senses like a warning bell. He stood and faced her, gritting his teeth at the pain that lanced both sides of his head. "She's like us."

"How do you know?"

"The same way I knew with you," he said.

That forestalled her next protest. Tom moved over and looked out the front door. "What's in the barrels?"

"Ale, by my guess," Darin said.

Evie frowned. "Ale."

"Yes, you know. What us *commoners* drink."

A mixture of hurt and shame flickered across her face before she turned away.

Oh, hells. Darin regretted the words instantly. He coughed. "Sorry, Evie. I didn't mean–"

She shook her head. "No, you're right. I'm the same as you now." She still wouldn't look at him.

He hated how small she seemed in that moment. He wanted to wrap his arms around her and pull her close, but settled for easing up next to her and lowering his voice. "No, you're not. You never will be."

She leaned back, resting her head on his chest for three heartbeats.

"I could never get along with the fancy clothes, for one thing," he said. "Too much silk."

She laughed, and so did he. Just like that, her spirit filled the room again.

"So, you said something about a witch?" she asked.

Uh-oh. Darin schooled his grin and put on a slight grimace. "Nasty woman. The last thing I wanted to see on deck."

"I see." Evie turned to look at him and straightened the collar of his shirt. Her nail scratched the nape of his neck. It felt sharp as a fresh-honed razor. "Was she... pretty?"

"She was unnatural. You know how I feel about them."

"Witches? Or women in general?"

That seemed like a dangerous question to answer, so he offered humility instead. "When they spotted that distraction of yours, she had me dangling out over the water on my belly," he said.

Tom guffawed.

"What for?" Evie demanded.

"Guess she didn't like the look of me." He elected not to share the fact that he may or may not have elicited such a feeling of dislike. "Which brings me to the uncomfortable news."

"She used metallurgy on you, and now you're cursed?"

Darin chuckled, but it sounded nervous to his own ears. *Too close to the mark.* "I wish that were all. But when she flipped me upside down, most of our hard-won loot fell into the water."

"That's not funny, Darin," Evie said, suddenly serious.

"I know it's not. But it's the truth."

She muttered a most inelegant curse that made Tom blush.

"I'm just relieved that you and Tom went separately with a good portion," Darin said.

Evie's face went stony. She looked at Tom.

The big man ran a hand through his hair. His nervous tell. "About that."

Darin's good humor plummeted into his gut like an anvil. Evie letting Tom give the news meant it was especially bad. "What?"

"We lost a little bit on the way back, too," Tom said.

"I don't see how." Darin couldn't quite keep the irritation from his voice. He'd set up their routes personally. "You should have had no trouble getting out of Eskirk."

"Eskirk was a breeze," Evie said. "It's the rest of this gods-damned crumbling queendom that gave us trouble."

"What kind of trouble?"

Tom shrugged. "The usual. Bandits, cutpurses, and thieves."

"Don't forget the pickpocket by the canal," Evie said.

"Yeah, her too," Tom said.

Darin rubbed his temples, which had started throbbing again. "You said you lost *a little bit* on the way back. How much are we talking?"

Tom looked at Evie. She lifted her skirts high enough to untie a slender purse there. Even in his growing sense of dread, Darin rather enjoyed the view. She dumped its contents onto the bar. Three jeweled rings, an emerald bodice, a handful of coins and other trinkets made a glittering pile, though a small one.

"Well, this isn't too bad," he said. "Where's the rest?"

"There isn't anything else. This is all we've got," Evie said.

Kat stepped into the common room and regretted it right away. There were three people inside, which was already borderline too many for her comfort in such a small space. But she'd unloaded the entire wagon, found the boys a nice spot in the hayloft, and so she couldn't put it off any longer. She had to make this thing stick, or she'd be back on the road again with the boys, wondering where they'd sleep each night.

She tucked the sample keg under her arm, grabbed the tap and mallet, and tried to walk in like she belonged there.

Darin looked healthier than the last time she'd seen him, if a bit unkempt. He stood beside the long wooden bar with practiced comfort. So it was his place after all. That was encouraging. With thieves, you never knew if anything they said was true. He smiled at Kat in a welcoming sort of way, and pretended not to see the way the pretty girl glowered at him. *She* didn't look unkempt, not in the least. She might be the most beautiful person Kat had ever seen up close. Tom, the big one who loved his horses, had situated himself along the wall and was keeping very still. Probably wishing he were back outside in the stables. She could empathize with that. *Wish I were back there myself.*

"Well, hello, Miss Kat. Welcome to the Red Rooster," Darin said.

"Just Kat is fine," Kat mumbled. "I can come back later, if it's a bad time."

"Nonsense." Darin gestured at his two companions. "I understand you met Tom and Evie already."

"Yes." Kat wasn't sure what else to say, so she hoisted the barrel. "Thought maybe you'd be thirsty."

"You come bearing gifts? How delightful," Darin said. "Isn't that kind of her, Evie?"

"Very kind," Evie said politely.

The big one said nothing; he didn't seem to be much of a talker. That didn't bother Kat at all. Now she had something to do, so she got to it. Heaved the cask up onto the bar. Drove the tap in with three deft strokes of the mallet. Then looked up, and quickly realized she had nothing to pour into. "So, any mugs?"

"I'm sure we can rustle up something." Darin ducked behind the bar and began rummaging for mugs with a surprising amount of noise. During this search, he set several random non-mug objects on top of the bar. One was a loaded crossbow. At least he didn't point it at her. After a moment, he produced five mismatched, dented tin cups. Kat shouldn't have been surprised. None of the tables or chairs in the entire room matched, and they all had at least a few dents or scratches in them. Most also carried a fine layer of dust, which suggested it wasn't really much of a common room.

"I brewed this myself," Kat said. She poured three fingers of ale into each mug with a little flourish. "Call it 'batch fourteen.'" She didn't spill a drop, and all five mugs ended up perfectly level when the foam cleared.

Evie gave her an appraising look.

Kat shrugged. "I get a lot of practice." Besides, pouring ale on a flat, sturdy bar was a holiday from sloshing it out from the back of her rolling wagon for a group of impatient freeriders. With luck, she might not have to worry about that anymore. Might not sleep with half an eye open and a sheathed dagger under her pillow. She took the nearest mug. The others claimed theirs. Now, who to toast first? Darin, who'd invited her, or Evie, who clearly didn't like her? Of course, it might also be that the girl had unfinished business with Darin. Their body language screamed of it. So, Kat settled on Tom and lifted her mug. "Here's to fast horses."

"To safe roads," Tom said.

Darin lifted his mug at Evie. "To moonless nights."

"And to unwatched purses." Evie touched his glass.

No one made a toast to the fifth mug of ale, but Kat didn't need an explanation. They'd lost someone and didn't want to forget. She drank a sip but did it slow so she could see the others' reactions as they tried batch fourteen. Tom's eyes bulged a little, but he drained his mug in a single pull. Evie took a delicate sip, made a face, and didn't try more. Only Darin showed no reaction, though he was watching Kat as if measuring her against some invisible stick.

Kat finished her mug and smacked her lips. "What do you think?"

"I've had worse," Tom said.

"It's a bit... rough around the edges," Evie said, swiveling her eyes to Darin.

"We all were, once upon a time," he said.

Kat couldn't help but think this conversation had taken on new meaning. "You know, if you sold ale here on a regular basis, you might turn this into a proper common room."

Evie snorted. "For coppers."

Darin clapped his hands to his chest. "You wound me, Kat. Are you suggesting this common room is somehow not proper?"

"I was more suggesting it's not a common room at all. You've got dust on the chairs and barely five mugs to pour into."

"It's a lot of work to run a bar," Darin said.

"Pouring ale and counting coins is a lot of work?"

"For us, at least."

"Now you've got me, and three healthy boys besides," Kat said, hoping it was true.

Darin blinked and looked at her. "Sorry, did you say *three* boys? I thought it was just Timmy and Abel."

"They made a friend."

"I suppose new friends can be useful," Darin said slowly.

"Agreed," Tom said.

A simple word, but Kat didn't miss the formality in it. This was a vote of sorts. Two for, one as-yet-undecided.

Both men looked at Evie, who sighed. "Fine. But don't expect me to play the barmaid if we start running a tavern."

"Of course not," Darin said.

"Wouldn't dream of it," Tom said.

Kat nodded along. "Besides, with the tips you'd get, it'd almost be robbery."

That was only the truth, but it won her a little smile just the same.

"Perhaps on occasion," Evie said. She seemed to sense Darin's grin and shot him a dark look. "*Rare* occasion."

Darin put up his hands in mock surrender, but there was a cool satisfaction to his countenance. He'd gotten his way.

Kat took the first full breath she'd tried since unloading the barrels. *We can stay.*

"That's settled, then." Darin took another swig of his ale and set the mug down. "Of course, it may not matter. I'm off to see the Dame tomorrow to explain why we haven't got her cut."

The little smile fell away from Evie's face. "How do you think she'll take it?"

"I'll put it this way: if I'm not back by nightfall, torch this place and do your best to disappear."

Kat started to laugh, but realized he was dead serious. *What have I gotten us into?*

CHAPTER NINE
A Visit to the Dame

Darin lived and breathed risk, but few situations brought more of it than meeting with his boss. The Gray Dame oversaw virtually all unscrupulous activity in this part of the Old Queendom. Every crew operating within two hundred leagues answered to her and paid duties. In return, she kept them from stepping on one another's boots and ran interference as necessary with the regional constabulary. She occasionally underwrote small criminal enterprises such as Darin's. It was the Dame who'd helped set up the heist at Eskirk's gala. That made her cut one-half, rather than the usual one-third.

When you didn't pay the Dame, she never seemed to react in overt fashion. She was too subtle for that. She didn't send couriered messages or summons. She knew that you knew that you owed. So she let you sit and worry about what falling in disfavor might do to you.

Once, Darin had known a rival crew operating in the southwest. Cunar, the fellow was called. He went in for more of the smash-and-grab style of heist. Get in loud, neutralize any guards, take the loot, and disappear. Rumor had it, he thought he'd mastered the disappearing part enough to stop paying his respects to the Dame. The fool even went so far as to brag about it in public. Soon after, he got word that a gem dealer was moving a valuable shipment overland by armored carriage. Right through his favorite territory.

Cunar led the raid himself. Isolated the armed escort, diverted the carriage to a patch of dense woods. Not long after, a woodcutter passing through heard men screaming. He followed the sound and came upon a grisly scene. Wheel ruts showed where the carriage had come to a stop. Bloody, almost unrecognizable bodies lay scattered in a ring around it. Cunar, his men, and their horses had been cut to pieces.

That's what it meant to cross the Gray Dame.

Owing her money wasn't exactly crossing her, but it hardly put Darin on her list of favorite subordinates. So it was with some trepidation that he rode Moody Mary toward the banks of the Icevine to meet her barge. The river flowed deep and frigid, fed by a slowly melting glacier high up in the mountains. The Dame's crimson-canopied barge was a constant fixture on it, either drifting downstream or being rowed against the current. Darin didn't expect a pass until late afternoon, which gave him a couple of hours. He let Mary graze on the tall grasses near the riverbank and settled under a tree to wait.

In the hour it took for the Dame's barge to appear upriver, Moody Mary had managed to crap on Darin's boots twice. The lookout in the barge's bow saw him, turned, and shouted something. Long oars slid out on both sides of the barge and steered it to the bank while Darin tied the end of the mare's reins to a shade tree. He approached the shoreline as the nose of the barge touched it. Someone threw a rope ladder over the rail. The climb up and over winded him, but not so much that he forgot to remove his boots and leave them on the mat provided. A clean-shaven man in crimson and gray livery appeared to offer him a washbowl and towel upon a silver tray. Darin didn't recognize him, but he was young and strikingly handsome. Quiet, too. He bowed and made an inviting gesture toward the canopy.

Darin stepped beneath it and into what seemed like another world. Dark polished wood shone everywhere he looked. It resembled the parlor of a wealthy noble, and it positively reeked of silver. So much that he tried not to think about how much cold spending metal was given over to mere decoration. A lean figure blocked his view, interrupting his moment of admiration for the decor. She was nearly as tall as Darin, and the chainmail added bulk to her shoulders. Were it not for the honeyed braid down her back, some might mistake her for a man. Her name was Areana and, as the fighting irons on her hips suggested, she was the Gray Dame's personal enforcer.

"You're late," she said, and made a curt gesture telling him to submit to inspection.

"Areana, what a pleasant surprise," he said smoothly, lifting his hands in the air, palms outward.

She confiscated his belt knife and searched the rest of his person with practiced efficiency. "You won't find it pleasant if you haven't got your nip for the Dame."

"Your concern for my well-being is–" He broke off as one of her gloved hands strayed uncomfortably high on the inside of his leg. "Ah, more touching than usual."

She smiled at him without warmth. "Might be my last chance."

"You worry too much."

"No, you don't worry enough."

Darin felt the barge shudder as the oarsmen backed it into the current. "As much as I enjoy our conversations, I don't want to keep her waiting." He didn't add that each moment in the current gave him a longer walk back to his ride home. It was the Dame's way of encouraging short meetings.

Areana tucked Darin's knife into her belt and gestured toward the center of the barge. He moved in that direction, conscious of the deep red tint to the weak sunlight that filtered through the canopy. As he moved amidships, a cacophony of chirps and chitters greeted his ears. Priceless divans and marble-inlaid tables gave way to an open area filled with birdcages mounted on wooden poles. Birds of every imaginable color and style perched inside them. The cage nearest him held a bright orange songbird with dark gossamer wings. The one beyond it contained an elegant gray bird with a dazzling white crest on its head. Its overlarge eyes seemed to watch him with a mixture of intelligence and pity. *And now I'm imagining things.*

The Dame herself was seated in a high-backed chair, slicing fruits on a marble pedestal table. She was just past middle age, by Darin's guess, and her once-dark hair had gone mostly to silver. That was part of what gave her the name. She sat with perfect posture – whether that spoke to high breeding or military training, he couldn't be sure – and moved the knife in swift, precise movements.

Darin swept into a bow. "Your servant, my lady."

She smiled at him in a grandmotherly sort of way. "Darin, how nice of you to drop by."

"Please forgive my lateness."

"Oh, were you late? I hadn't noticed."

He was and she had, but he didn't dare voice this particular fact. "I apologize just the same." He withdrew the offering purse from inside his jacket and placed it on the table, out of the way of the fruit-cutting operation. The Dame barely glanced at it. The stillness of her face said she knew the purse was light. She raised an eyebrow at him.

He winced. "It didn't go entirely to plan."

"Which part? The duel with an aristocrat's son, or putting the fear of plague into two hundred people?"

Darin grimaced. *There goes my reputation.* "I thought it had a certain flare."

"I don't care about style. I care about results." She hefted his offering purse disdainfully and tossed it aside. "These are surprisingly light results given how much you took from the people at the gala."

"We got out with plenty. Getting back home was the problem."

"Remind me, Darin. Who arranged access to a gala filled with drunk wealthy marks begging to be fleeced?"

"You did," Darin said, his voice tight.

"And who planned the getting away portion?"

Darin cleared his throat. "There were complications."

"There are *always* complications." The Dame took to cutting an apple, each movement sharp and precise. Each slice the exact same width. "Good criminals, successful criminals, plan for them and adapt as needed." She spun the apple without looking and resumed cutting from the core side. Every cut was still perfect.

"I'm sorry. I'll do better next time."

"You're assuming there's going to be a next time."

Darin fully expected her to make veiled threats, but even so, her words turned his gut to ice. "I'll make good on what I owe you."

"Really?" The Dame resumed her knife-work, only seeming to pay him half a mind. "Now there's something I've never heard before."

"I've got a good crew. We'll beg on street corners if we have to."

"I've got more than enough beggars on my payroll already, thank you," the Dame said. "And you're not pretty enough for it. No matter what Areana says."

Darin didn't quite know how to process that particular comment, so he set it aside. "You know what I mean. We'll do whatever it takes to put the silver back in your pocket." He didn't add that he was giving her the full score from the gala job – no need to make her wise to the full extent of their failure. It would mean tight belts at the Rooster, but survival came first.

"I'm confident you'll make good within a month."

"A month." Darin coughed into his hand. "I'm not sure it'll be quite that fast. For all of it, I mean."

The Dame gave him a measuring look. "I suppose I can give you an extension after that."

"That would be deeply appreciated, thank–"

"At the standard interest rate, of course."

Darin nearly choked. "You're charging me interest all of a sudden?"

"You're in deep, Darin. What choice do I have?"

He was already running the numbers in his head, and they didn't look good. Forget paying her back in a few months when he had some other gigs lined up. By then, with the *standard* interest, he'd owe double. The Dame knew that. Standard interest was her long-term plan to owning someone. "Gods, Dame. Save me the trouble and have Areana throw me over the side."

"You're always telling me you have big ideas."

"I have some irons in the fire, but... nothing like that." Nothing that would square them with the Dame before they drowned in her interest.

"Then it's time to work the bellows."

He'd have to line up something big. Maybe even bigger than the Eskirk gala. And they'd need smaller scores along the way, just to keep level. It was doable, but a lot of things had to go just right. Starting with this moment, because if he didn't convince her he'd succeed, she might very well let Areana drop him over the side. "I'll get it done. You have my word on it."

"Good." The Dame considered him a moment, then asked, "Would you be so kind as to bring me that bird from the corner? The yellow one."

Again with the birds. Still, there was nothing to do but comply. He walked over to the cage and opened it, muttering a silent prayer that the damn thing wouldn't escape before he could grab it. The gods knew how much the Dame paid to have these birds imported from the Scatters. Thankfully, the bird had a stiff leg, and didn't hop away fast enough. He cradled it in both hands to carry it to the Dame. Amazingly, the thing didn't peck him.

"Friendly little guy," he said, handing it to her.

"I've had him for years," the Dame said. "Lemonfinches are

rare, even in the Scatters. The coastal traders can't find me a second, no matter how much I offer."

Knowing full well the amount of silver the Dame could command – the wealth of hard coinage that sang to him from belowdecks on this barge alone – Darin guessed it made the bird rare indeed. One of a kind, and a long way from home. He could sympathize. "Sorry to hear that."

"Lemonfinches have a beautiful song, too. This one delighted me with his music every morning." She held the bird on her open palm. It showed no signs of fear, and in fact looked quite at home in her company. No surprise given that she fed all the birds by hand. "Unfortunately, he fell silent some time ago."

"Maybe he's lonely," Darin said.

"I'm sure he has a good reason." The Dame shifted her eyes from the bird to Darin. "Do you know what I do when birds no longer sing for me as they once did?"

"I wouldn't–" Darin began.

The Dame snapped her hand shut, crushing the bird's fragile body in a fist. The thing had no chance to make noise, even if it had wanted to. She opened her hand and its lifeless, crumpled form fell to the floor. Then she went back to slicing the fruit, paying it no further mind. "I expect you to keep Areana advised on your progress. Run along, now."

Darin couldn't think of anything to say, so he bowed and withdrew. He managed not to look at the bird, but its cage's door still hung ajar as he passed, a cold and empty reminder. He still had a month. He could do a lot in a month. Then again, if he failed to deliver a big score soon after that...

I'll wish I was the bird.

CHAPTER TEN
Broken Things

Tom didn't claim to have many practical skills in life, but he took pride in his ability to sense when trouble was coming. Growing up in the Scatters, he'd developed a sort of knack for it. Even as a boy, his unusual size had gotten him all kinds of unwanted attention. You didn't have to go looking for it. Lawless islands with few legitimate trade professions brewed trouble in batches. By the time he was ten, most of his friends had joined street gangs as junior members. Often as not, initiation required picking a fight with someone bigger than you. Tom got tired of putting his friends in the dirt. He started noticing the way people moved. The way they looked at each other, or looked at you. Once he could feel the undercurrents, he got a lot better at seeing trouble coming down the path.

Tom got a sense of that now from the thick air in the Red Rooster common room. Darin got back from seeing the Dame and hardly said a word. He poured himself a tall glass of ale and slumped on the nearest stool, brooding in silence. Evie tolerated this for a few minutes until she finally grew impatient. At last she stamped her foot and marched over to him. "Well?"

Darin didn't even flinch. "Well, what?"

"What happened with the Dame?"

"We spoke."

"Did you explain what happened after Eskirk?"

"I tried. We still owe her."

Evie's shoulders drooped. "How much?"

"Her full take."

"Her full–" Evie broke off. "We barely got back with our skins, and she wants her full cut?"

"Apparently so."

"How much is that, exactly?" Kat asked. "And who is the Dame?"

Darin opened his mouth to answer, but Evie shot him a look and he closed it.

"May I speak to you in private?" she said.

She and Darin retired to an upstairs room and closed the door. Tom didn't eavesdrop, but he doubted it was *that* kind of a meeting.

"So who's the Dame, anyway?" Kat asked.

"Darin's boss," Tom said, not knowing if he should say more.

"Didn't know he had one."

"Everyone's got a boss, they say."

"That they do." Kat barked a laugh. "Fancy an ale, while we act like they're not up there yelling at each other?"

"I'd better check on the horses."

"I'll join you. I want to make sure the boys are settled in."

They walked out to the stables together. The door was a massive slab of painted wood with poorly oiled hinges. Tom reached inside to unfasten the trip wire, then hauled it open. Mary looked out from her stall, saw him, and whickered softly.

"Good girl." He scratched her behind the ears the way she liked.

"Anyone home up there?" Kat called.

Three heads popped up in the hayloft.

"Everything all right?" said the bigger one. Timmy, his name was.

"Just fine." Kat gave a quiet sigh. She was smiling, though, when she looked at Tom. "What about that drink?"

It was a bit early for drinking, but Tom had heard it was impolite to turn down an offer of a drink. "Sure. Just let me…"

He reached up to the shelf above the door, found his tankard, and held it up for her to see. "Darin's mugs are too small."

Kat smiled again, even bigger this time. "You know what, Tom? You're all right."

They went back inside, where Kat filled Tom's tankard almost to the brim. He *was* thirsty, and after the first few pulls, he hardly noticed the aftertaste.

Evie slipped out some hours later, her face an emotionless mask. Didn't say a word to Kat where she stood behind the bar and didn't quite meet Tom's eyes as she walked out the door. Within a few hours, the skies outside grew dark, and it started to rain.

The rain lasted for a full week. In that time, Darin brooded. Tom rarely saw him, and when he did, Darin always had a strange look on his face. Like a boy caught stealing a pie from a windowsill. Tom didn't ask him how it had gone with the Dame. Darin would tell him when he was good and ready.

On the upside, Kat's home-brewed ale had started to bring more customers to the Rooster. Despite the horrible taste, they kept coming back. Cheap alcohol had become less and less common as the queendom became addicted to dreamwine. People didn't brew it as often anymore, Kat said. Something about economics. Whatever the reasons, the ale brought customers, and customers brought crowds. Which made it awkward when Darin finally came downstairs and wanted to talk. He came through the door and seemed surprised at the number of people sitting at mismatched tables, soldiering through mug after mug of Kat's brew. He eased up to an available spot at the bar, close to the door where Tom stood keeping an eye on things.

Kat caught a break in filling orders for the patrons, drew a half mug, and slid it down to Darin. "You look like you could use it."

"Much obliged." Darin took a long pull. He wrinkled his nose and gave a surprised grunt. "This a new batch?"

"Just tapped it yesterday," Kat said. "Tried something different this time, too."

Darin took another drink and grimaced. "What is that, cloves?"

Kat beamed. "Ah, what a palate you have! Do you like it?"

"It's different, I'll give you that."

"Not quite imperial dreamwine, eh?"

"I wouldn't know."

The rising timbre of voices across the common room drew Tom's attention away from his casual eavesdropping. Two men at adjoining tables leaped to their feet and got in each other's faces. Started having words. The untrimmed beards and patches of well-used chainmail made them out-of-work mercenaries. From rival companies, unless Tom missed his guess. Crow Makers and Steel Sorrows. One shoved the other backward, nearly knocking over a full table of mugs. The man regained his balance and came back swinging. In another minute, it would become a full-on brawl.

Tom took three steps and wrapped a hand around the back of their necks, clamping down on skin and hair. That was the nice thing about mercenaries: they never cut their hair short, and that gave them useful handles. Both men looked up, part in surprise, and part in the natural reaction of having your head tugged backward. Hard mercenaries or not, they might as well have been kittens. When Tom turned and started moving toward the door, they had no choice but to follow in small, unsteady steps. Both had the sense not to try drawing a weapon. Tom reached the door and threw them both out, ensuring that they ended up in a soggy heap in the wagon-rutted road outside. Then he went back to his post and resumed his watch over the room.

Darin and Kat were still talking. They'd barely registered Tom bouncing a couple of mercs.

"Business is decent," Kat said. "If we brought in some help, I'll bet we could do more."

Darin shook his head. "Ale brings in coppers. We need silver."

Kat grunted and muttered something to herself about "coppers count for something."

Not for the last time, Tom chided himself for not managing to make it back with more of the loot from the Eskirk gala. He'd focused on getting Evie back home. Back to safety. Whenever they ran one of Darin's games, that was Tom's job. Keeping people safe. It seemed easier to bargain for safe passage. Now he understood why Evie got progressively more upset as the silver evaporated. If he'd known keeping hold of the coin was so important, maybe he could have tried harder. Done things differently. Put more bodies on the ground and kept more coin in the purse. Too late for that now.

"How's the larder?" Darin asked Kat, in his most casual tone. Just hearing it made the hairs on Tom's neck stand up.

"Fine." Kat worked her cleaning rag across the bar, even though she'd already cleaned that part of it five minutes earlier.

"Looked a little low the last time I was in there."

"Did it?" Kat asked. Still not looking up.

"You picked up another stray, didn't you?" Darin asked.

"I caught 'em scrounging in the rubbish heap out back."

"*Them?*"

"Twin brothers."

"Damn it, Kat, the last thing we need is another set of mouths depending on us," Darin snapped.

He wasn't watching her, so he didn't see the way that she recoiled at the sudden anger in his voice. The kind of instinctive flinch that you only learned a certain way. Now when she looked at him, there was a guarded assessment in her eyes. Like a poacher watching a wounded animal, wondering if it was dangerous.

"Darin–" Tom started.

"They were starving," Kat whispered. "Hadn't eaten in who knows how long."

"We're not running a charity operation," Darin said.

His tone still carried an undercurrent of irritation. It probably had more to do with Evie's conspicuous absence the past two days than whatever Kat might have done. She wouldn't know that, though. Uncertainty flashed across her face. Tom could guess what she must be thinking: that she'd come so far, hoping to find a better life for her boys, and now she might have put them in harm's way. Darin didn't notice, of course. He could read strangers better than anyone Tom had ever met, but he had huge blind spots when it came to people close to him.

Kat straightened and stuck her jaw out in Darin's general direction. "You ever starved before?"

"Of course."

"I'm not talking about being hungry, Darin. I'm talking about your stomach pushing out because you can't get enough food. Your body starting to shut down. You ever experience that kind of starvation?"

"I have," Darin said quietly.

"So have I." Some distant memory of desperation haunted those three words.

Tom knew that sound. Knew that feeling. Hearing it again brought it all flashing back. Footsteps pounding toward him across the wet sand. A mob of boys shouting. The rough wood of the tiny boat's hull as he carried it out into the surf, waves slapping his face. It was barely big enough to keep him afloat, but it had gotten him out alive.

"Times are tight," Darin told Kat, jerking Tom out of the memory. "I'm not sure what kind of life we can offer them."

Tom cleared his throat, catching them both by surprise. "It's better than the one they've got."

Darin's eyebrows shot up. "Not you, too. Going soft all of a sudden?"

No, not soft. Not ever again. But Tom only shrugged and said, "We've room in the hayloft. Besides, someone needs to look after the horses whenever I can't."

Kat smiled at him. A big smile. The uneasiness fell away from her shoulders.

Darin looked from her to Tom and sighed. "I suppose we can use a couple of clever lads."

"Thank you. Both of you," Kat said.

"Don't let them get too comfortable, though," Darin said. "I'm not sure how long we're going to be here."

CHAPTER ELEVEN
Strange Invitations

The next day it rained harder. A wind-blown pelting deluge that seemed to come from all directions. The hard-packed dirt roads that ran past the Rooster turned to muck. Kat thought the Rooster might still get a drinker or two, but not a soul showed. She hoped it wasn't the new batch of ale. The cloves turned out stronger than she'd anticipated. She didn't mind the downtime, though. She and Darin scrubbed the bar to see if the acrid smell of old ale would come out of it. No such luck.

"Where'd Tom slip off to?" she asked after a while. The big man had made himself scarce when the storms picked up. Odd choice, that. Kat herself preferred a strong roof over her head.

"Guess," Darin said.

Kat considered it a moment. Thunder rumbled through the ceiling. The rain thickened to an energetic drumbeat on the tin roof. *Of course.* "The stables?"

"The horses don't like thunder."

That made sense. "He's good with animals."

"Speaking of which, how are your boys getting along?"

"Hey now, they're not *that* wild. Tom's been teaching them to look after the horses."

"That's good. Probably nice for them to have a role model."

Did he really just say that? Kat slammed down the mug she was cleaning. "What are you trying to say?"

"Ah, nothing, I just–"

78

"You meant *male* role model, didn't you?"

"That's not what–"

"I really hope you weren't implying that a man can do a better job raising those boys than I have."

"I wasn't!" Darin protested.

"Because that would be unwise," Kat said.

"Duly noted."

The door banged open to admit a thoroughly soaked man from outside. He shrugged off his sodden oil cloak by the door, a small gesture of politeness that also said he wasn't planning to stay. He approached the bar, smelling faintly of sawdust and wet horse. "Got a message for the Red Rooster."

Darin met Kat's eyes for half a second, in a clear signal that he intended to have some fun with this. "What's that, now?"

"Delivery for the Red Rooster." He brandished a leather satchel that he'd slung over his head and shoulder.

"What makes you think this is the Rooster?" Kat asked, in a bored sort of way.

"How about the sign out front with the rooster on it?"

"Is that supposed to be a rooster?" Darin tapped a finger against his lips. "Always thought it looked too round, myself."

"Mighty presumptuous to say you know what gender the bird was," Kat said.

"I know a rooster when I see one," the courier said.

"Really?" Darin leaned over the bar. "So you, ah, checked?"

"No, I didn't–"

Darin shook his head. "Checking our birds like he owns them."

"Unbelievable," Kat said.

The courier looked from her face to Darin's, and his lips twitched downward. "You want the message, or not?"

Darin sighed. "All right, who's it from?"

"I couldn't tell you."

"Then how do we know if we want it?"

The man straightened. "Are you refusing delivery?"

Darin pursed his lips and looked at Kat.

All joking aside, she'd never gotten a message by courier before, and the prospect of learning what it contained gave her a little thrill. She'd be damned if she let that show on her face, though. "Well, couldn't hurt to have a look at it, I suppose."

The courier flipped open his bag and withdrew an envelope in heavy parchment. It bore a prominent seal in red wax, stamped with the image of a bird perched on the edge of a wagon.

Darin ran his finger along the edge of the seal and gave a grunt of surprise. "Silver imbued."

"You think?" Kat touched the seal herself. It was solid enough, but she didn't feel anything to suggest precious metal. She must not have the same touch. She wanted to read it but doubted they could afford the price. Couriers didn't come cheap.

Darin clearly had the same line of thought. "What's the fee?"

"The sender covered it," the courier said.

Kat snorted. "Why didn't you say so?"

The man gave her a dead-eyed stare. "You never asked."

Kat shook her head. *Goddamn couriers.* They were technically on the queen's payroll, a relic of some long-forgotten time when the dukes and duchesses actually communicated with one another. Paid or not, they wouldn't take a message unless someone greased the wheels. To this one's credit, he hadn't tried to double-dip.

"Maybe lead with that, next time," Darin said sourly. "We'll accept the message."

Kat put a hand on his arm. "Let's offer him a mug of Red Rooster's finest ale. It's the least we can do."

"I think that's an excellent idea." Darin looked at the man. "Will you take an ale, on the house?"

"Very kind of you."

Kat set about drawing him one while Darin took the seal back behind the bar. He held it close to one of the lamps, peering at it. Then he stuck a hand into one pocket and began muttering to himself. He must not be accustomed to getting couriered messages either.

Kat slid a mug of ale over to the courier. "Red Rooster's finest, with our compliments."

Darin brought the envelope over. "I think it's safe to open." He dug out a paring knife from behind the bar and held it in the flame of the oil lamp until the edge glowed red. The hot blade slid beneath the wax seal, lifting it from the parchment.

"There's a nice little trick," Kat said.

"I try to keep seals whenever I get them." Darin winked at her. "Sometimes comes in useful later."

He used the knife blade to lift the flaps of parchment and flipped it over. A small coin fell to the floor. No, a half-coin. Someone had cloven a silver queenpiece right down the middle. A good clean cut, too. Professional job.

"Thought I felt something in there," Darin said.

"How good's the silver?" Kat whispered.

"Pure as it comes."

Kat whistled under her breath. First a couriered message, and now a free half-coin. If this was how the other half lived, she could start to get behind the idea.

The courier made a choking sound. He set down his mug hastily and pounded himself in the chest. The ale must have been too cold for him.

"Let it warm up a bit before you try again," Kat said.

The courier looked pale. "I'd best be on my way."

"No need to rush off. Take a minute and enjoy your ale."

He sighed and took a stool. He took another sip and swallowed it down without issue that time. Another satisfied customer.

Darin got the parchment unfolded and read the letter inside, which apparently was not long. "An invitation to meet someone."

"Who?"

"It's not signed."

"Where's the meet?"

"About a day's ride south of here." His lips twisted downward.

"Something wrong?" Kat asked.

"Nothing I can't handle. Besides, we need the work."

Kat didn't like the sound of his tone, but he clearly wasn't up for sharing. "Why don't you take Big Tom along? The boys can look after the stables for a day or two."

"I'll be fine."

"If you bring Tom, we'll know that for sure."

Darin sighed. "Fine, I'll bring him, but he stays out of sight."

Kat laughed. "Yeah. Good luck with that."

Darin slipped out to the stable half an hour before sunrise. He didn't particularly enjoy putting one over on Kat, but the note intrigued him enough that he wanted to meet the sender – not to frighten him off by bringing a half-giant who scared anyone with an ounce of survival instinct. Besides, it would be far easier to avoid detection in Harrison's territory without such a recognizable figure.

He unhooked the trip-wire from the stable door. It ran inside the stable and into a little cage, where it ended in a loop of cord tied to the leg of a Vlaskan screaming hen. She slept twenty hours a day, ate little, and screeched loud enough to wake the dead when disturbed. No less than three would-be horse thieves had been foiled by that little bit of security.

Darin slid open the stable door and stepped inside. He paused to let his eyes adjust, and to bring up the layout in his head. The first two stalls were empty. The third held Buttercup, who wasn't up for a journey this long. That left the borrowed palfrey in stall four, or Moody Mary at the end. Either would serve, but Mary liked to bite. *Palfrey it is.* He started down the aisle and stumbled right into a massive *something* in the middle of the floor. "What in the blazes?"

The form moved in the inky darkness.

Darin jumped back, fumbling for his knife. "Lord and Lady!"

"Is it time to go?" Tom asked.

Darin's heart felt like it might burst in his chest. "You scared the tar out of me."

Tom stood and stretched. "Didn't know there was much tar in you."

"What are you doing sleeping out in the stable?"

"I like to be by the horses."

He wasn't lying – Tom couldn't lie if he wanted to – but this had the feel of a Kat-planned ambush. Evidently, someone was bringing her up to speed on Darin's go-to moves, like slipping away before sunrise and *forgetting* the muscle.

"It's fine," Darin said. "Are you ready to ride?"

"Which horse?"

Darin sighed. "Take the borrowed palfrey."

They kept to the backroads and peddler's trails, which strung together the Old Queendom's smaller villages like beads on a string. Sure, the main road running south would've saved time and made for easier travel, but that highway also attracted certain groups to be avoided. Highwaymen, for one thing, most of whom would be deterred by the sheer size of Big Tom, but who might risk a confrontation to relieve them of their horses. Good mounts were hard to come by, as more and more of the hard-to-breed animals were exported to the budding economy of the Jewel Empire.

Of course, highwaymen weren't the worst monster they might encounter on a well-traveled road. There was always the risk of a royal tax collector.

So they kept to the backroads, and gave the tall stone keeps of queendom nobles a wide berth. The second highway, as it was called, was a windblown spiderweb of cart paths and old logging roads that could get you almost anywhere, as long as you didn't travel direct. There was no map, only the collective memory of generations of travelers who preferred avoiding the public eye. Burglars, kidnappers, con artists, paid assassins... not a one of them on duty, so everyone got along just fine. It was understood here that conflict drew attention, and attention paid dues to no one's benefit.

They reached Broadmeade a few hours past midday. Darin double-checked the half-coin in his pocket for what was probably the tenth time. Truth be told, he wouldn't be here if it weren't for that. It was good, pure silver. It spoke to wealth. He hoped there was a matching half and then a hundred more just like it.

"Listen, bringing you isn't exactly protocol for a meet, so I want you to lay low," he said.

"Lay low?" Tom asked.

"You know, try to blend in."

"Sure," Tom said, with the assurance of a man who had probably never blended in anywhere his whole life.

Broadmeade had a green, and grazing was allowed, so Darin left Tom there with the horses while he walked across the narrow lane to the rendezvous point. It wasn't an inn, but a free-standing alehouse with a long row of private booths in the soot-stained interior. A battered wooden sign out front called it the Lame Horse. An odd name for a village that appeared to have sold all of theirs, lame or not.

He settled into a corner booth with his back to the wall.

A big-shouldered man in a leather apron ambled over. "Fancy a drink?"

"What's on the menu?"

"Ale. We have a light variety, and a dark."

"Well, aren't you fancy? Three of the light kind," Darin said.

"One at a time, or–"

"All at once."

"That's a lot." *To pay for*, was the unspoken end of that sentence.

Darin let a leather purse fall out of his sleeve to the sanded wooden table. Soft metal clinked within. Three silver marks and ten copper bits. A barkeep might not know that the way Darin did, but soft metal had a certain sound.

Sure enough, the proprietor grunted and ambled away. He took a good ten minutes to turn up with the ales, and clunked them hard enough on the table that they sloshed over the rims. Somehow the man found his grace when it was time to pick up the coins.

"Love the service here, by the way," Darin muttered.

A man two booths up half-turned and looked back at him. Long-haired fellow with a scar on his cheek. Darin didn't recognize him and, fortunately, the man turned back to his business.

Three newcomers entered the alehouse. The man stepped in first. Middle-aged fellow, tailored jacket. He looked the wrong way to find the bartender, which meant he wasn't a regular. Then he beckoned behind him, and two women joined him. One was of a similar age, a stately woman with perfectly coiffed hair. She and the man cast glances around the tavern – he the left side, and she the right – unconsciously trusting one another's eyes like two soldiers from a veteran unit.

The other woman was younger, judging by her build. It was hard to be certain, though – she stood a pace or two behind, in the shadows, with a veil over her face. The older woman spotted Darin in the corner, with the three ales arrayed just so on the edge of the table. She exchanged a quiet word with the man, and they ambled toward him. They kept a casual air, but they gripped one another's hands with pale knuckles.

Darin smiled to put them at ease. "Come, friends. Have a drink."

CHAPTER TWELVE
True Colors

"So, how did you hear about us?" Darin asked.

"My Tal Orean business partner recommended your crew," the man said. "I believe you helped him with a problem four or five years ago."

Darin remembered it right away, a Tal Orean merchant by the name of Mardley who'd been accused of copper smuggling by the port authorities. He and Evie had bought round after round of drinks for sailors in port, and eventually figured out that it was a frame-job by Mardley's top competitor. Tal Oreans took a harsh view of smuggling coinage metals, so it had been a close thing. Evie managed to lure a confession out of the conspirator within earshot of the port-master, who'd set things to right.

"I remember that one," Darin said. "Framed for kidnapping. Mardley, wasn't it?"

"That's his name," the man said.

The woman's hand tightened where she held the man's. She reached up with the other one and re-coiffed her hair. Had to be some kind of signal between them. Maybe she sensed the test and was trying to warn him. Darin kept his face still, but found the handle of his belt-knife, and began to ever-so-slowly pull it from the sheath.

The man gave him a hard look. "It wasn't kidnapping charges, though. It was smuggling."

Thank the gods. Darin released his belt knife and gave them a genuine smile. "So it was. Copper, if memory serves."

Some of the tension drained from the man's posture. The woman shoved something dark and glittering back into her hair, and gave Darin a little nod.

Maybe not unarmed after all. Good. Clients who were competent in the hard ways of the world were rare indeed. He offered his hand to the woman first. "My name's Darin, by the way."

She shook it. "Damia Galcera. This is my husband, Alfon."

Darin shook his hand as well, and then gestured to the veiled woman who'd not yet said a word. "And who's this lovely lady?"

"She's our daughter," Damia said. "And I'd just as soon not tell you her name, until I know we're working together."

"Fair enough."

The unnamed daughter seemed to only be giving the conversation half an ear. She kept looking back toward the door, nervous as a mouse crossing an open field.

Darin saluted them with his glass and tried a sip of the ale. *Damn, that's good.* Light consistency, with just enough hops and a touch of honey. A far cry from the Red Rooster ale. Maybe the brewmaster offered lessons. "So, now that we've gotten acquainted, how can we be of service to you?"

Alfon glanced at his wife, who gave him a little nod and took up watch on the rest of the alehouse.

"There's a textile merchant based in a town called Stillwater, about a hundred leagues northwest of here," he said. He lowered his voice and leaned forward. "Jakub Purser. Do you know him?"

The daughter flinched when she heard the name. Damia put a comforting hand on her arm.

"I know the city," Darin said. Stillwater was in the northern portion of Caron, the queen's province. An industrial center, from what he'd heard. Lots of buildings. Lots of people. In other words, the kind of place he should avoid. "Never met the man, though."

"We've done business for several years. He imports fabrics from the Jewel Empire. Lovely materials, really. It's all hand-made."

By children. Darin fought a surge of irritation but managed to keep his face still. "Go on."

"Six months ago, my daughter expressed an interest in him as a husband."

That's how things worked in this part of the queendom. The woman chose the man, and if he wanted to accept, he had to offer something to her family in return.

"I see," Darin said.

"It was a good match for all of us," Alfon continued. "As part of the arrangement, Jakub began shipping some of his wares on my ships."

"It seemed like a better life for her as well," Damia said.

"Yes. A better life," Alfon echoed. "We were pleased and had no reason to believe this wasn't a fairy tale come true."

It never is. "Let me guess: he reneged on the shipping contract."

Alfon shook his head. "He made better than good on it. About a third of his shipments come through me, and we've kept up the margins."

"Must be nice," Darin said dryly, remembering the cost of the silk that their last job required. "So, what's the problem?"

"Well, he keeps her ensconced away in his villa in Stillwater, and never lets her out of his sight. We rarely see her."

"We're talking about *this* daughter?" Darin pointed. "Right here? You don't see her enough."

"She came on the ruse that her mother's brother died. Jakub thinks we're at the funeral."

Oh, perfect. No wonder the daughter kept watching the door. "How do we know he's not about to barge in and disrupt our little meeting here?" Darin asked.

Alfon made a placating gesture. "It's all right. We were careful."

They'd shown some cleverness thus far, so Darin gave them the benefit of the doubt – this time. But if mercenaries stormed the place, he'd be out the back door before anyone could blink. "What else?"

"He's rude and an absolute lout to her," Damia said. "She doesn't deserve this treatment."

Darin didn't like where this was headed. Odds were, this poor girl was just getting to see the man's true colors and didn't like them. "What do you want us to do?"

"We want you to get her out."

"Of the house? You did a fine job of that already."

"Of the *marriage*," Alfon said.

"This is a marriage that you initiated."

"It is," Damia admitted. "And it's our fault for not seeing the type of man he was. But we can't stand the thought that she'll spend her life unhappy."

Darin sighed. "Look, I understand your position. Your daughter married a man who turned out not to be a prince, and now you all regret it."

"But he's a monster!"

"You're still doing business with him."

"We're bound by the contract as well," Damia said, her voice tight with misery. "And he has our *daughter*."

"Spouses don't always get along, particularly in arranged marriages. It's the way of the world."

Alfon sat back and crossed his arms, glaring murder at Darin.

Damia glanced sidelong at him, then leaned over the table to whisper, "What if he were cruel to her?"

This was testing Darin's patience. "What do you mean?"

"He drinks, and he gets violent, and he hurts her."

Now there's a perfect accusation. Just the sort of angle to gain sympathy with a near-stranger. No way to prove it, and no one here to refute the claim. These two clearly knew their way around the game.

"It's hard for anyone to hear that their daughter is being mistreated by her husband," Darin said. "But I don't see how we can help. This isn't the sort of thing that we do." The Jewel Empire was the real threat, the real danger. Not some two-cart merchant who might or might not lay a hand on his wife.

"We want her freed from him, and we'll pay handsomely," Damia said. She nudged Alfon, who hauled out a heavy leather purse and slapped it on the table. The dozens of silver coins within called out to Darin like a chorus. He felt the current of their power humming up from the wood. There was gold in there, too. Gold and silver coins both, a small fortune. But the solid thump of the purse and the soft clink of those metals drew every eye in the alehouse.

Darin hunched down under the sudden scrutiny. "Put that away, before you get us all killed!" He shoved the purse back onto Alfon's lap. Part of that was for safety. The other part was to remove the temptation. The thought of all that silver... well, it might not square him with the Dame, but it would buy him a lot of forgiveness. Now that he knew it was there, it was all he could do not to bask in its alluring song.

He shook his head to clear it. "Look, you've said yourself that your son-in-law is a powerful man. And he held up his end of the contract."

"But the abuse–" Alfon said.

"Is difficult to prove," Darin cut in. "She says it's true, but I'm sure he'd deny it. That leaves me in the middle, not knowing whose story to believe."

Damia's lips twisted into a frown. She looked at her daughter and said, "Show him."

The still-unnamed daughter's eyes widened further, and she shook her head vigorously.

"I said, *show him.*"

The daughter cast one more furtive glance at the doorway. Then she lifted the long sleeves back from one arm. What should've been smooth, perfect skin was mottled with black and blue like thunderclouds in a spring sky. Some were old and faded grey; others bore the purple hues of fresh injuries.

Darin sucked in a breath across his teeth, aware of the noise but unable to stop himself. It reminded him of the time one of Evie's marks had thought to rough her up. Grabbed her by the arm, threw her around. Took a couple of swings at her, too. Darin would've killed the man if Tom hadn't stopped him. He felt that red-eyed anger boiling up in him now, a blind fury at someone who'd hurt an innocent lass like this one. Like Evie.

"Lady have mercy," he whispered.

"These are just the ones you can see," the mother said. "She's black and blue all over. Her arms, her back, her chest. Even her legs."

A dull ache in his palms helped Darin notice how hard he'd gripped the edge of the table. "Wherever the clothes will hide it," he said, gritting his teeth.

"That proof enough for you?" Alfon asked.

Darin didn't answer, but instead turned his attention to the girl's face. "What's your name?"

She looked at her mother, who gave a little nod. "Lisbet," she whispered, in a fragile little voice.

Four Gods, she's practically a child. "That's a lovely name. And you were brave to come here."

She straightened a little and stopped looking at the door. "Thank you."

"What's your husband's name?"

"You know his name," Alfon said.

"I want her to say it," Darin answered.

She trembled, but took a breath and answered, "Jakub Purser."

Fear shook her voice, but there was something else in it, too. Maybe a hint of pride. Darin sincerely hoped that wouldn't be a problem later. "He thinks you're in mourning?"

"He wasn't happy about it, but he let me go."

"I'm sorry to say–" Darin broke off as the long-haired man

from two booths up stood, paid his tab, and hurried out the door. Good. One less set of curious ears. "That is, you'll have to return to him for a little while."

She made a soft sound, a whimper. Her mother put an arm around her and cooed some reassurance.

"We rather hoped you could move sooner," Alfon said.

Darin wished he could, but a little pain now might save a lot later. "We have to be smart about this. If he's as controlling as you say, he'll already be suspicious. Might even have someone trying to follow you."

"We weren't followed."

"By traditional means, probably not. Otherwise my man outside would have warned me. But a man like your son-in-law may have access to... more arcane methods."

Alfon lowered his voice. "Metallurgy?"

"The services can be bought, for enough coin. Someone who's built a business empire would likely have encountered them before."

"Are we exposed, right now?"

"I don't believe so, no," Darin said.

"You have a metallurgist with you as well?"

"No." Not officially, at least. "More like a lucky feeling. Still, we need to be extra careful. If your daughter's husband has any suspicions of our intention, he can make things very difficult."

"We've kept our mouths shut this long," Damia said, with a cool look toward her husband. "We can make do a little longer."

"Good," Darin said. "Here's what I want you to do."

CHAPTER THIRTEEN
Slow Partings

Tom liked the look of Broadmeade. It was a good-sized village – about two hundred thatched-roof houses – ensconced in canal-watered wheat fields. Enough folks around that he might not be pegged as an outsider. Wonder of wonders, they had a decent harvest going, too. There was plenty of daylight left, so most of the workers were still afield. The adults swung scythes to cut the stalks near the ground, where the children could collect and roll them into long bundles.

The work had a soothing rhythm. Tom could have watched it all day but hoped he wouldn't have to. They rode far enough south to be across the unofficial deal line with Harrison, who ran a rival crew for the Dame. He and Darin shared some bad blood. Tom didn't know all the details but understood enough to want to avoid running into Harrison inside his territory. The less time they lingered here, the better.

Blend in, Darin had said. Easy thing to say – especially for him. Darin was average height, average weight, average nose. Average everything. He didn't have people always sizing him up. Thinking of picking a fight, just to see what he could do.

That was one of the reasons Tom liked horses so much. It was a comfort not being the biggest thing around. He let Moody Mary and the palfrey loose to wander the green. They'd find the best grass on their own, and they knew not to wander too far. He took up position in the shade on the wall of the building opposite the alehouse where Darin took his meeting. He focused on keeping still. Breathing slow. Willing himself to be invisible.

It didn't work. Some folks passed through the green without taking notice. Others glanced at him once, then looked again for a longer stare. There it was: the old size-up. Second only to the nudge-your-neighbor in Tom's list of least favorite stranger behaviors. He hoped Darin wouldn't be long. The area between his shoulder blades had started to itch. That wasn't a good sign.

The door to the Lame Horse flew open. Tom tensed but forced himself to remain calm. There wasn't a problem yet. And look, the fellow coming out wasn't even Darin. He was younger, for one thing, and apparently into his cups. He stumbled out into the sunlight and brushed a mop of too-long hair out of his face. Not visibly armed, and probably not a fighting man. He swung his head back and forth as if looking for something. Then he spotted Tom and moved right toward him.

Damn. Tom kept his hands where they were, but eased his weight off the wall. It was always better to seem less prepared than you really were.

"You got a friend in there?" the man asked when he was ten paces out. He wove a little as he moved, like a sailor trying to find his land legs after a long voyage.

Tom came up on the balls of his feet as he lumbered closer. "Maybe."

"Plain-looking fellow with dark hair. Sitting in the corner booth? Said his name was…"

"Darin?" Tom ventured.

"Yeah, that's it. Darin." The man cast a glance over his shoulder. "Listen, he's in trouble."

Double damn. That was the last thing Tom wanted to hear. Not many people had gone into the Lame Horse since he'd taken up his station. Definitely not any serious hitters. Then again, he couldn't see the back door. "What kind of trouble?"

"He was talking to some folks in the back. It got ugly." The man shook his head and looked back at the door again. "You'd better get in there quick."

Tom had already started moving across the street. He should have seen this coming. It was such an easy trap to spring. Send an anonymous note to the Rooster promising some kind of job. A fancy half-coin was enough to lure Darin across the deal line. Come to think of it, why *had* it been so easy to get Darin to this meet? It wasn't like him to take this much risk for a simple job. Tom would have liked a weapon, but he'd left his sword on the palfrey, now grazing on the far side of the green. It didn't matter. The alehouse would have chairs, stools, tables... everything he needed. But first, he had to get to Darin and find out what the hell had gone wrong.

Darin loved it when a client wanted to pay up front. That didn't happen a lot in his line of work. More often, the client conveniently forgot to bring payment even when a job was done. Not Alfon and Damia, though. When he'd finished giving their first set of instructions, Alfon hefted his purse, more surreptitiously this time. "Shall I give this to you now?"

Darin eyed it, felt the welling up of hunger to have so much silver in his hands, and shoved it away. Too much craving was dangerous. "Better keep that for now. Put it somewhere safe because we'll need it before long. I'd best get moving, but we'll meet again, seven days hence, like we talked about."

"Thank you for doing this," Alfon said.

"You can thank me when it's done," Darin said. *If we're all still breathing.*

Damia was already chivvying her daughter up out of her seat, no doubt to squeeze as much family time into this mourning ruse as she could. Then a massive shadow loomed over them, and they froze.

"What's the trouble?" Big Tom asked.

Damia stared up at him, her eyes as wide as her daughter's.

"It's all right, he's with me," Darin said. He looked up at Big Tom's wide face, which bore a mask of concern. The same way he looked at a horse when it was starting to go lame. *A poor joke to make in this inn.* "What's wrong?"

"What's wrong with you?"

"Wait, why'd you come in?" Darin asked.

"He said you were in trouble."

"What? Who said that?"

Tom scratched his head. "Long-haired fellow came out, told me you needed help."

Why in the hell would someone... oh, hell. Darin cursed. "The horses!" He pointed at Alfon and Damia. "Remember the plan. Come on, Tom!" They shoved the door open and barreled out into the street.

The village green awaited them, silent and empty.

"Where were they?" Darin called over his shoulder.

Tom pointed. "Near that edge over there. Where the grass is still decent."

Darin jogged over. The fresh hoof-prints and close-cropped grass plainly marked where the mare and palfrey had been grazing. Scattered among them were heavy boot prints. At least two distinct sets of them. Darin crouched to inspect them. "Horse thieves."

"How do you know?"

"They took our horses."

"Right." Tom ran his hand through his hair. "Sorry, Darin."

"It's all right. *Shit!*" He had half a mind to go back in and catch the new clients, maybe change his mind about taking some of the gold and silver as a down payment. No, that would draw too much attention.

"At least they took the feedbags, too," Tom said. "Horses got to eat, you know?"

Darin sighed. "Yeah, I know. Come on, we've got a long walk."

They set off along the northwest lane. Darin wished he'd

worn more comfortable boots, instead of his riding ones. They were more for show than long journeys on foot.

"What do you remember about the man who told you to come in?" Darin asked. "Did he use one of our code words?"

"Don't know," Tom said. "I heard you was in trouble. Things got sort of red and black in my head. Then I was standing over you and those other people, wondering what the problem was."

"You didn't think I could look after myself?" Darin asked.

Tom grunted. "Not as good as I can."

They made their way out of the village and walked in silence for a while.

"Really sorry about the horses," Tom said.

"Don't be." Darin put a hand on his massive shoulder. "I can't fault you for coming in to help out."

"I was worried."

"Yeah, you're a worrier."

Ten minutes later, they rounded a hairpin bend in the road and found their missing horses grazing in a little patch of weeds beside the road. Which would have been great news, if not for the band of armed men waiting beside them.

"Hey, it's the horses!" Big Tom said, about three times louder than he should have.

His booming voice brought toothy grins to the faces of the highwaymen. That included their leader, a red-haired and red-bearded barrel of a man who leaned against the palfrey, drinking out of Darin's wineskin.

Son of a bitch. Darin whispered, "Stay close to me, and ignore whatever they say."

"Why?"

"Because it's Harrison, that's why."

"Oh," Tom said, conveying all of the deep realization into that single syllable. All the rivalry and bad blood between two crews that vowed to wipe one another from the land. He cocked his head a little to one side. "Thought he'd be taller."

CHAPTER FOURTEEN
Deal Line

Tom had never met Harrison before, but he didn't need long to develop a dislike. The man had a scar on his face that gave him a permanent scowl. He and Darin stared at each other like feral cats in a tight alley. He carried no visible weapon, a brash show of confidence, but the five others were another story. Four swordsmen in chainmail and battered helms fanned out into a half-circle around him and the horses, their hands on sword hilts. They had the look of fever-wolves: lean, savage, and salivating into their tangled beards. Seasoned fighters, all. But the one that really gave him pause was the woman who stood apart, wearing form-fitting black leathers, and holding a horse bow like she was just itching to shoot someone. It had to be Annette, Harrison's top lieutenant.

"Well, have a look at this," Harrison said. "Couple of peddlers out for a stroll. On foot, as it were."

"Down-on-their-luck peddlers, you mean," Annette said. Her hair, a deeper garnet, was pulled back into a loose bundle with garrote-wire.

"Out of luck, more like," Harrison said.

"And out of silver, too."

"Harrison. Annette," Darin said, his voice tight. "Been a while."

"Not long enough." Harrison spat to one side. "Not nearly long enough."

"Looks like you found our horses. Much obliged for catching them, after they ran off."

"Oh, these horses?" Harrison leaned back and put an arm over Moody Mary, like she was a piece of furniture.

Tom's insides began to churn toward a slow boil. If he'd so much as scratched Moody Mary, or the borrowed palfrey, he'd tear Harrison limb from limb.

"Yes, those horses," Darin said.

"They can't be his horses," Annette said.

Harrison rubbed his chin. "No, because then he'd be across the line."

"In our territory," she said. "He wouldn't be that foolish, now, would he?"

"No one's that foolish."

Darin cleared his throat. "We're just passing through. We're not on a job."

"You're always on a job," Harrison said. "Might as well tell us about it."

Now that Tom could see the horses, and knew they were all right, his head started to clear a little. He still felt terrible that he'd been duped so easily. At least it wasn't common horse thieves who'd done it. Learning that a rival crew had run the scheme was almost a comfort.

Darin didn't look comforted, though. He was still on edge. It showed in the way he held his shoulders, and how he kept twitching his fingers like he wanted to dip them into a pocket. But his knife was on the other side, so if it was instinct, it was a poor one.

"Let's not make this more than it is," Darin said.

Harrison let his gaze slide over from Darin to Tom and pretended to notice him for the first time. "Good gods, is that a giant you've brought with you?"

"Leave him out of this," Darin said.

"You always did like big, dumb creatures."

Tom almost smiled. He'd lost count of how many times

someone tried to goad him with the "big and dumb" moniker.

"If that were true, I'd have liked you," Darin said. Then he put a finger to his lips. "Then again, the *big* part doesn't really fit."

Harrison's eyes flashed, but he regained his calm almost instantly. "So, where's Evie?"

"Probably got a crossbow trained on your back right now."

Harrison guffawed. "She wishes." Even so, he leaned a little bit into Moody Mary so his back wouldn't be exposed.

"How about giving us the horses, and we'll be on our way?"

"How about not crossing the line without warning us?" Harrison shot back.

"Fine. Next time I'll send a courier."

Harrison spat again. "Goddamn couriers. I'd rather you send the pox."

"Maybe I'll send both. You going to give us our mounts, or what?"

"Mounts?" Harrison feigned shock. "You actually *ride* these things?"

"Business must be worse than we thought," Annette said.

"What happened? Did that ramshackle inn burn down?"

Darin didn't rise to the bait. He just stared and waited for this to play out the way he wanted it to. Smart of him, really. Harrison probably wanted him to lose his temper and do something stupid. Tom admired that he could keep a cool head. Especially after Harrison had mentioned Evie.

"Guess it's only fair to let the horses choose." Harrison's oily grin made Tom's stomach turn. "They come to you, and they're yours. Otherwise, they're ours."

"Come on, now," Darin said. "Horses don't–"

"That's the deal."

Grinning, Harrison and Annette dropped the reins of the horses. They and their armed thugs took two steps back. Moody Mary and the palfrey just stood still. No surprise there. Horses that weren't being led or pushed *always* stood still.

"Well, this is a bit of a heartbreaker for you." Harrison's grin said it was anything but for him. "Then again, we're doing you a favor, sparing you having to ride these poor excuses for animals."

Tom put two fingers in his mouth and whistled three quick beats.

Mary turned her head ponderously, blinked, and whickered softly back at him.

That's it. Come on, girl.

Everyone else had fallen quiet, almost in disbelief. Tom almost smiled again. People always underestimated animals – horses especially.

Mary lumbered around and plodded toward him, like the good girl that she was.

The palfrey lifted its head, looked both ways, and then started to follow. But Annette casually stepped on the reins as they dragged past, and the palfrey held fast.

"That's cheating," Darin muttered.

Tom kept his focus on Mary as she made her way over. He kept eye contact, and when she was close enough, offered his hand. She licked his palm, her sandpaper-tongue a comfort. He did his best not to think about the palfrey.

Darin clapped Tom on the shoulder and whispered, "Mount up." He looked back to Harrison and his crew. "Well, then. Deal's a deal, isn't it?"

Harrison's face purpled. Annette leaned over him and whispered a suggestion. Tom couldn't make out the words, but guessed they were violent ones.

"I'd stay and continue this enjoyable conversation, but I don't want to," Darin said.

He turned and set off at a brisk walk, catching Moody Mary's reins to pull her and Tom along as well.

For his part, Tom kept his head down and whispered a prayer that Annette wouldn't put an arrow in his back. He made a nice, big target. He'd taken a couple of arrows in his time with the Sorrows. It was no picnic, even in chain mail. "What about the job?" he asked, once they were safely out of earshot. "Still want to take it?"

"Oh, we're taking it." Darin looked back over his shoulder, and there was a cold fury to his expression that Tom had rarely seen. "We're in. And the deal line be damned."

Evie had been fighting the instinct to punch Darin for half an hour. It felt like a losing battle. "You're out of your gods-damned mind," she said.

"He must be." Kat raised her eyebrows at Darin. "Tell me this is a joke."

Darin sighed and rubbed his eyes. He and Big Tom had taken three days to make the trip back, switching out turns on Moody Mary. "It's not a joke."

"What do we know about the husband?" Evie asked.

"He's a wealthy merchant working out of Stillwater, in Caron."

"That's across the deal line, isn't it?"

"A little bit, yeah," Darin said.

"Why are we even talking about this?" There wasn't much point to having a deal if you didn't honor it. Harrison and that monstrous woman of his would retaliate three times over, and then everything would revert to the way it was before the deal line.

"Because he's importing textiles from the empire," Darin said.

"So?"

"All of it's handmade, they said. You and I both know what that means."

It meant child labor, Darin's personal touchpoint. Kat growled wordlessly. She understood it, too. That wasn't terribly surprising given the motley crew of orphans she'd stashed in the Rooster's hayloft. Evie had broken down and told her about the rivalry. Still, the woman didn't know enough about Harrison and Darin to understand what crossing the deal line really meant. Or why it existed in the first place. "Harrison's already wise to us. That's one reason to refuse," she said.

"He got lucky, that's all," Darin said.

"What if he's tracking you?" Evie didn't use the word *metallurgy*. It was, as her mother used to tell her, not a topic for polite conversation in the queendom.

"I think I'd know," he'd said.

"Would you, though? If you weren't expecting it?" She couldn't draw magic from metal, but she could read his face like a cleanly copied scroll. And right now, he wasn't sure. He rarely was when it came to metallurgy.

"I'll look into it, all right?"

"I think that would be wise," Evie said.

"It doesn't mean we shouldn't take the job."

"Darin–" she started.

"We need silver, don't we?"

Tom, as usual, had nothing to say. Kat was suddenly interested in a stubborn dirty spot on the table.

Evie clamped her jaw shut and looked away. He didn't blame her, but she felt guilty anyway. When she'd learned how deep they were in to the Dame, she'd swallowed her pride and tried to call on some of her family's friends from way back before. Two countesses and a baroness. All of them had known her when she was a girl. They'd dined at her parents' table. Of course, that also meant they knew about her particular shame. That was certainly why none would see her, despite her calling at their gates in person. Practically begging for an audience.

Even the baroness had been polite but firmly distant. They'd likely suspected the reason for her visit. Even if they hadn't, none were willing to receive a person of no status simply because she'd asked. She'd been a fool to try, but she'd had to do something. Otherwise they'd all have sat around waiting for the Dame's axe to fall.

"That's my point. There's hard silver on the table and we need it. At least, I need it, so I've got to take the job. I could sure use some help."

"Count me in," Kat said. "And count on me dumping those textiles into the nearest harbor."

"A fine suggestion," Darin said.

"I'll come to make sure no one dumps Darin into the nearest harbor," Tom said.

"Thank you for conjuring *that* picture, but I'd prefer you stick around here to keep an eye on the Rooster." Darin looked to Evie. "What about you?"

Evie wanted to sigh. She couldn't let them go on their own. Darin knew that, but he still had the manners to ask. That didn't mean she couldn't torment him a little. She leaned back against the bar and put her legs on his lap, like a cat that wanted attention. "What about me?"

He pretended not to notice. "Are you in?"

"I am, but don't go thinking that it's due to your powers of persuasion. I'm only joining this fool's errand because of those two special words."

"Which?"

She gave him a predatory smile. "Wealthy merchant."

CHAPTER FIFTEEN
Imperial Moon

Early the next morning, before the others were awake, Darin slipped out of the Red Rooster's kitchen door with a shovel and satchel. Knee-high mists swirled around the little garden plots where Kat had planted hops. The cool air carried the earthy scent of fresh-turned soil. Beyond that lay a dense forest of green-needled sap trees. The trunks were only a foot or two apart, giving the appearance of an impenetrable wall. If you knew where to enter, though, there was a trail that wound through the timber out toward the foothills beyond. He and Tom cleared the path about once a year, in case they needed a quick escape route. Theoretically, no one who wished them harm knew the location of the Rooster, but that could change in a hurry.

After the third switchback, he started counting his paces. At thirty-four, he found the right gnarled tree trunk and dug. Truth be told, he could probably find the box without the map in his head, given what it contained. He found the top without trouble and pried it up with the shovel blade. This, truly, was their last-resort cache. He brushed off the dirt as best he could and lifted the lid. A pile of gold and silver coins lay within, all of them old. Some of them the rarest of their kind in all of Thyros. These went into his satchel, along with the best pieces of silver. Then he reburied the box and obscured the spot with fallen needles. No one had a reason to come back this way, but in his line of work you tried not to leave much to chance.

The Red Rooster still slept. Kat would be getting up soon to put a kettle on for breakfast and put the stable boys to work. Darin needed to see Seraphina, who lived in a hilltop cottage about half a league to the north. That was a fair walk, but he didn't want to wake everyone by trying to saddle Moody Mary. Besides, he could use the time to think. The plan for liberating the merchant's wife hadn't fully formed in his head. There were too many unknowns.

He reached the head of the trail that wound down to the cottage and paused. Faint, shimmering silver lines stretched across the trail. To his ears, it gave off a faint buzzing noise. Most people wouldn't see it, or sense it, the same way. It didn't have a malevolent feel to it, which meant it was probably just a ward. Seraphina liked knowing who was coming down her trail. He could have skirted around it through the trees but sneaking up on a silver witch seemed like a bad idea. So he held his breath and walked through the silver lines. His skin tingled from the metallurgy. He tried to ignore it.

Seraphina waited for him outside her little cottage. She was lean and rangy, nearly as tall as he was, but of smaller frame. Her hair was pale as bone. A thick pendant of silver hung around her neck. She sat at a worktable littered with bits of metal, glass beads, and animal bones – at least, he hoped they were animal bones.

"Hello, Darin," she called.

"Morning, Seraphina." He cleared his throat, suddenly uncomfortable. The necklace on her worktable continued to add beads, despite the fact that she'd dropped her hands to her lap.

"I thought it might be you." She furrowed her brow. "But then I wondered why you'd set off my wards."

"What wards?"

"You're a terrible liar."

"Hey now, that's my profession you're insulting."

"Maybe you should get a new one," she said.

He knew what she was implying, but he hadn't come here to have that particular argument again. "I was wondering if you'd be able to run the Rooster common room for a couple of weeks. We're going out of town."

"Where to?"

"Caron," he said.

"Going to see the queen?"

"Only if things go terribly wrong."

She grunted. "Don't you have some kind of deal line with Harrison?"

Again with the deal line. Apparently, it was the worst-kept secret in the queendom. "Let me worry about that."

She made a face that implied exactly what she thought about him handling Harrison, but at least she didn't voice her opinion. "What's the job?"

"Freeing a young woman from her rich husband."

"What for?"

"He's hitting her," Darin said.

She sniffed. "My first husband tried that. May he rest in peace."

"How many husbands have you had, exactly?"

"Don't ask questions you don't want to know the answer to."

He *was* idly curious, but also a touch concerned that the answer would terrify him. "Fair enough. There's another reason, though."

"There usually is with you."

"He's importing textiles from the empire."

"And you object to imperial fabrics?" she asked.

"I object to chaining children to a loom for fourteen hours a day to sell a few bolts of cloth." He didn't like that there was a growing demand in the queendom for such materials either, but that was a problem for another day.

"You've got that look in your eye," Seraphina said. "I wouldn't want to be the merchant."

"No, you wouldn't. Will you look after the Rooster?"

"Sure, sure. I'll look after it as I would my own husband."

"Now that's reassuring," Darin said.

"How's the current batch of ale?"

"She put cloves in it."

Seraphina barked a laugh. "Should be easy work minding the bar, at least."

"The next bit might not be." Darin poured the last-resort coins out into his hand. "Do you think you could render these coins so that I can find them easily?"

"Looks like you already found them."

"I mean if someone else had them."

"A tracking enchantment?" She narrowed her eyes at him. "That sounds almost like metallurgy, boy."

"Of course it's–"

"Not sure if you've heard, but metallurgy is frowned upon in the Old Queendom. Drawing power from coinage metal and doing strange things..." She gave a theatrical shudder. "Folks around here find it *unnatural*."

He ground his teeth. "You don't say."

"An old woman like me could get into a heap of trouble for the mere suggestion of such powers."

"You're not *that* old."

"Oh?" She fanned herself, as if suddenly flushed. "Is this the famous Darin Fields charm you're always telling me about?"

"Are you going to help, or not?"

"Which coins do you want to track?"

"All of them." He'd give one to everyone on the team and might have need of a spare or two. They'd be operating a long way from the Rooster. The more resources, the better.

"What are we going to draw from?" she asked.

"I hadn't given much thought to that," he admitted. Metallurgy required metal, pure metal. Good silver was valuable for a reason.

"So you thought you'd just use my silver, eh?"

"I suppose not."

"I've got more bad news for you, boy. If you want to be able to track the coins yourself, then you'll have to do the metallurgy yourself."

"What?"

"That's how tracking enchantments usually work. Yet another thing you'd know if you'd ever bothered to do any formal training."

Darin was still hoping to avoid that fight. He needed the coins, but he hated the idea that he might have to use metallurgy while on this job. It would be delicate enough. "Is there no other way?"

"Unless you want to bring me along on this little jaunt of yours, no. And before you get any ideas, I'm not interested in any long journeys by horseback."

Darin mumbled a curse to himself. This day kept getting worse and it had hardly even started. But his half-formed plan would require being able to know where everyone was. He didn't have much of a choice. "Will you show me how to do it, if I provide the silver?"

"Of course." She stood and gestured to her rickety chair at the table. "Have a seat."

"I can stand," he said.

"It's easier this way. Especially since you're going to need to take that boot off to get out the silver coin."

His mouth fell open of its own accord. "How did you–"

"I know you can probably get a toe on it, but you'll want to be holding the source metal for this."

Yet another open secret. Maybe she could sense coinage metals as well as he could. Or perhaps even better. She hadn't exactly told him the full extent of her abilities, and he hadn't asked. She was self-taught, except for a brief stint across the border, but she still had decades of experience on him.

He sat down and retrieved the coin from his boot. It was thick and perfectly round, almost too large to fit comfortably into his palm.

Seraphina gasped. "Is that an imperial moon?"

"I'm sure you've seen one before." Darin handed it to her. Some years ago, the Jewel Empire had begun cutting their coins in half. Uncut imperial moons were extremely hard to find, especially in the queendom.

"Not for a while." She turned it over and frowned at him. "You let it tarnish."

"I'm not in the habit of polishing things I keep in my boot." Not to mention, he got tired of looking at the empress's face. She was younger when the coins were cast, but no less cruel.

Seraphina set the coin down in front of him with a touch of reverence. "That will serve just fine."

Darin drew in a deep breath and let it out. "Guess I'm ready."

"How long's it been?"

"A while."

"How long, Darin?" she pressed.

"Since the gala."

She *tsked* him. "You're a fool. Why do you do it to yourself?"

He rolled his shoulders but the tension in them didn't ease. *Here we go again.* "You know how I feel about metallurgy."

"And you know how *I* feel about your feelings."

"Let's just get this over with, shall we?"

"Fine, fine." She cackled. "I suppose what you'll go through tonight will be punishment enough."

Kat was fairly convinced that Darin was dying. He'd apparently gone to visit the old woman who called herself Seraphina. It was nightfall by the time he returned, drawn and haggard, only to stumble upstairs without so much as a word of explanation. Kat tidied up the common room and hoped that everything was normal. It was hard enough trying to work up the nerve to leave her boys here while they were gone. She'd given the boys three stern lectures, seven minutes each, about expectations for while she was away. She needed to give about ten more to cover it all, but there probably wouldn't be time. That was assuming, of course, that Darin survived.

Tom had promised to keep an eye out, but still. Some things needed a woman's firm touch to get right. Big Tom, gentle as he was, would never fill that role.

There was another somewhat uncomfortable option in the form of the crone, Seraphina, who had come in tow with Darin and made herself comfortable in the common room as he convalesced. She had a disturbing habit of staring directly at Kat with her dark eyes, like a fox eyeing a hare coming out of its burrow.

"So," she said at last. "You are Kat."

"So. I am Kat," Kat said.

"We didn't get a chance to speak when you first turned up at the Rooster."

"No." *You were too busy poisoning Darin with sleeproot.*

"Darin said you're a brewmaster."

"Did he?" Kat didn't offer up what Darin had said about Seraphina, perhaps because it involved the word *witch*. Such things didn't seem like a good direction for their first conversation.

"Yes. Then again, Darin says a lot of things. Many of which aren't true."

"Well, that part is. Been brewing ale for years now."

"Good for you."

"Would you like to try some?"

Seraphina waved her off. "Very kind of you, but I don't drink much."

"How do you get through the day?"

"I have other vices." Seraphina winked at her.

Like what? Kat wondered, but didn't know how to politely ask.

Seraphina moved on before she had a chance. "Is it lucrative, selling your own ale?" she asked. "I've always been curious."

"If it were, would I be here?"

Seraphina barked a laugh. "Probably not." Her smile faded. "Still, there are worse places."

"You're not wrong. And I have to say, it's much easier to brew here than on the road." And that might be what worried Kat a little. She was getting comfortable here. Planting hops. Making friends. Sometimes comfortable became careless. Still, that uneasiness paled in comparison to the thought of leaving her boys here unsupervised. She'd tried to politely argue her way out of going at all, but Darin said it was a two-woman job.

"Darin asked me to look after the Rooster while you're away," Seraphina said.

"Ah," Kat said. "I wondered." She took a swallow of her ale to work up a bit of courage. "I've been charging two coppers a pint, if you're inclined to sell it while I'm away."

"That sounds like a lot of work," Seraphina said.

"It's not so bad." Kat bit her lip. "Matter of fact, there might be a few energetic young fellows around who can lend a hand."

"I assume you're talking about the noisemakers who've taken up residence in the hayloft."

"They're good lads," Kat said.

"Do they know how to run the tap?"

"Almost as well as I do."

Seraphina seemed to ponder this for a moment. "Very well. But don't let any of them fall in love with me."

Kat laughed. "I'll do my best."

"It'll be nice to have some young blood helping run this place. Sure beats having Darin moping around all the time."

"Speaking of Darin, is he, er... dying?"

"No." Seraphina smiled wickedly. "He just wishes he was."

CHAPTER SIXTEEN
Cold Metal

Darin felt like he'd drunk to excess, lost a fight, and stared at the sun for an hour the day before. The full body ache and throbbing in his temples were made worse by the recognition that this was probably his own fault. Seraphina had warned him that the longer he went without using metallurgy, the greater toll it would take when he took it up again. He tried explaining that it was hard to keep good silver around for his personal use when they were in so deep to the Dame, but it was no use. She wouldn't understand anyway. The concept of giving up all her silver – including the thick medallion that she wore constantly around her neck – was as foreign to her as Vlaskan hightalk. He'd get no sympathy there, just as he found none with Kat, who assumed he'd gotten into her ale. Evie might suspect the truth, but assumed that whatever afflicted him was somehow his own fault.

He allowed himself a day to wallow in misery. By nightfall he could keep some food down, which helped a little. He told Kat and Evie to be ready by sunrise.

Darin liked the fact that the Red Rooster was in disputed queendom territory. They weren't harassed by patrolling soldiers, or worse, pressed into military service. Such were the freedoms of living in the fringes of the Old Queendom. Owing to this lack of infrastructure, most settlements were small farming communities. The kind of places where locals could be bought, and knew to keep their mouths shut.

As they rode toward Caron, the central duchy and royal seat, the countryside slowly took on signs of civilization. Hamlets became villages, and then two-inn towns. They encountered more people on the road – most of them traveling on foot, a few mounted on animals that might drop dead at any moment. With two horses and a decent wagon, they drew more than a few lingering stares. Luckily, Kat had acquired two bushels of overripe sour melons that they'd piled high in the back half of the wagon to conceal the trunks beneath. Their pungent aroma caused most passersby to give the wagon a wide berth.

The creaking, bumpy ride in the front seat did nothing to help Darin's metallurgy haze, but after another half day it began to fade on its own. Enough at least that he set to making plans.

"What did you find out about our mark, this Jakub Purser?" he asked Evie, who rode a bone-white courser with a sweeping mane that she'd *borrowed* from a gentleman caller.

"That he knows his way around a coin."

"How so?"

"Five years ago, no one had heard of him. Now he's one of the most prosperous merchants in Caron."

"I assume he's well-connected," Darin said.

"A safe assumption," Evie said. "You don't get very far in the queen's duchy without lining some pockets."

"So basically, he's rich and powerful," Kat said. "You sure know how to pick 'em, Darin."

"I didn't pick this one, remember? They came to us."

Kat snorted. "You took the job, didn't you?"

"If you'd been there, you'd have done the same."

"Maybe. Course, we're going on this couple's word that he's really hurting her. For all we know, he cuffed her once and she made a big deal of it."

"You really think that's what happened?"

Kat shrugged. "How do I know? I'm hearing all of it third hand. I have no idea what this Purser fellow is like."

Darin was still reeling from the idea that Kat would suddenly question this entire mission, but that last bit helped slide a piece into place. "You know what? You're right."

"About what?"

"We'll get to know the mark first. If I'm wrong about what he's doing to Lisbet, we can break it off and go home."

Kat nodded, apparently satisfied for the moment. Evie nudged the courser ahead a few paces, either to avoid further arguments or get a break from smelling the sour melons. Probably both.

The foot traffic increased as they approached Stillwater, which was a proper city. It sprawled on Caron's northern border along the widest part of a slow-moving river called the Myre. Because of the tendency of river-trading vessels to become trapped in the eddying currents – known among the river workers as *getting myred* – Stillwater did a bustling trade business. With that trade came an ever-increasing flow of silver.

Of course, just like in any other part of the queendom – of the world, even – that silver didn't find its way equally to all pockets. The dock workers saw the least of it, followed by the sailors, and then the ship captains. Their piece of the cake was a child's midday snack compared to what the merchant-traders feasted on. The latter didn't set foot on the ships themselves, or even the docks, but conducted most of their business in the great trading hall that dominated the waterfront. That would be where their target, Jakub Purser, spent much of his time. Come sundown, he and his colleagues climbed into courser-drawn carriages for the short ride up into the foothills overlooking the harbor.

Darin dropped off Kat and Evie before parking his cart down the avenue – just another peddler hoping to sell out his wagon before the day ended. He lounged in the shade wearing a scowl to discourage any would-be customers. Not that it worked or anything. He sold four melons in the first half-hour. Three coppers each. At this rate he'd be out of melons and drawing attention uncomfortably soon. He'd no sooner had that thought when a well-to-do chap in a shimmering silk jacket glanced inside the wagon and stopped short.

Darin slouched down a bit lower and debated whether or not he should pretend to sleep.

"How much for a sour melon?" the man asked.

"Two silvers." That was easily six times a fair price, even when they were out of season. Nothing discouraged a sale like an exorbitant asking price.

"Two coppers, you mean."

"Nope, two silvers."

"All right, I suppose I could do five coppers."

Dear gods, this fool wanted to negotiate. "No sale."

"Work with me a little. Surely you're not going to stick at two silvers?"

"Changed my mind." Darin sat up and gave him a hard look. "Now it's three silvers."

The man frowned. "Think I'll take my business elsewhere."

"Good idea." Darin glanced up the street to where the flood of workers out of the trading house had slowed to a trickle. Still, none of the people coming out looked wealthy or gentrified enough to be the true powerbrokers here. Instead, it was young clean-shaven men or women with unbraided hair, the youthful types who served as runners throughout the day. They'd carry messages to the docks and the warehouses and even the harbor storefronts, all while their well-heeled clients sipped apple brandy and smoked those foul-smelling seaweed cigarillos.

Without realizing it, he'd set up outside an exchange house, the kind that handled the cold metal behind all of those transactions negotiated by traders. The traders themselves only dealt in paper and handshakes and letters of credit. When it came time to pay out the silver or gold, or to collect such earnings, a courier flanked by a pair of cudgel-armed guards visited the building at Darin's back.

He'd love to claim it was happenstance that he set up here – it was the right distance from the trading house to keep an eye on comings and goings without getting too close – but he'd be lying to himself. It was the vault of gold and silver at his back, the song of those pure metals that transmuted to him through the pavement.

The things I could do with that much cold metal. Forget about the little charms and enchantments Seraphina wanted to teach him. With that much silver, he could move mountains. Then again, that was the problem with metallurgy. It simultaneously drained away wealth and made you crave even more of it. He shook his head.

As the afternoon faded, business in the trading hall dwindled to a slow trickle, and the first of the traders began to emerge from their lofty den. These were the junior associates, judging by the modest clothing and the simple fact that they departed on foot. No fancy transports to the pinnacle of society for these youngsters; they were still earning their scars in the trading pit on the first floor. The aspiring bottom-feeders of the industry.

Not for half an hour did the first of the lacquered carriages pull up out front. These were four-wheel affairs pulled by matched pairs of dun-colored show horses. Their destination was the wealthy gated neighborhood of colonnaded manses and perfectly manicured gardens. On maps, it was called Uptown, and calling it such would immediately mark you as an outsider. The city's elite, who commanded such wealth as it took to live there, pronounced it *Upton*.

Dusk settled on the city. Attendants hung fish-oil lamps on the corners of waiting carriages, little globes of warm light that bobbed invitingly in the pool of growing darkness.

The light added a splash of daytime color to each carriage. Then came one that was pitch-black as a moonless sky. It seemed to drink in the lamplight. The trading house door banged open to disgorge a man garbed in silk and silver. Not the decorative silver plate, either. These were true metal accoutrements that breathed hints of hidden power. A broad-brimmed hat cloaked his face in shadow, but he moved with the spry agility of youth. The inlaid cane, which also glimmered with veins of soft metal, barely touched the ground.

He sprang into the carriage and pulled the door shut behind him. The driver flicked the reins, and the horses pulled the carriage in stately, elegant fashion down the lane to the corner. Darin nearly stood right then to follow, but decided to give it a ten-count first. Because you could never be too careful. And damn if he wasn't on eight when a shadow detached itself from the corner of the trading house, lumbered to the carriage, and hopped on the back. *A private guard.*

Well, this might prove slightly more interesting than he'd hoped.

CHAPTER SEVENTEEN
High Roads

Once upon a time, Evie had lived in a place like Uptown. It was half a lifetime ago and half the queendom away, but the carriage's rumble over cobblestones felt exactly the same. If she closed her eyes, she might even pretend to be in that life, seated across from Mother in one of her pretty tailored dresses. On the way to somewhere luxurious, somewhere exciting. Instead, the carriage halted suddenly, the door flew open, and there stood Darin in a ridiculous broad-brimmed hat.

"Follow the black carriage," he told Kat, who'd perched up on the driver's bench.

She tipped her hat, which had a brim even wider than Darin's. "Happy to oblige, m'lord." The carriage began moving again almost before he'd closed the door.

Evie wrinkled her nose. "You still smell like the melons."

"My deepest apologies, madam. A regretful necessity."

"Sell any of them?"

"More than I wanted to. The smell of the rest should keep folks away from the cart until we get back."

Evie snapped her fingers twice. "Where's my cut?"

"What cut?"

"You know." She laid claim to half of everything Darin stole on the side when they were setting up real jobs. She'd told him that at the start.

He sighed and flipped one of the coins end-over-end to

her. She smirked and opened her hand to catch it. But the coin never dropped. It hovered in midair between them, still spinning, as if tied to a string. Only the hint of a smile playing on Darin's lips gave away the cause.

She hated herself for the instinctive revulsion that welled up inside her. He knew how she felt about the things he and Seraphina could do. She punched his leg. "Stop that."

"I thought you wanted your cut." He was clutching the other coin between his thumb and forefinger. He wore an easy smile, but perspiration shone on his forehead.

"And I thought you wanted to keep a low profile."

Darin muttered something about "she says I need practice."

The coin fell into Evie's lap. She forced her fingers to pick it up, though they wanted nothing to do with something touched by metallurgy. Old lessons were hard to unlearn.

Half a dozen carriages and dun horse pairs glided peacefully here and there between manses, carrying their owners to dinners and soirées with their fellow elites. Kat took a bit to figure out how the rounded streets worked. Once or twice, Evie could have sworn they'd driven across someone's garden. Once Kat got a hold of it, though, they pursued their mark without ever seeming to, careening instead in wide circles that kept them hovering within view.

Then the black carriage disappeared down a private drive on a small, wooded lot surrounding one of the most impressive houses Evie had ever seen. And that was saying something. Jakub Purser's house was marble-on-the-porch kind of impressive. Statues-in-the-garden kind of impressive. Even Darin raised an eyebrow. "Business must be good."

Kat whistled loud enough to be heard over the rattle of the wheels on suddenly-more-prominent cobblestones.

Darin poked his head out. "What?"

"Should I follow him down the drive?"

"No. Go around back and see if there's another street on the far side."

"As you will, m'lord," Kat said.

"Stop calling me that," Darin snapped.

Evie giggled. "She's already figured out how to irritate you." Probably by accident – the woman couldn't possibly know Darin's lifelong enmity for the privileged elite – but she'd recognized a chink in the armor. She was already reading him, and Darin wasn't an easy man to read. Maybe Evie wasn't giving Kat enough credit.

"The real question is why she'd want to," Darin muttered.

"Because you make it so easy."

They lapsed into silence while Kat tried to find a less-conspicuous road up to their destination. There was a second driveway, more of a service lane, that divided their mark's property from that of his equally ostentatious neighbor to the south. Probably for deliveries of luxurious furniture, and for the servants to use as they came and went. Gods, Evie missed having servants.

The carriage rolled to a stop. They were in a shaded hollow, not quite up to the neighbor's house but as close to the mark's immense stone residence as they'd likely get. It might be fifty yards past the gardens and marble statues to the high wall, above which the mansion loomed like a mountain. With the master's arrival home, most of the windows glowed with soft yellow lamplight. That much oil burning at once, every night, had to cost a fortune all itself. Darin caught glimpses of activity through the lead-glass windows. Servants tidying things up, chefs at work on a meal. Lisbet holding her skirts as she fled up the stairs. Jakub following her, gesturing angrily.

The muted buzz of his shouting reached them even at fifty paces distant.

"What's his problem?" Evie asked.

"Don't know." Darin produced a palm-sized wheel of hard white cheese, broke it in half, and handed a piece over. "Can't see what he'd be unhappy about. Nice haunt he's got."

"Nicer than most," Evie agreed, and she even managed to keep most of the bitterness out of her voice.

"I'm clearly in the wrong business."

Evie snorted. "You want to become a trader all of a sudden?"

"I thought about it. But I hate the idea of sending something off, not knowing where it is. Or who's got it."

"I'm fairly certain that's the entire business model."

"I'd say it's not for me, but *damn*, Evie. Look around."

"I know." Evie sighed. "How much silver do you think is within a stone's throw of us right now?"

An odd expression passed over Darin's face as he looked at Jakub's massive house. "More than you can imagine. But I imagine some houses have coffers nearly as empty as ours." His eyes flickered toward a tall manor house with white stone walls that stood across the narrow lane. Putting on a facade, it seemed. Evie understood that.

They watched Jakub enter the uppermost room, heard the raised pitches of voices as husband argued with wife. He shouted ten times for every one of her softer protests, but that wasn't enough. Dull, fleshy thumps began to punctuate the sounds of the argument. Her pleas became a low, desperate wail.

Evie could feel Darin looking at her and muttered a soft curse under her breath. "I hate it when you're right."

CHAPTER EIGHTEEN
Mark Making

The next morning, Darin hired a carriage to carry them to the Uptown market, both to save a half-hour walk through crowded streets, and to better blend in with the patrons. If you walked here, it meant you were too poor to ride. There were options aplenty, for those with coin to spend. Carriages like the one they rode in. Sedan chairs with drawn curtains. Even the occasional hand chariot, pulled by husky laborers in brown wool jerkins.

The upper echelon of Stillwater possessed more wealth than they could spend in a lifetime, but they made it their business to try. Because a permanent market would be a scar on the face of the otherwise pristine Uptown, a traveling circus of wine merchants, gem traders, and other purveyors of luxury set up each day to ply their wares. A shifting revel-market that began at sunrise.

They set up, and the nobles came.

The hired carriage slowed to match the pace of the market, which moved in a slow dance among the circular pole tents. Darin scanned the other carriages for their mark, but everyone looked like a wealthy fop with too much time on his hands. Meanwhile, he'd underestimated the effect that so many objects of luxury so close would have on Evie.

"Ooh, look at those furs," she cooed. "Can we stop?"

"We're not here to buy things," Darin said. In truth, he felt a certain longing himself. The sheer amount of silver and gold here astonished him. So many coins moving about, changing hands, being slapped down on tables, or shaken out of purses. And the strongboxes, sweet gods. Nearly every tent had one. He'd been close to great piles of silver before, but the complex tapestry of coin around him, the way it all *moved*, conspired to make him dizzy.

"Come on, just a touch?" Evie asked.

"Focus, Evie." *Focus, Darin.*

She huffed at him and slumped back into the carriage. "You never let me have fun anymore."

"You'll get your moment, I promise you."

A fortuitous gap in the revel-shoppers saved Darin from further promises. He didn't see the entire man, but the silver-veined cane helped pick Jakub Purser out of the crowd. A few more heads bobbed out of the way, and there he was. Not in the main thoroughfare through the bustling market, but out on the periphery.

Darin leaned around and tapped the shoulder of the driver – a bearded Tal Orean who hadn't spoken a word more than necessary since picking them up. The man looked at him expectantly.

"Could you take us into the outer aisle?" Darin pointed with his elbow in the vague direction of Jakub's sedan chair. In Tal Orea, pointing with a finger was a crude gesture. No doubt, the driver had adapted to the savage ways of the Old Queendom, but he inclined his head in appreciation even so.

"Much obliged." Darin ducked back into the carriage, where Evie and Kat were giving their mark a look-over.

"He's younger than I'd imagined," Evie said.

"Maybe, but he's got some coins to his name," Kat said. "That's a wardrobe's worth of hand-embroidery on the shirt he's wearing. Expensive cane, no surprise there. What do you think those boots are made of?"

Darin squinted. "Rethaltan leather?"

"No, they'd be duller."

"Sharkskin," Evie said.

"I'll be damned. Good eyes," Kat said.

She rolled her shoulders. "It helps if you've worn it."

"Let's figure out what's piqued his interest," Darin said. "What's that vendor selling?"

"Something shiny," Evie said.

"You'd know."

She punched him in the arm, but not ungently. "You asked."

The carriage driver eased them into the outer lane, about three carriages back from Jakub's sedan chair. The pace was slower than an old man trudging uphill. Darin grated at the delay, but used the time to watch their mark, to see how he shopped.

Jakub's sedan chair moved in fits and starts, halting whenever he stopped to point at something on one of the vendor tables. Then his bearers stood patiently while he examined it, always asking a question or two of the seller. These had to be veteran salesmen, to do enough business to justify a slot at the Uptown market, but few of them made any impression. Most often, Jakub put the trinket back and told his bearers to move on.

"Here comes the tent he was at when you spotted him," Kat said.

She, Evie, and Darin leaned out to examine the merchandise. It looked like a traveling peddler's knapsack had burst open on the table: great heaps of silk scarves were piled around the edge of the table. The rest was tableware: knives and forks, ladles, spoons. Much of it dipped in silver or bronze, but nothing solid.

"Where was he looking?" Darin asked.

"Middle of the table, toward the back," Evie said.

That particular section held some of the fancier pie-servers, along with the merchant herself, a gnarled old woman in a top veil and shawl. She greeted them with a glare and an unfriendly expression. Darin thought about asking her what Jakub had looked at, but decided against it. She'd probably curse them out of her way for wasting her time. He knocked twice on the front of the carriage, a pre-arranged signal that told the Tal Orean to carry them on. A glance to the left told him that Jakub's sedan chair had made the turn, and begun a stately march down the center of the market. Jakub himself sat back in the chair with the curtains drawn, though. Easily the mark of a man done shopping for the day.

"Shit, did he buy anything?" Darin asked.

"Not that I saw," Kat said.

"Here's the shiny vendor," Evie said.

Neat folds of fabric covered the front table in a dizzying array of colors and patterns. Too small to be bolts of cloth for linens, and the material seemed too smooth for that, in any case. Nearly every solid color was dyed a cringe-worthy bright hue. Green. Goldenrod. Royal blue. The colors climbed on top of one another to shout their brightness over their neighbors. Others bore floral designs or exotic patterns that made Darin's eyes ache.

"What are these?" he asked.

Evie snorted. "Guess you don't know everything, do you?"

"Come on, just tell me."

"They're dress materials, you oaf."

"So Jakub was buying dresses?" That might open a surprising and not altogether uninteresting line of inquiry into their mark.

"I don't think he was. It was shiny, remember? And small, too."

The cloth vendor was a dark-haired young man; his loose-fitting robes were a color of orange that knew no counterpart in nature. He offered a wide, friendly grin that seemed almost genuine. "Come, friends, come and see my wares."

"What a lovely display you have here," Darin said, the lie flowing easily from his tongue.

"Maybe a nice new dress for the pretty lady?"

"Aww..." Evie preened like a peacock at his praise. She

poked Darin's chest. "What *about* a dress for the pretty lady?"

He shook his head. "We're just looking."

"It's not for looking, it's for touching," the merchant said. "Put your hands on that maroon silk, and you'll never want to wear anything else."

Darin complied out of sheer politeness. The silk slid around his fingers like a stream around a rock. It *was* soft. "Not bad," he said.

"Just as I promised. Now, try the cloth-of-silver."

Darin obliged him, but stopped short just before his fingers brushed the shimmery pile of cloth beside it. A tingling sensation swept from his fingertips up his arm, like the shock of hitting a stone with an axe on a cold morning. He recoiled, and brought the hand to his mouth to cover the reaction. He coughed twice. "Perhaps later."

A hint of disappointment flashed over the merchant's face. Something told Darin that if he'd touched the cloth-of-silver, he'd feel a sudden impulse to buy things.

"I thought I saw Jakub over here earlier." Darin made his tone conversational. "Did he buy anything?"

"Afraid not," the merchant said. "Didn't even lay a hand on any of my silks, either. He saw me counting change and wanted my Orean double-silver."

"Did you sell it to him?"

The merchant shook his head. "Normally I'd be happy to, but that particular coin is my only piece of home."

"I'm sure he understood," Darin said.

"He doubled his offer twice, then called me a fool and stormed off in a huff."

"Pleasant of him."

"I've encountered his type before."

"What type is that?"

"The type who only want to buy what's not for sale."

"Ah. Of course."

The man's grin returned. "Unlike you, my friend. Surely

you've spotted something to put a smile on your lady's face."

Even if he had, Darin was certain he couldn't afford a hand's width. "I'm afraid not."

"Even after the help I've given you?"

Darin couldn't ignore that the man had been useful, but he couldn't afford his wares, either. "How about a word of help in kind?"

"Words won't feed my fam–"

"You went too soon to the cloth-of-silver," Darin said.

The merchant's face became a mask of caution. "Not sure what you mean."

"Let's ask the market guards, then, shall we?" Darin made as if to wave one over.

"All right, all right," the man said hastily. "I take your meaning."

Darin smiled. "First one touch, then a second. Then when you have a bit of the mark's trust…"

"Third time's the charm," the man said. "Never thought about it much that way before." He winked at Darin. "Much obliged."

"Good luck to you." Darin knocked twice on the roof of the carriage.

They lurched forward into the slow traffic, where the cacophony of half a hundred ongoing negotiations afforded them some privacy.

"You've got it already, don't you?" Kat asked.

"What?"

"Jakub's vice."

"Not sure yet. The next merchant will tell us for sure," Darin said.

The vendor in question sold tiny brass instruments small enough to fit into a pocket – absolutely the kind of novelty to make yourself a nuisance at dinner parties, but that didn't seem to match Jakub's personality. Fittingly, he'd only paused his sedan chair long enough for a peek in the merchant's change box. He'd paid handsomely for an old Vlaskan dram, the kind that was mostly copper. Vlask had produced a small number of these before switching to a mix of softer metals. The old copper ones were numbered, though, which was why a certain kind of hobbyist sought them out.

"This is good," Darin said. "He's a coin collector."

"Isn't every trader?"

"Not just any coins. Old ones, and rare ones." And by chance, Darin had grabbed a fistful from the reserve fund. He wanted to believe that was luck, but the Lady had rarely shown him kindness.

"So he uses money to buy other money?" Kat shook her head. "What a gods-damned waste."

"He *is* a trader. It makes a certain kind of sense."

"If you're a lunatic," Evie muttered.

"The why of it doesn't matter. We've got a fistful of old coins, and one needs to end up in his pocket," Darin said.

"I assume you have some kind of plan for making that happen," Kat said.

"That depends. Can you act?"

"Act how?"

"Like someone other than yourself," Darin said.

Kat frowned at him, to show how little she appreciated how *that* came out. "If necessary."

"Tomorrow, you're going to make an enemy."

Kat snorted. "Is that all? Been doing that for years."

CHAPTER NINETEEN
New Vendors

Of course, having something the mark wanted and being able to sell it to him were two different things. Darin nearly had a stroke when he learned the cost of a vendor stall at the Uptown pop-up market. The entry fee alone ran more than most shopkeepers made in a year, and you had to pay that before you even sold two bits. It went beyond their crew's normal operating budget for a pre-mission like this, so they'd had to call on Lisbet's parents to cover it. Alfon and Damia weren't in Stillwater but had relocated to within half a day's ride. Their eagerness to see this done was plain on their faces when he met them to collect the coin.

"How is she?" Damia whispered.

"I haven't spoken to her since our first meeting."

Alfon pressed a heavy purse into Darin's hand. "When will this be over?"

"It's too soon to say."

"We should be there with you. We can come to Stillwater."

"No." Jakub almost certainly had a network of informants. If he had any idea what was coming, this whole thing would collapse into a bloody mess. "The risk is too high."

"But we're useless here," Damia protested.

"That's not true." Darin shook the purse. "If you weren't here to back us up, we'd be trying to find a new plan right now. Trust me."

The Galceras looked at one another, clasped hands, and nodded. Realists. Darin awarded them a notch of respect.

Back in Stillwater, Darin and Evie arrived an hour before dawn at the designated square for the pop-up market. This rotated among four locations in Uptown, to add to the illusion that the market wasn't permanent. You paid your fee and had your tent set up before the sun broke the horizon, or you didn't set up at all. Evie's outer garments looked plain enough – a solid wool overcoat, knitted cap, and fur-lined boots – but that would change soon enough. She smelled like lavender this morning, a faint and familiar perfume that reminded Darin of the early years. A period he liked to call "our time of innocence."

Evie liked to call it her "time of foolishness."

They worked in quiet efficiency, setting up the tables and squaring them to the planned flow of traffic. As newcomers, they got the worst location on the outer rim of the marketplace. Nothing to do about that – they had to hope that Jakub would venture this far out into the periphery. Darin set up the merchandise while Evie pranced off to pay their fee. The collector's name was Tobias, and on that information alone, she nominated herself to carry the money over. A lavender-hinted coldness lingered while she was away, but Darin ignored this as best he could and laid out the inventory.

Ten years of taking odd jobs across the queendom – along with the occasional gambling windfall – had produced an esoteric collection of trinkets. More recently, Kat had begun taking barter for her brews. Two ales for the hand-carved bird in corkwood, three for the brass finger-flute, and five for a grandmother's spice jars. Darin stashed away the odd tokens in a trunk for the next time the crew needed to "play the vendor."

Evie returned with decidedly less bounce in her steps.

"How did it go?" Darin asked.

"Not well."

"No discount off the fee, then?"

"As it turned out, we probably should have sent you."

"Me?"

She made an irritated scoff. "You'd think that even someone more interested in men would have at least a platonic appreciation for my gifts."

"Ah."

"It's not natural."

"It's perfectly natural. You just don't like the idea of a man who's immune to your charms."

She threw her arms around his neck, her eyes playful. "At least I still have you."

He snorted. "Your power over me wore off a long time ago."

She pulled him close and stood up on her toes to whisper in his ear. Her breath was hot, and her sultry voice stirred some very primal instincts below the waistline. "Save the acting for the mark, darling."

He exhaled with intentional slowness while she slipped away from him, and began rearranging what he'd laid out so far on the tables.

Day broke first on the slanted cloth rectangles that formed the roofs of the market stalls. As it marched down to paint the rest of the market in daylight, the first of the morning's patrons appeared. The early shoppers came mostly on horseback, riding directly to a certain stall for a quick haggle over some essential item. Wine, weapons, and herbal witchcraft, for the most part. The foundations of a society that regretted its previous night, or planned to ruin someone else's coming day.

"Here comes another one." Darin took another swig of the piping hot tea and passed the leather flask to Evie. They hadn't brought anything to sit on, so they perched on the edge of the open wagon and shared a loaf of day-old bread.

The approaching rider was an older man, stout fellow, on a lovely black gelding with white fetlocks. He swayed in the saddle a little more than he should, which meant he'd been in his cups. *And not quite out of them, by the look of it.* Darin had a hunch on this one, but it was Evie's turn to pick first.

"One of the wine merchants." Evie tilted her head, examining the horseflesh. "Maybe even the imperial dreamwine."

Darin let his gaze flicker to the opulent circular tent in the center of the market, the one he'd avoided looking at all morning. The one flying imperial colors from its pinnacle. "He's not *that* wealthy."

"So you say."

"So I say," Darin agreed. "I think he drank too much already, has started to sober up, and realized he might've diddled his life away last night. He'll want the herbalist."

The man rode up the middle lane, paused to get his bearings, then turned left. Distinctly *away* from the herbal tents. He slowed in front of the imperial wine sellers, but then pressed on to a local vintner, where he bought a leather-wrapped bottle for a fistful of coins.

"Now there's an expensive breakfast," Darin said.

"But it was wine, not herbs."

He sighed. "So it was." He flipped her a silver penny.

She snatched it deftly out of the air and added it to her pile. They'd split eight of them and begun this little gambling game to pass the time; at the moment, she was winning six to two.

Traffic picked up as the morning took hold, and the rising sun pressed away some of the persistent chill that lurked in the marketplace. The stream of lookers riding or being carried by the tent grew from a trickle to a steady current. The bird-carving brought eight silvers, which would thrill the hell out of Kat when she heard about it. Evie's natural persuasiveness, though mostly under wraps, brought in handsome coin for a few other items.

Jakub arrived shortly after midday, still sporting the cane but now wearing a jaunty sailor's cap – feathers and all – in place of his usual broadbrim. It proved a better match for the garish riding jacket, a patchwork of no less than six different hues, each one more brightly unnatural than the next. He rode the same sedan chair with the same bearers, probably a standing contract. To Darin's frustration, he made his first pass down the center aisle of the marketplace, which put their cramped location neatly in his blind corner.

"Damn," he muttered.

Evie chewed her lip, one of her anxious-but-not-showing-it habits. "Wish we'd gotten a better booth."

"It's not by chance that they put us here. They know where the wealthy do their looking."

"All he needs is a glimpse."

She was right, but that window of opportunity would be narrow if it came at all. Two of the busiest vendors held the last positions of the main row. The carpenter who built odd-shaped furniture in dark tropical wood would turn Jakub away from Darin and Evie's little setup. The butcher who'd slaughter any number of brightly plumed birds right before your eyes, to take home for the evening meal, would bring him around toward them.

"Get ready," Darin said. *Let's hope he's more into tropical slaughter than hardwood.*

The Lady of Fortune was merciful, because Jakub paused long enough to purchase an emerald-green hen with brilliant yellow eyes. The butcher grabbed it about the body from its cage, ignored its squawk of protest, and clove off the beautiful, feathered head with a single blow from his cleaver. Darin winced, suddenly reminded of the Dame's demonstration with her songbird. Jakub counted out a few gold coins for the man while he bundled the bloody carcass up in leak-proof paper. They made the exchange. Jakub tucked the package behind him on the chair and turned right in the necessary direction.

"All right, Evie. Light the signal fire," Darin said.

She loosened the clasp of the riding cloak, drew down the hood, and let it slide off her. Darin caught it and tucked it beneath his chair. A single, conservative movement to ensure that all eyes remained on her. The silken dress beneath glittered in the sun, bright as any of the trinkets on their table. The material was called glittersilk, in fact, and it conjured a visual illusion under the right conditions. The further you stood from it, the more transparent it became. So you'd wander in closer, hoping to get a better look at what lay beneath. Yet the dress remained frustratingly opaque, always teasing, never revealing.

She'd been wearing glittersilk the very first time Darin had laid eyes on her, half a lifetime ago. That was also in a market square, in some nameless village on the Far Wyld. What were the odds of two like-minded grifters hitting the same market on the same day, both of them hoping to do their part to spit in the eye of the empress? The glittersilk had caught his eye, as it was meant to do, and pulled him in like iron filings to a lodestone. Over the next two days he'd been robbed blind, stabbed twice, and nearly drowned. *Happiest time of my life.*

"Aren't you going to look?" Evie asked, tearing him back to the present.

Darin knew he shouldn't, but stole a glance at her anyway. Seeing Evie in glittersilk was like looking at the sun – dangerous to do, and best done quickly. He sucked in a sharp breath.

"Do you like it?" she asked.

"Every man within a hundred leagues likes it." Darin half-wished he were exaggerating, too. The radiant material on Evie's slender form, combined with her dark hair and suddenly quite-visible face, might as well have rung a dinner bell for every able-bodied man within view. Casual glances became second appraisals, and then outright stares. Their boots carried them almost unwittingly toward her. Questing hands found the purse-strings and hefted them for an approximate count of the silver they'd use to impress the pretty little thing in the diaphanous dress.

The nearest such interloper, a hatless young man in a cream fur overcoat, practically ran up to the table. "What's for sale over here, then?"

"A few trinkets from far-off places," Evie said. "I like to find *stimulating* new things when I travel, don't you?"

She was using the voice again, the tone that put up hairs on the back of Darin's neck.

"I'll take a few things," the man said. "How much for–"

"Ten silvers," Evie said.

He frowned. "I haven't even told you what I wanted yet."

"What about that brass owl over there?" she asked.

Darin hid his smile. They'd found it in the saddlebags of an abandoned mule that wandered up to the Rooster a couple of years back. The animal was three-legs-lame by the time it reached them and had to be put down. They kept the owl in case the owner ever came by to claim it, at which point Tom intended to have a stern word about caring for burden animals. No one came, though. The owner had probably toppled dead out of the saddle somewhere in the wilderness that seemed to be expanding as the duchies grew apart. Not that Darin minded these rifts in the Old Queendom. A bit of chaos served his purposes.

"It's a bit burnished compared to what I'm used to," the young man said.

"Ten silvers are just a pittance for a man of your means," Evie purred. She brought the owl up to her lips and kissed its head, ever-so-alluringly.

The man seemed to choke on his own tongue as his clumsy fingers ripped open his purse. "Just the sort of thing I'm looking for, actually."

Darin wrapped it up for him in an old bit of scrap cloth, while Evie took the man's silvers and declined an invitation to dinner. The man left with sagging shoulders, but the wrapped owl clutched tight against his side.

So it went with the ten or twelve other men who approached their booth for the sole reason that Evie stood there. Every smile, every laugh of hers reached some poor fellow who was on the fence and brought him heedlessly into range of Darin's ridiculous inventory.

"What about the spice jars, for that gentleman over there?" Darin would ask.

Evie scooped up the item, gave the approaching customer her best come-hither eyes, and swapped out their junk for solid spending-metal faster than you could say "overpriced."

The flurry of activity became a force in itself, drawing eyes from across the market – and a few envious stares from their competing tables. Still, Jakub's sedan chair remained frustratingly distant in the coveted center ring of the market. Two laps around, then a third. Darin wanted to kick himself. He should have figured out a way to get a better booth. All this preparation, and the man probably wouldn't even see them.

The midmorning sun came out from behind a cloud. Evie's glittersilk dress shone like polished silver. And that, somehow, was what brought the sedan chair around a corner and up the aisle toward them.

"Crowded today, isn't it?" Darin asked casually.

Evie got the message and started turning away a few would-be customers to clear out the line. Meanwhile, Darin spread the true merchandise into a visible spot on the sales table in front of her. First, he piled the silver half-moons together in haphazard fashion, as if to be used for change. Then the Ganari golden oat, better known as a *goat*. There were a couple of Vlaskan drams, though not the numbered copper ones. He'd also brought a trio of iron korunas from the Scatters. A good mix of the old and exotic. With Evie feeding so many sharks for silver, keeping the enchanted coins on the table took most of Darin's efforts. There was no way to know which he'd choose, so all of them carried the tracking enchantment. That meant not passing one off to anyone but their mark, unless they wanted to be following the wrong people across the middle queendom. And that was just one concern. The other was that Darin would tuck the silver into his own pocket without even meaning to. He'd had some of these coins for years; it would be hard letting one go.

Evie's sudden brusqueness thinned the line out considerably. The sedan chair moved with purpose toward them now.

"Here he comes," Darin said.

CHAPTER TWENTY
Old Coins

Evie had played this game before. She'd lost count of the times Darin hatched a scheme that required her to deploy her charms on some unsuspecting man. It bothered her, in fact, that he was so quick to cast her in this particular role. Even if there was no denying that she had a knack for it.

Now she ignored the mark as he approached. Men like him were accustomed to getting people's attention. When they didn't get it, they began to act rashly. She kept her eyes on the hopeful young man who'd just spent a small fortune on dented brass tumblers. "I hope you'll enjoy them. As for tomorrow, I'm afraid I won't be around any longer."

The young man frowned. "Surely you can delay–"

"It's simply not possible."

"Then I'm not sure I really should be buying–"

Jakub chose that moment to interrupt by rapping his silver-inlaid cane twice on the merchandise table. "Afternoon."

The young man snapped his mouth shut and left, with his dented tumblers in hand.

Darin put on his stage smile and replied first. "Afternoon, good sir."

Jakub paid him no mind and took a dignified posture, the cane angled out so that Evie wouldn't miss the inlay of silver. Or the jewel-encrusted rings on his fingers. "New to the market, are you?"

Evie leaned toward him and gave a little smile. "What makes you say that?"

"I make it my business to know the pretty faces around here."

"That must be... exhausting."

"Not for those of us with the stamina for it."

Darin cleared his throat. "We're just passing through. Here today, back home south in the morning."

He might as well be a piece of furniture, for all the reaction he got from Jakub.

"Whereabouts are you from?" he asked Evie.

"Oh, you know, all over," Evie said. She twirled her hair around one finger, half tease and half invitation. "A few years in Tal Orea, another couple in the Scatters. I never stay in any place for long." She used the singular *I* on purpose, a part of her enjoying the way Darin's lips twisted downward as she implied that they might travel separately.

"We'd like to sell whatever we can, even so," Darin said. "Perhaps something here would interest your lordship?"

Jakub's eyes slid down Evie's torso to the table in front of her, where he couldn't miss the careful display of old collectible coins. A moment of excitement flickered across his face and disappeared so quickly that she nearly missed it. "I'm not much one for trinkets."

"Surely a man of your experience can find a little something to take home," Evie said.

"Perhaps." He nudged a carved statuette with the boot of his cane. "How much for the statue?"

Diverting away from what he really wants. It was clever, she had to admit. "Eight silvers. That's what we got for it."

Jakub grunted and pretended to peruse the other wares on the table. Evie started counting down in her head. *Three, two, one...*

"Any interest in selling an old coin?" Jakub asked, in a perfectly casual tone.

"One of these old half-moons?" Evie asked. "I'd been using them for change, but…"

Jakub shook his head. "I've a fistful of those already."

"How about an iron koruna?" Darin offered. "You won't find many of these beyond the Scatters."

"Not interested."

"Which one, then?" She let just the right hint of impatience enter her tone.

He pointed at the faded golden coin Darin had positioned out front. "What is that, a golden dram?"

It was the Ganari goat, as they all three knew. Ganar had stopped minting goats almost a century ago, and this once-prevalent coinage had all but disappeared from both continents. Every goat was inscribed with the likeness of a long-dead Ganari king, and numbered in their equally dead native tongue. They all spoke Imperial, now, and the Ganari ruler was little more than a national puppet for the empress.

"That's not a dram," Evie said.

"But it's also not for sale," Darin added.

Evie blinked out of turn. He'd gone off script.

Jakub allowed a tight smile. "Everything has a price. And I'd pay handsomely, too."

Darin shook his head. "This here's a family heirloom." He made as if to slide it off the table.

Jakub snapped his cane atop Darin's wrist, not painfully, but firm enough to hold it in place. "Ten silvers."

Exactly what I've been charging, Evie couldn't help but think. And it was a princely sum even for a goat in good condition. She hadn't given the goat a close inspection, but given the way Darin liked to bury old coins, it was probably in poor shape. "Come, brother, be reasonable." She leaned between them, cutting the tension with her silken-clad form.

"But Father–" Darin protested.

"Father wouldn't fault us for selling it to a good home." She looked pointedly at Jakub. "You have a good home, don't you?"

Jakub's lips curled into a smile. "The finest in Stillwater, I assure you."

"I suppose I might be willing to let it go," Darin said. "But not for so little. Not after Father handed it to me on his deathbed and told me I should take care of you with it." He grinned at Evie and pulled her close, his arm around her waist. The gesture could have been brotherly but left plenty of room for other interpretations.

She swept his arm down from her side in a casual way. It was all she could do not to strangle him.

Jakub's mouth tightened, but whether at the price or the girl-grabbing, it was hard to say. "It sounds like quite a hardship. Perhaps another eight-piece would salve those old wounds, however fresh they may seem."

Evie squeezed Darin's hand as hard as she could. Maybe she could break a bone or two. It'd serve him right. "Eighteen silvers for the old family goat is a generous–"

"Ho now, hold on!" A sedan chair had come up behind Jakub's, and the sturdy woman in it waved her arms to get Darin's attention. "What's this about an old goat?" Her hair was in total disarray about her face. She wore the grey robes of a traveling minister, with the sigil of the Four Gods emblazoned on the front in thread-of-gold. A *golden nun,* most called them. For the right donation, they claimed to put in a "good word" to the higher powers. She arrived at the table accompanied by the unmistakable smell of sour wine.

Jakub's glare was like ice, and his tone had a frostiness to match it. "This isn't your concern, sister."

The nun shook a heavy purse that clinked with soft metal. "I've been looking for a goat for years."

"You'll need to keep looking," Jakub said. "This one is spoken for."

"It's an open market, isn't it? I'll pay the eighteen, plus another eight." She leaned in and whispered, "Along with a quiet blessing, from our benefactors above."

Evie gasped softly. "Twenty-six silvers *and* a blessing?"

"That's a lot of coin in your pocket. Let's have a look." The nun lurched in her seat as if to grab the Ganari goat from the table.

"Beg pardon." Jakub spun his cane so fast that it blurred. The end of it caught the nun square in the shoulder, shoving her back to her seat.

She spluttered something that might have been a curse. "I'm a woman of the Four Gods! Get your filthy walking stick off me."

Jakub held her fast to the chair and turned back to Evie. "Four pieces of eight in pure silver, right now. That's my *final* offer."

Evie took a breath, looking from Jakub's cool, confident visage to the ruddy face of the nun. "I'm sorry, good sister, but this gentleman promised it a good home." She met Jakub's eyes. "You have a deal, sir."

Jakub's smug grin returned to his face. He released the nun from the pinion-hold and paid her no further mind. He untied the heavy leather purse from his belt and tossed it unceremoniously onto the table in front of Darin. "You don't mind counting, do you?"

Darin bit back what would undoubtedly have been a rude response, and pulled open the purse. He counted four pieces of eight for Jakub to see and palmed a fifth when the man glanced away. Evie wrapped the goat in a square of lambskin. She pranced around the table and close enough to press it into Jakub's waiting hand. "I hope it brings you good fortune, your lordship."

"It has already," Jakub said. He gestured vaguely at Darin to return his purse. But he kept his eyes on her, wandering up and down her body like a prized calf.

Jakub's purse came sailing back and struck him hard in the chest.

"Whoops," Darin said.

Jakub glared at him. "Watch it!"

Darin offered a smug grin of his own. "Pleasure doing business, m'lord."

Jakub stared at him another moment longer, perhaps trying to decide if he'd been insulted. He tapped his cane on the sedan chair to have the bearers carry him away.

Evie whirled on Darin and short-punched him in the arm. "Why did you do that?"

"Do what?"

"He almost *walked.*"

"He wasn't going to walk," Darin said. "He took a coin and overpaid for it, so he's that much more likely to keep it with him."

"Why couldn't you leave your ego out of the con for once?"

"I'm sorry, Evie."

She harrumphed and had to look away from him. *The fool nearly ruined everything.*

"I liked how you told him it was lucky. That was a clever touch," Darin said.

An obvious attempt to placate her, but it softened her temper a little. "Thank you."

The stout golden nun hadn't moved from her position by the table. "By the Four Gods, upon whose intercession we both rely, and sometimes curse, that was quite a show."

Darin chuckled. "You played the nun part well, Miss Kat."

Surprisingly so. Evie gave her a smile. What Kat lacked in stage training, she made up for in sheer enthusiasm. Then she remembered how Darin's childishness had nearly ruined everything, and she fixed him with a frown.

"The marker's in play," he said. "That's what matters, isn't it?"

"I suppose. But next time, *you* wear the dress."

CHAPTER TWENTY-ONE
The Butler

Once a year, Stillwater's entire trading fleet doffed their normal plain canvas for brightly hued sails and assembled in the deep-water harbor for a two-day regatta. By tradition, the city's wealthiest merchant hosted the event. That was Jakub Purser by a significant margin. Word was, most of the ships in the harbor belonged to him. Word also was that the man had fired his butler the previous morning for a minor infraction. Not just fired him, but thrown him physically out into the street and refused to pay him his final wages. And then he'd fired his private guard, for refusing to do the throwing out.

The timing, of course, was terrible for Jakub with the regatta coming. He'd put out a call for a new butler immediately. But Stillwater being a relatively small town, and Jakub's temper being rather widely established, there were no responses.

More accurately, those few who might have responded were talked out of it before they set foot on Jakub's walkway.

The house was easily the most massive dwelling Kat had ever seen in person. Almost like a mansion out of a child's story rather than a place where one man and one woman lived without any children. It wasn't enough that Jakub normally had a pair of hired guards out front to keep away beggars and distant family members. Fortuitously, they'd received carefully forged orders instructing them to ride down to the waterfront and inspect each one of Jakub's vessels from bow to stern.

Thanks to Lisbet providing some old shipping manifests, the orders matched the master's handwriting perfectly.

Everything was set. Everyone was out of the way. Of course, there was the obvious problem that Kat and Jakub had recently met in the market. Evie had cut her hair and put on a thick layer of powders and paints. Darin somehow acquired a jet-black suit of the lightest, softest silk Kat had ever seen. With a few adjustments, it fit her perfectly. Kat hardly recognized the woman in Evie's looking-glass. Hopefully, Jakub wouldn't either. Of course, that was only the start of it. Evie spent over an hour teaching Kat how to talk as a servant. Basically, it amounted to kissing asses and not saying what you really thought. Kat figured she could stomach that for a single night.

Now, on the path to Jakub's massive wood and steel front door, she fought a rising sense of panic. What if Jakub refused to hire her? Worse, what if he realized she was the golden nun from the market? Darin seemed confident that this wouldn't happen, that men like Jakub saw the clothes instead of the person. But Darin didn't know everything. Hell, he didn't know that Kat wouldn't fall apart in the middle of this scheme and give it all away.

She took a calming breath. Sixty-four paces up the walkway to Jakub's house. Eight steps up to the massive front door. Despite her nearly overpowering apprehension, she found this amusing. Eight was the coinage number, something moneylenders and merchants both found extremely lucky. Of course there'd be eight steps. Maybe people were as predictable as Darin said. The thought gave her enough confidence to lift the massive iron knock-ring on the door and rap it three times against the wood.

Muffled shouts came from within. Then footsteps approached the door, and a man cursed as he fumbled with the locking mechanism. Gods, if it took Jakub this long to open a simple door, he stood little chance of putting a child in Lisbet.

DAN KOBOLDT   147

The door flew open at last to reveal a red-faced and half-dressed Jakub. "Yes?"

"Jakub Purser, please," Kat said. It sounded less odd a phrase in the moment, though when she and Darin had practiced it, she could hardly believe someone would initiate a conversation this way.

"That's me," he said, with an air of impatience. "What do you want?"

"I'm told you're seeking a butler."

"And?"

"My name is Ronna Goldan." Kat bowed from the waist the way Evie had showed her, and offered the neat stack of letters that Darin had forged that morning. "I come highly recommended."

Jakub took them with obvious reluctance and looked her up and down, frowning. "You're a woman."

"Very astute of you, sir. Is that a problem?"

"It's just that I normally hire a man for a butler."

"Oh?" she asked. "And how's that been working out for you, sir?"

His eyebrows shot up and, for a moment, she thought she'd pushed too hard. Then he laughed. "Not well, I suppose."

"A man like you, a man of means, needs a woman serving him. If you don't mind my saying so, sir." Kat's stomach twisted saying this.

Jakub smirked a little. He liked that. Then his brow wrinkled. "You seem familiar."

"I used to be in Brinley Pendergast's service, sir," Kat said. "You'll find a letter from his steward in that stack, there. I wasn't able to get one from the master himself, for obvious reasons." This was the part that made her really nervous. Pendergast had been the top merchant in Stillwater before Jakub's rise to prominence. A bitter rivalry emerged, it was said. Jakub won out. The night before signing over his last ship to Jakub, Pendergast had jumped off a high bridge.

"Pendergast." A complex mix of expressions crossed Jakub's face. "I don't remember seeing you."

"I prefer to work in the background, sir. That's a woman's place." It grated her to tell him this. The very thought went against every fiber of her being. But Darin had said it would probably seal the deal, and he was right.

"The job pays two coppers a day. I can't afford more with the severance I'm giving my previous butler."

Two coppers a day was an insult, and the bit about severance a bald lie. Kat frankly didn't care about the salary for this position, but she also knew this was a test. "I'd hoped for four a day, if I'm being honest."

Jakub put on a pained expression. "Would that I could afford to offer more."

"Surely a man of your stature could do three a day."

Jakub gave her a thin smile. "These are hard times."

"Very well, then. Two coppers a day." Kat watched Jakub's face and saw the look of disappointment. "Of course, I'd want triple that amount every fourth day, on account of the gods."

"On account of the—"

"Gods, yes. I'm a devout woman, and the Four will be needing their nip," Kat said brightly. "So that's two a day for three days, and six on the fourth."

Jakub's eyes narrowed. "That happens to work out to three a day."

"We can call it that, to make the accounting easier."

Jakub gave her a sidelong look, as if revising his initial opinion. "How soon can you start?"

Now that's better. "Right now, if it pleases you."

"It pleases me." Jakub pushed open the door wide enough for her to enter and looked out past her. "Where are my guards?"

"Do you normally have guards, sir?"

"A pair of them." His brow furrowed. "They really should have stopped you before you got to my door."

"I'll get to the bottom of it, sir." Kat straightened her jacket collar with both hands. Evie should be watching; she'd make sure Darin got the guards ordered back. "What else needs doing?"

"A hundred things. But first, you might start with my wife."

Kat felt a spike of consternation. "What about her?"

"She's upstairs, taking far too long to get dressed."

"I'll see if I can help out." Kat's boots clicked on granite as she crossed the threshold. Several overlarge pedestals stood along the walls, each holding a sculpture carved in white marble. Some were ships, some were women – not Lisbet, though – and no less than three were statues of Jakub Purser himself. There were eighty-two ships in the Purser fleet at last count, and it probably took all of them to hold the man's ego.

Kat ascended the broad main staircase to the upstairs of the massive house. Soft lamplight bathed every chamber, even though no one was in them. *What a waste.* She crept down the hallway on the thickest hand-woven rug her feet had ever trodden upon toward the only door that lay swathed in darkness. A lamp with a low-trimmed wick waited on the elegant table outside. She took it with her through the door into a spacious bedroom, only it wasn't a bedroom. The closet held more clothes than she'd ever seen in one place in her life.

A wall on her left bore women's gloves. Gloves! There had to be fifty, sixty pairs. Kat had exactly two pairs of gloves, a thick leather set for making ale, and a lightweight fingerless pair she wore when she was feeling ornery. The next section held scarves; beyond that were shawls. And beyond those stood a slender young woman rummaging through two massive heaps of dresses. She was young. Too young, really, to have a mess like this. Certainly too young for the mottled bruises on her upper arms.

"Are you Lisbet?" Kat called.

The woman jumped like a startled hare and pulled a fistful of dresses up to cover herself. "Yes. Who are you?"

"Ronna Goldan, mistress," Kat said. "I'm your husband's new butler."

"He found one already?"

"He got lucky. I'm a friend from back home."

Lisbet's furrowed brow went smooth, and her eyes flat. "Where is he?"

"Still downstairs, I believe."

Lisbet tiptoed to the doorway, peered out, and then sagged in obvious relief. "He's quieter than you'd think possible, when he wants to be. So, what's the plan?"

"I'm to help you get dressed," Kat said.

"And then what?"

"And then I'll do whatever else your husband needs." *Within reason*. There were some things she'd never do for that pig of a man. Or any man, for that matter. "As will you."

"Of course." Disappointment marred Lisbet's face, but only for a heartbeat until she schooled it again.

The poor thing had been living this nightmare for far too long. But Kat didn't want to rush things and ruin Darin's carefully laid plans. "What dress will you be wearing, mistress?"

"I don't know. I-I can't pick the right one."

"Perhaps I can be of assistance," Kat said, the way Darin had suggested. The dress mattered. She perused the long line of dresses still hung along the closet's back wall. Every hue, every material she'd ever imagined was represented. Most of them looked as though they'd never been worn. Now she understood why Darin hadn't sent Evie for this job. They'd never have made it out of the closet. He told her he wanted something flashy. Something memorable. Gods knew why.

She was two-thirds down the row of dresses when she saw it: a silver garment that shone like polished metal. It was a simple enough gown, but the material seemed to bring its own faint, silvery light. She lifted it from the rack and held it up. "What about this one?"

Lisbet shook her head. "That? No, I could never–"

"What's wrong with it?"

"Nothing. It's simply a bit bold for my preference."

"We want bold."

"We do?"

"Yes. Trust me, this is the dress. Come on, I'll help you try it on," Kat said.

"I can manage, if you want to wait out–"

"And fail my first duty as Jakub's butler? I don't think so." Kat gestured impatiently for Lisbet to come closer. She pressed her lips together at the sight of the bruises. *The poor girl.* No one deserved a husband like that. She knew she shouldn't ask, but as she helped Lisbet slip on the silver dress, her mouth betrayed her. "What happened here?"

"I asked if we could invite my parents to the regatta," Lisbet said, in a small voice. "I miss them terribly."

"I'm sure they feel the same of you, mistress." Kat busied herself with the straps and tried not to think about it. If she let all of this in, it might break her. She had to be strong.

"I told him I don't want to go months without seeing them. If not for my mother's sister's funeral, I wouldn't have seen them at all."

Mother's brother, you mean, Kat nearly said. *Gods, we need to get this girl out of here.* "What did he say?"

"He said his captains spend years at sea, without ever complaining. But I'm lonely here."

"It's just you in the house, then?" Kat asked.

"There are servants. And a cook. But none of them will talk to me." Lisbet leaned closer and whispered, "They're all deathly afraid."

With good reason, Kat thought, remembering what had happened to her predecessor. "I see. Well, let's have a look at you." She took a step back and admired how well the dress fit Lisbet. Jakub must have had it tailored. "You're a lovely thing. You know that, don't you?"

Lisbet nodded, though her eyes glistened. She picked out

a shawl and wrapped it around her arms just so, making the bruises disappear. She must have practiced it.

Kat bit her lip so hard it would probably start bleeding. "Well," she said at last. "I'm probably needed downstairs. I'll see you soon, all right?"

"Yes. Thank you," Lisbet whispered.

Kat nodded and turned to march downstairs, where she vowed to try her best not to throttle Jakub's overlarge neck.

CHAPTER TWENTY-TWO
The Wife

On Kat's long list of regrets in life, agreeing to infiltrate the Purser home quickly rose to the top of the ranks. There were three primary reasons for this. First, it confirmed all her worst fears about how the ridiculously wealthy lived. Jakub wasted money on *everything*. The ridiculous sculptures, his wife's clothes, even the gala itself. The sheer amount of coin that he threw about on food nearly put her into a rage. The guests lucky enough to be invited aboard his ship would want for nothing. Unless they amounted to a small army, Jakub would probably end up throwing most of the food away. Such a waste. Then again, that seemed to be the regatta's entire theme. More than a hundred ships from the Stillwater fleet were taking part. They could be carrying grain down to Tal Orea or hunting slavers out in the Scatters, but no, it was more important to put on a spectacle.

Second, she did not enjoy the deception nearly as much as she expected. Playing the golden nun in the market had brought such a thrill. Part of that was because it was brief. She showed up, helped squeeze more money out of the mark, and disappeared again. Today was different. She had to spend hours in this role, actually working on Jakub's behalf. His former butler had taken care of many of the arrangements – the man seemed perfectly competent, as far as Kat could tell – but there were still last-minute invitations to send and the order of ships to decide. Then Lisbet needed help picking out shoes. And no one had ordered a gods-damned carriage to take them to the harbor! It was real work. *Actual* work. Far more than she wanted.

Third, and most importantly, these hours taught her that Jakub Purser was one of the worst people she'd ever met in her life. What he did to Lisbet was horrific, but that was just the beginning. The tip of the dogfish fin. In the short time she'd spent with him, he'd managed to insult Kat's accent, size, and supposed parentage. These weren't intentional jabs meant to demean her; they simply came up in conversation. Interspersed with those remarks were strings of curses that even made Kat blink a few times. They only got worse as he drank throughout the day. It turned out, with Kat handling the logistics, the man had little to do.

At last, she'd gotten the household squared away and the carriage was trundling down Jakub's long drive. The merchant himself stood rather unsteadily against one of the huge stone pedestals, ironically the one that bore a sculpture of him at the wheel of a ship. The contrast between the tall stone captain and the half-soused, overweight reality made Kat want to smile.

"Are you ready, at last?" he called up the stairs.

"Almost," Lisbet replied.

"You've been 'almost' for half an hour!"

Kat pulled open the huge front door to wave to the carriage driver. Jakub still lingered at the base of the stairs.

"Lisbet!"

"Coming. I'm coming," she said.

She crept down the stairs a minute later, stepping awkwardly on the new steel-heeled shoes. Kat had twirled her dark hair up in a series of tresses, each one held in place with a glittering metal comb of a precious metal. Copper, gold, and of course, silver. The set had belonged to Damia Galcera, and probably cost a small fortune. Lisbet had done her own paints and powders – a good thing because Kat was useless in that department. The cloth-of-silver dress flowed with her as she descended. Even Jakub, in his near stupor, stared at her in slack-jawed amazement.

"How do I look?" Lisbet asked him quietly.

Jakub grunted. "Still wish you had more meat on your bones. But I like the dress."

He had his back to Kat, which was a good thing. It gave her time to wipe the snarl from her face before he turned around. Lisbet reached the landing, still walking like a drunken sailor crossing a narrow bridge.

"Come on, then," Jakub said. "We're going to be late." He turned without another word and walked briskly to the door.

Kat elected not to point out that since he was hosting the gala, it could hardly start without him. As it was, she barely had time to get the door open before he lurched past. According to Evie's instructions, she should have escorted him down the eight steps to the carriage door and made certain he got seated comfortably. Kat preferred to forget this bit of decorum and waited for Lisbet to make her way to the door. "You went with the silver shoes."

"You were right, they do suit the dress better," Lisbet said. "I just feel a bit unsteady."

"That's what I'm here for." Kat offered her arm.

Lisbet took it gratefully. They descended in lockstep while Jakub looked on with an air of obvious impatience. Kat didn't rush. It was foolish to break with procedure, but after the day she'd had, she savored moving slowly downward, Jakub's pretty wife on her arm while he waited below. Lisbet's hand was incredibly soft. She smelled of lilacs. The loathsome brute didn't deserve her.

They reached the ground, where she helped Lisbet climb up into the dark-lacquered carriage.

"Is that the fastest she can move in this getup?" Jakub groused.

"It is, sir. But think how lovely she'll look beside you tonight," Kat said.

He nodded and leaned back into his seat, apparently mollified. "Meet us at the harbor."

"Of course, sir." It never occurred to Jakub that she might have no means to get herself down to the harbor, which was a ten-minute ride and three times longer to walk. Men with his privilege didn't think about the everyday challenges of the common folk. Or maybe Jakub did, and this was his way of punishing her for lingering on the steps. No matter. Kat had summoned a queendom-style carriage, the kind with the jump bench on the back. As the driver got it under way, she side-stepped the rear wheel and vaulted up onto it. It was a bit bumpy on the cobblestone sections, but years of driving her own wagon gave Kat the muscle memory to move with the bench. On the whole, it was almost as comfortable as riding inside the carriage.

She couldn't see inside the cabin, but she could hear them.

"Stop fidgeting!" Jakub snapped. "What's got you so nervous all of a sudden?"

"Nothing." Lisbet hardly sounded convincing.

"Gods, woman, it's our wedding night all over again."

Kat realized she was grinding her teeth and forced her jaw to keep still.

"Things got a little out of hand last night," Jakub was saying.

"It's fine."

"It's not that I don't want you to see your parents," he continued. "Hosting them now would be very hard on my schedule. I've got ten deals that I hope to finalize over the regatta."

"I understand," Lisbet whispered.

"Perhaps next year, after the harvest feast."

"Of course," she said, her voice faint.

With luck, there won't be a next year, Kat thought.

As if on cue, they hit a bump in the road and the impact nearly jolted Kat from her jump seat. She flailed for the carriage wall to steady herself. A heavy thud and muffled curses from inside suggested Jakub had lost his balance as well.

He pounded on the roof with a fist. "Watch the road, man!"

They rode in injured silence through the winding streets, past the smaller but still impressive houses of Jakub's competitors. Stillwater, on the whole, appeared to be prospering. Well, this part was. Eventually they passed out of Uptown proper and into the middle town. The houses were what Kat might call normal size here, and there were far more of them. Skilled workers lived here, and perhaps the occasional ship's officer. Still not a bad roost if you could get it. They kept rolling downward into the harbor district, which was far shabbier by comparison. The buildings lost their discrete edges and became a long wall of nondescript tenement buildings. Sailors and dockworkers called this place home. Kat saw more families here. More children. They roamed the streets in boisterous packs under the watchful eye of two or three adults per group. Communal child rearing was a necessity in port towns, with so many of the able-bodied men and women working at sea.

The carriage rumbled to a merciful stop at the shoreline, where Jakub and Lisbet mounted separate sedan chairs to be carried down to the docks to board his flagship. Kat trailed after, marveling at the sight of more than a hundred ships in the harbor. They'd swapped their usual plain canvas for brightly colored sails. It was like watching a massive flock of exotic birds upon the water. They zoomed and swooped the same, clustered together the same. Even though the back of Kat's mind knew that so many ships with empty holds represented a colossal waste of resources, the visual effect didn't fail to impress her. If even half of those ships belonged to Jakub, she began to understand how he lived like he did.

That didn't make it right, though.

The sun had begun to drop toward the horizon. If all went well, by the time it rose again, Jakub would be a new man, and not in a good way.

CHAPTER TWENTY-THREE
Dock Workers

The wind all but died as the sun dropped below the horizon, allowing the city of Stillwater to live up to its name. The great ships in the regatta set anchor in the harbor to begin the real festivities. Their bow and stern lanterns twinkled like hundreds of fireflies. Among them was the *Queen of Profits,* Jakub's flagship. Not the most subtle of names, Darin had to say.

Darin and Evie prowled the docks, looking for the right opportunity. A roving fleet of dinghies and sailing junks ferried revelers between ships and shore. More than a few departing boats spotted them in their bright, colorful garb, and called out offers to carry them forth. On the land side, dock workers clustered around large barrels mounted on wooden frames, with taps at waist-level. A few of these groups beckoned them as well. Everyone was welcome everywhere. Darin had never seen anything like it. He and Evie kept smiles on their faces, and declined all offers with an air of polite regret. A boat leaving the docks would make a beeline for the nearest ship party that had room for them. They needed their own craft to get to a singular destination. One that probably wouldn't welcome a dinghy full of partygoers.

Trouble was, nearly every craft was either on the water, or otherwise occupied. The entire damn city must have turned out for this thing.

"What about that one?" Evie asked quietly. The oversized hood of her cloak muffled her voice to a whisper.

Darin glanced ahead to the little rowboat. "No oars."

"None of these have had oars."

"Probably because no one wants their boat taken by people like us," Darin said.

"Do we need them?"

"What am I to paddle with, my hands?"

"How about your head?" she asked irritably.

He didn't acknowledge the barb. She'd been on edge all morning. Both of them had. They'd gotten a late start – turning away would-be applicants for Jakub's sudden job opening had proven more work than it should have – and now they couldn't find a boat.

"There's one with oars," Evie said.

Darin glanced casually to the side. The rowboat was a bit smaller than he wanted, but there were oars in the oarlocks. An iron chain and heavy padlock secured it to the piling. "The lock will take some time."

"Not if I do it." Evie climbed down before he could protest. The rowboat hardly shook when she boarded it. She pulled back her hood and withdrew two long, slender pieces of metal from her hair. Revel costume or not, you'd never catch Evie without her favorite lockpicks.

Darin leaned against the piling and dug into a pocket for his leather flask. That way if someone came asking his business, he'd have an excuse. He'd probably need it, too. A group of half a dozen revelers was making its way down the docks in their direction. It looked to be a mix of sailors and merchant marines. A tough group, to be sure, and not one they wanted getting interested in what he and Evie were up to.

"What's taking so long?" he hissed.

One of Evie's picks slipped, and she cursed. "It's rusted."

"We're going to have company in a minute."

Evie made an exasperated sound and brushed an errant

strand of hair out of her face. "You want to climb down here and do this?"

"Just hurry."

She muttered something decidedly uncomplimentary under her breath, but it looked like she redoubled her effort. Darin couldn't see very well in the dark, and he hated that. As the light faded, keeping track of Jakub's ship among all the others in the harbor grew difficult. Frustratingly, the man refused to drop anchor. Maybe it was a prestige thing. Maybe he wanted to show off the skill of his crew. Or maybe the man was just a fool who didn't recognize the danger.

The noise from the sailors grew louder. With luck they'd pass along their merry way and be none the wiser. Darin took another swig from the flask. Tried to be nonchalant. *Nothing to see here. Just keep on moving.*

Only they didn't keep moving. They slowed down and fell suddenly quiet.

"I heard Stillwater had a harbor rat infestation, but I didn't think it was this bad," a man said.

Darin's gut twisted at the sound of the voice. He knew the rough, sneering tone the moment he heard it. Four's sake, Harrison sure seemed to turn up at the worst of times. And here Darin was with only a flask in his hand.

He'd dressed like a dockworker, as had his men. From their sudden grim expressions, Darin guessed that the laughing and merriment had been part of an act. A ruse designed to get them close to Darin undetected, and it had worked. Which, working backwards, meant that this was no chance encounter. Harrison knew he was in Stillwater. Knew right where to find him vulnerable, too.

"What do you want?" Darin asked.

"What do we want?" Harrison snickered and looked around at his men. They wore a motley assortment of plainclothes and finery, none of it matching, all of it probably stolen. Irregular bumps and sharp bulges in these articles suggested that most of them were armed to the teeth. "He wants to know what we want, boys."

The men laughed, but not in a kind way.

"Funny thing," Harrison continued. "Last time I checked, Stillwater's well on our side of the line."

"We're not working," Darin said.

"*We*, is it?" Harrison stalked across and looked over the edge of the dock. "Hello, love."

"I'm not your love," Evie said.

"Still wasting your time with this flea-wagon?" He looked back at Darin. "And looks like you're making her do all the work!" He clucked his tongue. "You're as disappointing a criminal as you are a man."

"Believe it or not, Harrison, not everyone gives two shits about your opinion," Darin said.

"I know I don't," Evie volunteered, catching his eye. She gestured at the now-loose chain. She'd gotten the lock open.

About time, too. He wouldn't say that, of course. Evie looked mad enough to spit as it was. If Harrison was here, it meant Annette was lurking somewhere nearby. The two of them in the same city didn't bode well.

The scar on Harrison's face darkened. "Big talk for a man and woman here alone, without their hitter, working mighty far into someone else's territory."

"Already told you, we're not working." Darin vaulted himself into the rowboat. He hit the hull hard and slammed both his knees into it. Hurt like hell. Nearly swamped the boat, too, but it pushed them out into the harbor.

One of Harrison's men made as if to follow, but Harrison held him back. "No, let him go. Like he said, he ain't working."

Darin took up the oars and set to rowing. He'd lost sight of Jakub's ship, but Harrison offered the more immediate threat. He wasn't the type to let things go. Certainly not with Darin operating this far across the deal line. More disturbingly, Harrison and his crew had continued down the docks to where a good-sized ship waited. A sleek cutter, with sails rigged and ready.

"What the hell is Harrison doing here?" Evie said.

"Nothing good." Darin rowed faster.

"Which one is the *Queen?*"

Darin grimaced. "I lost track of her."

"Are you serious?"

"I was a little distracted by Harrison."

Evie stood and scanned the harbor. "Everyone's anchored now. Oh, this is simply *perfect*, Darin!"

"We'll find it."

"How? How will we find one ship out of a hundred in the dark?"

"I'll figure something out," Darin said. He glanced over his shoulder, though, and saw that she was right. Hundreds of lanterns bobbed up and down in the inky darkness that was Stillwater Bay. That didn't begin to count the smaller craft moving in between. Music drifted across the water from several directions. Flutes, for the most part, and the occasional thrum of a stringed instrument. The weather was perfectly ambient, the breeze faint and salty. Any other time, if he weren't facing the crushing pressure of indebtedness to the Dame, he might take a minute to enjoy a night like this.

Instead, he ignored the music and cursed the breeze that fought his progress out to the middle of the bay. Here, by some unspoken agreement, none of the ships had anchored. Nor had any of the flotillas of smaller crafts drifted into this area. It was a void of growing darkness in the otherwise festive waters. The exact middle, as it were. Points of light floated gently all around.

Evie spun in a slow circle, peering out at them. At last she sat down in a huff, nearly tipping their boat over. "It could be any of them."

"Gods, would you be more careful?" Darin snapped, hurrying to steady the rocking hull.

"This is hardly the time to be careful. She's counting on us."

"Who is?"

"Kat! And Lisbet, too, of course."

Darin blew out his cheeks. "Didn't know you were fond of her all of a sudden."

"Are you complaining?"

"Not at all."

He tried figuring out the size of the ships by how far apart their bow and stern lanterns were. An old mariner's trick. There were too many of them, though, and to his eyes most of them were fuzzy.

Evie slammed her fist into the transom in frustration. "We have to do something, Darin!"

"Give me a second," Darin said.

"For what?"

"Just wait, all right?" Darin closed his eyes and focused on the silver queenpiece in his hand. The same queenpiece that had whispered promises to him since the moment he put it in his pocket. It was pure silver, untarnished and never tapped. He took a deep breath and let go of that tiny bit of willpower that kept the silver at bay. The moment he opened himself to it, the power flowed into him. Life flowed into him. He tasted every grain of salt on the breeze. Smelled the faint floral perfume that Evie denied she wore. Every wavelet that slapped the side of the tiny rowboat sounded like a thunderclap. He sent his senses questing outward. Across the water in every direction. Searching for metal. There were little clusters of it everywhere. A lot of copper, some gold, even the occasional piece of silver. He wanted a certain one, though. An old golden coin with a particular twist of metallurgy on it.

Seraphina had said it would call to him. Like a friend in a crowd, waving at him. He wished he'd tried it back at the Rooster before they'd gone on this fool's errand. Where was it? There were too many pieces of metal. He took a deep breath and forced his perception wider. A new pressure started pulsing at his temples, as if someone were jabbing both sides of his head with a finger. He could sense so much more metal now, all over the harbor and on the edges of the dock besides. *They're all the same!*

A pinpoint of light flickered, catching his attention. It was distant, but only a few points off the starboard bow. He fumbled for the oars with his hands, not willing to break his concentration. His fingers found one. He turned the boat slowly until its bow was dead on the golden pinprick. "There."

"What?" Evie asked.

"Right there, straight off the bow. See the ship there?" He couldn't really make it out himself, but the coin pulled at him like a beacon.

"I think so."

"That's it."

"Are you sure?" she asked.

"As much as I can be."

To Evie's eternal credit, she didn't ask how. She fixed the handful of ships in the direction he was pointing and said, "I've got them. Row."

He turned back and rowed, falling quickly into a rhythm that sent them steadily across the gentle swells.

"A little to starboard," Evie said. "Yes, perfect."

Darin put his trust in her and focused on the rowing. Good, long, smooth strokes. The rowboat handled fairly well for a booster. Good craftsmanship. *Focus, Darin.*

"Stop!" Evie said, startling him.

They couldn't have closed the distance already. "What's the matter?"

"There's a ship coming."

"They'll yield to us."

"I don't think they will," Evie said.

Darin snorted. For a highborn girl with so much privilege, Evie showed some surprising gaps in her knowledge of the world. "It's the law, Evie."

"Something tells me he doesn't care."

A cutter was bearing down on them. Now that they were close, they threw open the lantern shutters that had let them get so close. Darin caught a glimpse of Harrison's scarred, leering face. He threw himself into the starboard oar and spun the rowboat out of its path. The cutter shot past them, less than two yards from the transom.

"Beg pardon," Harrison called.

Then they had the wake to deal with. It struck right away, tossing the little rowboat back and forth in a dangerous wobble. Evie gasped and clutched at the hull. Darin fought the oars to keep them from tipping over. And Harrison's cutter was already turning.

"Darin–" Evie started.

"I see him!" Darin took a chance that the boat wasn't going over and set to rowing. He needed momentum. A small part of his brain told him this was pointless – a cutter with even the faintest breeze would always have more speed than he could conjure with two oars – but he ignored the voice and rowed as hard as he could.

Goddamn Harrison. The man just couldn't leave things be, could he? Thing was, it could have just as easily been him and his crew trying to rescue Lisbet tonight, only they hadn't gotten the gig. Which probably was for the best, because they'd have just killed Jakub, burned his mansion, and probably scuttled his ships for assurances. That was how Harrison operated. No subtlety.

The man himself bore down on their starboard side this time, a perfect example of this. The cutter's hull actually struck them this time. Only a glancing blow, but it sent splinters flying. Nearly snapped one of Darin's oars in half, too.

"You've made your point. Leave off!" Darin shouted in anger.

If Harrison heard, he didn't care to reply. The cutter was already turning in a wide circle to make another pass. Moonlight glinted on its long rudder as they made the turn. Darin got a flash of inspiration. His hand snaked into his pocket again and found the silver queenpiece. It might be enough. Especially with the way Harrison was turning so hard, putting pressure on the rudder. Darin let the power flow into him and sent it barreling across the water to the iron bolts reinforcing the rudder's long wooden spine. Adding to the already significant strain where the wooden tiller met the water.

The crack of splitting wood was almost deafening. The tiller handle snapped free, and pieces of it fell into the water. The rest of the cutter shuddered and then calmed as the ship spun gently with the breeze. It was a dead stick, now, at the mercy of the wind and currents. That would keep them busy for a while. Maybe they'd drift into another ship or, better yet, the shoals on the leeward side of the harbor. Harrison's shouts and expletives were almost enough to soothe the growing discomfort in Darin's body. He hadn't used metallurgy this much in a long time. He was close to his limit, in fact. He could feel it. And given how much of a toll it normally took on him, this was bound to be painful. But he couldn't quit. Not yet. Kat was counting on him. So he clung to the silver coin and the power within it, found his beacon, and pointed. "There's our mark. Don't let me stray from it."

He took up the oars again and rowed. His shoulders ached with the renewed effort. It must have shown on his face because Evie made a noise and stood. "Move over."

"I can do it."

She chose to ignore this, and wedged herself on the bench beside him, taking over one of the oars. "Fool man. You'll kill yourself through idiocy one of these days."

"Don't be silly," Darin said. "I know you'd never let that happen."

"I might."

Darin laughed. "Just don't wear yourself out. You'll still need to talk your way onto Jakub's ship."

Evie looked at him sidelong. "Jakub will be pouring me a drink before the next bell."

She was not wrong.

CHAPTER TWENTY-FOUR
Ghost Ship

Evie lay on the bed in the ship's main cabin, waiting for the fat man to wake. She'd slipped in here just before sunrise. Now it was almost midmorning, and the sunlight streaming through the porthole – it must be Tal Orean glass to be so perfectly clear – should have woken him already. Somehow the man continued snoring. Granted, he'd drunk more than his share of fine liquor the previous night. That wasn't even counting the powders she'd slipped into his drink to exacerbate the effects. He was no stranger to alcohol, this one, but the combined doses of merriment, drink, and powders had done their work well. He'd be fuzzy at best about how the night ended. Just how she wanted him.

She took a moment to savor the thrill in her stomach that had been with her since the night before, when Darin piloted their skiff through the swarm of regatta ships directly to Jakub's schooner – barely managing not to be sunk by Harrison along the way. She still wasn't entirely certain how he'd managed that. It had something to do with the coin, and silver, and that old witch Seraphina. She could have asked him about it, but she feared the answer. Beyond that, she'd had to focus on her approach, on talking her way aboard a ship full of strangers. That had been *her* moment. A few uncomfortable tasks still lay before her – most notably, this disgusting lump of a man – but the most challenging work was done.

At last, Jakub Purser's snoring came to an abrupt end. Evie nestled herself in the bed with her back to him. All she wore was a tiny gossamer shift. Jakub was silent for a moment, and then groaned. Evie smiled to herself. Served him right. He muttered something that might have passed for "morning." She grimaced as he pawed at her side with a meaty hand. His fingers had no strength to them. Gods, she hated him.

He gave a surprised grunt. Maybe he noticed that her frame was different from his wife's, or wondered why the brown and black splotches that normally mottled her back and shoulders had all disappeared. She sighed and stretched slowly. "Oh, Jakub! What a night that was," she whispered.

"Yes, quite a night," he said, after a moment. His addled mind couldn't make everything fit.

She rolled over to face him. "You were insatiable." Men loved hearing that, though few of them truly met the bar. She doubted Jakub did, and she never planned to find out.

He stared at her, his face a mask of confusion. He squeezed his eyes shut, winced in pain, and opened them again. "Who the hell are you?"

She huffed. "You've forgotten my name already?"

"Where's Lisbet?" he demanded.

"Who's Lisbet?"

"My *wife*!"

She half-shrugged and closed her eyes, as if going back to sleep. "Haven't seen her."

He grabbed her by the shoulder and shook her roughly. "Answer me!"

"How should I know?" she snapped.

He cursed and threw himself out of bed. He moved gingerly in the semi-darkness, and occasionally halted in his frenzied attempt at dressing to clutch his head and mewl in pain. Evie watched this through slitted eyes, in case the man thought to try something foolish.

"Never drink like that again," Jakub muttered.

"Aw, didn't you have fun?" Evie stretched again, posing just so across the coverlet. Daring him to look.

He did, and his eyes lingered in a few particular places. Then he looked at her face, and his eyes narrowed. "Where do I know you from?"

"Probably last night, when we–"

"*Besides* last night." He snapped his fingers then, remembering. "The market. You're the girl from the market."

Well, he had a better memory than Darin did when faced with her naked form. She had to give him that. "Of course I am. That's how we knew each other. I came to try to get our family goat back, you refused, we got to drinking…" She shrugged to leave the rest unsaid.

Jakub shook his head and grasped the bar across the door. "The door is barred. That's good. She – maybe she doesn't know."

"Know what, Jakub?" Evie couldn't resist a little jab.

He scowled and lurched out into the passageway. Evie stood and slipped into her dress, a black and red little number that some called a *black widow*. Which was exactly why it was her favorite. Jakub was calling for Lisbet up on deck, his voice sounding both concerned and fearful at once.

Evie left the cramped little cabin, pausing only long enough to palm Jakub's gold cufflinks from the bedside table. No need to leave such fine metal here, where it would only go to waste.

"Where the hell is the crew?" Jakub shouted, almost to himself.

"They're probably still ashore," Evie said, coming up on deck. The sun felt warm on her skin. The salty breeze was a vast improvement on the stuffy air from below. The river was calm; most of the ships from the previous night's revel had returned to their moorings for the night. The *Queen* was still anchored at the south end of the river's wide harbor area, her sails luffing about the mast without purpose.

The serenity of the morning was lost on Jakub, who

muttered something unpleasant and said, "Who told them they could go ashore?"

"You did."

"That doesn't make any sense."

It probably didn't, since Jakub hadn't granted his crew leave in over six months. Which, undoubtedly, was why they were so eager to take a night off. They'd have scattered to the shore bars, the gambling houses, even some of the other ships.

"I'm certain you were only trying to get me alone," Evie said. "Did you find your wife?"

Jakub winced. "No."

"I'm thinking about our conversation last night – lovely party, by the way – but I don't recall anything about a wife."

"I'm sure I mentioned her," Jakub said, with a hint of defensiveness.

"Jakub. I'm not naive. It's hardly the first time a man has invented some reason to see me off the next morning."

He made a choking noise. "She's real. I promise you."

"Was she the one in that silver dress?"

He whirled around to face her. "You saw her?"

"Of course. She's hard to miss, that one."

Discomfort flickered across his face. "You don't think that she saw us–"

"I'm not sure, Jakub. You told me to wait for you in your cabin."

He rubbed his eyes with his fingertips. "Can't remember a damn thing."

Good. "Perhaps she went ashore with the crew."

"Perhaps." Jakub wandered up to the wheel deck and began setting the rudder to rights. He paused there and looked down, no doubt noticing the dark stain across the wheelhouse. "Some fool's spilled his drink."

He put a finger in the smear that had ruined the fine wood. He frowned, and his fingertip came away bright red. He clamped his other hand over his nose and mouth. Backed away on shaky legs. He stumbled on something on the wheel deck. A dark rag of sorts, crumpled on the wood.

He nudged it with his boot, spreading the mess out across the deck.

"No," he whispered. The lighter colors beneath stretched out and caught the sunlight, shimmering in that unmistakable silver color. It lay in a river of blood that ran over to and across the rail, as if something bleeding had been dragged and thrown over.

"Something wrong?" Evie asked, keeping her voice cheerful. She pranced up to him, looked down, and gasped. She made her eyes as wide as she could and brought them up to Jakub's face. Then she turned, as if to flee.

"No!" He grabbed her arm.

She squirmed against his grasp. "Let me go!"

Desperation had brought strength to his fingers. "It's not how it seems!"

She kept squirming. He snarled and caught her wrist. Yanked her hard up against him. "I said *stop!*"

She brought her wrists together and down to loosen his grip. Then snaked a hand around and grabbed the little finger on his right hand. Bent it down and away. He gasped and lurched upward instinctively. No one wanted a finger broken. That opened him up nicely. She drove a knee into his crotch. He groaned and crumpled to the deck like a rag doll. She smiled down at him. "And I said, *let me go.*"

"Hello, the *Queen*!" someone shouted. "Permission to board?"

"Why, that sounds like your first mate." Evie raised her voice. "Granted!"

"No, no..." Jakub was muttering. He lay on the deck with Lisbet's bloody silver gown beside him. The only thing missing...

"Oh, nearly forgot." Evie found the bundle of rags behind the wheelhouse, unwrapped it, and let the blood-smeared dagger fall to the deck. It had a ruby the size of a gull's egg in the hilt, and *JP* engraved on the blade.

Jakub didn't notice.

"What happened here?" demanded a man's voice. The first mate must have seen something was amiss.

"Well, that's my cue," Evie said. "Good luck with the murder charges." She skirted around the mast as boots pounded toward the wheel deck.

"M'lord?" called the mate. He was a stout fellow with an oarsman's shoulders. Dark-haired, with a full beard and a voice like distant thunder. Two equally burly crewmen stood behind him. Hard, sun-leathered seamen all of them. They stared at Jakub in slack-jawed horror like he was a monster from the deeps.

The mate took a step forward. "Are you bleeding, m'lord?"

"I'm, I'm fine," Jakub managed to say. He struggled to find his feet. "It's not my blood."

"Whose is it?"

"No one's."

The mate's face darkened. "Where's Mistress Lisbet?"

"I don't know."

"Don't know, or don't want to say, *m'lord*?" He pronounced the honorific with a sneer. "She was here when we left last night. We all saw her."

The other two sailors murmured darkly in agreement. The mate stumped forward around the wheelhouse and paused, staring at the deck. He bent to pick it up.

"Don't touch that!" Jakub said.

The mate ignored him and lifted the dress so that a few bits of silver showed. Cloth-of-silver, to be exact. They'd all seen her in it the night before. It was the kind of dress you didn't soon forget.

The mate turned to face Jakub. "Why, Jakub? By the Four Gods, *why*?"

Jakub bolted feebly for the stern of the ship. The sailors caught him with rough hands before he'd taken two steps.

"Throw him in the brig," the mate said.

Evie stepped over the rail and climbed down the rope net to the skiff that had brought the sailors, which was empty save for the oarsman.

"Need a lift, miss?" Darin asked.

"As a matter of fact, I do. How fortuitous."

"Love the dress."

Evie laughed softly. "So did he."

CHAPTER TWENTY-FIVE
Bitter and Sweet

Darin met the parents at a different drinking-house in a different village, but still felt exposed. Kat had once again insisted he bring Tom along, who drew attention wherever he went. Darin resorted to taking the wagon, with Tom riding in the back. The big man made no complaint. Then again, he never complained unless someone forgot to feed the horses.

"I want you to keep an eye out for Harrison's crew," Darin said.

"Think they'll be around?"

"We're still fresh off the job and vulnerable. So absolutely I do."

They made a riding pass of the rendezvous point, a dilapidated stone and mortar building called the Pump Handle. Nothing to worry about from the front – this hour of midday meant few patrons coming in and out. A curl of dark smoke out of the chimney promised something decent might be roasting inside.

Darin slipped in the door. Comforting dimness awaited him inside; the only light came from the hearth, where flames licked up the sides of a haunch of lamb. The savory aroma made his mouth water.

A woman in a white cloth apron poked her head out of the kitchen. "Well, well. An early customer!" She had a friendly red-cheeked face and a smile with almost no teeth. The proprietress, probably. "Give me a minute and I'll put a lamp on."

"I don't mind the dark." Darin found his way to the table in the far back corner. He had almost an hour before the clients arrived, and thought he'd use that time to spook other patrons out of the place. *No need for that, apparently.*

She bustled over and wiped down his table with a corner of her apron. It remained spotless white, which made this about the cleanest drinking room Darin had ever seen. "I'm just trying to save on lamp oil. You wouldn't believe what the stuff costs."

"I might, actually." That was why he was taking this risk. The job was done and they needed the silver. "How's your ale?"

"My husband makes it in the cellar. How do you think?"

Darin chuckled. "Sounds like my kind of drink."

"Might be a little rougher than you're used to."

That's impossible. "I'll try a bit, just the same."

She swung around the bar, filled a mug from the dusty hogshead on the back of the wall, and slid it in front of him. "That'll be two coppers."

He plunked a silver mark on the table and slid it over to her with his thumb. "This ought to do for a few rounds."

She picked it up, tried biting it with her mostly absent teeth, and nodded. "Suppose it will."

"Meat sure smells good."

She wagged a finger at him. "That's for my evening patrons, not the day-drinkers."

He held her eyes and gave her his most charming smile. "Evening's a long way off, and I'm hungry. How about a little slice?"

She glanced at the roasting haunch, then back at him. "I might be able to find a sliver that's done enough. Just a taste, mind you."

"I promise that's all I want."

"And I promise I don't hear *that* five times a day." But she sighed, and fixed him a little plate.

The lamb was perfectly roasted, crisp on the skin but tender and juicy beneath. The savory-spice and hickory smoke gave it a good flavor, which the ale did its best to burn away. To the innkeeper's stark disbelief, Darin ordered a second one while he carried a plate of the meat out to Big Tom.

He found the big man brushing the horses and humming a song to them in his rumbling voice.

"Brought you something," Darin said.

"What's this?"

"Try it. You'll thank me later."

Tom took the plate in one massive hand, tucked it inside the wagon, and got back to brushing. It'd be long cold before he remembered to eat, but there was no point in badgering him. Darin slid back inside, toasted the proprietor with his new ale, and sat back to wait.

The clients turned up a few minutes later, easily ten minutes before the appointed time. Alfon entered first, pausing to let his eyes adjust to the interior. He spotted Darin, nodded to him, and made a quick survey of the rest of the room. Then he ducked out and returned with Damia. By prior arrangement, they came and took the table beside his without eye contact. Without a word of greeting.

For his part, Darin stood and poked his head out the door, to make sure no one else lingered there. He spotted Tom who sat relaxed but alert on the edge of the wagon. Tom scratched his ear, the signal for *all's well*. So they hadn't been followed, nor had they brought anyone. *Good.*

"Is all this really necessary?" Alfon asked.

"Caution is our friend," Darin said. "I ran into some of my least favorite people after our last meeting. I don't want that to happen again."

"Who was it?"

"Bastard by the name of Harrison."

"Oh, him."

Darin half-glanced behind him. "You *know* him?"

"We'd have gone to him if you said no. He has a reputation."

For violence and greed, Darin almost said. "Well, I think you made the right choice."

Damia grabbed his arm and pulled him close. "Please. How is she?"

"She's safe."

The woman closed her eyes and sagged against Alfon's shoulder. "Gods be praised."

"When can we–" Alfon started but broke off as the proprietress stopped by to offer them slices of the roasted lamb. Darin swore under his breath. *So I'm a day-drinking interloper who has to beg for lamb, and they get it offered straight out.* Then again, it wasn't hard to guess why. The Galceras looked like they had money.

Alfon declined with perfect graciousness. The proprietress took her leave and went back to the bar to wash some of the drinking mugs. Which were already cleaner than the Red Rooster's had been when new.

"When can we see her?" Alfon whispered.

Darin sighed. *I hate this part.* "Jakub's set to see a queen's magistrate next week. It doesn't look good for him."

"He should hang," Damia snapped.

"Let us hope that he will." Yet in his heart of hearts, Darin knew that wasn't likely. *Money is power.* "At the very least he'll be tossed into a dungeon."

"Then he can rot," she said.

"We agree on that. But if he catches even a whisper that Lisbet might still be alive, she'll be in danger. All of us will. He's not the kind of man to take that lying down."

"We'll be careful," Damia promised.

"I'm sure you would. But given your son-in-law's connections, there's only one way to guarantee Lisbet's safety."

Alfon let out a long, painful breath. He knew.

"What?" Damia demanded.

"She needs a fresh start. No one can know where she is."

"For how long?"

"For as long as you want her to be safe."

"Wait a gods-damned minute," Damia hissed. "We can't *see* her ever again?"

"Can't see her, can't write to her. Can't go looking for her," Darin said. "For as long as Jakub lives." *And in my experience, the least deserving live the longest.*

"But–" Alfon began, but words failed him. He and Damia sat in shocked silence. They were smart people; they saw the logic behind it. But that didn't make it any harder to let your daughter go.

Especially when you worked so hard to get her free.

"She'll be safe." Darin slid a folded piece of parchment across the table. "She left you this."

Damia pulled it close to her, looked at the words in Lisbet's flowing hand, and broke down into sobs. She buried her face in her husband's chest, her body shaking. Alfon held her with one arm and handed Darin a heavy purse with the other. Thick, heavy coins. Good quality. The ever-present temptation started to rear its head. He shoved the feeling away. He had plans for this silver. He swore it would be a crossbow bolt to the heart of the Jewel Empire. "I wish it had worked out differently. Be well."

He paid the glaring proprietress and made his way out the door. Big Tom waited out front with the horses already back in their traces.

"All right?" Tom asked.

Darin climbed up the wagon. "As much as they can be."

"Get the money?"

"Yeah." The Galceras had paid well, but not nearly enough to square them with the Dame. *The less I think about that, the better.* "Come on, Tom. Let's go home."

CHAPTER TWENTY-SIX
Carrot and Stick

Darin knew something was off about the woman the moment she stepped into the Red Rooster common room. It wasn't the clothes; they were sturdy-looking homespun. Easily plain enough for the crowd here. Maybe it was how she ignored Big Tom, who loomed just inside the door. Or maybe it was the way she held herself. Like she owned the place, and everyone here was beneath her.

She approached Kat and asked a soft question. Didn't order a drink. Kat pointed her to where Darin stood cleaning the last of the pewter mugs. Maybe his luck was about to turn. The silver from the Galceras had bought him another month's patience from the Dame, but each passing day felt like a new weight around his shoulders. Normally, he maintained a low profile after pulling off a job. Kept to himself, closed the common room early, and generally avoided any situation that encouraged talking. But they couldn't afford to hide while the days ticked away, so they'd spread word around that the Red Rooster crew was looking for work. In the past week alone, they'd recovered a merchant's prized horse, rigged two card games, and redirected a shipment of lumber from Tal Orea. At the moment, Evie was out collecting payment for a couple of those jobs. Darin would have gone himself, but she tended to get paid in full.

Gods knew what this newcomer would want. The woman

made her way down the bar toward him at a leisurely pace. Her boots rang on the cracked wooden floor. She positively reeked of silver.

"Are you Darin?" she asked, in an imperious tone.

Darin slid a hand beneath the bar, and let his fingers brush the handle of the crossbow hidden there. "Who wants to know?"

"You may call me Zora." She said it with a lilt, as if she were granting him a wish. "You might say that I'm – what's the phrase – a friend from back home."

That was the newest code phrase, the one they'd adopted during the Stillwater job. Maybe the Galceras had given a referral. Darin exhaled a breath he hadn't realized he was holding. He brought his hand above the bar and gestured at the stool in front of him. "Come then, friend. Have a drink."

Zora gave a small nod and sat, but not on the stool he'd gestured to. "Red wine, if you have it."

"I said a drink, not a decoration." Darin filled a mug almost to the brim and slid it across the bar. "Ale."

She tried a sip and grimaced. "It's got a… memorable taste."

"We brew it right here at the Rooster."

"I'm not surprised." She took another long pull. "Cloves and cinnamon are certainly a bold combination."

Someone else with a palate. And careful, too. "So, what brings you to the Rooster?"

"I want to talk about hiring your crew."

"What crew would that be?"

"The one that made it look like a merchant murdered his wife."

Shit. No one should know about Jakub this soon after the job. They were still hunkering down, avoiding attention. Certainly not ready to take credit. The girl was safely ensconced where no one would find her, but to even acknowledge involvement carried too many risks. "Don't know who or what you're talking about."

Zora rubbed her chin and put on a confused look. "Merchant out of Stillwater, name of Jakub Purser?"

"Doesn't ring a bell."

"It was less than a fortnight ago."

Darin raised his voice to be heard over the din of the common room. "Where was I last month?"

"You were here!" shouted every single patron.

"See? I was here." Darin filled a mug of his own, took a drink, and smacked his lips. "Ah, that's good."

The woman called Zora pursed her lips. "Very well, then. How about the time you boosted every crate from a Ganari spice trader while he was taking a bath?"

Four Gods, she's well-informed. That job had been over a year ago. The more Darin denied, the more hazardous this dance became. He decided to throw a bone instead, just to see where that would take it. "That was never proven," he said. "And anyone who takes two-hour baths is just asking for it."

"I couldn't agree more. That's why I came to you."

"For what?"

"To engage your services for a most delicate operation."

"Even if I were to have a crew, this isn't how it works," Darin said. "You don't walk into someone's establishment and tell *them* the operation."

"How does it work, then?"

"Pretty simple, really. People come to us with a problem. Sometimes we help out."

"Like a woman whose husband beats her," Zora said.

And we're back to Jakub. Darin stared at her unblinking. He knew, and Zora knew, but admitting something like that could change the tone of the conversation. It was far more important to learn how she'd found out. If people started connecting fresh jobs to the Rooster, they'd all be in serious trouble. Torch-the-inn-and-go-to-ground kind of trouble. "I can't remember anything specific, but that sounds like a problem we'd love to handle."

"I suspect it does." Zora slid something onto the wooden surface between them, a small gold coin. Not just any coin, either, but a faded Ganari goat. Even now it sang to him, a soft golden lullaby of ownership. "In fact, I'm quite certain of it."

Darin knew it was *that* particular goat. The one he'd sold to Jakub, which had helped him find the man's yacht in that ridiculous regatta. Strange that he hadn't felt the coin approaching. Something about his tracking enchantment must have changed. That unsettled him, but the odd woman's purpose here was a more immediate concern. "What do you want?" He hoped she hadn't come all this way to ask about the girl. They'd never find her. He didn't know where she was himself. That's what intermediaries were for.

"You had no way of knowing this, but Jakub was a key element of some of my plans," Zora said. "Your little scheme landed him before a magistrate."

"I don't know the man, but I'm sure he'll be missed."

She laughed softly. "If you think men that wealthy are executed, you know little of how the world works."

Darin clenched his jaw. "Actions should have consequences."

"His reputation is tarnished, and he's lost his freedom. I daresay he won't find another wife."

"Some might call that a good thing," Darin said. Still, it worried him that she was speaking of Jakub in the present tense. It would have been far safer if the man had hanged.

"I'm not among them."

"Then why don't *you* marry him?"

Zora didn't rise to the bait, but drummed her fingers on the bar. "He will, of course, remain a powerful man."

"Well, no job goes perfectly. Or so I'm told."

"I imagine that kind of wealth could hire quite a few knives and torches, to destroy those who'd wronged him."

"Was he wronged, though?" Darin asked. "Sounds to me like this fellow got what he deserved. Caleb, you said his name was?"

"Jakub."

"Right. Jakub."

She pressed on in the same dangerously casual tone. "The full picture of how his life took such an awkward turn might drum up some bad blood."

"We all have it in us. The blood, that is." Darin considered reaching again for the crossbow whose stock still pressed into his knee. But he couldn't imagine that a woman this well-informed would walk so easily into a death-trap. It gave him pause. "In situations like these, I find it's best not to go kicking any dogfish."

"I happen to enjoy kicking things," Zora said.

"I'm sure you do." He gave an expansive shrug. "Then again, a crew talented enough to do what you described... well, they could be *anywhere*. Don't know how you'd even find them."

"That's a shame, because I hope to make them very rich," Zora said.

Darin relaxed a shade. He'd had some interesting preludes to contract offers before, but the veiled threat wasn't his favorite. Still, if she wanted to make them rich, she didn't plan to kill them. Right away, at least. "You're finally saying things I understand."

Zora gave a thin smile. "I knew you'd catch on eventually."

CHAPTER TWENTY-SEVEN
Silver Promises

Tom never claimed to be one of the smart ones, but he liked to think he had good instincts. Those instincts told him this Zora woman meant trouble. Anyone who walked into a strange common room like it was their own parlor was either a great fool – which she clearly was not – or had ice running through their veins. As far as Tom could eavesdrop, Zora knew about their past activities, too. She laid them out for Darin like a gambler showing her hand. That was risky. Darin could utter a single word and the room would clear out. Tom would bar the door. Then the woman would either be very good, or very dead. Tom gripped the handle of his cudgel and thought about what he'd do if that happened.

She'd hit Darin first. Probably wouldn't kill him, but she'd want him out of play. She'd know Tom was coming. He didn't see any weapons on her. That meant blades. She'd have a pair in each sleeve. Tom had no delusions about his own size. He made the best target by far. He might knock the dagger aside, he might not. It wouldn't slow him down. Only a fool would charge within reach of her knives, though. He'd use the table. The big square one. Pin her against the bar. That would bring her arms down. It had to. Then he'd club her with his cudgel, and that would be it. At least, that's how he thought it would go. Instead of giving him the signal, though, Darin stared at the coin on the table between them and kept talking.

"Tell me about the job," he said.

Zora traced a finger around the rim of her mug. "Have you ever had imperial dreamwine?"

"Seeing as I'm not even independently wealthy, or highborn, I have not."

"I would have thought that your line of work allows for certain... indulgences."

"I indulge in putting food on the table, and hay in the stables before winter," Darin said.

"What about its manufacture? Are you familiar with any parts of the process?"

"You might say that."

Tom nearly guffawed. Darin grew up in a labor camp on the hot, sun-drenched slopes of the imperial vineyards. Watched most of his family die there, or so Evie had said. There was no way Zora could know this.

"How familiar?"

"Not nearly enough to copy it, if that's what you're thinking," Darin said.

"I'm content to let the imperials keep their secret little process. It's the wine itself that interests me."

Darin seemed to find that amusing for some reason. "How much do you need?"

"A dozen barrels."

The smile fell away from Darin's face. "That's... quite a bit. Enough to fill a wagon."

"Just so," Zora said.

"The last time I checked, the empress wasn't in the habit of sending such quantities of her precious wine into the Old Queendom."

"She does once a year."

Someone who didn't know Darin, someone who hadn't spent years scheming and gambling at his side, might not see the flash of recognition in his eyes. Tom spotted it, and something more. Whether it was fear or hunger, he couldn't be certain.

"Is this a gods-damned joke?" Darin asked quietly.

If it was, Tom couldn't help but think it was a poor one. Everyone was as tense as wound-up springs. Kat had stopped pretending to clean the bar.

"Do I seem like the joking type to you?" Zora asked.

"The queen's dreamwine? That's practically treason."

"It doesn't belong to the queen until it arrives in her palace."

That seemed like a technicality, but Darin let it pass. He had a more obvious concern. "No one has stolen a single barrel of dreamwine and lived long enough to brag about it."

"Just because a thing has not been done, doesn't mean it can't be done."

Tom thought that was exactly what it meant, but he didn't want to intrude on the conversation.

"At least four crews have tried. I knew two of them."

"Were they as good as you?"

"Better. It didn't matter, not with the Groktar."

Groktar. The word rang in Tom's head like a dinner bell calling him to the table. Word was, the Jewel Empire's finest mercenaries were the best fighters on the continent. Trained since childhood, it was said. Tom had met a couple in the fighting pits in the Scatters before he got out. They'd actually *volunteered* for the lists, and left a trail of bodies in their wake. As a boy, he'd felt only relief to never draw their names.

"How would you go about it, out of curiosity?" Zora was asking.

Darin shook his head. "I wouldn't. I like my head attached to my shoulders."

"Perhaps you'd be willing to speculate." Zora untied the purse on her belt and poured out a stream of coins onto the bar in front of Darin. Not the grubby trade-coppers that usually slid across the wood. These were real silver. Tom could tell from the sound they made, and from the quiet hunger in Darin's eyes when he looked at them. Of course, he was hardly the only person in the common room. There were two mercenaries sitting at the small table in the far corner. One with gray in his dark beard, the other still trying to grow one. They'd been drinking since late morning – the way only out-of-work swords could do. The soft clinks drew a flat-eyed stare from both of them. They looked at one another. Tom shifted his weight against the wall to remind them of his presence. He'd hate to bludgeon the paying customers.

"Don't show silver like that in here unless you plan to lose it," Darin hissed.

"It's yours now, if you indulge me," Zora said.

"Done." Darin didn't touch the coins, though his fingers twitched oddly toward them. He'd warned Tom more than once about touching strange metal. Silver, especially. That made plenty of sense, but Tom wouldn't relax until someone dropped that into the strongbox. There were too many people in the common room trying very hard not to look at them.

"So, how would you do it?" Zora pressed.

"I'd hit them out in the country, as far away from Caron as possible," Darin said. "Not too close to the border, though. Somewhere in the middle, where there aren't many prying eyes."

That made sense. If you tried to boost a shipment of dreamwine, folks would gather around to watch for pure entertainment. It was as good as watching an execution. Or it had been, for the last few fools who'd tried it.

Zora nodded as if this were obvious. "What would you do about the Groktar?"

"I'd try to avoid a fight. Maybe draw some of them off with a feint attack, and then distract the others while someone goes for the horses." He shrugged. "But none of this would work unless you knew exactly where the shipment would be, and when. Last time I checked, the Empress doesn't put up notices about it."

Zora said nothing. Darin had kept a casual tone, but he was watching her face.

"You know the when and where, don't you?"

"What happens after you have the wagon?" Zora asked.

"The Groktar will come after us. We'd have a couple of egress routes at the ready."

"They might not come for you, if they all happened to be dead," Zora said.

Darin scowled. "I have no love for the empire, but if you want an entire squad of foreign mercenaries killed, you'd better find a different crew."

"Does the thought of bloodshed make you dizzy?"

"No, but the thought of being marked for death might. The empress has a long memory," Darin said, with just a hint of bitterness. "Besides, any fool can use violence to get something. We pride ourselves on avoiding it whenever possible."

"You'd avoid bloodshed. With Groktar mercenaries," Zora said flatly.

"There's undoubtedly a way. Infiltrate their ranks. Deceive from within. Maybe hedge our bet in case it does come to blows."

Tom found himself interested again. Deception was Darin's specialty. Usually, blows belonged to Big Tom.

Zora's lips twisted into a half-smirk. "This is becoming quite a plan for someone who claims he's never thought about it."

"Anyone in this profession has daydreamed about boosting dreamwine. But that's all they are. Daydreams. In reality, it's an invitation to suicide."

"You don't strike me as the kind of man who's afraid of a challenge."

Clever. Trying another tack, to play on Darin's emotions. It wouldn't work, but Tom admired Zora for trying. She couldn't know what it meant to ask Darin to steal something that came from the Jewel Empire. No matter how great the reward or how minimal the risk, he wouldn't touch it. Not unless it meant a chance to spit in the empress's eye, a dream that Darin had spoken of more than once.

Sure enough, he was already shaking his head. "It's not just me I have to worry about. It's my whole crew, and there's no way they'll sign on to this mission. Even if I thought it was a good idea. Which I don't."

"You haven't heard the best part yet," Zora said.

"Better lay it on me quick, then."

"I'll pay you two hundred pieces of eight."

Tom must have heard wrong. That was more coin than he or anyone here – except maybe Evie – had seen in a lifetime.

Darin shook his head, as if he'd had the same problem. "For a second, I thought you said–"

"Two hundred pieces of eight."

"Gold or silver?"

"Silver."

Kat made a sound, almost a choked gasp. Her cheeks colored, and she went back to pretending that she wasn't listening.

Darin's face showed no emotion. That, more than anything, told Tom how much the sum must be.

Darin glanced at the pile of silver on his bar. He must be thinking about it. Or maybe about how much they owed the Dame. Tom wasn't good with sums – never had been, as a matter of fact – but from the way Kat reacted when she heard the number, he knew it was significant. They didn't have much time, either.

"The answer is no," Darin said at last.

But two hundred pieces of eight, Tom thought. Zora had said it with such conviction, she might actually mean it.

Darin took a drink of his ale. His face was unreadable, but Tom knew what he was thinking. That much coin bought a new life for all of them. A retirement in luxury, with no concern for food ever again. And beyond that, a chance to strike at the empress from a distance. But it couldn't be this easy. "I've gone up against the empire and lost before. I'd be a fool to do it again. For that price, at least."

"I suppose I could add a bit more to the pile," Zora said. "Call it two hundred and fifty pieces of eight."

"I was thinking more like four hundred."

"Four hundred?" Zora scoffed. "For that much, I could practically buy the wine outright."

"If you wanted to buy it, you wouldn't have gone to all this trouble," Darin said.

Tom had no idea how Darin knew that, but he was right. The look on Zora's face confirmed it.

"Three hundred. That's as high as I'll go."

Kat was gesturing at Darin now, her excitement poorly hidden.

Run, Tom's instincts told him. *Run as far from this as you possibly can.*

But Darin was nodding. "I'll discuss it with my crew."

Zora's lips twisted downward. "Is it not your decision?"

"Everyone gets a vote. We're progressive like that."

"How long will this discussion take?"

"I'll have to track them down because they could be anywhere. Could take a week."

Tom smiled to himself. Gods, but Darin could lie to the queen with a straight face if he needed to.

"I'll be back two days hence. I expect an answer." Zora turned on her heel and stalked to the door.

Darin gave Tom the nod, and he stepped aside so the woman could leave. The moment she walked out the door, Darin ducked into the kitchen. He emerged with Timmy in tow, and was whispering instructions to the lad. Tom missed most of it, except for the end where Darin said, "Don't let her see you."

Darin flipped a copper into the air. The lad caught it and was out the door in two heartbeats.

Kat marched over. "What's that about?"

"Just following a hunch," Darin said.

"With my Timmy?"

"He said he was the quietest of them." Darin wilted a bit under Kat's stare. "What? You said you wanted them to learn a trade. This is part of it."

"Thieving is not a trade."

"It's the only one I know enough to teach."

Kat jabbed a finger into his chest. "Anything happens to him, and I'll take it out on you."

Tom didn't doubt for a second that she was serious.

CHAPTER TWENTY-EIGHT
Fraught Decisions

"Last call," Kat announced. It took every bit of self-control she could muster to keep her voice level.

The two soldiers in the corner signaled they'd take another ale each. She filled two mugs, brought them over, and received two coppers in return. No tip, apparently. Then again, they'd all watched Darin scrape the pile of silver coins into the strongbox with a dagger, so this was hardly a surprise. Now he stood down at the corner of the bar, counting its contents and muttering to himself.

Kat flipped a copper into the box and put the other in her pocket. Half and half, that was the deal.

Four minutes and ten seconds had passed since Timmy scampered out the door on orders to do gods knew what for Darin. She loved all her boys, but she'd had Timmy the longest. She wouldn't delude herself into thinking that she'd keep him around until old age, but he was still a boy. Someday he'd grow tall, awkward, and stupid in the way that boys do, but he still had good boy years left. If he got hurt tonight, she'd take it out on Darin just as she told him. But she'd also never forgive herself.

The door to outside banged open. Kat's heart lifted, but it was Evie. She handed Big Tom her riding cloak as she glided past, wearing the little smile that meant she'd charmed some hapless soul out of a small fortune.

"Good night, Evie?" Kat called to her.

"I've had worse." Evie sighed and pushed back her hair. Gold and rubies glinted on the bracelet around her wrist.

Kat whistled. "That's new, isn't it?"

"Oh, this? It was a gift." Evie cast a baleful glance in Darin's direction and spoke loudly. "Some men know how to *appreciate* things of value."

Darin didn't look up. "If that's part of our payment, it goes in the strongbox just the same."

Evie turned back to Kat. "I don't think he understands how gifts work."

"There's a lot he doesn't understand," Kat agreed.

"Evie." Darin rapped his knuckles on the rim of the strongbox.

Evie rolled her eyes and sauntered over to him, but made no move to produce the coins. "Hmm... I can't seem to remember where I put it."

Darin still didn't look up from his counting, but pointed with his free hand at Evie's midriff.

"I don't know what you're implying," Evie said.

At last Darin looked at her, and whatever he saw on her face made him lose count. He moved around the bar and right next to her. Evie turned with him, wearing a mischievous smile. Darin put his hands on her shoulders and spun her around, so that her back was to him. He pulled her against him with one arm, and sent the other searching down the front of her dress. Kat looked away out of habit. She'd have to be blind and deaf not to sense that the two of them had a history, but she'd thought it was *ancient* history.

"Ah ha!" Darin held a purse triumphantly and shook it. Coins clinked softly within.

Evie pouted and made a grab for it, but he held her fast with his other arm. He emptied it into the strongbox, a pleasant stream of coppers and gold. Looked like a good take, as far as Kat was concerned, but Darin's lips still twitched downward. "You're a little short."

"Maybe you didn't search hard enough," Evie said.

"I could try again." Darin made as if to move around the bar.

Kat didn't think she could stand another ridiculous display. "Gods, Evie. Either hand him the coin or take him upstairs."

Evie's smile vanished. She flushed prettily and extracted a small purse from somewhere under her skirts. She handed it to Darin, who cleared his throat loudly and accepted it, muttering his thanks.

Good. Here they were flirting shamelessly while Timmy was outside. Alone. Probably lying in a ditch with his throat cut. Whispering for Miss Kat while his life poured out.

Kat shook her head to clear it of that image and resumed scrubbing the bar. Trying not to think about Timmy or what he was doing. He'd always been clever, and brave to the point of foolishness. Some day, not too far off, she'd have to watch him leave to start his own adventures. It would be good if he learned a few things from Darin first, she supposed.

Darin finally finished counting and slammed the lid of the strongbox closed.

"How bad is it?" Evie asked.

"We're a long way off." He glanced up at Evie and Tom. "Even with the… latest infusion."

"Do you think the Dame will give us more time?"

"At this rate, it doesn't matter. We need a big payday."

Kat opened her mouth to ask if he was ever going to bring up Zora and her offer. Big Tom caught her eye, though, and gave his head the tiniest of shakes. Maybe he was right. Evie was the tough sell, and no one handled her better than Darin.

"Where in this cursed queendom are we supposed to find a serious job on short notice?" Evie asked.

"It just so happens that something did come up earlier, while you were out."

"Really?" Evie tilted her chin up. "Were you ever planning to tell me?"

"Of course." A pained expression found its way onto Darin's face. "It's just…" He trailed off.

"Just what?" she prompted, with an air of impatience.

"It's something we've never tried before."

CHAPTER TWENTY-NINE
Hard Lines

Evie brought out her boot knife and began to sharpen it with the whetstone Kat kept behind the bar. The rasp of steel on stone helped her think. She needed a clear head. "So let me see if I understand this. This woman–"

"Zora," Darin offered.

"Yes. Zora. She knows about us and our past jobs. But rather than selling us out to our enemies, she wants to hire us."

"So she says," Darin said.

"All we have to do is steal something that's never been successfully stolen. From the queen."

"Technically, it won't belong to the queen until she takes possession in Caron."

"Oh, thank you, Darin. I'll be sure to bring up that nuance when they're fitting us all for nooses on the gallows at Caron Square."

"I sincerely doubt the queen will be offended if we steal something she doesn't yet own."

Evie neglected to point out that what Darin didn't know about what offended nobility could fill a book. Several books, perhaps. "Do you realize the significance of what this Zora wants us to steal? Every noble of consequence will be at the gala, and most of them are there for the dreamwine. If you succeeded, you'd make an enemy of every highborn in the queendom."

"I haven't even told you how much she's offered," Darin said.

Evie shrugged. "It doesn't matter. This is sheer foolishness."

The silence stretched for a minute. Evie fought the urge to ask, because she could tell Darin would just love to tell her. It had to be a princely sum, otherwise he'd know better than to waste their time with this. At last, her curiosity won out. "All right, how much?"

"Three hundred pieces of eight."

"Gods above!" Kat whispered. "I thought I heard it wrong."

"Me, too," Tom said. His eyes had gone a little wide at the number, which was as close as Tom came to shouting.

Evie kept her face still. She felt Darin's eyes on her. Knew he'd see it if she reacted. If she dared show what the thought of that much silver meant. She wouldn't give him the satisfaction, even if a tiny part of her dared dream about buying back the life her father had gambled away. Gabled manor houses and hired seamstresses. Stables full of horses. Most of all, never having to worry where your next meal came from, or what you might have to do to get it. She shoved that burgeoning hope away because the hunger in Darin's eyes worried her. "That's a lot of gold," she said.

"A lot of *silver*."

Evie felt her mouth fall open but was powerless to stop it. Three hundred pieces of eight in silver was, quite literally, a fortune. Even divided four ways, it would mean Darin and Tom never had to work again if they didn't want to. Kat, too, though she seemed to enjoy peddling her gods-awful ale. It might not be enough for Evie's dreams – which were more expensive than most – but it would take her a long way. Certainly that kind of silver bought access to a new social circle within striking distance of the one she truly craved.

Darin read her reaction correctly, and spread out his hands in half-apology. "Now you understand why we're even talking about it."

Evie needed a minute. Words had deserted her. She could feel all of them looking at her, but she wasn't ready to react in some way. In any way, really. Money mattered to everyone, but for her, this kind of wealth carried so much baggage.

"Have you tasted dreamwine before?" Kat asked Darin, breaking the silence.

Darin shook his head. Tom shrugged; he wasn't the kind to indulge in much of anything.

"I have," Evie found herself saying.

"What was it like?"

She exhaled softly. "Do you know how fine-woven silk feels when you touch it for the very first time? Not the cheap stuff we use on jobs, but pure gossamer?"

"I suppose," Kat said.

"When I was a girl, my mother bought an entire bolt of it to have dresses made. Before she gave it to the seamstresses, she let me wrap myself up in it. Head to toe." She sighed softly, remembering. "It was pure luxury."

"Is there an end to this story?" Darin asked.

"Yes. *That's* what dreamwine tasted like."

"Like pure luxury?"

"No. Well, yes." She struggled to find the words. "It tasted like the joy I'd felt in that moment as a little girl. When life seemed so perfect and full of promise." It ached her heart to think about it now. To know the things that the little girl would soon endure.

"I've brewed two dozen batches of ale, and I can't begin to guess how you'd achieve that with wine," Kat said. "Might explain why no one else can make it."

"And because no one else can make it, the empress can charge whatever she wants for the stuff," Darin said.

There was something odd about his voice, and Evie felt a pang of sympathy. Darin knew all too well what the Jewel Empire's most valuable export cost the common folk of the empire.

"Still, the amount this Zora is offering is ridiculous. Not many in the queendom have that kind of silver. What do we even know about her?"

"Not much, at the moment," Darin said. "Though I have some suspicions."

A knock sounded at the door, which Tom had barred after Evie burst in. Kat took two hopeful steps toward it and halted, listening. Three more knocks came, then one. Big Tom lifted the bar with one hand, and cracked the door enough for a skinny boy to slip in.

Timmy grinned at Kat, then looked from her to Darin as if unsure where to go. Kat tilted her head at Darin. The boy ran over to him and straightened.

"Well?" Darin asked.

"She met some men on the north edge of town," the boy said.

"Soldiers?"

Timmy shrugged. To a boy his age, grown-ups were grown-ups and that was distinction enough.

"Were they wearing uniforms?" Darin asked.

"Nope. She got on a horse, and they rode off behind her."

"Retainers," Evie said. She gave Darin a meaningful look.

Darin ignored her. "Well done." He flipped him another coin.

Timmy caught it in midair on his way through the kitchen door. Kat was smiling, too, though she probably didn't realize it.

"So this woman who wants to hire us has her own retainers, and she knows where to find us," Evie said. "This keeps getting better and better, doesn't it?"

"If she's got retainers, she's got money," Kat said.

"Oh, she's got money." Darin rummaged in the strongbox, and produced a handful of flawless silver queenpieces. There had to be eight or ten of them. "Here's your proof."

"You took silver from her?" Evie asked sharply.

Darin held up his hands to placate her. "She paid that just to hear my *ideas* for taking a shipment."

"Seriously?"

"She emptied an entire purse on the bar. Didn't even count it."

Evie shook her head, not ready to buy in. "She could hire mercenaries and take a shipment by blunt force, if she really wanted it."

"Something tells me she wants a softer touch than that," Darin said. "She knew about Lisbet."

Evie cursed in what her mother would have called an *unladylike* fashion. That job was too recent for anyone's knowledge to be good news.

Kat muttered something and wiped her brow with the bar-rag.

"It's not necessarily a bad thing. It's part of why she wanted to hire us," Darin said.

"Would you even be considering this job if it wasn't imperial dreamwine?" Evie asked.

"Like you said, it's a lot of money."

"That's not what I–"

"I know what you meant." His lips twitched into a frown, and for a moment his eyes were distant. Thinking about his brother, perhaps. Darin hadn't spoken of him in years. It was an older brother, she understood, and he'd kept Darin alive when they were young. He never made it out. Darin did. Now, half a lifetime later and in another country, he still looked for small bits of vengeance.

Evie slid the knife back into her boot-sheath and straightened. "Does Jakub know about us?"

If the answer was yes, she was gone. She had a go-bag hidden in the stables, a small trunk buried in the woods, and enough tucked away to last her almost a year. She'd scraped and saved for too long to have it all come crashing down. If Jakub figured out who she was, who she'd *been*, he could ruin everything.

"No," Darin said quickly, as if he sensed her edge. "Even so, if we refuse to do the job, Zora could make our lives difficult."

"Oh, well then this is *perfect,* isn't it?" Evie spat. She hated this. Hated not being in control.

"I don't understand," Kat said. "Why is she giving the job to *us*? Why not someone else?"

"She was working with Jakub on something. Maybe she thinks we owe her for messing that up. Or maybe she was impressed by our handiwork."

"Or she's working against us, and knows the perfect bait to dangle in front of you," Evie said.

"I'm hardly the only person who likes silver."

"I don't mean silver." *How can he not see it?*

"Say what you think, Evie," he said.

It was on the tip of her tongue, but she didn't want to out his past in front of Kat. "She might know where you were born."

Kat frowned. "Where's that?"

"In Vlask," Darin said curtly. He never liked to call it the Jewel Empire. He kept his eyes on Evie. "So what if she knows it? It won't affect my decisions."

She snorted. "It already has. Or we wouldn't even be discussing this."

"I won't deny that taking a shot at the empire's golden goose appeals to me," Darin said. "Besides, think of what we could do with the silver. We'd not only send a message, but change the game entirely. Really put them on notice."

"It's too risky," Evie said.

"Everything we do is risky. And if you haven't noticed, we need silver."

She knew that, but this was pure insanity. "I vote against."

"Aw, Evie, come on," Darin said.

"That's how I come in on this," she said. "You should too, if you value your necks."

"Not all of us are up a gold bracelet tonight," Kat said. "And we could use the money. You think she'd be willing to put some of it up front?"

"She can afford to," Darin said.

Kat gave a short nod. "Can't believe I'm saying this, but I'm in."

One for, and one against. They all looked to Big Tom, who fingered his cudgel the way he did when pondering something. Usually it was whose head to thump. More than a few Rooster patrons had learned that habit the hard way.

"I hear the Groktar are pretty good fighters," Big Tom said.

"Not just good. Some of the best in the world," Evie said.

Tom drummed his fingers on his great wooden cudgel for an almost uncomfortable period of time. "Then Darin and Kat are going to need me."

Evie sighed. *So much for the voice of reason.* They all had their reasons for wanting to take a job of this size. It tempted her, too. Even so, she couldn't help but feel it was too easy. A woman with dangerous knowledge of their past, offering too large a sum for what historically amounted to a suicide mission. Not even queendom nobles threw around that amount of silver unless there was some bigger game afoot. But she'd never find out what it was if she forced them to say no. And besides, Darin might just opt to do the job without her.

So she ignored the little voice telling her to run, and gave in. "I suppose I'll have to come along, just to make sure you lot don't get killed."

CHAPTER THIRTY
Down Payment

Darin hated when clients ran late. Zora was due half an hour ago. Even with Kat's boys watching every crossroad, the uncertainty made him nervous. He sat by a table in the corner and tried to take his mind off it by sanding out some of the worst knife-marks. It was good simple work, sanding tables. He appreciated things that were simple. Things that didn't take planning or strategies. Things that didn't get people killed.

He wouldn't mind a simpler life. If Zora came through with her job, he'd be able to have one, too. Even a fifth of the promised sum – after getting square with the Dame – would buy any kind of life they wanted. For Kat, it meant food and shelter for as many orphans as she wanted to take in.

At last, a boy came running with word of horsemen. From the south, even though she'd ridden off to the north when she met her retainers. She was careful. At this point, Darin wasn't sure if that was good news or bad.

Big Tom had cleared out the Rooster's common room. He was gentle about it, but anyone too drunk to stand on his own got tossed in the gutter out front. He'd just resumed his post by the door when Zora strode past him. Something about the woman's appearance had bothered Darin last time. Now, he thought he knew what it was: her clothes fit her too well.

Dressing down for the Rooster, but won't give up the tailor. Finally, a crack in the facade.

She approached Darin's table, eyed the empty chair that he'd set out for her, and dragged over a different one instead. She sat down with a straight back, and her hands on her knees. One finger tapped a steady beat against her leg. Curious. Darin hadn't noticed that little tic the last time she was in here.

"Thought maybe you weren't coming," he said.

"Thought, or hoped?"

"A little of both."

Zora nodded, as if his answer satisfied her. "Do you have an answer for me?"

By her tone, she considered all this a formality. She knew she had him on the rope when she offered the ridiculous sum of silver. Still, he didn't have to make this easy on her. The more he did to assure their success now, the better off they'd be. "We want half the silver up front."

"You think I'm a fool? You'll be paid once it's done."

"Then the answer is no. We need hard coin just to set the first parts of the plan in motion." *Hard coin we don't have,* he did not say, because anything they could scrabble together went to the Dame.

Zora had coin, though. The song of gold and silver radiated from her, mostly from a large purse tied to her belt, but also from other bits of coin hidden about her person. It was easily the most money that the inside of the Rooster had ever seen. Not enough to square them with the Dame, but enough to make a serious dent. And it was *right there.* Within reach.

Zora stared at him; her face was unreadable. The only movement came from her ever-tapping finger, counting its beats in a rhythm. What was with the tapping? He'd sure like to know. This was a delicate moment. If she refused to put down any cold silver, it meant she wasn't really serious about the job. Or she didn't think they'd succeed, so she'd never planned to pay. Neither boded well.

"One fourth up front," Zora said at last.

Thank the Lady. "A third," Darin said.

"Done." She tapped her finger three more times, then stopped with finality. Something new entered her posture. A coiled readiness. It gave Darin an uneasy feeling.

A shrill whistle sounded from the kitchen. A warning, from one of Kat's boys. Darin reached for the nearest hidden weapon. Kat started for the kitchen door, but it was kicked open. Armed men poured into the room. Five, no, six of them, dragging in Timmy and Abel with knives at their throats. Kat snatched up the hidden crossbow from behind the bar. Evie wrapped her in a bear hug so she couldn't bring it up. Big Tom's club appeared in his hand like a metallurgist's trick. He took two steps forward, but three more men ran in from the kitchen, spears already leveled. They backed Tom up against the wall, spear tips pressed against his belly. He glanced at Darin. There were too many, even for him. Darin gave him the signal to stand down. Then everyone went still.

If this was a robbery, Darin couldn't help but think, it was a poorly planned one. The strongbox behind the bar wasn't half full, and most of that was copper or gold. This many hired swords cost a fortune. Then again, the leader hadn't announced himself. It occurred to him at that moment that Zora hadn't even flinched when the men stormed in. But she had stopped tapping her finger. Now, she smirked at him in a way that twisted his stomach.

He managed to keep his tone casual. "Friends of yours?"

"You might say that."

"I suppose they're a reminder that you're not to be taken lightly," Darin said.

Zora leaned back with the confident air of someone who felt they owned the room. "They're a reminder that I won't be *taken* at all."

"You sure about that?" Darin tapped the inside of her thigh with the stiletto he held there.

She glanced down, and pursed her lips. One flick of his wrist, and she'd bleed out before she got to the door.

"Funny thing about highborns," Darin said. "They think having a bunch of hired swords makes them untouchable."

If being outed as an aristocrat surprised Zora, she didn't show it. At least he'd wiped the smirk off her face. "My men know their business."

Part of him wanted to try it. Slice her open from knee to hip, and watch the surprise bloom in her eyes. If he could get a hand on her silver, maybe that would give him an edge with her men. Trouble was, he couldn't count on the metallurgy. Not with his friends facing cold steel. Damn. *Should have listened to Seraphina.*

He let the moment of madness pass, and moved the tip of the stiletto away from her thigh. "Good thing we have an agreement."

Zora hesitated just long enough to give him a twinge of panic. "So it is." She snapped her fingers twice.

The men lowered their weapons. Kat finally stopped fighting Evie to bring up her crossbow, but the snarl remained on her face.

"Gopher," she snapped. That was one of the code words, the first one anyone connected to the Red Rooster crew learned. A simple word with a simple meaning. *Go to ground.*

The boys scampered pell-mell through the press of bodies, some escaping into the kitchen, and others out the door. One of them even scrambled up the coal chute, a feat Darin wouldn't have thought possible if he hadn't seen it with his own eyes. They all disappeared within seconds. At least two of Zora's guards had been quietly relieved of their purses. Darin bit back a curse. They certainly learned fast. *But maybe that's what armed men got for threatening children.*

He plunked the stiletto down on the table. "Now, let's talk about that down payment."

CHAPTER THIRTY-ONE
White Knuckles

The only thing Tom liked about crossbows was that they took time to reload. As long as the archer didn't put the first bolt through your gut, it gave you a nice chance to kill him. Still, he couldn't fault Darin for keeping one under the bar. Or Kat for snatching it up when the men charged in holding knives to her boys' throats. Hells, it took every ounce of self-restraint he possessed to keep from knocking those spears aside and clubbing their bearers to the floor. He'd start with the one on the right. He was the shortest of the three, seemed the most distracted, and his guard was too low.

But no, he had to push those thoughts out of his head. Darin and the woman who called herself Zora had both relaxed their postures. He no longer held the dagger against the artery in her thigh. Clever move, that. Tom had worked in the Rooster for years and still hadn't found all of Darin's little hidey-holes for weapons.

"Every shipment of imperial dreamwine enters our borders on the queen's highway," Zora was saying. She'd unrolled a large hand-drawn map on heavy parchment. It was, even from a distance, the finest map Tom had ever seen. Must have cost her a fortune. By the way Darin was staring at it, he'd probably had the same thought.

"The first ten leagues of that are a flat, straight highway that runs due east," Zora said.

"I know it," Darin said. His voice sounded oddly tight.

"That's where you'll take the shipment."

"It's far too close to the border."

"Nevertheless. You must take the wine before it reaches this point here." She jabbed her finger down on the parchment.

Darin made a pained face. "We don't usually operate under such strict conditions."

"I'm hardly a usual client, though, am I?" Zora said.

"You seem to know about our past. So you must understand that our work involves a certain amount of..." Darin trailed off, as if unable to find the right word.

"Nuance?" Evie called over her shoulder. Most of her attention remained on Kat, who had yet to relinquish the crossbow.

"Yes, nuance," Darin said.

"The terms of this contract are not negotiable," Zora said.

"They'll need to be, if you want us to actually do it," Darin said. He allowed enough ice into his voice that everyone felt it. Some of the retainers stiffened. Others, like the ones closest to Tom, gripped the handles of their weapons more tightly. For his part, Tom kept very still. If they made to point steel at him again, he would act. No matter what Darin said or signaled. Coming into someone's home with blades drawn had already caused nearly as deep an insult as Tom could bear. Blood feuds had started over less in the Scatters.

Zora stared at Darin, her face unreadable. "Are you backing out of the job?"

"No, I'm telling you what we need to get it done. And part of that is being more than a ten-minute ride from the Jewel Empire."

Zora held her silence a moment longer while everyone else held their breath. At last, she slid her finger east on the great parchment map to nearly the middle of the border duchies. "I suppose it would be acceptable if the wine were to go missing before it reaches this point here. But no farther east."

"We can work with that," Darin said.

"Good. Send word when you have the wine." Zora stood and stalked to the door. Tom was careful not to move toward her, though his hands itched with the instinct. She snapped her fingers as she moved past, hardly sparing him a glance, and her men fell in line behind her. Tom settled for watching how they moved as they departed. The ones who'd held spears on him left first and took up positions flanking Zora just beyond the door. It spoke to their training, and probably her trust in them. The ones who'd barged in holding knives to Timmy and the others, however, were another story. They hurried out in a careless fashion, not even watching to see if anyone followed them. Amateurs. Tom filed this away for later consideration – he had a feeling he'd encounter Zora's retainers again – as he shut the door behind them.

Tom looked at Kat, who looked at Evie, who turned to Darin and said, "So. We're really doing this?"

"It seems that way," Darin said.

"It's a long way off," Kat said.

Darin nodded. "I don't love the terms either, but she undoubtedly has her reasons. Besides, it might be better pulling this off a long way from the Rooster."

"How do we even start?"

Darin pursed his lips and stared off into nothing for nearly half a minute. That was his "thinking" face, and Tom knew better than to interrupt.

"We start with the wine," Darin said at last. "We need to understand everything we can about its manufacture and transport."

"It's not going to be easy to steal imperial dreamwine," Evie said.

"I realize that. That's why first, we're going to steal a vintner."

CHAPTER THIRTY-TWO
The Gambler

One of the few upsides of living out of a wagon for so many years, Kat decided, was that she met people all over. She kept in touch with them, too. Many of them operated inns or taverns, the kind of places where you could set up and sell ale for a few days without getting in trouble. Turned out, that was a good way to keep your finger on the pulse of the queendom. People who ran common rooms knew what was happening where. A few days of casual inquiries among her contacts to the west revealed that there was a village in southeast Brycewold where the wagons carrying imperial dreamwine – and the Groktar soldiers who protected them – often stopped for a night. If the schedule held, they were expecting another one through any day. There was only one inn, so that pretty much narrowed it down. It went by the name of the Popped Cork, which even Big Tom found amusing.

"How many of these informative friends do you have across the queendom, anyway?" Darin asked, when she surprised him with this information.

"Too many to count."

"Do they all write back?"

She shrugged. "Not always. Sometimes I'll ask if they're in need of another barrel of ale. That usually brings a response."

"I'll bet," Darin said.

Kat felt nearly certain that he meant that as a jab, but she saw no hint of it on his face. She didn't know anyone at the Popped Cork, so she sent a couriered missive. She kept it short and to the point: the Red Rooster brewed ale, and they'd like to send a free cask for the Popped Cork's customers to try. This wasn't uncommon among two-horse villages; sometimes it led to a service contract that profited both sides. Maybe the Popped Cork brewed their own ale, or maybe they didn't. Free ale. Only a fool would say no to that. Darin even paid in advance for the reply. Sure enough, an enthusiastic response came within a couple of days. This wouldn't be the actual heist – Zora had specified a time and a place for that already – but more of something Darin called a dry run.

Before she even got to the Popped Cork, she understood why the Groktar liked it. The road was wide and straight leading in and out of the village that clustered around it. The place looked more like a fortress than an inn: two square, stout stories, a large stable, and a heavy stockade fence enclosing it all. A single entrance, with blind corners going in. It was also the tallest structure around; from the upper rooms, they'd be able to see for half a league in each direction.

Kat parked the wagon out front, hobbled the old plow horse to keep it from wandering. She hoisted the half-cask with the Red Rooster emblazoned on the side. They'd all taken a crack at re-creating the image from the Rooster's sign on test barrels, since whoever painted it had died years ago. Made it into a little contest and let the tavern regulars pick the best image. Big Tom won handily. Kat still wasn't sure how.

The door to the common room felt heavier than it should have. Kat got it open enough to slip inside and saw why. Steel bands crisscrossed the back of the door, lending it weight and strength. Nothing short of a battering ram would bring that down if you barred it from the inside. She let the door swing closed behind her and surveyed the room. The low-set wooden tables had mismatched chairs, most of which were empty this early in the afternoon. A few men and women sat dicing at a velvet-topped table set up in the corner. *Not bad*. Kat wouldn't mind a game or two. She never gambled when the boys were around – didn't want them picking up bad habits any sooner than they had to – but they'd stayed home. It had been a two-day journey here, even with Moody Mary pulling the wagon. Normally she'd have taken her time, selling ale as she went, but Darin had insisted on speed. The man's patience seemed to be running short on everything and everyone of late.

"Can I help you?" called a man. He stood behind a long split-trunk bar along the back wall, washing glasses with a filthy rag. He might have been forty; he might have been sixty. He'd put a few extra meals away in the middle. No gray hairs in the dark beard and hair, but he might be dyeing them. Men did that sometimes. A few of them even got away with it.

"Got a delivery for you," Kat said.

"From the Rooster?" He grinned, showing a few gaps in the teeth. "Been waitin' for that."

Kat held up the barrel. "The wait's over."

The man helped her lower it to the bar, a gleaming darkwood affair that had been polished to a high sheen. There weren't even any knife-marks in it.

"So, do you work out of there? The Rooster, I mean."

"More or less."

"What's it like?" he asked.

"What do you mean?"

"I hear stories sometimes."

"Yeah?" Now Kat's curiosity was piqued.

"More than a few," the proprietor said. "Lots of interesting things."

"You gonna say what about, or do I have to guess?"

"I shouldn't. It's not proper stuff for a lady to hear."

Kat snorted. "I'm no lady. Speak freely, man."

The man beckoned her close to the bar, and lowered his voice to a whisper. "Is it true you've got a real looker who works there? Dark hair, eyes you could lose yourself in?"

Evie. Not many run-down common rooms had people like her around. "The words don't even do her justice."

The proprietor barked a laugh and slapped his palm against the bar. "I knew it!"

"She'll even take your purse if you get too close."

"Now that I believe," the proprietor said. "Say, how about a drink? We can try this ale you've brought."

"No, I couldn't. That's for you and your customers."

"Come on, just a nip."

Kat grinned. "You twisted my arm. Name's Kat, by the way."

"Mathias."

They clasped wrists in the way of the Old Queendom. Mathias dug out a tap and used a mallet to pound it in. Kat took the liberty of flipping over two of the cleanest-looking glasses.

Mathias poured two fingers for each of them – less than Kat would have liked, but she took it as a sign of politeness – before they touched glasses and drank. She couldn't help but watch the man's face to see what reaction the ale brought. He didn't flinch like some folks. His reaction was hard to read at all.

"What do you think?" she asked at last.

"I think I could pick that one out of a crowd," he said.

Kat decided to take it as a compliment. "It'll wake you up in the morning, too. We have a few regulars who find that appealing."

"Hair of the dog that bit 'em, eh?"

She smiled and shook her head. "They never learn." She drained the last of her ale, smacked her lips, and set down the glass.

"Another?" he asked.

"Thank you, but no." She tilted her head in the direction of the dicing table. "I wouldn't mind a game or two, though."

"Got any coin?"

Kat shook her purse by way of answer. Soft metal clinked from within. Copper, mostly, and a few gold pieces. She'd wanted to bring a silver in case there were higher stakes, but Darin seemed to want to keep the silver coins in the strongbox.

Mathias walked her over and made the introductions. The dice players, who were deep into a game, offered a lukewarm reception. That changed when Mathias announced that Kat had brought cheap ale and a full purse. In short order, they'd scrounged another creaky wooden chair from a nearby table and made room for her between the two women. They had the same thick mops of too-curly hair, the same wide noses. They had to be sisters, she thought, even before learning their names were Lena and Rena. Strangely enough, they didn't make any such disclosure during the introductions. So that's the kind of game it was going to be. The third player was a man named Georg, and by the sour expression on his face, he wasn't having a good night. Still, that might be what they all wanted her to think. These three were regulars. She saw it in the way they spoke to Mathias, and how they always seemed to get their ales replaced with fresh ones when they ran low. So this was a local game with people who knew each other and, as a newcomer, Kat had a serious disadvantage.

Well, fine. She wasn't here to clean them out anyway.

She set about losing her money in slow, steady attrition. A bad toss here, a foolish bet there. Not that she had an endless sack of coins waiting at home, but a handful of coppers were well worth the view of the establishment from the gaming corner when the Groktar mercenaries arrived. The first two had to duck to enter, they were so tall. They were wide, too, though the leathers and armor no doubt added to that. Half-helms shaded their eyes; heavy beards covered the rest. They rested their hands on sword hilts and surveyed the common room in grim silence.

Lena nudged Kat. "Your toss."

"Right. Sorry." She scooped up the dice into the leather cup, shook it, and spilled them out. All while pretending not to watch the door.

Lena and Rena grunted in surprise. She looked down, and realized she'd actually won a round. *Damn*. She forced a grin. "Hey, look at that!"

Another mercenary strode in, this one a woman but nearly as tall as her male companions. She hardly spared a glance for the common room. Such was her trust in her men.

"Evening, captain," Mathias said.

"We'll need the usual accommodations." She had short, clipped speech. Not a word wasted.

"That'll be–"

"I know the tally." She produced a small, tied leather purse and tossed it on the bar.

Mathias hefted it and had the wits not to count it. At least where she could see. He produced a ring with five iron keys on it. Apparently, they were renting out half the building.

"Just one night, I take it," Mathias said.

"Just one." She turned on her heel and strode back outside, where a rising commotion made it sound like the rest of her party dismounted. Before long, these new arrivals filled most of the empty seats in the inn. They were hard pieces cut from the same leather: veteran mercenaries, heavily armed, and dust-covered from a long journey.

Kat hit another lucky roll, and smiled.

Another man entered, but he lacked the soldier's swagger. The two guards escorting him had an air of resignation. The man himself was jowly and big-bellied, a few years short of middle age. He slid onto a stool with exaggerated care and summoned Mathias. They conferred quietly in low tones. Mathias produced an honest-to-god glass and poured three fingers of a dark, colorful liquid into it. Grape wine. Not of Vlaskan make, by her guess, but some sort of country wine. The customer paid two coppers for it and made a pinched face at the first sip.

Kat forced her eyes back to the dice. *Well, now I'm just offended.*

CHAPTER THIRTY-THREE
The Vintner

Evie would never admit it in polite company, but she rather enjoyed interrogating a hapless mark. There was so much variety in how you could extract information from someone. Fear and physical torture, while effective, were so pedestrian. Even seduction, which had served her purposes on numerous occasions, failed to elicit the thrill that it once had. Anyone who understood animal instincts could exploit these avenues to get what they wanted and leave only the husk behind. An artist, however, could get the mark to tell them things voluntarily, often without even realizing what they were doing.

Evie's mother had always told her she could be an artist, though Evie doubted this was exactly what she had in mind.

Find out everything you can, Darin had told her. *The route, the Groktar, the wagons they use. Everything.*

First, she had to find this tiny backwater inn where the caravan spent the night. There were too many nameless little one-inn towns in this part of the queendom. She missed Eskirk.

When at last she found the Popped Cork, its exterior did nothing but disappoint her. The angles were too blocky, the windows too small. The stables took up far too much space for an inn this size. It was an inn like Darin might have designed. Still, this had to be the place. She took a step inside and paused to let her eyes adjust. It took a conscious effort not to draw down her hood, but she didn't want to bring attention to herself. Which was a pleasant change. Sometimes it was easier not to be the person everyone had their eyes on.

She made out the vintner right away. He slumped over his stool as if someone had poured him onto it. Not a fighting man, certainly, but middle-aged, married, and a father to girls. She couldn't say how she knew these things, but she did. Chalk it up to a decade of reading people. Friends, enemies, allies, marks. She slid onto an empty stool at the bar, not next to him, but one away. The man behind the bar was fiddling with his apron, scrubbing at some imperfection. Either he was distracted, or she'd been too quiet for him to notice. She shifted in her seat and cleared her throat softly.

He glanced up and then nearly fell over himself to approach her. "I'm terribly sorry, m'lady. Welcome to the Popped Cork."

Evie smiled. "No trouble at all."

"What can I get you?"

"Do you have any bottles of Tal Orean red? The seventy-two?"

The bartender's face fell. "Would that I did, m'lady."

"What about a Ganari white?"

"Oh, I've plenty of those."

"From *before* the invasion," she said.

He shook his head. "Haven't seen one of those in years, I'm afraid."

"A shame." She sighed. "I'll take the newer Ganari. But it won't be the same."

"Have it in a moment for you, m'lady," he said, and disappeared into the kitchen. No doubt he'd have to go down to the cellar to find a bottle of Ganari white that someone actually wanted. After the Jewel Empire took over, they made certain that nothing remotely palatable came out of Ganar's vineyards.

The vintner was looking at her. She let her eyes drift in his direction, and offered him the half-smile of a stranger greeting another. Nothing more.

"You know your wine," he said.

"Oh." She pretended to notice him for the first time. "Yes, well, I'm in the business."

He turned on his stool so that he was facing her, the universal signal of a man who's suddenly *quite* interested. "You're a winemaker?"

"A brewster, actually." Which was a complete lie, of course. With luck, Kat's brief introduction to the topic would be enough to sound convincing. The woman herself was deep into her gambling, and losing steadily by the looks of it. Too far away to be of use, in any case.

"Yet you ordered wine," the vintner said.

"We all have our weaknesses. Besides, I like dabbling in other forms of fermentation."

The bartender returned with her bottle of Ganari white. Judging by the new smear on his apron, he'd hastily cleaned the dust from it on his way up from the cellar. Clever fellow. He poured it with a bow and left the bottle beside her, in a not-too-subtle indication that she'd bought the whole thing. "I hope it's to your liking."

"We'll know soon enough." She made no move to touch the glass, though, and when he seemed disappointed, she added, "I'll let it breathe a while, first."

"A wise decision, m'lady." He turned to the vintner. "Fancy a drink, Jerry?"

"Why not?" said the vintner. "I'll have a mug of your finest ale."

"Ale?"

"Yes, ale." The vintner glanced at her sidelong. "I like to dabble, you know."

"Since you're feeling exploratory, I've got just the thing," said the bartender. He filled a mug from a familiar-looking cask on the end of the bar and slid it across.

The vintner made a big show of taking out his purse. Gold and silver coins spilled out when he untied it. He shoved a handful across, hardly counting them. The bartender swept these up and managed to be several paces away when the vintner took a first sip. He made a sound like a drowning animal, coughed, but managed to keep it down. Then he inspected his mug as if he thought it were poisoned.

The Red Rooster's finest, and you're welcome, Evie thought. "Is it safe to say you work in the business as well?"

The vintner was still recovering from his taste of Red Rooster ale. "Ah, yes. I'm a vintner, as a matter of fact."

"What kind of vintner travels with his own set of armed mercenaries?" Evie asked.

"A very important one."

"Oh?" She smiled wickedly. "Or maybe the wine you make is so bad, you feel the need for some protection?"

He guffawed. "I make imperial dreamwine, m'lady. The finest substance in all of Thyros."

"You jest."

"I'm serious as sin." His chest looked ready to burst, he'd puffed it out so far. In his strutting, he instinctively took another swig of ale and nearly choked.

Evie pretended not to notice. "An imperial vintner!" She shook her head, as if in disbelief. "You're a long way from home, aren't you?"

"Part of the job," he said. "I'm accompanying–"

The tall woman who'd taken the stool on the other side of the vintner cleared her throat pointedly, and his voice faltered. He glanced at her, and then brought his attention back to Evie. "That is to say, I certainly am."

Evie gasped, her eyes as wide as a country lass seeing the city for her first time. She leaned toward him, conscious of how the neckline of her riding dress gaped just so. It could've been accidental, but it wasn't. "That sounds exciting!"

"It's interesting work, if you can get it."

"I tried my hand at winemaking a time or two. Never seemed to get it right, though."

"It's a subtle art."

"With ale, I have a good sense on balancing the bitterness." Evie furrowed her brow. "With wine, it's like every batch I tried came out tasting sickly-sweet."

The vintner nodded. "That means it's not fermented enough. Give it more time in the cask."

"You think?"

"I'm certain of it." The vintner hazarded another drink of ale and winced. "To think, this is the best they can offer here."

Evie shrugged. "What do you expect? There probably aren't three horses in this village."

"Oh, I know there's more than that. We alone have half the stables with–"

The mercenary woman cleared her throat again.

"Well, it's not the smallest village I've seen. Let's leave it at that," he finished.

"I'm guessing it's not the largest, either," Evie said.

"You guess correctly."

The mercenary captain woman clearly planned to keep this an uninteresting conversation, so Evie tried a different angle. "Is it true what they say about dreamwine?"

The vintner offered a little smile. "What do they say?"

"That drinking it whisks you to another place and time, however briefly," Evie said, and the appeal of that sentiment gave her a moment's pause. "I've heard it offers you a glimpse of another person's life."

"In my experience, the life it shows you is your own. A dose of nostalgia."

"What kind of nostalgia?"

"It varies by the person. Sometimes it's a cherished memory. Other times, a bittersweet experience."

"Is it always the same for you?"

"No." The man's eyes shone as he thought about it, but whatever vision the dreamwine gave him, he didn't seem to want to share.

"I'm almost afraid of what dreamwine might show me," Evie said.

He frowned. "Afraid?"

"I've had more than my share of... indiscretions." She giggled with a touch of playfulness.

"Ah. Now, that I don't find hard to believe."

"I'd love to know how you manage such an effect with the dreamwine."

The vintner glanced at his guard captain. "I probably shouldn't say too much about that."

"Aww." Evie pouted. "Isn't there *anything* you could teach me?"

Loud and chaotic as the room was, half the customers still heard her. Turned in her direction, or elbowed a neighbor. Most of them would like to teach her a few things themselves. The vintner drew in a sharp breath. His brow glistened with perspiration. Evie's eyes pulled him like an anchor chain. He leaned in.

The captain inserted herself between them. "I think it's time to call it a night."

"Hey now, we're just–" the vintner stammered.

"Call it a night, I said."

Her voice cut like a knife. The vintner crumpled under it. He muttered an apology and slid from his stool. The mercenaries stood at some unspoken signal, leaving half-drunk ales behind on their tables. They flanked the vintner and the captain on their way upstairs, leaving no room for further conversation.

Evie wanted to kick herself, but returned to her drink and did her best to look bored. Darin said they might have someone watching the common room. No need to seem overly concerned if that was true.

A few minutes later, Kat laughed and said loudly, "Well, you've cleaned me out. I'm done for tonight, I suppose."

"Come back anytime," said one of her fellow players.

"We'd love to have you," said another.

Kat slid onto the vintner's now-empty barstool, claiming his half-full mug of ale before the bartender could get to it. She took a large swallow and sighed. "Now, that's a quality drink right there." She lifted her mug toward the bartender, who returned the gesture.

"Get what we came for?" she asked more quietly.

"Probably not," Evie said.

"So, what now?"

"We'll have to find another way."

CHAPTER THIRTY-FOUR
Hit and Run

Darin leaned against a nondescript building opposite the door to the Popped Cork, watching for any signs of trouble. In the yard to the side of the inn, his prize taunted him. The Groktar's wagon looked more like a siege engine than simple transport – the frame was Ganari nightwood, the spoked wheels nearly as tall as a man. They'd stacked the barrels in a precise arrangement in the middle of the wagon. There were only three.

All this security for three barrels?

Two of the men had already taken the heavy draft horses around to the stables. Two more had gone in with the captain. Four of them had taken up positions around the wagon, leaning on spears or halberds. One of them had a bow, and two had horns clipped to their belts. It said something that they were all standing and alert, not playing cards or smoking pipes like your typical off-duty mercenary. Nine well-armed, well-trained soldiers for three goddamn barrels of dreamwine. And Zora wanted him to take a dozen.

Those were the things he saw. There were probably twice as many little details that Big Tom would make note of. It should be him here assessing the security, but Darin hadn't wanted to take the risk. People tended to remember someone of Big Tom's stature. Experienced fighters certainly would. For all he knew, these same guards would work the security detail on the dreamwine shipment he did try to take. So he did his best to memorize the details without trying to.

Don't mind me, I'm just a fellow out having a smoke. Wishful thinking, as it turned out. The nearest mercenary did take notice of him, and fixed him with the dead-eye stare of someone who wanted you to know they saw you. He wasn't as memorable as Tom, but he saw no need to draw the attention. So he tapped out his pipe against his boot and turned to walk away. In doing so, he nearly barged right into a well-dressed man with a cane who was walking down the avenue.

"Well, look who it is," Harrison said.

Darin took a step back. "Gods, you turn up like a case of the flux, don't you?" He could feel the eyes of the men guarding the wagon. If a fight broke out here, they might get involved just for the fun of it.

Harrison wore a nobleman's long jacket and button-up shirt. Fancier dress than Darin had ever known the man to wear. Something was odd about this. The infuriating smirk, however, was unchanged. "What brings you to town? Looking for something better than Red Rooster ale?"

"As a matter of fact, the Popped Cork just started serving our finest."

"That so? Guess I should send for the healer."

Darin ignored the insult, though he was glad Kat wasn't here to witness it. "You want to explain what you're doing on our side of the line?"

"What line?"

"The deal line."

"Oh, I see. You think we're still doing that, even after Stillwater."

"I told you, we weren't–"

"Yeah, you weren't working," Harrison interrupted. His voice was level, but the whites had begun to show around his eyes. "Now it's my turn to say the same."

Darin took a deep breath to stave off the usual mindless

anger at seeing Harrison's ugly, scarred face. In doing so, he had a sudden realization. The man had silver on him. *A lot* of silver, in a purse at his belt. Pure stuff. "I suppose you're just here on holiday."

"Yeah, well, got a lot of silver to spend. It's not something you'd know about."

Darin nearly shuddered to think of what Harrison had done to earn it. Then came a sudden and disturbing thought. Maybe it wasn't so much a reward as a down payment. *Oh, hell.*

"Got a new patron, have you?"

"As if I'd tell you."

"Let me guess," Darin said. "A hard-nosed highborn with more silver and retainers than she knows what to do with."

Harrison's eyes got even more white around them, which Darin didn't think was possible. How he did that and managed to false-face when a job required, Darin still couldn't understand. Some people saw the clothes and the manner, but not the man.

"How in the gods–" Harrison muttered.

"How do you think?" Darin interjected. "She hired both of us."

"No one's got that kind of scratch to burn. Not even her."

"She only pays whoever succeeds. So you're not going to cost her a penny."

"That a fact?"

"That, Harrison, is a fact."

"You'll stay out of our way, if you know what's good for you."

"The sooner you realize you're in over your head, the better off you'll be," Darin said.

Harrison straightened, and took up his cane again. It was a ridiculous accessory. The strangest part was that he somehow pulled it off. He looked just like some too-rich dandy out for a stroll. "Well, I'm off. S'pose you'll see who's in too deep soon enough."

He strolled off down the street, whistling to himself. He even had the gall to wave at the Groktar. Then he called out to them, "I'd keep my eyes on this one." He pointed with a cane back in Darin's direction. "Takes an unhealthy interest in cargo, if you know what I mean."

The mercenaries shifted slightly in their stances, tightening hands on weapons. They weren't sure what was happening, but they were ready to bring violence to the situation if needed. Darin forced himself to look away. *Goddamn Harrison.* He was supposed to meet Evie here to see her back to the horses, but if he stuck around, he'd soon be talking to sword points. So he held up his hands and kept moving. Down the street. Not looking at the wagon or the horses. He kept his ears tuned, though, and heard the door to the Popped Cork fling open. That would be Evie. No one made an exit like she did.

He stalked around the corner of a row-house and broke toward the west end of town at a fast clip. The smells of each craft-house marked the profession, even if the signs didn't. The tanner's place reeked of animal fat and harsh chemicals, the smithy of steam and sulfur, the carpenter of sanded wood and sawdust. Not a whisper of silver in any one of them, which made these lean times for a modest village. No wonder Mathias had been so eager to take some free ale of dubious origin.

He turned into the alley past the carpenter's place – their agreed-upon meeting point – and relaxed a bit when he saw Evie standing there. "I was worried you'd–"

She put a finger across her lips and pulled him back into the shadows of the alley. He stumbled after her, confused. Then he heard the rustle of leather, and the steady clump of boots coming down the lane. Ten men in mail and black leather moved with grim purpose past the mouth of the alley, heading down past the smithy. Gold in their pockets, and cheap steel in their hands. *Sell-swords.*

He and Evie stood like statues for another half-minute. Then Darin hurried forward and craned his head around the corner.

The sell-swords were turning right past the row-houses. On their way to the Popped Cork. Harrison wasn't in town to make Darin's life more difficult. He was doing his own scouting, in this very town.

"We need to get out of here," he said.

"What's going on?"

"Not sure yet. I just ran into Harrison."

She grabbed his arm. "Wait, he's *here*?"

"Just saw him five minutes ago. Looking especially smug about something."

"He's across the gods-damned deal line."

"Yes, we had words about that."

Evie muttered something about "having daggers rather than words" but otherwise kept her peace. They crept down the street by the blacksmith's place, past the tannery, to get a view of the Popped Cork. The wagon was still there, and so were the Groktar. Of the sell-swords there was no sign.

"Was Kat still in there when you left?"

"The bartender asked her to stick around for another drink," Evie said.

Darin shot her a sidelong look. "Kat? Not you?"

"They're talking about ale."

"Oh, is that all?"

"If it's more than that, he's laying siege to the wrong castle," she said flatly.

So I'm not the only one aware of Kat's preferences. Or lack thereof. "Did she tell you–"

"Of course not," Evie said. "She doesn't have to."

Dusk began to fall on the little village. Few actual villagers were about; now that Darin thought about it, he hadn't seen many locals out on the streets here. Even in late afternoon, which was unusual for a settlement this size. Without warning, the Groktar guarding the wagon started moving. They were looking at something across the street.

Shouts sounded from the far end of the street. Boots

pounded, and then a wave of fighting men in leather and mail boiled out of an alleyway toward the inn. Had to be eight or ten of them. Ten men against four Groktar. Good odds for the sell-swords. And they had to be sell-swords. They charged in a ragged line, all of them shouting at the top of their lungs. Maybe they thought the guards would retreat inside the inn, leaving three barrels of priceless wine for the taking.

Unfortunately for them, the female Groktar by the back of the wagon had a bow. She dropped two of the attackers before they even entered the yard. Good shooting, Darin had to admit. It did nothing to shape the sell-swords' ranks. Then the two groups met with shouts and a clash of steel. The bow-woman leaped atop the wagon, brought a horn to her lips, and blew a long, wailing note.

The door to the inn flew open. The captain charged out first, helmetless but with her sword in her hand. The two massive soldiers who'd gone in with her were right behind. She pointed. They split up left and right around the wagon to attack the sell-swords on their flanks.

"Hey look, it's almost a fair fight," Darin said. Seven on eight. Only it wasn't exactly that. The Groktar quickly formed two groups. One covered the wagon. The other counterattacked, isolating the would-be raiders from one another. One of them went down. Then another.

More doors banged open on the row-houses and craft-halls. Groktar poured into the street with drawn steel. Not just the area of the innyard, either. Two men in mail and steel helms barged out of the building not ten paces to Darin's left. In short order, he found himself confronting a pair of sword points.

"We're no trouble." He put Evie behind him and backed up against the wall, hands raised.

He could only watch as nearly a dozen Groktar swarmed the sell-swords in the yard, cutting down four of them in a matter of seconds. The two surviving mercenaries threw down their swords and put their hands in the air. Groktar seized them, forcing them to their knees. The captain, still helmetless, handed her sword to one of her men. There was blood on the blade. She bent low to speak to the nearest sell-sword. It didn't look like a question, though. More like she told him something. Then a dagger appeared in her hand.

"Look away, Evie," Darin said.

Groktar mercenaries with their blood up and a reputation to protect wouldn't look kindly on surrender. Evie closed her eyes. He did the same, but he couldn't shut his ears to the short, brutal sounds followed by heavy thuds.

Darin opened his eyes. The Groktar swordsmen were still watching him, trusting their fellows to handle the business at the wagon. They were young like most soldiers, with hard lines to their faces and no beards. The unmistakable high cheekbones and coal-dark eyes of imperial natives stirred something in Darin, and a snarky comment sought to force its way from his mouth. He clamped his jaw shut against it. *Now's not the time for risk-taking.* Instead, he addressed the older of the two, guessing him to be in charge. "Her father's expecting us."

"You don't want him to come looking," Evie said. "He's the local magistrate."

The swordsmen conferred briefly in quiet voices. The elder one pointed unambiguously down the road away from the innyard. *Go that way, or you won't go at all.* Darin gave him a tight nod and herded Evie around the corner.

"Did you see Harrison with them?"

"No."

"It was hard to make out anything. I won't get my hopes up that he went down with those men." Harrison didn't put himself in the line of fire when he could hire some poor sod to do it for him.

"Why was he here?"

"Probably just to muck things up for us. They'll change their schedules now, and be on alert. The job Zora gave us just got twice as hard."

Evie said nothing. She walked slowly, staring straight ahead. Her lips quivered with each indrawn breath.

"Hey," he said softly. "You all right?"

"For a minute I thought that they were going to... That *we* might..."

"They wouldn't dare. After all, you're the magistrate's daughter."

That won a little smile.

"Please tell me you learned something from the vintner."

She shook her head. "The captain had him under close watch. What about you?"

"Oh, I learned one thing."

This is going to be harder than I thought.

CHAPTER THIRTY-FIVE
Reluctant Plans

When Kat heard what happened outside the Popped Cork, she was ready to call this whole thing off. It was bad enough that the escorts for a three-barrel shipment lived up to the Groktar reputation. When that horn sounded, the she-beast of a captain had nearly knocked Kat over on her way out the door. It may have been a blessing, since her even larger and more solid companions charged past a moment later. She'd never seen anyone move so fast. The carnage in the innyard – when she finally got the courage to leave the common room – left little doubt as to the Groktar fighting ability.

It was bad enough. Harrison's involvement made everything worse. Now they'd be looking over their shoulders at every step. Wondering when Harrison would turn up to smash Darin's carefully laid plans with a war hammer. She wasn't alone in these grim thoughts, either. For the entire two-day ride back to the Red Rooster, Darin and Evie hardly spoke a word.

Darin, of course, had sent an angry letter to Zora via courier, demanding an audience and explanation for Harrison's involvement in the heist. They waited an entire day for her to show up at the Rooster. Which she did not. Instead, a messenger arrived with a brief missive confirming the bad news. Zora had hired a "provisional crew" for the job. Whoever delivered got paid.

Now here they were, sitting in the common room with the door barred, trying to figure out how to proceed.

Evie rattled her nails on the bar. She hadn't even gone for her usual freshening up process before calling this meeting, which said something about the urgency. "I can't decide if I hate Zora for putting us in this position, or admire the sheer gall of her terms."

This just keeps getting better. "How much do we have of the down payment?" Kat asked.

"Some of it," Darin said. "Sixty pieces of eight."

Kat divided that sum in silver by the current price of grain, allowing for some fluctuations. Divide that by two meals a day – three for Tom, of course – and it came to a not-entirely-unsatisfactory number. "That'll keep us going for a long while," she said. "Even with eight or nine mouths to feed."

"Excuse me, did you say eight or *nine*?" Darin asked.

"Eight, I mean," Kat said, kicking herself for the mental lapse. Truth be told, she hadn't the strength to turn away another desperate young boy. Especially with the promise of a big score on the near horizon. And if that didn't come through, one boy a day could skip a meal, with all of them taking equal turns. It would be enough to keep another belly somewhat full. They'd get by. "I say we cut our losses."

"And leave the Rooster?" Darin asked.

Kat grimaced at the spike of visceral pain in her belly at the thought of abandoning the place she'd finally started calling home. She'd be lucky if she could even find all of the boys in the hayloft, much less get them to board the wagon, if they believed they were never to return. "If that's what we have to do."

"But the full payout–" Darin started.

"Would be nice, sure," Kat said. "But only if we deliver, and that's not guaranteed. Whereas the silver we have now is already in our pockets."

"It won't last as long as you think," Evie said. A cloud passed over her face. "It never does."

"Which is why I think we should do the job like we agreed," Darin said.

"Sure, look how it worked out for Harrison's sell-swords," Kat said.

"I'm not him. I'd plan better than that."

"How close did they get to the shipment?"

"I don't know, maybe ten paces."

Evie snorted. "Not even that close. Twenty paces at least. Once that horn sounded, there were Groktar everywhere."

Kat grunted. "How many?"

"At least a dozen. Maybe more."

"That's more than you said were on the wagon."

"I know," Darin said. "I can't reconcile the figures."

Kat couldn't either. One guard per barrel, one scout, plus the captain made five. Even if you counted the vintner – not a fighting man, according to what she'd heard – it was half of the number that showed up to cut down Harrison's ill-fated paid swords. "So where did they all come from?"

"The men that got the drop on us didn't come from the wagon or the inn," Evie said.

"Wait, someone got the *drop* on you?" Kat demanded.

Darin shot Evie a look. "For a moment."

"How long of a moment?" Kat couldn't remember the last time someone had gotten the better of Darin. Yet another sign that perhaps this job wasn't for them.

"We were close to the action, but they never saw us as a threat," Darin said.

"Oh, is that why they almost put us both to the sword?" Evie asked sweetly.

"They weren't going to kill us."

"They weren't going to kill *me*." Evie smiled. "With you, they could have gone either way."

"And they might go a different one, if you're not careful," Kat added. "How bad is this going to be?"

Darin shrugged. "Dicey at best. We'll know more when I finish the plan."

"You don't even have a *plan*?"

"I've got a plan," Evie said. "We tell Zora we have a shipment, invite her here, and then we ambush her and her men. Cut them all down, burn the bodies."

"Evie!" Darin chided.

"It's not the worst plan," Kat said. "Nets us the rest of the silver and removes the threat." The threat wasn't just against the four of them, either. She had to think about the boys in the hayloft, depending on her to keep them safe.

"That's not the kind of crew we are, and you both know it," Darin said.

"Maybe it's the sort of crew we should become," Kat said.

"You don't mean that."

"Don't I?" Kat had been fourteen when the blood plague swept through her home village. Practically a child, but somehow the oldest one still alive. Somehow in charge of dozens of orphans who'd looked to her to keep them alive. Darin knew the generalities of her story, but not the specifics. Not the terrible things she'd seen, or the haunting memories of the nine orphans she'd failed. "Tell me why we shouldn't."

"For one thing, it's a terrible example for pairs of young eyes," Darin said.

Damn. He'd scored a touch with that one, she couldn't deny it. "Fine. We won't kill her."

Evie threw up her hands. "Well, if we can't kill her and we can't run, we're back where we started."

Darin held out his hands in mock surrender. "I'm not completely without ideas here. We don't know enough to make an informed decision right now. I think we should get into things a little bit, and see what we uncover."

"About Zora, or the job she wants us to do?" Kat asked.

"Both."

Kat hated that the wheels in her head were already turning. "I'll want the full story of your scouting expedition again. Every detail you two can remember." Even the best protective details had vulnerabilities.

"I can work a few contacts to find out more about our mysterious patron," Evie said.

"About time you put those lovely eyelashes to work," Darin said.

"You never said you liked my eyelashes." She batted them in come-hither fashion.

"What do I do?" Big Tom rumbled, from the back of the room. The sudden words startled all of them.

Gods, I'd forgotten he was there. Big Tom could mimic a piece of furniture when he wanted to.

"You get the fun job, Tom," Darin said. "You figure out how we fight Groktar mercenaries without getting ourselves killed."

"Already got an idea about that," Tom said.

Kat smiled to herself. There was the Tom she knew, working on things quietly in the background. It was why he ran a good stable, and why he'd be useful on a job like this.

"Really?" Darin didn't entirely manage to hide his surprise.

"Sure do. But you ain't gonna like it."

CHAPTER THIRTY-SIX
Deadly Roads

Three days later, Tom and Darin rode at a brisk pace on a narrow country lane in the southwest tip of Hulscot. Tom didn't like pushing the horses this hard, but he didn't want to be late, either. Just getting this meeting had been hard enough.

The War Maker's compound was located somewhere in the foothills of the Iron Mountains on the border between Chillston and Caron. The exact location was something you generally found out only when the War Maker wanted you to. He enjoyed that luxury because he made the best weapons in the queendom.

It wasn't easy to get this meeting. They asked Evie to write the letter of introduction. Tom told her what to say, but the thing looked like a work of art by the time she was done. He had asked her how she could write like that. She'd said she learned as a young girl, but didn't seem eager to tell more. Then they had to deal with a haughty queendom courier who'd wrinkled his nose and charged a small fortune for delivery. Darin reluctantly paid for reply postage as well. It was a lot of work but at least it got a response, including an invitation to call on the War Maker the following day.

A scramble to find another mount followed, which led them to the present moment, riding too fast to admire the rolling, tree-topped hills around them. They were evergreens, straight as spears and nearly a hundred hands tall. Not harvested in this generation's lifetime, that was for sure. Tom couldn't remember the last time he'd seen trees so large and in such great quantity. He liked being around them – feeling smaller than something for once. Darin kept muttering something about "fortune in uncut lumber." Tom paid it no mind. They were good trees.

The sun seemed weaker this far north, and a chill to the air promised storms later. They'd ridden a full day northeast in companionable silence, enjoying the rise of the foothills around them.

Darin broke it at last. "So, just so I understand you correctly, you let me try to land a meeting with the War Maker cold, and never thought to mention that you *knew* him?"

"It never came up," Tom said. "Besides, knowing isn't what I'd call it."

"What would you call it, then?"

"Professional awareness. We're both in the same trade." In fact, Tom owned two weapons made by the War Maker – a dirk and a poleaxe – and they remained his prized possessions. The reputation of making the best weaponry in the queendom was well-earned.

"Killing is a trade?"

Tom gestured at the pristine woods around them. "Seems to have worked out for some, hasn't it?"

"You've got a point there."

They rode on for a while, Darin lost in thought, Tom still enjoying the view. As a boy in the Scatters, he'd only known the short, scraggly trees that clung to the thin soil covering the islands' rocky terrain. Whatever decent wood anyone had went into building ships and boats. It seemed the farther away from his homeland he went, the better the trees got. The ones here were tall and straight and thick as canoes. Anyone from the Scatters would have killed for just one of them. The War Maker had *thousands*.

"How much do you know about him?" Darin asked.

"Who?"

"The War Maker."

Tom considered this for a moment. "Probably as much as everyone knows. When it comes to making weapons, the War Maker is the best."

Darin gestured at the virgin landscape around them. "And the richest, judging by this. Anything else?"

"Heard it's a good idea to pay on time," Tom said.

"How so?"

"Something about the last person to stop paying what they owed bit into an apple that cut his face open like a butcher's apprentice."

"Lord and Lady, *this* is who we're going to meet?"

"It's just a rumor."

"Not a good rumor, though, is it?"

"Guess not," Tom said.

Darin had been in a bad mood since they'd left the Red Rooster. He kept putting a hand to his waist and then half-looking behind them, as if he'd forgotten something. Granted, some of his bad mood might come from his ongoing battle with Pasture, the plowhorse they'd borrowed for the ride. He'd cinched her saddle too tight, and things went downhill from there.

Tom sighed and went back to watching the lovely trees slide past. That's how he noticed the carvings on the trunk of a scent-pine. Five vertical slashes marred the trunk at eye-level, as if someone had come by with a belt knife and notched them out. Another tree a few paces beyond bore similar markings, though these were older and there were two rows of them. Right at shoulder height, so you couldn't miss them. There were more notched trees on the other side, too.

Darin saw him looking. "They're tallies," he said.

"Of what?"

"Nothing good. Probably lives the War Maker has taken."

Given what he'd heard about the War Maker, Tom was

surprised he could see any bark on the trees at all. "Didn't know we're supposed to keep tallies."

Darin barked a laugh. "You got enough that you need to?"

"I have a few." Tom didn't enjoy killing, but sometimes it couldn't be avoided.

"I'd just as soon you not go advertising that."

"Why not?"

"Plenty of reasons. First of them being, the more dangerous you seem to be, the more inclined men are to try you."

"They hear I've killed people, so they want to fight me?"

"More or less," Darin said.

"Why?"

"Because men are fools."

Tom shook his head. He believed Darin, but the world just didn't make sense sometimes.

They were still an hour's ride from their destination – and running late – when he noticed the change on the horizon. "Got some haze up ahead."

His words jolted Darin from some dark thought or other. "Where?"

"Due ahead, maybe half a mile out."

Darin shaded his face and squinted against the sun, but he didn't have the same eyes as Tom. "What *is* that?"

"Horsemen, probably."

"Which way do you think they're moving?"

"I'll know in a minute." Tom kept watching the horizon, trusting his knees and Mary's instincts to keep them on the road. The haziness stretched upward. No slant to it. "Coming at us, I think."

"Damn."

"Think it could be trouble?"

"That's been our luck lately," Darin said.

Tom found his hands drifting to his weapons out of habit, and forced them to stay on the reins. "Shouldn't this be neutral ground?" He couldn't imagine that anyone would risk offending the War Maker by picking a fight anywhere near the compound.

"It should, but I'm not sure I want to meet someone who's just left the War Maker's place."

"Good point," Tom said.

"Not thrilled about anyone seeing us headed there, either."

"Better point."

Tom took stock of the terrain alongside the road. They might be able to squeeze the horses into the evergreens and get off the road. It would be tight, though. "We can try the woods."

"Will the horses fit?"

"One way to find out." Tom nudged his mount to the tree line and dismounted. The mare hesitated but he coaxed her in. Darin was struggling to get Pasture down the hill. He hurried back and took the reins. Once no one was fighting her, she came right along of her own will. Darin muttered a few unkind words under his breath. He really didn't get horses. The hazy cloud got thicker. They'd have company in a minute at most. He led Pasture into the start of the trees as far as she'd go behind Moody Mary. As it was, things were tight. The foliage got so thick ten paces in, the horses could go no further.

"We're not hidden enough," Darin hissed from the edge of the trees.

Tom looked, but didn't see another inch of room in the thick trees. "That's it." He wished he could go back to five minutes ago. Why had he thought it a good idea to cram everything into the trees? They were sitting like ducks in a puddle. Exposed. If someone came for them, he might not be able to get out in time to protect Darin.

"Can you get me another pace?"

"Honestly? No."

Darin cursed. "Someone glances down here, and we're going to look like..."

The thought came, and Tom couldn't resist. "Horses' asses?"

Darin barked a laugh. "Damn it, Tom, not the time." He

sucked in a deep breath and dug for something deep in his pocket. "I've got an idea."

"Is it back out of these gods-damned trees and face whoever's coming like a couple of men? That's what I'm thinking, too."

"No. Just hold as still as you can, all right?"

Tom decided not to say that he couldn't move if he wanted to. He focused on keeping the horses calm while Darin did... something. He stopped mumbling to himself. His breathing slowed. Then the hair on Tom's arms stood up. He looked back out toward the road. The view was muted now, as if someone had drawn a sheer curtain across the openings in the tree line. He didn't have time to ask Darin what it was. Up on the road, a party of armed men rode into view. Experienced fighters, based on how they handled their horses. Plus, they'd set two outriders ahead, and probably had two more coming up behind.

Fighters were always interesting. The wagon intrigued him more, though. It held a wood and steel framework taller than a man. Must be some kind of war machine. Maybe a compact scorpion. Which was curious, since no one outside of the queen's army was supposed to own siege machinery. Tom made a mental note to come up with an excuse to need one of those on the next job. If these men could quietly take possession of a scorpion, why couldn't he? With a big ranged weapon like that, you wouldn't have to besiege a city. You could sit outside and knock down the walls as much as you pleased.

The men rode out of sight around a turn in the road. Darin let out his breath like he'd been holding it. The air shimmered behind him and started to return to normal.

"Don't move, Darin," Tom said quietly.

"What?" Darin gasped. "Why?"

"They'll have a rearguard."

Darin gritted his teeth. The air held its dimness, and just in time. Two more riders came down the road almost silently. Must have muffled their hooves. They were on alert, too, scanning the trees on both sides. Horse bows in hand, like they expected trouble. The moment they'd disappeared around the bend after their companions, the odd dimness to the air dissipated. Darin slumped against Pasture like he could barely stand.

"What was that, exactly?" Tom said.

"Looked like a group of professional mercenaries, if you ask me," Darin said. "Glad we got off the road. Anyone openly transporting siege weapons wouldn't want us riding past them."

"I meant the other thing."

"Just a trick."

Tom didn't press the issue. He'd never seen a trick that could make ordinary light seem dark, and caused that tingling sensation on his arms. But Darin never told anyone anything until he was good and ready. Besides, you started asking someone too many questions about things, they might turn around and start doing the same to you. Minding your own pint was sort of a rule at the Red Rooster. "You don't look so hot."

"I don't feel so hot."

"What do you want to do?"

"I want to be on time. Even if you have to tie me to the saddle."

Tom really hoped it wouldn't come to that.

As so often happened in his line of work, Darin was feeling like shit. He hadn't needed to be tied to the saddle – not really – and by the third time Tom offered to do it, he got the distinct impression the big man was just having fun with him. Gods, but he hated this trip. Two days lost just traveling, and then they'd had to get off the road in a hurry to avoid one of the War Maker's gods-cursed customers. He didn't regret using metallurgy to keep hidden from them. He hadn't even been sure it would work. Still, they had to ride twice as hard to make the War Maker's appointed meeting time, all while he fought wave after wave of nausea.

The private road narrowed to less than a cart's width. Beyond that, Darin could have sworn the place carried a faint hint of metallurgy. Maybe that explained how the last customers had ridden out with a wide cart, and now he and Tom couldn't even fit side by side. They had to ride single file, with Darin in front. He'd have preferred to give Tom the van, but he wanted to see what lay ahead. At last, the trees fell away on both sides to reveal a wide clearing. A large manor house took up most of the hilltop, encircled by a high stone wall with horseshoe towers at the corners. The wall itself bristled with catapults, ballistae, and a couple of machines Darin didn't recognize.

"Well, now I understand why we needed an appointment," he said.

They kept the horses at a walk across the cleared ground to the fortress. There was no better word for it. A steep ravine prevented access to the wall itself. A thicket of rusted iron spikes lining the bottom discouraged any uninvited crossings. There was a drawbridge in the fortified wall, but it was up. Opposite, on their side of the ravine, was a tall hitching post supporting a cast-iron bell. They dismounted beside it. Darin rang three times.

There was no response, but movement flickered high up on the curtain wall, close enough to the siege engines to make Tom uncomfortable.

"Should we ring again?" he asked.

Darin frowned at the ramparts a moment. "No, let's dismount."

Tom did so, and slipped Mary an apple from his pocket. She nuzzled his hand in appreciation. Such a gentle horse. He looked up to find Darin staring at him. "What?"

Darin looked away. "She's never done that to me."

"Maybe you never gave her a reason to."

Darin muttered something under his breath, shook his head, and put his attention back on the fortress. "Masters Darin and Tom," he shouted. "We have an appointment."

A dull clunk answered him, and then the drawbridge began to lower on a pair of massive chains. Despite their size and the clear heaviness of the door, it made hardly a sound as it settled into place across the ravine. Still, the ponderous weight of it made Mary shy away. Tom patted her flank in reassurance. Then he saw the dark opening of the fortress that waited across the bridge, and felt a tickle of warning. "You sure we should go in there?"

Darin laughed, but he wasn't smiling. "Not at all. But if this goes sideways on us, I want you to remember one thing."

"What?"

"This was your idea."

CHAPTER THIRTY-SEVEN
Deep Wagers

Tempting as it was to take a long ride on horseback to trade barbs with a warlord, Evie greatly preferred her task of learning more about their patron. Zora, she called herself. That wouldn't be her real name, of course. Given the hazardous and highly illegal nature of the contracted work, she wouldn't want anything easily traced to her. Still, there were things she hadn't managed to hide. Her money, for one thing. Not many in the Old Queendom could afford to front a hundred pieces of eight in silver to a band of outlaws.

Zora hadn't flinched when she handed it over, either. That meant not just wealth, but someone accustomed to it. Someone, more than likely, who grew up in it. Evie knew what that was like. It had been years, but she hadn't forgotten. The highborn traveled in different circles than queendom commoners. That's why Zora stuck out so much when she walked into the Red Rooster common room. Why Darin spotted her right away. The wealthy had their own places to congregate.

Evie knew the nearest such haunt. She hated going there. Even so, if she was right about Zora, it would be the place to start asking questions. So she dedicated two hours to the necessary preparations. First up, retrieving the moonstone-inlaid trunk that she kept hidden away with the few remnants of her old life. She had three gowns, but she'd worn two of them already. Most crowds might not remember, but this one would. That left the sapphire silk, which she'd been saving for… some occasion. She wasn't sure what.

There was jewelry as well: her finest remaining pieces and the few gifts she hadn't pawned for hard coin. No metal other than silver, and no gemstones other than fine. She not only had to wear these baubles, but also pretend that they meant very little to her. That was the true luxury of being fabulously rich. You never worried about losing something that cost more than most people made in a year. You never worried about putting food on the table, or hay in the manger. You never had to sell all but the last few remnants of a life stolen from you.

She carried her shoes and wore heavy boots – incongruent with the rest of her attire, but necessary for the long walk back to the Rooster. Kat already had the horse and cart out front. She and Seraphina were speaking in low voices beside it, neither of them looking happy. Their faces brightened when they saw her, though.

Kat feigned confusion. "You must be lost, my lady. This here's a common establishment."

"The queen's palace is that way," Seraphina added, gesturing vaguely toward the south.

"You're both terribly clever," Evie said. "Seraphina." She gave the older woman a nod. "How was your sojourn?"

That's what the ancient woman called her yearly trip up into the mountains with her equally ancient friends. The women spent a month at some hidden cabin, doing only the gods knew what. Evie strongly suspected it had something to do with metallurgy, but didn't ask. Some things called for a certain propriety. Magical powers, like a family's wealth or a woman's age, were things not openly asked about.

Seraphina sighed. "Perfectly rejuvenating." Silver glittered at her neck.

"New necklace?" Evie asked.

"This old thing? It's ancient."

Evie had a knack for jewelry. She knew in her bones that

she'd never seen that necklace before. Gods knew how she'd made it, or what it did. "Well, it's lovely."

"I'd offer to lend it to you, but you're positively sparkling."

"All necessary for tonight." She looked at Kat. "Are you ready?"

Kat gestured expansively at the wagon. "Your chariot awaits."

Climbing into the wagon in her gown required a special kind of acrobatics. Evie was glad Darin wasn't around to see it. Once she was settled, and Kat had cracked the necessary jokes, they set out.

"Did your boys learn anything of our patron's origins?" Evie asked.

"Not a whisper."

"I suppose it was too much to hope for."

"She must not be from around here," Kat said.

"I suspect she is, and she isn't. That's why I'm headed where I am tonight."

"Are you sure I can't drive you all the way there?"

"In this?" She gestured at the cloud of dust that billowed around the wagon as they drove. *Thank the Lady I thought to bring a cloak.* "I wouldn't even get past the stables."

Kat sniffed. "This wagon's done all right by us, if you ask me."

"I'm not insulting the wagon," Evie said quickly. "It's saved my hide a few times."

"And been your bed a few times, from what I've heard."

"I choose not to remember those nights, thank you," Evie said.

"It's good to remember where we came from. Then we know how much better things are."

Not all of us came from the same place, Evie didn't say. She'd been born into a house that dwarfed the Red Rooster – sixteen rooms, each more opulent than the next – and wanted for nothing for most of her childhood. There was no reason to point that out now.

"Is this fellow really going to let us use his carriage?" Kat asked.

The fellow in question was an up-and-coming perfume merchant named Tarnek. Young, handsome, and already bringing in more money than he knew what to do with. At Evie's encouragement, he'd bought a bright lacquered carriage in anticipation of needing transport to high society events. As the invitations to such events had yet to materialize, Evie took it upon herself to make sure the carriage saw good use. "If we leave the wagon as collateral, and return before morning."

"What if he needs it?"

"He won't."

"And what is the cost of this magnanimous, if temporary, trade?" Kat asked.

Evie gave her a flat look. "Nothing I wasn't willing to pay."

At last they trundled into an old wheat field. The carriage was tucked into a corner under the protective cover of a towering oak tree.

"Well, there it is," Kat said.

"You don't have to sound so surprised," Evie said, mostly to cover her relief. The danger in keeping so many gentleman callers on the hook was that every now and then, one of them slipped free. Tarnek had grown a tad more possessive of late. It wouldn't be too much longer until he gave her some kind of clumsy ultimatum.

Kat shook her head. "The things men will do for a pretty face."

Evie batted eyes at her. "Oh, but the face is only part of it."

"I'm sure." Kat reined in beside the lacquered carriage and gave it a once-over. "A bit over the top, isn't it?"

Evie only paid her half a mind; she was doing her best not to fall in the dirt beside the wagon. "That's the point."

"Wonder if it's half as nice on the inside." Kat pulled the carriage door open, only to leap back cursing when a man's head appeared. "Gods!"

Tarnek ignored her and spread his arms out for Evie. "Elsbet!"

Kat looked at her and mouthed *Elsbet?*

Evie gave her the hand signal for *game afoot*. She never let her gentleman callers know her true name. Hells, she didn't even tell Darin for more than a year. "What are you doing here, Tarnek?"

"I thought perhaps you'd reconsider my offer to–"

"I'm *not* reconsidering. As I told you before, I'm not looking for such an arrangement at the moment."

"Give me a chance."

"The lady said no, Turnip," Kat said.

He seemed to notice her for the first time, and coughed into his hand. "It's Tarnek, actually. And who might you be?"

"I'm the driver, and we're running late."

She was right, though Evie couldn't ignore the delicacy of the situation. If she turned him away too harshly, he might take his carriage and leave. She wouldn't get anywhere near an enclave of the rich and powerful in Kat's secondhand wagon. Then all of this prep time would be wasted. Worse, she'd miss her chance to collect intel on the woman who called herself Zora. Darin would be back before long. He'd insisted on taking Big Tom instead of her. Gave her some line about matching the performers to the crowd. That was fine and good, but she fully intended to remind him how useful she could be.

"I beg of you," Tarnek was saying. "Let me accompany you to the enclave tonight."

"Have you received an invitation?" Evie asked.

"Well, no, but I thought I might–"

"You thought you might get in on my arm," Evie finished for him. This was taking too long. As much as she wanted to avoid the burden of carting a man around all night, at least Tarnek had dressed appropriately. The dark silk jacket was newly tailored, and had just enough hand stitching around the collar to convey that its owner was well-to-do. Perhaps more importantly, a velvet purse hung heavy at his belt. He undoubtedly had even more coin secreted about his person in little throw-purses; hunting for those after a night of drinking ranked highly among Evie's favorite pastimes. She looked at Kat, who appeared to be giving young Tarnek a similar appraisal.

"Will you be taking on any baggage, m'lady?" Kat asked.

"One package only," Evie answered. "If it behaves, I might even bring it home with me."

Tarnek smiled triumphantly, and nearly fell out of the carriage in his haste to offer Evie his arm. "Allow me, m'lady."

Evie accepted his arm and settled herself in the carriage's middle seat while Kat switched the horse over. She climbed up into the driver's seat outside.

The interior of the carriage was as plush and luxurious as Evie had imagined. The cushions threatened to swallow her. Dark silk draped every other surface. Tarnek opened a small compartment to reveal a chilled bottle of wine and two glasses.

I could get used to this life, Evie couldn't help thinking. She limited herself to tiny sips, feigning a touch of motion sickness. In truth, the carriage offered a far smoother ride than the bumpy wagon. But she couldn't afford to let the wine dull her senses. Darin might be off to visit the War Maker, but the crowd that she'd mingle with tonight could be far more dangerous.

CHAPTER THIRTY-EIGHT
The War Maker

Darin hadn't seen much of the War Maker's abode, but what he saw worried him. And he hadn't even been inside.

It took Tom five minutes of fussing with the reins until he was willing to leave the horses. This included his tying of a slow-slip knot, which would let the horses work free of the hitching post in time if this meeting went poorly.

Darin ground his teeth at the delay and prayed that the drawbridge didn't start going back up. They crossed at last to enter the shadowed atrium. They saw no one, but the drawbridge rose ominously behind them. Darin wondered if he'd made a mistake to put them so completely in a dangerous man's control. But they needed him and his arts, or else they'd meet an undoubtedly worse fate at the hands of the Groktar.

They left their weapons with the horses as a sign of good faith. And so, armed only with confidence, Darin strode down the dim hallway to the lamplit doorway at its end. This opened into a wide chamber, one wall lined with books, and the other with weapons. There were blades, polearms, ranged weapons... every device ever conceived for maiming and killing. The flicker of torchlight on all that metal drew Tom like a moth to a flame. Darin put out an arm to hold him back, but kept his eyes on the man sitting in the center of the room. No, not sitting, lounging in an overlarge chair, one leg hooked over the arm. This undoubtedly was the master of the house.

He appeared unarmed. A woman stood a few paces behind him, openly cradling one of those steel-belted cudgels that city guards liked to call *thumpers*. She looked like she could use it, and with the way she was glaring at them, she might want to.

Probably best to ignore her. Darin took a step forward to address the man. "You must be the War Maker."

"You must be Darin and the giant."

"We are. Thank you for receiving us."

The man considered them both for a moment. "So, you think you're War Maker material."

"I don't know about that, but we need the best," Darin said. "Rumor has it, that's you."

The War Maker didn't argue. "You speak as if you know of our work." He gestured to the long wooden table at the side of the room. "Perhaps you can tell me which of these swords was forged by the War Maker's own hands?"

Tom moved right to the table, which held no less than twenty blades of various lengths and styles. He glanced at Darin and pointedly drew his gloves from his waistband, tugging them on before he touched anything. That was as smart as it was disturbing, the thought that the War Maker might have poisoned some of the sword handles as a test. Tom spared hardly a glance for the pretty weapons with gold plate or inset jewels. He picked up a long scimitar with a leather handle, then tossed it aside. A longsword and a pair of dueling épées got the same treatment. Darin knew he should probably help, but standing up straight took all of his concentration. That little trick on the roadside had drained him. Tom spent some time with a short sword, peered closely at the blade, tested it on his own arm, and finally set it back. He looked at Darin and shook his head.

None are the War Maker's? The moment Darin had that thought, he realized it made sense. Most people could pick out the best-crafted weapon in a pile. It took something else to recognize that the whole set was trash. He looked at the

War Maker. "If any of these are your work, then I think we've made a mistake."

The man gave a little nod. Apparently, this was the right answer. "What about this one?" He held up another sword, a one-handed job with a slight curve to the blade. He tossed it to Darin, and several things happened at once.

Tom moved out and caught the sword in one hand. With his other hand, he shoved Darin backwards. The War Maker drew his own sword and leaped forward. Tom parried his downward slash as Darin tumbled over the table and to the floor on the other side. None of the swords cut him, but his body screamed in pain. When his head stopped spinning, he saw two sets of boots dancing in the open area beyond the table as steel rang on steel. He pushed himself off the floor. The effort brought darkness to the edges of his vision. He clawed for purchase on the table and hauled himself above the rim.

Tom and the War Maker circled one another, both of them breathing hard.

What in the Four Gods? He should do something. He grabbed one of the dueling épées. A whistle drew his attention to the back of the room. The woman had a weapon trained on him. It looked like a longbow, but with wheels at the top and bottom. And three strings, one of which held a mean-looking arrow with a barbed steel tip. She shook her head in a clear message that he wasn't to interfere.

Damn. He set the épée down and could only watch as the War Maker pressed his attack. A high slash. Tom parried. A thrust at the middle. Tom spun to the side. A nasty, low kick at the groin. Tom managed to catch it with his thigh. Then he counterattacked. His sword flashed left and right. The War Maker knocked these aside. Tom went left again. Another parry. Tom started to attack right. Even Darin could predict it. The War Maker was no different. He sidestepped and slashed down at where Tom's wrists were going to be.

Flat-bladed, but even so, it would have ended the fight… if Tom had gone right. Instead he feinted right and swung left. The War Maker's sword clanged against the stone floor. Tom brought his blade down sharply and knocked it out of the other man's hand.

That's it, then. Darin started to heave a sigh of relief when the War Maker threw himself bodily at Tom. Drove a knee into his midriff. Tom grunted and bent double. The War Maker got him around the back of the neck. Too close for the sword to matter. He drove an elbow down into Tom's back once, twice. Darin winced with each dull, meaty thud. Tom's sword clattered to the ground. He started to crumple down after it. The War Maker bent over on top of him, then was heaved up, high off the ground. Tom wrapped both arms around him, broke his hold, and then threw him bodily against the stone column. The War Maker struck about five feet up and tumbled in a heap to the floor. Tom stooped and reclaimed his sword.

Surely that's *it,* Darin thought.

Then, impossibly, the War Maker scrabbled to his feet. Tom moved sideways, eyes on him, to where his sword had fallen. All he had to do was pick it up, and this thing was over. No matter what. Instead, Tom kicked it by the hilt and sent it skittering across the floor to the War Maker's feet. The War Maker kept his eyes on Tom, but picked it up.

Four's sake, they're still not done. "Never should have come here," Darin muttered.

"Enough," the woman said.

Darin couldn't have agreed more.

The War Maker looked at her, shrugged, and put his sword back into his belt. He moved back up to his overlarge wooden chair – moving a bit tenderly, Darin couldn't help but notice – and took his seat again. Darin shuffled around the table, stepping carefully among the blades that had fallen when Tom shoved him unceremoniously across it. He really could have been stabbed by any of these. He made a mental note to bring that complaint to Tom the next time they were in private. For the moment, though, he walked over to make sure the big man didn't have any lasting injuries.

"You all right?" he asked.

"Decent. How about you?" Tom asked.

"Somewhat emasculated, but I'll live."

Tom nodded. "Exactly."

They turned and faced the War Maker, who was looking at the woman behind him. Something unspoken passed between them. She'd lowered the odd wheel-bow, at least.

"So," said the War Maker. "What do you want with me?"

"We'd like to order some special weaponry," Darin said.

"I rarely do business with people I don't know."

"Then let's get to know each other," Darin said easily. *Because not all of us have that luxury.*

"Heard you might be affiliated with a place called the Red Rooster."

That was a chancy accusation. If he'd heard good things about the Rooster, that was one thing. But if he were on the receiving end of one of their jobs, well... confessing might be the last thing Darin wanted to do. *I still need his help.* "That's right."

The man smiled. "I've heard rumors about you."

"Not too many, I hope. We try to keep a low profile."

"You were at the siege in Tal Orea."

That had been during the Orean conflicts, a series of unofficial skirmishes between the Old Queendom and Tal Orean military factions. These culminated in an equally unofficial siege at a Tal Orean border village. Tempting as it was to let the starvation and disease determine the outcome, Darin helped a considerable bribe make its way into the hands of the two Tal Orean guards on midnight gate duty. Queendom forces controlled the village by dawn. They disarmed the militia, treated the wounded, and then left. Both sides went home, and denied that the whole damn thing ever happened. "Not so much the siege itself. More like the ending."

"Ha! I knew it."

"Someone had to put an end to that nonsense," Darin said. "As it happens, we're good at endings."

"Whereas I tend to be more involved at the beginnings," said the War Maker.

Something about his tone helped Darin make the connection. "You *started* the siege?"

"In a manner of speaking."

"May I ask why?"

"Sieges are good for business."

"Sorry to have cut it short for you," Darin said.

"No, you're not. You wanted that siege over, so you forced the issue."

The man's cavalier attitude put Darin's back up a little. "Another week and both sides would have starved."

"And?"

"And last time I checked, the dead don't buy weapons."

The woman behind the War Maker snickered. The man made a sour face, but said, "A fair point. So, what do you want?"

"Well, I had this whole speech about how your reputation precedes you and all that, but I sense I should skip it," Darin said.

"You're smarter than you look."

"Thanks," Darin said dryly. "We're hoping to commission an unusual weapon."

"Those are my specialty."

"Which is why we've come."

"The real question is whether or not you can afford my rates."

"Are they so high?" Darin asked.

"Not if you're royalty."

"Right. Well, I thought perhaps this project might intrigue you."

"How so?"

"I need a heavy crossbow. For use against cavalry."

"Bah!" The War Maker gave a dismissive wave. "Nothing special about those."

"The kind I need has never been made before." Darin gave a quick summary of what he had in mind. He left out the reason why.

"Sure is an interesting concept," the man said.

Darin glanced back at Tom. "See? I told you he'd be interested."

Tom looked at him and coughed twice into his hand. Which also happened to be one of their signals, but *false flag* didn't exactly apply here. So it must have simply been a cough. Of embarrassment, perhaps.

"Interested, yes. And quite possibly offended, too," said the War Maker. "You do understand the concept of *war*, don't you?"

"Oh, leave off, Sal," the woman said, in a tone without apology.

The man turned. "You're really into this?"

"He's right about one thing. It's never been done before, at least on purpose."

"Suit yourself." The man heaved himself out of the chair and wandered over to the bookshelves. He chose a leather-bound volume, and flopped down on a divan there to read it, paying them no further mind. When Darin looked back at the woman, she'd taken his spot in the massive chair.

Lord and Lady, don't tell me. "*You're* the War Maker?"

"Oh, you were expecting a burly fighter?"

Darin started to stammer an apology, but she waved him off.

"Save your breath. If I were truly offended, you'd already be bleeding out on the floor."

Darin brought his palms together. "Your tolerance is most appreciated."

"How many of these crossbows do you need?"

"At least four, and within half a month's time." He added hastily, "If you can manage."

"We can manage."

Then she told him the price, and his day got even worse.

CHAPTER THIRTY-NINE
Colton Downs

Colton Downs hardly resembled the stone fortress that had been built on these grounds almost a century ago. The bloodline of the highborn family that owned the castle had long since petered out, leaving its rightful ownership among a field of perpetually squabbling descendants murky at best. While the queen's inheritance courts took their sweet time deciding who had the best claim, a local businessman had converted the place into a sprawling gambler's dream. In this part of the queendom, with so few forms of entertainment available, he might as well have built a silver mine. The horse tracks on the western side were the main feature; a new race ran on the hour every hour during daylight. Racehorses from all over the continent came here for a chance at the winner's purse, and to be wagered upon by society's well-heeled.

By design, all guests arrived at the eastern gate and faced a gauntlet of dice games, card tables, and other distractions to reach the horse tracks. Most of the peers congregated in the central keep, which featured both the high stakes tables and a fabulous view of the finish line. You could enter the left-hand door with a minimal weapons check and no particular fuss. If you entered by the right-side door, however, a herald announced you by name to the mildly interested crowd. When Evie climbed out of the carriage and accepted Tarnek's arm, of course he tried to steer her right.

"I'd like the left door, please."

"Come on, Elsbet. Let's have them announce us to the crowd."

"I'd just as soon not draw attention, thank you."

"But Elsbet–"

"No."

He sighed a touch over-dramatically, but gave over and led her to the left. There was less of a wait here, Evie told herself, and she kept her eyes forward so as not to see the pout on Tarnek's face. A silk rope stretched across the door. Behind it stood a man who was big enough to be Tom's brother. If his size didn't deter a casual interloper, the port wine stain covering half of his face usually did. And if for some reason *that* failed to intimidate would-be gamblers, the man had metal teeth.

"There's my favorite customer!" he called, when she stepped into the lamplight. He grinned, his entire mouth glinting.

Tarnek faltered a step.

Evie pretended not to notice. "Good to see you, Walter," she told the doorman.

"Not as good as it is to see you, m'lady. It's been too long."

"Oh, did you miss me?"

"Terribly." He unclipped the silk rope and pulled it open so she could pass.

"Good boy." She patted his cheek on her way past.

Tarnek made to follow her, only to have the silken rope clicked back in place, barring his way. "Uh, Elsbet?"

"Walter, he's with me," Evie said. "Tarnek, introduce yourself." *Like I told you.*

Tarnek did so in a low voice, and offered his hand. Walter enveloped it in his own. Silver flashed between them.

"Good luck to you, sir," Walter said, pulling the rope aside.

Tarnek practically danced through the opening to offer Evie his arm again. "Does this mean I'm in?" He didn't manage to conceal the undercurrent of desperate hope from his voice. Colton Downs remained selective about their walk-in clientele.

Tarnek's mother had been born poor before making her fortune. Name recognition generally took at least two generations to build in the Old Queendom, even with considerable wealth. *Whereas poverty will lose it in half that,* Evie thought bitterly. "When you accompany me."

He was breathing heavily, probably at the thrill of seeing the inside for the first time. "Which I will do whenever you ask."

"I should hope so." It saddened her to think that she might need *his* name to come here someday.

The inside of the gambling house proper reeked of silver. That's what Darin would say, at least, if he were here. Piles of it sparkled on every table, every counter. Her father had taken her to a gambling house once. He was so proud to show her his latest passion. Everyone there greeted him with a smile and called him by name. Even the dealers, who would all beckon him toward their tables. That's when she knew something was wrong.

The memory came flooding back unbidden. Evie swallowed hard and tried to focus. There was a good crowd for so early in the evening, which meant better odds that someone useful would be around. *Speaking of odds.* "Drat. I've forgotten my coin-purse."

"Consider your entertainment covered." Tarnek produced a small but heavy purse from inside his jacket and pressed it into her hand. It was embroidered with daisies, what he believed to be her favorite flower. "What would you like to play first?"

"Have you gambled in a house like this before?" she asked. "No."

She nodded in the direction of a low-stakes dice table. "You will go to that table and try not to lose too much too quickly."

"I think we should stay–" he started.

"I'm going to the fouracre tables. Do you know the game?"

It was a cruel question, because of course he didn't know. Highborn children learned the complex betting and cardplay on their parents' knees. They taught it to no one else, which was the best way to ensure that the game maintained a certain exclusivity.

"No," he said, with a sag to his shoulders that made her feel even worse. "But I'm a quick learner."

"I won't be long. Then we'll play together."

He perked up a little. "By the time you return, I'm sure I'll have doubled my coin. We'll celebrate."

"That's the spirit."

She left him and didn't look back, hoping not too much damage had been done. Not to their relationship, of course – she knew how to soothe a man's wounded ego – but to the casual onlookers who'd seen that they came in together. Who might have seen that he'd given her the coin. Some might take it to mean that "Elsbet" was spoken for. The sight of her walking alone back to the fouracre tables would hopefully put that notion to rest. She could feel eyes on her, their owners following her progress among the crowded tables. Her sapphire dress drew attention as well, since the color had been notoriously difficult to find in the past few years. Anyone who saw it would assume that she had the money and connections to get enough for a dress commission. They'd never guess the truth, that it looked new only because she'd never taken it out of her cherished trunk.

An elegant older woman waited at the entrance to the fouracre section. She held herself with the posture of good breeding. The podium in front of her held two objects: a leather-bound ledger and a polished silver lamp to read it by.

Evie gave her a big smile. "Hello, Grace."

The other woman frowned and furrowed her brow. "Do I know you, miss?"

Evie plucked a fat silver coin from Tarnek's purse and set it on the podium. "Here's my name card."

Grace swept the coin up and made it disappear into her sleeve. "Starts with an E, doesn't it?"

"Just so," Evie said. "Elsbet."

"Looking for a game?"

"Perhaps. What do you have?"

"A lively table of minor players."

Lively meant drunk, and *minor* meant cheap. Hardly the type of table Evie needed. She gave Grace another coin. "Anything else?"

"A quieter game with..." Grace consulted the ledger, and made a surprised little sound. "A baroness and the imperial ambassador."

What in the gods is an imperial doing here? She covered her surprise with a laugh. "Quiet indeed. That sounds promising."

Grace escorted her over to a table that was partially obscured behind a cloud of smoke and occupied by three players. "Ladies, ambassador. Have you room for a fourth?"

"That depends on who it is," said one of the ladies. She had to be the baroness. Her emerald gown glittered even more than the tremendous pile of coins in front of her. The lines on her face put her at about middle age, though there was no hint of gray in her dark hair. Instead, there was a small fortune in jeweled pins. Evie's fingers twitched just looking at them.

"Miss Elsbet is a regular," Grace said, gesturing toward her.

The baroness gave Evie a lingering inspection, and quirked an eyebrow. "What do you think, ambassador?"

The ambassador was an older gentleman with shockingly bright green eyes. He wore a plain but finely cut jacket in dark red, a color that marked him as a representative of the Jewel Empire. "I defer to you in this, milady."

"What kind of player are you, Miss Elsbet?" asked the baroness.

Evie met her eyes defiantly. "Try me and find out."

The baroness laughed. "I think we will."

Grace tilted her head in acknowledgment, then made the introductions. "May I present Kane Arus, ambassador of the Jewel Empire. You've already spoken to Velora, Baroness of Wheatcroft." She gestured to the third player, a younger woman of darker features whose canary yellow dress featured a spectacular plunging neckline. "This is her companion, Ivette."

The ambassador and the baroness offered warm smiles, but Ivette greeted her with a cool stare. *So it's that kind of companion, is it?* No wonder she wasn't thrilled at having another woman at the table.

Evie settled in the open chair and set about losing Tarnek's silver with the appropriate amount of decorum. Ivette had won the deal before she joined, and used that control to make sure Evie never got a decent card. Stacking the deck for or against other players was allowed in fouracre, as long as the perpetrator did so without being obvious. Ivette handled the cards with deft confidence. Most casual players would miss her sleight of hand entirely.

Evie did not.

Wait until I win the deck, girl. There was nothing to do about it until that happened. She focused her attentions instead on the table's two primary information sources, the baroness and the ambassador. Darin would want her to start with the latter; for someone who claimed to have left his life in the empire behind, he spent a lot of time worrying about it. It *was* peculiar that an imperial ambassador had turned up in the middle of the queendom's forgotten middle country, but that curiosity could wait.

She turned to the baroness. "Wheatcroft. That's in Brycewold, isn't it?"

The baroness glanced up from lighting her next smoke. "Just across the border."

"Grow a lot of barley and hops over there, if I'm not mistaken."

"Well, aren't you well-informed?"

"I like to keep tabs on our neighbors." And in Brycewold's case, it didn't hurt that Kat and Darin were constantly rambling on about where to get the next batch of hops for brewing Red Rooster's finest ale.

"That's industrious of you," said the baroness, but it wasn't a slight.

"Some might call it intrusive," Ivette said. She made an aggressive bet, too, effectively forcing Evie out of the hand. A warning shot, and poorly veiled.

"There's nothing wrong with staying abreast of things happening in the queendom," Evie said tartly. "For example, I'd be curious to learn what brings an imperial ambassador out to the forgotten middle."

Ambassador Kane offered a prim smile. "I go wherever her majesty the empress orders me to."

"Did she order you to come here?" Evie asked. Perhaps a little too direct a question, but he'd opened himself to it.

The ambassador glanced at the baroness, looking for help.

She merely folded her hands under her chin and said, "I'd like to hear how you answer this one."

"We've been playing fouracre for nearly a week, my good baroness. What brings about this sudden curiosity?"

"It occurs to me that you never said what your orders were. Implied, certainly, but never stated."

"What passes between the empress and myself is not for others to hear," he said calmly.

The baroness's mouth fell open; she'd taken some offense. Her eyes flashed, but he raised a placating hand.

"That being said, madam, I assure you that I'm exactly where she wants me to be."

Evie saw the opening and took it. "So where are you staying, ambassador? Perhaps it's a place I've been before."

"He's staying with me," the baroness said.

"With *us*," Ivette said, in a slightly petulant tone.

The baroness rolled her eyes. "Yes, with *us*."

The knot of intrigue dangled tantalizingly in front of Evie. All she had to do was reach out and begin to pick at it. Gods knew what she might find. Yet it wouldn't help with their present plight, or the task Darin had given her. She suppressed a sigh and took another direction. "I apologize if my questions were too forward. It's only that I've seen a number of new faces lately, and wondered what the reason might be."

"Oh?" The baroness swiveled back toward her and quirked an eyebrow. "What new faces?"

Evie paused for just a moment, as if about to divulge something secret. Which, to be fair, she probably was. "There's a woman who's been coming around. To my... friend's common room."

"The way you said *woman* just now makes me wonder if it's merely a friend," said the baroness.

That hadn't been Evie's plan, but the angle held some appeal. *Let her think I'm vulnerable.* "Yes. He's more than just a friend, as you guessed."

"He?"

"He," Evie confirmed.

The baroness sniffed. "Pity."

Ivette's face thawed to a smile, and she even went so far as to pat Evie's hand. "How would you describe this woman?"

"Frightening," Evie said. She told them what Zora looked like and how she'd handled herself. Even under threat of harm. "Part of me suspects she served in her majesty's armies."

"She does sound like a dangerous woman," the baroness said. "I don't suppose you know her name."

"I'm sure it's not her real one. She calls herself Zora."

The baroness and Ivette shared a look.

Lord and lady, they know *her.* "What?" Evie asked. "Surely that's not her real name."

"It's more of a nickname," said Ivette.

"You'd be more proper to refer to her as *marquess*," said the baroness.

Evie had to be careful about the next question. Too direct and they wouldn't answer. Too subtle and she'd learn nothing. "What is her–"

A man's voice intruded. "Elsbet."

Tarnek. Hells. She turned her head slightly to give him an ear, but didn't look at him. A cruel thing to do, but ever so important because of who was watching. "Yes?"

"You said we were going to play together." His tone mingled accusation with hurt.

"When I'm finished."

"Would you at least like to introduce–"

"No. Wait for me at the concierge." Sweet Sister, she was going to *maim* Grace for letting Tarnek in to interrupt. Ivette and the baroness wore impassive expressions. They both knew how these conversations went. She didn't enjoy being so cold, but the less that her fellow players knew about her business, the better.

Tarnek stomped out of the fouracre room without another word. Evie let out a long breath and felt the color rising in her cheeks.

"He's handsome, I'll give you that," Ivette said.

The baroness gave her a frown, then looked at Evie. "Somehow I don't sense that this is the fellow you're so worried about."

Damn. "I needed a distraction."

"Burning two candles at once, it would seem."

"Nothing I haven't done before." She smiled. "So, this Zora woman. Should I be worried?"

"About your fellow?" The baroness glanced at her companion again. "I should think not. Even so, I should offer a word of advice."

"What's that?"

"Stay as far from her as you possibly can."

CHAPTER FORTY
Hard Lots

Darin and Tom got back late from the meeting with the War Maker. All Darin wanted was a hot bath and his warm bed, in that order. He smelled like horses and the road, but he was exhausted. Come to think of it, he could skip the bath. He sent Tom into the stable to tend the horses while he went inside to clear out the common room. Turned out, there was no need. He walked in to find Seraphina setting out four glasses of ale. She'd already evicted the night's patrons. And swept up, by the look of it.

"Welcome back," she said, before he'd even spoken.

"Thank you, Seraphina. The place looks good."

"Why shouldn't it? I run a tight ship while you're away."

"Closed up early tonight, did you?" he asked.

"I didn't think you and Tom would enjoy coming home to a room full of strangers."

She was irritatingly correct in this; Darin hadn't relished the thought of resuming his duties as barkeeper straight off. Red Rooster ale had a mean bite, but once the customers got past it, they resisted being shown the door. And he wouldn't have had Tom's big arms to enforce any such request, either. At least not until the horses were unsaddled, brushed down, and fed. That would take half an hour yet.

"I don't recall sending word ahead."

"Probably because you didn't." Seraphina jabbed a poker

into the fire. The flames danced and flickered green wherever the metal touched. Her casual use of metallurgy for so menial a task bothered him.

"A little strange that you knew when we'd be returning."

"You're not the only one who knows how to keep track of people, boy," Seraphina said.

"I didn't feel anything."

"Maybe if you agreed to further instruction–" Seraphina began to say.

"I told you I have no interest in that."

"And I told you that there'd be a price to pay for ignoring the craft."

"It's not a craft."

"What would you call it instead?"

"A curse." One that had nearly cost him his life a few times, and robbed him of plenty of other things besides. He saw the affront on her face and added quickly, "It is for me, at least. I don't want the metal to speak to me."

"And I don't want to be an old woman, but what choice do I have?" she answered. "We all have to play the hand we're dealt, Darin. Yours is hardly the worst I've seen."

"Easy for you to say," he said. Seraphina lived a fairly comfortable life from what he could see. She had food, shelter, and a common room where she got to boss people around every time Darin went on a job. And every year she got to prance off with her silver-witch friends to a bacchanalian retreat up in the mountains.

"Oh, think we should compare our lots, then?" she asked lightly. Her tone warned him he'd overstepped, but she was already ticking items off on her long fingers. "First, I've buried *three* husbands, whereas you haven't even been married."

"Well, not because I–"

She continued right over him. "Second, I've experienced two significant wars, a category for which your count is, again, zero."

"I know, but–"

"Third, I actually endured the metallurgist training that you've worked so hard to avoid."

"Only for two years," Darin muttered. Seraphina, like many queendomers, had answered the call when the Vlaskan Empress had offered amnesty to any with metallurgical ability. Darin had considered it himself, but very briefly. It wasn't just for the opportunity to learn from the fabled master metallurgists that reputedly served the empress. To be actually *welcomed* rather than shunned held tremendous appeal. He didn't begrudge Seraphina for going. She'd obviously not liked it enough to stay.

"That's two years that you don't have," Seraphina said. "Two years that I spent building up a tolerance for it, which is why only one of us whines like a mewling babe after using metallurgy. The other one did her time, damn it."

He raised his hands in surrender. "Leave off, Seraphina. I grant that your lot was worse than mine."

She harrumphed, but pushed a mug of ale in his direction.

He took a drink, so thirsty that it almost didn't burn his throat as it went down. "I should get Tom out of the stables."

Seraphina shook her head and pointed at the door. It banged open to admit Tom not two seconds later.

"Have a drink, Tom," he called.

The big man lumbered over, bringing with him a waft of horses and road dust.

"Come to think of it, maybe we should wait for Kat and Evie," Darin said.

Seraphina pointed at the door again, and it opened. A goddess in sapphire silk swept in. She'd coiffed her hair in piles of elegant curls, and she sparkled with enough gems to rival the queen herself. Darin had trouble breathing, and couldn't even find a word to say.

Naturally, Seraphina was not at a loss for words. "How many men followed you home? We can send Tom to sort them out."

Big Tom started to rise from his chair, but Darin put a hand on his shoulder. "She's kidding." *I think*. The last thing he wanted to deal with tonight was a string of Evie's admirers trying to talk their way into the common room. He told himself it had nothing to do with how she looked in that sapphire dress. He'd never seen one like it before, and probably never would again. Gods, but she was beautiful.

He stood, nearly knocking his chair over in the process. "You look, just…" Again, he couldn't find words that seemed enough to convey the warmth that spread in his chest when he looked at her. Maybe there weren't any words.

Kat stumped in and plopped down onto a stool. She swung the nearest mug of ale up for a long draught, and smacked her lips afterward. "I think what Darin's *trying* to say is that you look nice, and he hopes you didn't screw us all over."

Evie scoffed, "Of course I didn't."

"Oh, really? So then you did not offend an up-and-coming merchant and our best source of a halfway decent carriage?"

"He'll get over it," Evie said.

"He hardly said a word to us the entire way back."

"Maybe he was tired," Evie said.

"He looked like a wounded puppy, so I hope whatever you found out was worth it."

Evie took a while to find a way to settle herself on the stool, but eventually accomplished it in a feat that acrobats would envy. "Zora is the nickname of a marquess in Brycewold."

Darin sucked in air over his teeth. That couldn't be a coincidence. "Anything more to suggest that it's our client?"

"Beyond the word of a baroness?"

"Ideally, yes." He trusted most highborn about as far as he could throw them – Evie being the obvious exception, both because of their history and the fact that he could probably throw her a fair distance.

"She and her consort described almost the same woman. A veteran of her majesty's army, now a marquess and looking to move even higher."

"Is she married?"

"Widowed."

"How convenient for her," Darin said. Then again, if you were married to someone like Zora, perhaps death was a mercy.

"My thought exactly."

"Like I already told Evie, I don't see how this helps us," Kat said. She'd already finished her mug of ale, and stomped over to the bar to refill it. The woman could drink like it was her profession.

"I think it helps a great deal," Darin said. "We know how she can afford to hire us, and we know what she has to lose. That's key leverage for when we have what she really wants."

Kat waved this off. "She wants imperial dreamwine. Just like everyone else in the queendom. No matter if there are decent alternatives that don't cost a fortune."

Darin shook his head. "If all she wanted was the wine, she could buy it for what she's paying."

"Maybe she's just bored."

"That's a big gamble for mere entertainment."

"There's a certain appeal to stolen goods." Evie stretched backward. A pair of jeweled gold bracelets jangled at her wrist. Of course, that was hardly the only spending metal on her. Her earrings were pure silver and the pendant necklace hidden beneath her bodice was silver *and* gold. Her slender belt was buckled with a golden clasp, and below that... Darin drew in a quick breath and forced himself to look away. Some things were better kept hidden.

Which, undoubtedly, was how Zora felt about this heist. She was putting down an awful lot of silver to have something done by a crew whose reputation was, above all, discretion. The highborns liked diversions, but this didn't feel like one. Playing games was one thing. Hiring an entire team of throat-cutters to intimidate a hired crew in their own common room was another. The thing was, she'd left the manner of the heist up to him. She'd only really stipulated two conditions, that it be this particular shipment, and that it happen in Brycewold. "It's about the wine. We know that much," Darin said. "I wonder if it's about the place, too."

Evie pursed her lips. "There was an imperial ambassador at the Downs."

"Doing what?" Darin asked.

"Gaming with the baroness."

"Where's she from?"

"A little barony in Fairhurst."

That had to be important. Darin felt like he was trying to solve a puzzle with too many missing pieces.

Kat drained the last of her ale. "Who'd want to steal something that you end up drinking?"

"And for what deeper purpose?" Evie asked.

"I don't know yet," Darin said. "Let's steal it and find out."

CHAPTER FORTY-ONE
The Duke

Big Tom liked it when he could be sure about something. Even things that weren't necessarily good. It was certain, for example, that if they didn't pay the Dame what they owed her, she'd have them all killed. It was also certain that the Groktar guarding the Jewel Empire's largest and most expensive shipment of dreamwine would be the best of their lot. And it was certain that in order to succeed, the Red Rooster crew would need good fighters of their own. Since they weren't highborn and didn't serve in the royal army, that meant mercenaries. And since Darin wanted the best, that meant the Sorrows.

Like the War Maker, the Sorrows had a number of official contracts with the queendom's elite. Escorting merchant vessels through dangerous waters. Hunting down bandits along the queen's highway. Fighting off the occasional raiding tribe out of the Ganari mountains. And, like the War Maker, the Sorrows also catered to *other* sorts of clients. If you had coin, you could hire them. That was how it worked.

To be fair, there were some contracts the Sorrows wouldn't take for any amount of coin. For example, they didn't touch the highborns, and they wouldn't take a job that put them in contradiction with the queen's army. *Direct* contradiction, at least. Tom hoped the duke had no such stipulations about Groktar soldiers who were inside the queendom's borders.

More importantly, he hoped he could afford them. As the best and most experienced mercenaries in the queendom, the Sorrows demanded the best pay. The man who set those prices and took those jobs was called the Duke of Sorrows. Tom didn't know if he was really a duke, but he probably had the money to be.

The duke wanted to meet at a riverside alehouse called The Oarsman. It was hardly Tom's first choice of venue, given the place's reputation for impromptu violence, but that was probably why the duke had chosen it. He knew this would be a negotiation, and he wanted it to happen on his turf. Tom arrived half an hour before the agreed-upon time. It was more crowded than he expected, and with all the wrong sorts. Stout dockworkers sat elbow to elbow with sailors and grizzled mercenaries. The only open booth was just inside the door, which the duke wouldn't love. So he made his way to the table in the back corner. It had a wall behind and on one side, along with a view of the door. That meant it was the booth the duke would prefer. Unfortunately, it already held three hard-looking women in fighting leathers. The table boasted an impressive collection of empty ale mugs. Gods, what would Darin do in this situation? *Talk them out of it, probably.* Talking had never been Tom's strong point, but he needed this meeting to go well, and the table would help. So he took a breath and approached the women at it.

One of them saw him coming and muttered something to her two companions, who erupted in laughter.

"Afternoon," Tom said. "Looks like you're having a good time."

The woman in the middle – who'd made the joke at his expense – leaned back to give him an open inspection. She was lean and rangy. Probably as tall as Darin, and with an air of casual violence about her. "We were. What's it to you?"

"I was wondering if I could persuade you to switch tables," he said.

"That so?" She took a healthy swig of ale and slammed the

mug down on the table. "How would you *persuade* us?"

What would Darin say here? Something cheeky, most like. "I thought I'd start with my good looks, and go from there."

They guffawed with laughter, all three of them.

Maybe that had been a little too cheeky. "All right, how about the next round of drinks?"

She looked at the woman on her right, whose strawberry blonde hair was tied with a strip of black leather. "What do you think, Sonia?"

"I don't know, Dannie. It's a pretty cozy booth. What say you, Dawn?"

Presumed-Dawn was the oldest of the three, fair-haired and rather pretty. She was also a trained fighter. It showed in how she held herself. At the moment, however, only mischief sparkled in her eyes. "Seems like moving might be worth three rounds of drinks."

"My thought exactly," said the first woman.

"Two rounds," Tom countered.

"Pass."

Three rounds was robbery, but at least Tom had the coin. What he didn't have was time. The duke would arrive in less than twenty minutes. He could offer the coin instead, but these three would probably shake him down for all he had. "Fine. Three rounds, for the booth."

"Done," said Dawn.

"I'll be right back." He hurried over to pay the visibly amused bartender for three rounds for the women – delivered to the empty table – and two ales for him and the duke. He returned to the corner booth, where the three women hadn't moved. "It's all set."

"Good of you," said Sonia. "Know what, though? We were talking, and we'd rather prefer to have the ales delivered here. Wouldn't we, Dannie?"

The woman in the middle, the one called Dannie, smiled wickedly. "That *does* sound better."

"We had a deal," Tom said.

"We're changing the terms."

"I already told the barkeep to send them to your new table."

"That's easily fixed."

Tom's patience had started to wear thin. It had been a long ride here, he was thirsty, and he'd already talked a lot more than he usually did in a week. "Have it your way. When the Duke of Sorrows arrives, I'll let him know why he can't sit at his favorite table. Sonia, Dawn, and... what was it?" He looked at the one who'd made the joke. "Dannie."

Dannie was mid-sip of her ale, and choked. "You're meeting the duke?"

"Did I forget to mention that?" Tom glanced at the door. "He'll be here any second."

The three women moved quicker than he'd have thought possible, evacuating their seats and clearing their empty mugs from the table. Dannie paused to give Tom a new appraisal. "So you know the duke, eh?"

"You could say that. I used to work for him."

"Maybe lead with that next time." She disappeared in a swirl of hair and leather.

Tom took a seat behind the table and stretched out. *This is more like it.*

The duke entered the alehouse two minutes later. Ten minutes early. He checked both of his corners, and then paused to let his eyes adjust to the dimness. He didn't have armed guards. Didn't even have a weapon on him that Tom could see. Even so, his presence had a quieting effect on the otherwise rowdy alehouse crowd. The three women in leather greeted him as he passed. At the next table, four rough-looking men gave him polite nods. One of them even knuckled his forehead and offered their booth. The duke laughed and declined; his sharp eyes had picked out Tom in the back corner. He stomped over just as the barkeep showed up with the ales.

"Good, you've got my favorite table," the man boomed.

Tom found his feet and grinned. "Of course I did, m'lord."
They'd all called him that in the Sorrows. It was strange how
easily the honorific rolled off his tongue again. "You look
well."

"And you look too thin. What's that witch Seraphina been
feeding you?"

"You don't want to know."

The duke laughed. They clasped arms. Tom offered him the
seat facing the door, a courtesy he offered very few people
in this world. The duke's nod said he knew it. They sat and
tried their ales. It was light and bitter, just the way Tom liked.
Maybe he could buy the recipe off the bartender. Kat might
like that. Or then again, maybe she wouldn't. She seemed to
be touchy about ale.

"How's business?" Tom asked.

"Can't complain. A lot of travel, but it keeps the men lean
and hungry."

"That's good for sell-swords, isn't it?"

The duke cleared his throat. "Don't care for that term,
actually."

"Sell-sword?" That was news to Tom.

"Yeah, we're trying to get away from it."

Tom would have thought it was a jest, but the man's face
was serious. "Why?"

"It's just not accurate. Did I come in here and ask, 'How's
my favorite merchant bath robber?'"

Tom felt his mouth fall open but couldn't do anything to
stop it. "Guess not."

"Sorry, maybe you prefer horse-fixer?"

"Gods, man, keep your voice down!"

"Now you know how I feel, don't you?"

Tom raised his hands. "All right, all right. What would you
prefer I call you instead?"

"Soldiers of fortune has a nice ring to it."

He wasn't wrong. Tom even found it a little funny. "Fine,

soldiers of fortune. You're the best, or at least you were when I was with you."

The duke stiffened haughtily. "I like to think we still are."

"I'm supposed to hire your services."

"Where's the job?"

"Fairhurst, near the border with the empire."

"That's a little out of the way, isn't it?"

"It's not our choice," Tom said. He hated the idea of not getting to pick the location of the heist, but Darin said Zora insisted on it.

"Must be important, then."

"Oh, I know what you're going to say."

"I doubt that," said the duke.

"It must be a high-paying job to bring us that close to the border, so you're about to double your usual rates."

The duke guffawed. "Damn me, but you did know what I was thinking."

"I haven't forgotten everything you taught me."

"I'm glad to see it. Now's the part when you tell me you can't even afford the Sorrows' normal rates, so you're hoping to get some kind of discount."

"Sounds like I don't have to."

"Just like you don't have to teach me how to do business. So let's talk about what you want, versus what you can afford."

"I think you're going to like this one. Very low risk," Tom said.

"What's the target?"

Tom checked the space around them to be sure no one was eavesdropping. "Groktar soldiers."

The duke stared at him. Then he drew out his purse and flipped a coin on the table. "Drinks are on me. Good seeing you, Tom."

"Come on, duke. Aren't you a little curious?"

The big man shook his head. "Not if I heard you correctly. Because we only operate inside the queendom. Last time I checked, the only Groktar this side of the border are the ones guarding imperial dreamwine."

"We're not asking you to boost the shipment."

"No, but you want us to attack the guards, which is essentially the same thing."

"I'm not sure it is," Tom said. "As long as you don't try to get to the wine, your risk is minimal."

"Minimal?" The duke barked a laugh. "These are *Groktar*, Tom. They know what they're about. Believe me when I say that. I've no love for the Jewel Empire, but I'm not a fool, either."

"I know you're not. That's why I didn't come to make the request until we had something to even the odds."

"Yeah? What do you got?"

"The War Maker, for starters." *Along with Kat's numbers, Evie's looks, and Darin's brain.* It didn't sound that crazy when he said it in his head.

The duke's easy smile fell, and his eyebrows went up. "You got the War Maker signed onto this madness?"

"We do."

"I see." The duke leaned forward and lowered his voice. "Tell me, what's he like?"

Better to ask what's she's *like.* Tom bit his tongue rather than give away the War Maker's carefully guarded secret. If the duke ever got to meet her, he could figure that out for himself. "You wouldn't believe me if I told you."

"Come on, Tom! Give me a hint."

"Well, we'd hardly walked in the door when the man tried to kill me."

It was the duke's turn to have his mouth fall open. He drained his ale and signaled the barkeep for another. "Now *this* is a story I've got to hear."

CHAPTER FORTY-TWO
Pieces

For as long as she could remember, Kat had been on her own. She'd been looking after the boys, of course, but there had never been anyone watching her back. Helping her do whatever needed to be done. The Red Rooster crew worked as a team, and it was a marvel to behold. Somehow, they'd gotten the best illicit weapons maker in the queendom. That alone was an accomplishment. Then last night, Big Tom had come stumbling home from his meeting with the Duke of Sorrows, drunker than she'd ever seen him, but bringing the good news that the Sorrows agreed to be hired. It was no small thing, that. Getting hired swords to take a swing at foreign soldiers in peacetime undoubtedly took some persuasion. How Tom managed it, she'd probably never know.

Everything was coming together. She could sense it, the same way she knew her numbers were closing in on zero when she did her monthly tallies. Beyond that, anyone could sense what this job meant for the Red Rooster crew. If they failed, they'd never get the money to pay the Dame. Based on what Kat had heard, and the way Darin talked, such a failure did not bode well for anyone's long-term health. But she'd cast her lot in with them regardless, so it was her problem, too. On the bright side, if they succeeded, they'd not only be able to get square with the Dame, but also invest in their own futures. That wasn't to discount the major challenge they faced in boosting the dreamwine. Yet if anyone could pull off a ridiculous job like this, it was Darin and his crew. Kat had never known anyone like them in her entire life. Evie, who talked like a princess on one day and a sailor the next. Tom, who could lift two men clear off the ground without breaking a sweat, and still spent most of his free time sneaking apples to the horses. Seraphina, who looked after all of them like a cantankerous grandmother. And Darin, who had the strange ability to change personas as some men changed clothes.

Kat herself had made some contributions to Darin's various schemes, but it didn't feel like enough. Certainly not when she accounted for herself *and* the boys. So once Evie had departed and Tom went out to feed the horses, she sidled up to Darin where he stood cleaning glasses. "Need to talk to you."

"Well, I'm here." Darin drew a splash of her clove ale into the glass and used it to scrub the inside.

"Sorry, are you using my ale to *clean* the ale glasses?"

"Works great, doesn't it?" He gestured to the row of already-cleaned glasses. Kat had to admit, they were spotless.

"Kind of a waste of ale, isn't it?"

"The minute you can mix up lye for as cheap as you can ale, I'll switch to that."

"Fair enough."

"So, what's on your mind?"

"Just wanted to put a bug in your ear about something. We're all in on helping boost the dreamwine. Anything you need, just ask."

He looked up in surprise. "Very good of you to say, but it's not necessary. You and Evie and Tom have already proved–"

"No, not them. I mean me and the boys."

"*Your* boys?"

"Timmy and Abel are clever lads. You've seen it. They might be useful," she said.

"This isn't children's games, Kat. It's going to be dangerous."

"Oh, you think we've never been in dangerous situations before?"

"Well, it's not that I–"

"Last year, in Chillston, an out-of-work mercenary took a swing at me because he didn't like the price of my ale," she said. "The year before that, we got caught on the road by a black cloud storm. Had to take shelter under the wagon while fist-sized hailstones hammered the wood over our heads."

Darin bowed. "I surrender! You've been in more than your share of tough spots. That's good to know."

"The boys have, too. They'll step up when you need them to."

"What can they do?"

"I've been teaching them their letters and sums. It's still a work in progress, especially with Timmy, but they're coming along."

Darin smiled as if amused. "Not sure we're going to have need for much of that on this job."

"Timmy's quick on his feet as you know. Abel's not afraid of anything."

"Do they know how to fight?"

The question surprised her. "Only to defend themselves." Beyond that, she'd always preferred they find ways to avoid a fight.

"What about weapons?"

"Abel's comfortable with the crossbow."

"Oh, I remember," Darin said sourly. "What about a regular bow?"

A lot of young boys learned to shoot bows and got pretty good at it but, given her lads' dubious upbringing, it was hard to say. "I'm not sure."

Darin pursed his lips in that thoughtful way of his. "We might be able to use some bowmen on this job."

"How much danger will they be in?" Kat asked, even though part of her didn't want to hear the answer.

"Some," Darin admitted. "But not nearly as much as the rest of us."

Kat hesitated. If she agreed to this, she'd be able to bring the boys with her on the job. Of course, she might also be putting them in harm's way. At least she'd be with them. She could keep a close eye, and maybe ask Tom to do the same. "Just Timmy and Abel. They're the oldest, and they need to do more to lend a hand. The others can stay here and help Seraphina with things."

"Are you sure?"

"Yes." Kat spit out the word before she could change her mind.

Darin nodded. "You should ask Tom to show them a few things, in any case. Might come in handy."

She didn't like that idea very much, but he was probably right. Times like these, places like the Old Queendom, there was never a guarantee of safety. Best if the boys learned how to take care of themselves from a professional. "I don't love the idea, but I suppose you make a fair point."

"We don't have enough horses for them, though, so they'll have to ride in the wagon."

"Taking the wagon again, are we?"

"We'll need it," Darin said.

"For what?"

"Clothing, supplies and, if we're lucky, some very specialized weaponry."

CHAPTER FORTY-THREE
The Neck

For all their sprawling size across their respective subcontinents, the Jewel Empire and the Old Queendom did not share a large common border, at least one that could be traveled by land. Jagged mountains separated the two nations everywhere but a central plateau that provided the only crossing point with decent terrain. Two provinces – Brycewold and Fairhurst – controlled the border on the queendom side and maintained the road that ran into Vlask. As the only practical overland trade route, it was perpetually choked with travelers and merchant trains. That's why it was called *The Neck*. Within two hours' ride to the imperial border, the pace at times could slow to a crawl.

Once, when Darin was a child, an imperial soldier had ridden past the vineyard where he and his family worked twelve-hour days. The man's warhorse was the largest animal he'd ever seen. Eighteen hands, at least, and that animal wasn't fully grown. Imperial warmblood horses were bred in the highlands of the empire's northernmost reaches. They were tall and deep-chested, towering over queendom horses by a fair margin. In battle armor with their blood running hot – a behavioral trait that gave the breed its name – the animals were twice as dangerous as any soldier atop them. Now, hours away from the imperial border, Darin stared at the press of bodies along the road and imagined what it might be like to ride a charging warmblood over the top of them.

Naturally, this was where Zora wanted them to boost the wine. In the queendom's neck, on a crowded road, where armed border guards from two different countries made regular patrols. Not on some secluded country lane where Darin could set a perfect ambush, far away from prying eyes.

Kat rode beside him, her knuckles white where she gripped the reins. "This is never going to work."

"We've pulled off harder jobs before," Darin said, though none came to mind.

"There's too many gods-damned people."

"Or maybe not enough road."

"How do the wine caravans even get through this mess, anyway?"

Darin heard a commotion and shaded his eyes. The line ahead rippled, bulging away from the road like a school of minnows fleeing a pike. A cloud of dust rose from whatever was causing it. *Horses.* "I think we're about to find out."

She'd seen it, too. "They wouldn't have decided to move the shipment early, would they?"

Darin shrugged. "If they did, we're already out of luck. We have to hope this is a regular load coming through."

"How much dreamwine do queendomers drink, anyway?"

"More than what's good for them."

He and Kat nudged their horses off the narrow road, doing their best not to trample any of the other travelers who packed into the gutter with them. The drumming of many hooves announced the approach of incoming riders. Three of them rode in a wedge down the middle of the road, shoving aside any who lingered in the way. An elderly man, stooped beneath the weight of a large burlap sack, failed to move fast enough. The lead rider never slowed, never flinched from his course. The crowd emitted a collective gasp as the old man crumpled beneath the horse's hooves.

"What a bastard," Kat hissed. She took half a step forward.

Darin clamped a hand on her shoulder. They dared not draw

the attention of Groktar mercenaries. Not here, not now.

The caravan drew close. So close that they caught glimpses of the wagon with its barrels piled high. Heard the rustle of leather and clink of steel as the Groktar mercenaries trotted past. Beyond the three in front, there were two outriders on the side of the wagon, and another two serving as rearguard. Seven riders in total, and all of them bristled with weaponry. Swords at their belts, polearms in their hands, and the occasional horse-bow tied behind a saddle. No heavier weapons than that, though, which suggested they might be underprepared to face mounted attackers. Darin made a note of that as he tried to get a better glimpse of the wagon itself.

There wasn't much to it. Three barrels were stacked in orderly fashion, their heads pointed at the front of the wagon. There was something else, too. A webwork of heavy iron chain stretched between metal loops screwed into the sides of the wagon. *Now there's an unwanted complication if I ever saw one.* Most of his plans relied on moving the barrels out quickly and quietly. Now they'd have to either deal with the chain or take the whole wagon. Neither option held much appeal. And then there were the Groktar mercenaries, who would undoubtedly frown upon either.

"Lot of guards," Kat said under her breath.

"Seven for three barrels. Got to figure two or three times that for the real shipment."

"You see the chain?"

"I saw it." But one problem at a time. Secondary security only mattered if he could figure out a way past the soldiers.

Kat chuckled mirthlessly. "Some might call this a gift."

"How do you figure?"

"We just got a free glimpse of exactly what we're up against."

"I guess that's true."

"So, any impressions you want to share?"

"Yes." Darin watched the wagon disappear behind a cloud of dust and the press of people on the road, then pulled down the brim of his hat to better shade his eyes. "We're going to need a gods-damned miracle."

They set up a base of operations in a village called Far Doran, a few leagues southeast of the border. A shoulder-high rock wall encircled the settlement, a relic of less peaceful times with the queendom's westerly neighbors. Darin would have preferred to camp in the rural country, but Evie insisted on a "modicum of civilization" during their time in Fairhurst. Given that it was a small village, finding enough space for all of them was a bit of a challenge. The tiny two-story inn had only two rooms, both of them already rented. In the end, Darin managed to rent them a thatched house on the outskirts of the village, squashed between the wall and the tannery. It was a drafty building that smelled like old hay with an undercurrent of vinegar. In a few weeks, every square inch would be stuffed with fresh-cut hay to dry it out for thatch over the winter. As such, it was poorly insulated, and the doors didn't lock from the inside. On the bright side, it certainly had room. They were able to stash the wagon and its valuable contents out of view of prying eyes. The villagers here, like everyone in Fairhurst, apparently, took an uncommon interest in other folks' business. Big Tom had to turn away three sets of well-wishers and would-be greeters before sunset on the first day.

Finally, Darin told him to stand outside the door and look mean so that he, Kat, and Evie could examine the map of the two provincial regions that shared the imperial border. He'd bought it from a silk merchant nearly a year ago. It was a copy, like most maps, but it showed the western duchies and the eastern portions of the Jewel Empire with reasonable detail. Rumor had it, the silk merchant made a good living selling fabrics dyed with hard-to-find colors.

Darin had had the manners not to comment that such a business all but required avoiding the customs agents along the official highways. As a matter of fact, that made the map all the more valuable to him. Sure enough, it contained a number of routes that weren't on maps produced by the royal cartographers. Worth its weight in gold, which is about how much Darin paid for it.

There was a reason the Groktar soldiers liked the road between Fairhurst and Brycewold. It ran straight and flat for almost ten leagues from the Jewel Empire's border toward the capital province of Caron. The road dated back to a time when labor laws were nonexistent in the queendom, and those in power had taken full advantage. The road wasn't just flat; it was graded, allowing a mounted party that cared little about riding on top of pedestrians to make very good time indeed. From what Darin could gather, this portion of the trade route took wine caravans the least time, and they'd be loath to give it up.

Yet the transport would have to be diverted. The main route was too heavily traveled, too crowded, too open. No blind turns or choke points that might host an ambush. No natural cover to help them melt away into the surroundings. The only opposing force that might help Darin was time. Given how many soldiers it took to escort a shipment of imperial dreamwine – not to mention the empress's recent troubles along the Vlaskan border in the southwest of the empire – Groktar resources were, by most accounts, stretched thin. The rigorous timetables helped ensure that as many shipments as possible made their way to queendom cities. If Groktar compromised security for anything, it would be speed.

"All we have to do is slow them down," Darin said.

"Good luck with that," Kat said. "Remember that poor old man?"

He did, and she wasn't wrong. It would take a serious blockade to reroute Groktar soldiers bent on their mission. Furthermore, it had to look incidental. If the Groktar sensed the shipment was in danger, they might just as easily turn back and cross to the safety of the Jewel Empire's territory.

"What about a wounded rider routine?" Darin asked.

"They won't care about someone on the side of the road."

"Even a wealthy damsel in trouble?"

"Ooh, I like those two words together. *Wealthy damsel,*" Evie purred.

"The wine they're protecting is worth at least twenty of them," Kat said.

Evie glared at her.

"No offense intended," Kat said.

But still a fair calculation, Darin thought. "What about the reverse hostage gag?"

Kat shook her head. "We don't have enough people."

"Wagon off its wheels."

"They'd just go around," Evie said.

"Well, it's a trade route. What else do we think might be coming through?"

Kat had been working her contacts in both duchies to learn everything she could about transportation. "There's a load of iron heading east tomorrow," she said.

"Ingots?" Darin asked.

"No, raw ore."

"What else have you got?"

"Might be a spice trader coming through behind it. And then there's a couple of silk merchants heading west, same day."

No help there. "What about the day after tomorrow?"

"A load of lumber moving west, and two cartloads of goats or sheep coming east to graze."

"Which one is it, sheep or goats?" Darin asked.

Evie sighed. "Are you sure we can't do something with the silk and spice merchants? They sound... cleaner."

Kat ignored her. "Could be one, or could be both."

"Let's hope it's goats," Darin said. Goats were meaner. They needed mean.

"Even if we manage to divert them, it's not clear what the plan is," Kat said.

"We pick a spot for the Sorrows to hit them. Use that as a distraction to grab the cargo."

Kat looked at the map and frowned.

"Something wrong?"

She traced the road westward across the Vlaskan border and stopped. "What's this symbol?"

Darin looked where she was pointing. There was a hand-drawn symbol just inside the border, two rectangles right by one another. "Not sure."

Evie scoffed and shouldered them both out of the way. "Let me see it."

Kat had managed to keep her finger on the exact spot despite being jostled. She opened her mouth to say something, hesitated, and closed it again.

"That's a barracks," Evie said.

Kat swept her finger from the barracks back into the Old Queendom, to the junction of the road they'd selected for the diversion. "That's not very far. Perhaps an hour's ride at pace."

"So what?" Darin said.

"You don't see the problem?" Kat asked.

"Enlighten me."

"Reinforcements," Tom rumbled from across the common room.

"Tom sees it, and he's not even looking at the map," Kat said.

"Would they really send a rider for help back across the border?" Darin wondered aloud. He didn't want to do it, but he swept his eyes to Tom.

The big man thumped over to look at the map. Kat showed him the barracks and the planned ambush site.

"It's what I'd do," he said at last.

"Well, then fine. We'll hit it somewhere else," Darin said irritably.

Trouble was, after another half-hour of searching and arguing, they came to realize that there *was* nowhere else. There were other bridges and choke points on the main highway, but few had nearby alternative routes. Of those, every one was close to a small town – which probably explained why the route existed in the first place – and that proximity would be problematic for keeping their heist quiet. Zora had been most insistent on that. She wanted the wine taken in this part of the queendom, it had to be this shipment, and no one could be the wiser. That last bit was pure common sense, from Darin's point of view, so it was odd that she stipulated it as a condition.

"All right, so we have no other options," Darin said at last. "It has to be here."

"What about the barracks?" Kat pressed. She'd been unusually concerned about safety on this job. Darin supposed that was a feature of bringing her ragamuffin orphans along. At the moment, they were up exploring the mostly empty hayloft in the roof of the building. The occasional bits of laughter, thuds, and clouds of dust reminded everyone of their presence.

"I have an idea for that, if it is a Groktar barracks," Evie said.

"Let's hear it," Darin said.

Evie's dark eyes glittered. "We kill them."

"What?"

"If they're dead, they can't reinforce anyone."

"She has a point," Kat said.

"Yes, brilliant. Let's just start a war with the Jewel Empire," Darin said. "I'm sure they…" He trailed off as an idea hit him. Evie was right about one thing. They had far greater odds of success if there were no reinforcements to send. "You know what? It might be doable."

"Finally, we can have some fun." Evie rubbed her hands together. "How do you want to do it? Arson?"

"The War Maker sells catapults," Tom offered.

Darin held out his hands for silence. "Don't go getting ideas. That's not what I meant. If we change the word 'dead' to 'incapacitated' then we might have something to work with."

He looked at Evie. "Remember how we handled that coin-counter who never left his desk?"

"Of course." Evie shuddered. "Still gives me nightmares."

"Think that would work?"

Evie stared at him. "Are you serious?"

"It's better than killing them all," Darin said.

"Oh, sure," Evie said. "They'll only *wish* they were dead."

CHAPTER FORTY-FOUR
Infiltration

A direct attack on the imperial garrison would be suicide. Evie knew that the moment she laid eyes on it. The garrison's design followed the layout of most military outposts in the Jewel Empire: a central tower, a free-standing armory, and a large stable with two mounts for every soldier stationed inside. A ten-foot wall encircled the compound, topped with vicious-looking steel spikes. The empress's engineers had built in a single access point, a massive iron-banded door. This currently stood ajar, but once you walked through you had to circle the tower to its entrance in the back. You'd pass no less than four murder holes, giving the guards inside plenty of time to see whoever came a-knocking. Or put a crossbow bolt into them. If you somehow got past those to the rear entrance, there was a stout iron portcullis to contend with. The mechanism, too, looked to be inside the tower, making it all but impenetrable. By men, at least.

Men seemed to think brute force could solve any problem. If you sent Big Tom to take out this garrison, he'd probably call up a hundred men from the Sorrows and storm it in the dead of night. There would be heavy casualties, of course. Five for every man inside the fortress. If you sent Darin, he would probably spend a fortune on siege machinery and level the entire complex from afar. Which might work, assuming you could do so before the Groktar mustered their cavalry. If you sent Kat, she'd probably bring in a wagonload of her awful clove-ale. Anyone who drank that in sufficient quantity would hardly be in fighting shape the next day.

Evie planned to get in with nothing more than a skimpy silver dress.

She still needed a ride across the border, of course. Since neither Kat nor Big Tom spoke Vlaskan, that meant Darin had to take her. He knew this as well as she did, and went all quiet. For Darin, that represented true displeasure. They rode most of the way in silence. As they approached the border checkpoint, his reluctance became almost palpable.

"Swore I'd never come back," he muttered to himself.

"We don't have to do this," she said. "We can find another way."

"We've been over it. There is no other way."

"Darin."

"It's fine, Evie." He offered her an unconvincing smile, one that became more mischievous and convincing. "Besides, you have the harder job tonight."

"Getting into a building full of lonely soldiers? Surely you jest."

The late afternoon sun was setting more or less in front of them, casting long shadows from the few trees that lined the road. The line of travelers headed into the empire side was blessedly short this late in the day. A few shepherds steered their animals back home, probably after bringing them in to graze. These must be familiar to the Groktar manning the border station; they were waved right on through. Single travelers got a brief interrogation. Perhaps ten places ahead in line, coincidentally, was a Groktar wine caravan, apparently on its way back after a successful delivery. Two Groktar rode on each side of the empty wagon. Evie nudged Darin and nodded.

He cast a cool appraising glance at them, then looked away as if disinterested. "Gods, it's like we're seeing them everywhere now."

"How many riders do you count?"

"Four."

She'd counted the same. "Do you find that strange?"

"Must have been a small shipment. One barrel."

"Why would anyone think it's a good idea to move dreamwine into the queendom one barrel at a time?"

"Not sure. Be certain to ask the soldiers, won't you?"

Evie snorted. Then she sat up straighter, as it was their turn at the border checkpoint.

Two Groktar soldiers stood on either side of the road. The one on the right waved them forward. Darin flicked the reins gently to send the mare forward, but kept a tight hold on them. Evie took a deep breath and steeled her face to passivity as the wagon came to a stop. Left-hand Groktar, a man young enough to be adopted by Kat, moved beside them to inspect the wagon. Right-hand Groktar was older, bearded, and had the bored impatient look of a duty soldier.

He gave them a cursory glance and rightly chose the queen's tongue. "What brings you to the Jewel Empire?"

"It's our honeymoon." Darin wrapped an arm around Evie's waist and pulled her up against him as if she were a side of beef. "Promised the little lady I'd show her some vineyards."

If the Groktar guard was amused, he gave no sign of it. Very little amused border guards. He looked at Evie and said, "Is this true, miss? If you're in danger, you need only say a word."

It was a surprising but gratifying question. A country that asked it of a woman traveling alone with a man perhaps deserved more credit than she gave the Jewel Empire. It made what she planned to do that much more regrettable. "How *dare* you?"

"I meant no offense."

"It's an insult, that's what it is."

The Groktar held out a hand as if to placate her. "It's our duty to–"

"Your duty to insult everyone who crosses the border?"

The Groktar looked to his junior officer as if for help, but the other man's eyes were equally wide. He put on a frown, stepped back, and waved Darin forward. "Carry on, then."

Darin lifted the reins, but Evie put an arresting hand on top of his. "Wait." She looked up at the Groktar who'd spoken. "I would know the name of the man who's caused this affront."

The Groktar stared at her for a moment. "Second Lieutenant Tomasz."

"Well, Second Lieutenant Tomasz, expect me to send a *very* strongly worded letter to your commanding officer."

"I look forward to it," the man said flatly.

Darin shook off her hand somewhat firmly at that point, and got them moving again. He waited until they rumbled out of earshot before remarking, "So that was slightly terrifying."

"It got us through, didn't it?"

"Are you really going to write them a letter?"

She sniffed. "You'll be lucky if I don't send one to *your* superiors."

The ride from the border to the Groktar fortress was not far; they'd marked the building before even crossing over. Darin pulled the wagon over to the side of the road and whistled. "Now *that* is a fortress."

Evie climbed out of the wagon and retrieved her bottle of spirits from beneath the seat. That had been another reason not to encourage a longer inspection.

"Come back an hour before sunrise," she said.

"You don't want me to wait?"

"Why would you?"

Darin's eyebrows went up, and he looked away. "No reason."

"You don't think I can get in," she said.

"Come on, Evie. When have I doubted you?"

"Never," she said. *Until now.* She rapped on the edge of the wagon with her knuckles. "An hour before sunrise."

Darin bowed from the driver's seat. "I live to serve you."

She sauntered down the lane and into the shadow of the

Groktar fortress. The sun was setting, but it was light enough that no one should mistake her for something threatening. She noted signs of movement on the wall as she approached, but no one challenged her at the gate. She moved through the open door and around the edge of the tower. Trying not to think about the murder holes she passed. She reached the back and found the portcullis, which was closed. A single Groktar soldier stood on the other side, at attention, as if he expected her. Interesting. Maybe his fellows on the wall had signaled him, but if so, she couldn't say how.

"What business do you have here?" he asked.

"Um…" She draped a strand of hair across her mouth, and chewed it as if nervous. "Is Second Lieutenant Tomasz around?" The Vlaskan tongue rolled smoothly from her mouth. It helped that she and Darin had practiced on the way here.

"He's on duty."

"Oh." She looked down and away.

"What's that you have there?" the soldier asked.

"A bottle of spirits." She held it up, so he could see the quality of the glass. Good glass meant good spirits. Well, not in this case, but most others. "It's a gift for Tomasz and his friends, to thank them for protecting the empire."

"I'm a friend of Tomasz," said the man.

She gave him a shy smile. "Are all his friends this handsome?"

The soldier stepped forward and leaned on the portcullis. "Would you like to come inside?"

"I thought you'd never ask."

CHAPTER FORTY-FIVE
Life Serum

Despite his promises to the contrary, Darin was shocked at how quickly, how *easily*, Evie managed to talk her way into the central tower of the Groktar garrison. He drove the wagon off as promised to see what the border checkpoint looked like from the imperial side. The same two guards were having a go at everyone who came in, but the traffic had dwindled considerably. Across the road, a small number of people, most of them traveling on foot, moved east into the Old Queendom. None of the Groktar paid them any mind. Evidently, they were far more concerned with who came into the Jewel Empire than who moved out of it.

For a brief moment, staring from imperial soil out into the Old Queendom, he was a boy again. An orphan with blistered feet and rags for clothes, stealing eastward toward freedom. No one challenged him as he'd scampered down the dirt road. One or two of the Groktar might have noted his presence, but he didn't dare look back to see. The moment his feet hit queendom soil, he ran as hard as he could for as long as he could – half a league inland, he would learn later. Not the most impressive sprint, but he'd been at the brink of death after years of malnutrition. He didn't remember falling into the ditch beside the road, or being pulled out by Seraphina. She was old even then, but still strong enough to haul him up into the bed of a wagon.

An owl hooted somewhere close by, pulling him back out of the memory. He pulled the reins and wrestled the mare around to head back toward the barracks. This time, he circled around to approach it from the north, so as not to look conspicuous. He found a spot atop a small hill that had a decent view of the tower's back door, parked the wagon, and settled in to wait.

The fatigue must have set in then because the next thing he knew, he'd woken with a start in the pre-dawn grayness. Stars still shone above, but it was late. Or early. He sat up and peered through his groggy eyes at the Groktar fortress. They'd set torches out along the wall every ten paces or so. That was clever, for two reasons. First, it lit the ground around the fortress well enough to see if anyone was slipping close. Second, torches didn't last, so it forced the guards on patrol to replace them every couple of hours. The current torches had burned low, almost to the point of sputtering. They looked due for replacement. Perhaps overdue. Darin took that as a good sign.

Evie emerged a few minutes before actual sunrise. Waiting in the shadows, Darin had a moment to admire the way the moonlight painted her in every shade of grey. Dark hair, darker eyes. Pale skin, of which very little remained hidden by the diaphanous gown. He knew right away that she'd done well. Evie could walk like anyone she wanted – highborn lady, hip-swaying temptress, even a hobbling old crone – but this was her own gait. One that few ever saw, and she did it because she knew he'd be watching.

"How'd it go?" he asked, when she'd neared his position.

"They liked me," she said.

"In that gown, who wouldn't?" he said. He helped her into the front seat of the wagon and threw half his cloak over her. The chill night air already had her shivering.

"The garrison commander didn't want to play." Evie pouted in a way that suggested she'd tried to persuade the commander otherwise. "But come sunrise, the rest of them will need a doctor."

Darin handed her the reins. He stood to doff the riding cloak
in which he'd slept – or kept watch, as it were – and retrieved
his leather satchel from the hollowed-out cabin below the
wagon's bench where Kat normally kept her crossbow. "I'll
make sure they find one."

Evie put a hand on his arm and spoke in Vlaskan. "The
commander's no fool."

"Then I will be no fool either," Darin answered. He climbed
down.

"Just be careful." Evie flicked the reins and got the wagon
moving again, trundling back toward the border checkpoint.

Darin watched her until she dipped out of view beneath a
gentle rise in the land. With luck, she'd be back at the base
camp by midmorning. Dawn was already fast approaching, yet
no one came out to snuff the torches. There was a flurry of
activity near the stables, and then a rider emerged from the
main gate. He clung to his saddle like a man with a mortal
wound, but managed to steer his mount down the road to get
help.

Darin waited another half-hour. Then, as the sun climbed
above the horizon, he made his way toward the garrison at
a jog. The door in the outer wall remained open. He passed
through this, half-expecting to be challenged, but encountered
no one. He slowed as he neared the tower proper. He held out
the leather satchel in one hand, and kept the other in plain
view so they'd see he wasn't armed. Still no challenge. He
made his way around the portcullis and found it raised almost
a foot off the ground. A tall woman leaned against the wall on
the other side. She had the sharp countenance of a Vlaskan
bloodline, all right, but her face looked pale. There were bags
under her eyes.

"Please tell me you're the doctor." Despite her clear
exhaustion, she spoke the Vlaskan tongue with a precision that
spoke of schooling. A second child of a noble family, perhaps.

"I am." Darin held up his leather satchel, and the woman all but sagged with relief. It continued to amaze him how a simple symbol of office – lost by a real doctor in a dice game at the Rooster two years ago – convinced people he had medicinal training. "The man you sent offered few details before he fainted."

"Korval was the healthiest we had, other than myself." She placed a hand on her chest, palm over her heart. "I'm Commander Berus."

Darin copied the gesture. "Altrio, of the mediciners' guild. Korval said something about a night sickness?"

She nodded wearily.

"What are the symptoms?"

Berus pulled down the lever that released the counterweights, lifting the portcullis. It raised with agonizing slowness. "Best if you see for yourself."

Darin ducked under the portcullis when it was at shoulder height. Berus leaned against the wall still, her eyes closed. She almost looked asleep.

"Commander?" he said softly.

Her eyes snapped open and she straightened. "My apologies, doctor."

He smiled and gave her a sympathetic touch on the shoulder. People usually responded well to such a thing, and the physical contact added trust. "That's all right. I understand you've had quite a day."

"This way." She launched herself upright and moved up a narrow stone staircase just inside the wall. They climbed past two murder holes, where the narrow passage opened up into a room. There was a stout wooden door here, shut and barred. That didn't stop the smell, though, which hit Darin like a wall. Even knowing what to expect did not make it any more pleasant. Nor did it stop his insides from roiling up and threatening to spill out. He brought a kerchief to his face and inhaled deeply. It was soaked in citrus juice, which Kat had promised would help. "What is that?"

"They all started losing their guts in the middle of the night. From both ends," she said.

Darin brought the kerchief down long enough to look at her. "Is everyone sick?"

"Everyone but me."

Good. "Any idea what caused it?" he asked. "A new food, perhaps?"

"The rations have been the same. And the men have been on duty for weeks without leave."

"No visitors?"

She started to answer in the negative, but caught herself and pursed her lips.

"Commander?" Darin pressed.

She sighed. "There was a girl here last night."

"Was she ill?"

"No. Quite healthy, I'm told."

"Did she bring anything in? Food or spices?"

"Just a bottle of liquor."

Darin frowned in what he hoped was a medically condescending sort of way.

"The men practically begged," Berus said. "We're shorthanded lately, so everyone's been pulling double shifts. I gave in."

Darin held his disapproving expression for another moment. "I'll see the men now."

Berus moved to the door, lifted the bar, and heaved it open. Inside was a bunkroom. Darin barely had a chance to register it before the stench hit again, so much stronger and more rancid that he did gag. It smelled like a dead horse in a puddle of its own piss, left out in the summer sun on a hot afternoon. He put his fist in his mouth and bit down to keep himself centered. The worst part was, a doctor in this situation would step into the room and make his examination. He sucked in a breath, held it, and did just that.

About a dozen Groktar lay within, most in their bunks, a few on the floor. Each man dwelled in private misery. Some lay still, others tossed about in a futile effort to get comfortable. At least they were breathing. Darin half-feared they'd come in to find them all dead. No one seemed to notice him, or the garrison commander. He leaned close to the nearest fellow, a Groktar private. The man had a fighter's build, but was curled in his bunk in the fetal position, his face ashen. Flecks of vomit covered his beard. His eyes flickered open. He groaned, and looked ready to vomit again. Darin straightened and hurried from the room, beckoning furiously for the commander to follow.

"Close the door!" he whispered, the moment she came out. "Can you bar it again?"

"Won't you need to–"

"Just do it, please!" he hissed.

Berus obliged him with a hint of reluctance, despite the fact that she'd had it barred when he got here. A jaded part of Darin wondered how hard it had been to lock them in the first time, not knowing what they had. Not knowing if they would live to see the dawn. "You've got me worried, now," she said. "What is it?"

Darin refused to look at her, and tried to turn away. "I– I need to check my library."

She grabbed his arm. "Curse it, man, you know something! I can see it in your eyes. Tell me."

"Gray fever," he whispered.

She drew in a sharp breath, as if a block of ice had formed in her belly. "Are you certain?"

"The signs are unmistakable."

"That's a death sentence for half the men in there!"

"Not to mention one of us, if we tarry," Darin said. "We've been exposed."

He pulled a pair of glass vials from his bag; they were each half-full with a blue, inky liquid. "I've seen it before, so I always travel with serum." He plucked the cork out of a vial and handed it to her. "Drink."

She took the vial with eagerness, but then paused. He fiddled with his own, watching her out of the corner of his eyes. Maybe she was starting to distrust him. So much of this ruse relied on him getting in and out before the *actual* doctor could arrive.

He put on a look of concern. "You won't help anyone if you fall ill yourself, commander."

She let out a long breath, and gave a nod. "You're right." She upended the vial, draining its contents in a single swallow.

As she did so, Darin palmed his full vial for the empty one up his sleeve. He smacked his lips. "If the gods smile on us, that will be enough."

Berus made a face. "It tastes metallic. Is that silver?"

"Copper. Staves off the infection so the medicine can work. I'll prepare enough serum for the men. There were twelve of them, weren't there?"

"Yes. Twelve."

He set his satchel on a table and began taking out a mortar, pestle, and various jars of powders. A moan of true misery, muffled by the door but no less pitiful for it, made Darin glance up. In doing so, he snagged his arm against the side of his medicine bag. The vial of blue medicine came loose. He made a grab for it but missed, and it clattered out onto the table in full view.

The commander looked at it, then up at him. "What is that?" Comprehension dawned on her face. Her hand went to the hilt of her sword.

Seven hells. He had only one moment to head this off, and with no better plan, he went for honesty. "That was my vial of serum. I switched it out when you weren't looking."

Her brow furrowed. "Why?"

"I had it as a boy."

"You're one of the stricken."

"Yes," Darin said, allowing a touch of shame to show in his face. Survivors of gray fever were viewed with disgust, especially in the Jewel Empire. Those few who survived by some miracle were forced out of their communities into colonies of the stricken. *If she buys it for long enough...*

"But you don't have any of the signs," she said.

"None that you'd be able to see. I was lucky."

She frowned at him, still unconvinced. She took a step forward and swayed.

"Are you well, commander?" Darin asked. "You look a bit peaky."

"I feel–" she began. She wavered, and caught herself on the wall. "That's odd."

He took a few quick steps to reach her before she fell. He took her elbow and ushered her gently down the hall. "Let's get you to your quarters."

"I think I just... need to lie down."

"Yes, yes. A fine idea. Right this way."

She was practically sleepwalking by the time they found her bunk. She collapsed into it face-down.

"Sleep well, commander," Darin said. "I'll take it from here."

CHAPTER FORTY-SIX
Queen's Highway

Convenient as the queen's highway was, it had subtle weaknesses. Dozens of creeks and streams crisscrossed the route. Most carried little more than a trickle outside of the rainy season – just enough to water horses or burden animals on the hot, dusty journey. The deeper ravines required bridges to allow wagons and carts a safe crossing. Half a league ago, Kat had fallen in with the goatherd as he brought his animals east. They got to talking, as travelers often did on a long monotonous journey. The man's name was Joaquin; he was a fourth-generation goatherd. Childless, apparently. The end of his line. Kat felt for him, but didn't mind that the man took a liking to her.

"Why bring your goats so far to graze?" she asked.

"Goats gotta eat," Joaquin said.

"You don't have any pastures closer?"

"Used to." He paused to holler at a goat that had begun to stray. "Sweater! Back in with you!"

"What happened?"

"Her imperial majesty needed the land."

For vineyards, he didn't have to add. According to Darin, that was always why the empress took someone's land.

"Sorry to hear that," Kat said.

"Luckily, my wife's brother has an orchard in Fairhurst."

Kat chuckled. "Married a queendomer, did you?"

"S'not uncommon in these parts. We talk the same, we eat

the same." He broke off again. "Pantaloon, I got my eyes on you!" He coughed and looked back at her. "Doesn't matter which side of the line you're born on."

Not sure the queen and the empress would agree with that. Kat looked ahead; they were approaching the agreed-upon bridge. It had taken forever to get here, but still she didn't see the lumber shipment coming from the other direction. Damn. She took off her hat and mopped her brow with a sleeve. "Hot one today, isn't it?"

"Been that way for a while now."

"Got anything to drink?"

"Not on me. There's a crick coming up 'fore long."

A little brown goat with white markings had taken up position behind Kat as she walked. It kept ramming her thigh at sporadic intervals. "This one's an energetic fellow. What do you call him?"

"Boot. Bet you can guess why."

"He looks thirsty."

"Yep. Might be able to give him a nip in a minute here."

Ten minutes and three thigh-rams later, they came to the bridge over the ravine. This was narrow enough that the traffic in each direction had to cross it single file. The bottleneck caused a serious slowdown; lines of impatient travelers stretched out in both directions. *There.* A good ways back, behind thirty or so hot and weary travelers, was a long four-wheeled wagon hauling lumber.

Kat made a show of looking over the ravine as they stopped at the bridge. "Bit steep, isn't it?"

Joaquin frowned. "Hate to let him walk down by himself."

"I'll take him. Going for a drink myself anyway."

"Much obliged."

Kat took her time leading Boot down the slope. The animal drank noisily from the stream. As bad as some of her boys, and that was saying something. *Gods, I hope they'll be safe during this madness as Darin promised.*

"Easy now, don't gorge yourself." Kat pulled him back and made him wait before he took a second drink. Then she helped the pudgy goat climb back to the road.

"Know your animals, don't you?" Joaquin asked.

"I've been around a few." Kat cast a surreptitious glance toward the lumber wagon, which had inched closer, but not by much. "Looks like Sweater over there could use a nip, too."

"That's Scarf, but I take your point. Do you mind?"

"Not at all." Kat led an ancient-looking goat down the steep slope. This one knew not to drink too much too fast. She let it take its time, which seemed like a good idea until she had to carry the damn thing back up. The lumber wagon was closer now, maybe ten travelers back. A huge man lumbered behind it, traveling on foot to help hide some of his height. The brim of his straw hat tilted up, and Tom caught her eye. He looked in puzzlement at the goat she was carrying, but hefted the wood handle tucked into his belt.

"Appreciate that," Joaquin said. "Think we'd better get moving now. They're hungry. Boot! Lay off the lady a minute."

Lady. There's one I don't hear often. "You sure?" She needed to buy another couple of minutes. "I have to say I'm surprised at you."

The man paused. "Why's that?"

Kat gestured at a solid black goat. "Well, Tunic over there looks ready to faint."

"Seems fine to me."

"He had his tongue hanging out just now. Looked a little pale." Kat walked toward the animal. "What do you say, Tunic?"

The gods smiled on her, because when her shadow fell across the little goat, it fainted cold and keeled over.

"Told you." Kat picked it up and made her way back down the ravine. A splash of water roused the little thing. It drank, weakly at first, but roused after a gulp or two. For a minute, Kat wondered if maybe she *did* have a special eye for animals.

The gods knew she'd tamed more than her share of half-wild orphan boys.

"They've had enough now," Joaquin said. "Need to get moving."

"Better let this guy come first," Kat said, nodding at the massive lumber wagon that was trundling toward the bridge. "He doesn't look like he's stopping."

Joaquin called his herd over to the side to keep them out of the way. The wagon started across. The bridge trembled beneath its ponderous weight; the wood had to weigh a ton. It wasn't quite halfway across when Big Tom stepped up beside it.

A wheelspike had proven a useful tool on a few of the crew's jobs, or so Darin claimed. It had a stout handle as long as a man's arm, and heavy steel head with sharp squared-off edges. Strictly speaking, they weren't entirely legal in the queendom, the country ostensibly being at peace. Like weighted dice, they were something you didn't want to be caught holding. Wheelspikes really only served a single purpose, one demonstrated aptly by Big Tom. Two hard swings of it shattered four spokes on the right front wagon-wheel, causing it to buckle. Tom fell back to the far side as the wagon teetered over and fell. The great pieces of lumber were apparently not lashed tightly – or more accurately, *no longer* lashed tightly – and tumbled out onto the bridge with a deafening crash. The noise spooked the two draft horses pulling it. They tried to bolt, but the wagon was held fast by the jumble of timber pinning it neatly in the midst of the bridge. All they accomplished was shaking loose the largest timbers – which were entire tree trunks, these – and that only added to the chaos.

Joaquin and Kat managed to keep the goats out of the fray, but when the dust settled, gourds and carrots and other vegetables lay sprinkled among the fallen timbers. The half-starved animals ignored their goatherd's protests and leaped in.

"Get those goats out of our lumber!" Big Tom bellowed, even though it wasn't really his lumber. He no longer held the wheelspike, but stood with one leg uncomfortably straight.

"Tell him to leave the goats alone," Kat said quietly.

Joaquin raised his voice. "Leave my goats alone!"

Then the lumber wagon's driver clambered out of the ravine and started cursing at everyone with vitriol. A buzzing discontent rose among the travelers on both sides as they realized they wouldn't be crossing the bridge anytime soon. *Beautiful.*

Hooves pounded from the western road. The pedestrians scattered as Groktar horsemen pushed through. They reined in at the sight of the jammed bridge. The woman on the largest of the horses pressed forward. "What's going on here?"

"Do your eyes work, or do you need a gods-damned–" The lumber driver caught himself when he saw who he was addressing. He cleared his throat. "That is, lost a wheel and the wagon went over."

"Get it cleared."

"Happy to oblige, but I need the goats out of there first."

"Whose goats are these?"

Joaquin took off his hat. "They're mine, and I'm trying to get them clear, but some fool has put–"

"We'll get it cleared," Kat broke in. *No need to give away how well it worked.* "Might go a lot faster if you lent us some able-bodied men."

"That is not our purpose."

"Getting across the bridge isn't your purpose?"

"Cleaning up messes isn't our purpose. Making our timetable is. Even if it means riding over a man's livelihood. Or cutting down those who've caused a delay."

The image of the elderly man getting trampled under hooves leaped into Kat's mind. The simmering anger made her reckless. She leaned over and spat, not enough in the Groktar's direction to make it an insult, but damn close. "If you do that, who's going to clear the road?"

Laughter rumbled among the travelers close enough to hear their exchange.

The Groktar commander gave Kat a cold stare. "Be careful in how you speak, woman, unless you have no desire to keep your head on your shoulders."

Kat stared at her defiantly. "On queendom soil? You wouldn't dare."

"Queendom soil," the commander said, with contempt. "Speak another cross word, and you'll learn exactly what I dare to do."

Kat opened her mouth to let loose another taunt, but spotted Big Tom looking at her with panic in his eyes. *I'm being selfish,* she chided herself. Worse, she was putting the whole operation at risk. So she clamped her jaw shut, pulled down the rim of her hat, and walked away.

"That's better." The commander spun her horse and rode back to her men. They consulted a map, which hopefully showed the old cart path and ravine-spanning bridge half an hour's ride north. They discussed it, and Kat would've killed to hear what was said. More than once, the Groktar commander looked back and seemed to be staring right at her. Or Joaquin, as if she suspected one of them had done this on purpose. At last, she glanced at the sun in its relentless march across the sky, and signaled her men to mount up.

They rode north, their precious cargo neatly ensconced between them, away from the prying eyes of the queen's highway.

CHAPTER FORTY-SEVEN
Command Post

Darin had just managed to squeeze himself into the garrison commander's uniform when hooves thundered in the yard. That would be the escort's messenger, and right on time. Darin tried to loop the belt around his waist, but it wouldn't fit. He tore it off instead and stuffed it under the table. The messenger began pounding on the portcullis, which Darin had taken the liberty of lowering again to keep out any unwelcome visitors.

The rider was fair-haired and young, no more than twenty. Two stripes on his collar made him a corporal. "I need the commander!" he said.

"You have him," Darin said.

The man frowned. "Where's Commander Berus?"

"I relieved her this afternoon. I'm Commander Dolan."

The man had the gall to try to look past Darin's shoulder into the barracks. "Uh–"

"Name and rank, soldier!" Darin snapped.

He straightened his back and saluted. "Corporal Hegum, sir."

That's better. "What's the problem, corporal?"

"They just hit the transport, about a league north of here," the corporal said. He put his hands on his knees, trying to catch his breath. His horse, too, was panting. And well-lathered in sweat.

"Who did?"

"Bandits, but they were well-armed. Came out of nowhere."

314

"How many attackers?" Darin asked. Gods, but it was fun to play the brusque military officer.

"Ten or twelve mounted men. No auxiliaries that we could see."

"That's it?" Darin scoffed. "I'd think you'd be able to handle it."

"We drove them off. They never got near the barrels," Hegum said.

"Then why are you here, exactly?"

A look of confusion marred the corporal's face. "It's protocol."

"What?"

"In the event that a transport is threatened by any serious force, the commanding officer shall send a fast rider to the nearest garrison or outpost, both to raise the alarm and garner reinforcements to meet the threat with overwhelming–"

"Right, right. That protocol," Darin interrupted, silently thanking the Four that Kat had known as much by looking at the map. "Good man. Just wanted to make sure we were talking about the same thing."

"Our captain would like a dozen fast riders, if you can spare them."

"That's going to be a problem." Darin dug the red kerchief out of his pocket, fed it through the bars, and tied it off. "The whole outpost is under quarantine."

"*Quarantine?*"

"An outbreak of the cruelest sort. I'm the only one who can stand on his feet right now."

"How soon will they be up again?"

"It's hard to say." Darin lowered his voice. "We think it's the gray fever."

"Gods!" The messenger's face paled, and he took an instinctive step backward. "Are you sure?"

"A doctor was here earlier. He confirmed it."

"And… you're the only one not infected?" He gave Darin a dubious look.

"I had it as a child," Darin said, choosing to ignore the flash of revulsion on the corporal's face. "I've got the men locked in their barracks. The doctor made them a tincture, but..." He let his words fade, as if uncertain of the results. Truth be told, he didn't know if a proper doctor could do anything for someone with gray fever. It *might* be possible. The trick was probably finding someone who lived long enough to drink medicine.

"What about our caravan?" the corporal asked. The reality of delivering bad news to his captain was starting to sink in. He'd already been gone an hour; his companions were undoubtedly hoping for assistance.

"We've sent to the next garrison for reinforcements." Darin brought out the wide parchment map that he'd liberated from the real commander's office. "Based on your rate of travel, I'd guess you're right around here. No more than an hour's ride down the queen's highway." He pointed to the gorge with the narrow bridge where Kat and Tom would have caused a minor catastrophe. It sounded like they'd succeeded.

"The empress's highway, you mean, sir?"

Now there's an interesting name for it. Darin cleared his throat. "Right, of course."

"Well, no matter what you call it, we had to deviate north."

"What the hell for?" Darin demanded.

"The bridge was blocked. Some sort of accident."

Curious. Given the opportunity to point out a questionable decision by his commanding officer, Corporal Hegum had given her a pass. Most queendom soldiers Darin had met would sell their own mothers for a shot at a promotion. "So where are they?"

"There's another bridge to the north, or so we believed. The map said so. We rode north, but there was nothing to be found."

Because it's a lot easier to destroy a bridge than to build one. Darin pretended to ponder the map. "We should use the terrain to our advantage. Have your captain take up a defensive position at the mouth of the canyon here."

"She won't like having her back to a wall."

"That's the most defensible position. I can send word for our reinforcements to come down the canyon to reach you."

"Everything you're saying sounds reasonable, but I'm saying, the captain won't like it."

Damn, this fellow was loyal to a fault. Knew his commanding officer's mind enough to predict how she'd react.

"How long have you been serving with her?"

"Four years last month."

"That's a good while. Has she ever made a mistake?"

"Fewer than most, I'd say."

Darin ground his teeth. "Well, has she ever lost a shipment of the dreamwine?"

"Of course not!" The man looked suitably offended.

"Do you want her to lose one today?"

"No, but–"

Darin snapped his fingers against the parchment. "This is the best plan, corporal. It's my job to tell you that, and to make sure you get the reinforcements you need to hold out. It's your job to convince your captain to do the right thing."

He sighed. "I'll do my best, commander."

"Off with you, then," Darin said. "As soon as we're relieved here, I'll send men your way."

Just not the ones you think.

CHAPTER FORTY-EIGHT
Dubious Reinforcements

The Groktar had already set up in the mouth of the canyon when Darin reached them. Four of them were behind the wagon; the other eight formed a tight semicircle in front of it. They were all mounted, with hands on the hilts of their swords. Sending a clear message: *don't trifle with us.*

Darin approached them at a canter, holding tight to the reins of the packhorse behind him. The heat already had him sweating into the too-tight commander's uniform. He noted the Groktar soldiers' defensive postures, the tension in their shoulders. No apparent casualties, but they looked nervous. The duke and his Sorrows had done their job well.

The first touch has to be just right, Darin had told him. *Enough to alarm them, but not so drastic that they turn back for the empire.*

The Groktar captain was easy to pick out; she waited at the center of the guards on a massive black warhorse. She had good posture, and perhaps a few years on the youngest men in the party. A long scar ran across one cheek. A few of her soldiers looked at her as he approached. They might as well have pointed.

"Captain," Darin called. "I'm Commander Dolan." He saluted.

"Captain Guirao. Where the hell are those reinforcements?"

Darin reached the circle of guards and dismounted. "They'll be here within the hour. I told them to ride down the canyon," Darin said.

Guirao signaled to one of the rear escorts, who rode around the closest bend in the canyon for a better look.

"Did the corporal advise you of our situation, captain?" Darin asked.

"He did. Gods, the gray fever. I hoped I'd not hear of it again."

The Groktar shifted in their saddles, none of them quite willing to look at Darin. They'd have heard the stories about gray fever, of course. Everyone in the empire lived in constant fear that the "queen's curse" might one day leap the border. Or that they'd have extremely bad luck and run into one of the infected.

"That makes two of us," Darin said. "In the meantime, I brought what I could."

He pulled a sheet of burlap from the packhorse. Beneath it and lashed in pairs across the animal's back were six of the deadliest anti-cavalry weapons the world had ever seen. Their stocks were hand-carved in dark wood, the limbs still perfectly varnished. Every one had a quiver of white-fletched bolts. With these, six men could hold off a small army.

"Heavy crossbows?" asked the captain.

"Just got these into the armory," Darin said. "Perfect timing, wasn't it?"

Some of the men gave low whistles of appreciation. They were warming up to him already.

"Good work, commander," the captain said. "We'll hold the rabble off with ease, if they show themselves again."

She sent five men to arm themselves, an unspoken invitation for Darin to take the sixth crossbow.

Don't mind if I do. He rather wanted to try one anyway.

The Groktar scout returned to report a dust cloud, of the kind that a party of horsemen might kick up when thundering down the canyon.

"The reinforcements, as promised," Darin called to the captain.

The soldiers relaxed visibly – settling their shoulders, patting their mounts – because after the crossbows, they took him at his word.

Guirao, it seemed, was unconvinced. "Hegum!"

The young corporal handed his crossbow to the man beside him and nudged his horse over. "Yes, captain?"

"Ride around the next bend and make sure–"

She broke off as the Sorrows charged into view. They'd muffled the hooves of their mounts to approach in near-silence, and used the terrain to get close. Now a full fifteen of them bore down on the guards' position, their horses snorting and white-eyed, their swords and spear-points glinting in the late afternoon sun. They also happened to have chosen an angle of attack that put Darin and his packhorse in the way.

"Move those horses!" Guirao shouted.

"Right away, captain!" Darin scrambled to find the reins, and led his mount and packhorse through the line of Groktar soldiers. They snapped back into formation behind him like the jaws of a well-oiled trap. Steel rasped on leather as they drew swords. Darin couldn't help but admire how calm they were, in the face of a dozen charging attackers.

"Ready crossbows," the captain said, her voice level.

Darin put his cocking stirrup on the ground and drew the crossbow. The mechanism felt smooth. The tension was perfect. He slid a bolt into the groove and it stayed on its own. Most crossbows didn't fit so perfectly, which meant you either had to jam the bolt down into a tight groove or keep a thumb on it, so it didn't flounce out. The wooden stock was engraved on both sides to help his fingers keep a grip. It was a gods-damn work of art, this killing machine. Almost a shame what he'd asked the War Maker to do to it.

"Crossbows, hold to thirty paces," Guirao said.

Easy for you to say. The attackers were at sixty and closing. Darin dropped his horse's reins and ran back to join the line of Groktar, his crossbow at the ready. He'd always been a better shot while on foot. Two of the soldiers parted wordlessly to make room for him. He earned no nods of gratitude, but then again, this was supposedly his job.

The so-called soldiers of fortune had nearly closed the gap. This close, from the ground, they looked like a horde of charging giants. The duke himself led them, brandishing a warhammer over his head. All of their horses foamed red at the mouth. It was a terrifying sight if you didn't know about the wildberry that stained the animals' gums. An old mercenary trick to strike fear into the enemy. They loomed like rabid beasts, practically on top of the Groktar line. Still the captain didn't give the order to fire.

Not her first skirmish, Darin thought grimly.

Finally she dropped her arm and shouted, "Loose!"

Six crossbows thrummed in answer. At thirty paces, each one should have dropped an attacker or killed his horse, reducing the attacking strength by a third. Yet all of the bolts somehow failed to find a target. Darin caught a glimpse of his bolt careening skyward, as if flicked up at the last moment by an invisible hand.

The other crossbowmen cursed. He did, too, mimicking their tone of surprise and disgust. No one seemed to have noticed that *all* of the crossbows had missed by a fair margin.

"Reloading!" Darin shouted, and dropped back behind the line of horses. He drew the string and fumbled the bolt, dropping it below the wagon. He cursed again and scrambled after it. Then the Sorrows hit the line with a wave of steel. The rearguard moved up to engage them.

Which left Darin alone with the wagon and its vintner, a jowly middle-aged man with gray hair and a round, bulbous nose.

"This thing's worthless!" Darin shouted, and tossed the crossbow aside. He climbed up into the wagon and took the reins. "Let's move this wagon deeper into the canyon. Our reinforcements should be here any minute."

"Shouldn't we stay by the escort?" the vintner asked. He was sweating profusely. His breath smelled of wine.

"Trust me. We'll be safer in the canyon," Darin said. He flicked the reins; the wagon trundled into motion. He felt the heaviness of the barrels – every one worth a small fortune – but kept his face still.

The vintner muttered something under his breath; it sounded like a prayer. "Gods, please help us."

Prayers from a Vlaskan. Darin shook his head. "How about a little liquid courage?" He took a small flask from beneath his jacket. "I just happen to have some brandy here."

If the vintner thought it odd that a Groktar officer was packing spirits, he didn't say so. He instead clasped Darin's wrist. "You're a savior, do you know that?"

Darin uncapped the flask and passed it over.

The vintner tipped it back and took two large, disgusting gulps. He broke off and wiped his lips. "Tastes a little bitter for brandy."

Darin shrugged and took it back, shoving the cork firmly into place. "The garrison commander liked it well enough."

"I thought *you* were the, the–" the vintner began. His eyes rolled back in his head. He slumped over.

Darin caught him and lowered him to the wagon seat. "You know, that was the commander's reaction, too."

He flicked the reins to get the wagon moving. Given the rising noise of the melee behind them, the four draft horses needed little encouragement. They tossed their heads and rolled their eyes back, trying to see the source of the conflict. Darin spared it a glance himself. The Sorrows had engaged the Groktar lines with pole weapons, keeping themselves at a distance and largely out of bodily harm. After the first volley missed, the Groktar tossed the lovely but ineffective crossbows aside and engaged with swords.

Despite the Sorrows' greater numbers, it was an even contest because the Groktar held their positions. That wouldn't last long, though. Darin had paid the duke for ten minutes' combat with minimal casualties. He hoped he might get fifteen. But he'd barely rounded the first blind turn in the canyon when hoofbeats announced the sound of pursuit. Five Groktar swung into view, riding hard.

"Traitor!" the captain shouted.

Even with four horses pulling it, there was no way the wagon could outrun lone riders. The Groktar closed quickly. They were less than fifty paces back when Darin shot through the narrow chokepoint in the canyon and shouted, "Now!"

A boulder slammed to the ground right behind the wagon. Then another one, and a third. They rained down from both sides of the canyon's rim. The Groktar sawed their reins, horses wheeling, to keep back from the avalanche. Darin pumped a fist. Kat and her boys had timed it perfectly. He gained ground for a few precious moments, glancing back in time to see the first soldier press forward. The horse stumbled on the loose rocks. It snapped an ankle and went down hard, its screams echoing off the canyon walls. The rest of the Groktar left their horses and charged after him on foot.

The canyon narrowed until it nearly scraped the wagon on both sides. It forced Darin to slow the horses to a walk. If he got stuck here this whole operation was blown. He'd have to run on foot, or else face the mercy the Groktar had shown Harrison's hired swords – which was to say none at all. The right side of the wagon scraped against stone.

"Hang on, hang on," Darin muttered. He snapped the reins down again to give the horses an extra push. A break in the stone appeared ahead. *The end of the canyon.* Trouble was, the horses were struggling to pull the wagon against the scrape of the wall. He'd slowed to a walking pace, and the Groktar were running full tilt at him. Light bloomed ahead; the mouth of the canyon was *close.* But so were the soldiers; he could hear their boots pounding. If one got hold of the wagon–

He snapped the reins hard. "Come on, heya!"

The wagon shot out of the canyon's mouth. Darin pulled the reins to bank to the right as planned. The Groktar shouted and put on a burst of speed and would have followed, were it not for Big Tom stepping around the corner to bar their way. He wore one of the most expensive things Darin had ever purchased, a suit of armor plate. Custom-made, too. It had to be to fit a man of his dimensions. The last thing Darin saw as the wagon careened behind a boulder was Tom spinning his two-headed halberd like it was a child's toy.

Hold them as long as you can, Tom. They weren't out of this yet.

CHAPTER FORTY-NINE
Groktar Mercenaries

For as long as he could remember, Tom had lived in awe of Groktar soldiers. The Scatters were a long way from Vlask, but they still heard the stories of the legendary soldiers who guarded the Jewel Empire's most precious commodity. A Groktar was worth three good men on his worst day, it was said. Tom wanted to know if that was true.

The halberd wasn't his favorite weapon, but this one was special. The War Maker herself had designed it. The shaft was ironwood – nearly as hard as metal but much lighter – and fit perfectly in Tom's hands. The business end featured a wide hook at the base of a triangular spear point. The perfect combination for pulling an enemy from his horse and punching a hole through him. On the other end, the halberd had a stout cap of hammered metal. It didn't have the sheen of pure steel. Felt harder, too. While he waited, Tom had been using it to knock holes in the canyon wall. Doing so hadn't so much as dented the metal cap.

Hooves echoed from down the canyon. Hard to say how many. Two horses would be good. More than that, very bad. He wished he could have been with the Sorrows when they made their sneak attack. Not just to make sure it bought Darin some time, either. He'd have enjoyed fighting with his former brothers again. Even in a ruse like this one.

A wagon barreled into view down the canyon. Tom moved

out and put his back to the rock right beside the mouth. The pounding hooves rose to a thunder as the wagon drew close. A loud grating noise joined the cacophony. Tom hazarded a glance around the corner. The wagon was close, but one side of it had already begun to scrape the wall. It was going to be tight. A man in a Groktar uniform held the reins. Damn. That was supposed to be Darin. Plan B, then. The hook should let him reach the driver, but it wouldn't be easy. He'd have one shot. He gripped the halberd tight and took another glance. There were *two* men in the wagon. One of them was Darin. Why was he wearing a Groktar uniform? At least he had the wagon. And the wine. That gave Tom a moment's respite. The horses were two of the largest he'd ever seen. They had the bits in their teeth and were running free. Darin probably had little control. Maybe that was a good thing, given his history with burden animals. It didn't matter, as long as he got away.

Tom had to buy him some time.

He swung around the corner and started forward. The full plate armor slowed him down. Not a whole lot, but enough for him to notice. He hadn't wanted such heavy armor, but Darin insisted. Gave the Groktar too much credit, in Tom's opinion. No one was that good. Well, he'd know soon enough, because here they came. Seven, no, eight soldiers with swords drawn. If the count was still a dozen, that meant the Sorrows had cut down four. Which they weren't supposed to do, but asking mercenaries not to kill was like asking the sun not to rise. Still, eight soldiers incoming. At least they were on foot.

The lead two faltered a step when Tom stepped into view. To their credit, they sped up again. Tom got about ten paces into the canyon. Set his feet.

Nine times out of ten in this scenario, one would feint while the other attacked. Sure enough, that's what they did. Right Groktar made as if to swing and dropped back. Left Groktar attacked, or would have, but Tom hadn't waited. He took another step forward before the feint and lashed out with the halberd's business end, catching right Groktar in the armpit as he raised his sword. Tom heaved left. Sent the man sprawling headlong into the left-hand wall. He crumpled in a heap just in time to tangle up his partner. The man stumbled and went down. He kept hold of his sword and tried to recover. Tom brought the blunt end around. Rang his helmet like a bell. The next two Groktar were almost on him. Tom expected another feint. Planned for it, really. He made as if to attack high on the right-hand Groktar, but changed his angle and swept low to the left. Knocked the legs right out from under left-hand Groktar. Right-hand didn't feint, though, and swung his sword under Tom's arm to hit his side. The armor caught it, but it still hurt. By instinct, Tom brought his arm down and trapped the blade. The man tried to wrench it free. He was too close for the end of the halberd, so Tom struck him with the shaft. His head snapped back. The halberd didn't even break. Left-hand Groktar was still moving, so Tom kicked him in the head with a mailed boot.

Four men down. The other four slowed at a hand signal from the one in front. She was a woman with captain's stripes on her shoulder. She spoke a quiet command to her men. They held back while she came forward alone. Tom awarded her a point for courage. Coming forward on her own against an unknown figure with the sun at his back who'd just felled four of her men. She approached slowly. He was glad for that; it gave him a chance to catch a few breaths. A sharp pain in his side suggested the sword blow would leave a hell of a bruise. Might even have cracked a rib. The captain climbed right over one of her men without a glance. She kept her eyes on Tom. Her sword was out low, at a strange angle. Too low of a guard.

Tom held his ground. The moment she tried to step over the last two men, he'd strike. She kept her sword low still. What was she–

Light flashed on her sword right in his eyes, blinding him. She'd caught the sunlight and used it against him. He squeezed his eyes shut to rid them of the aftereffects. When he opened them, she was leaping right at him, sword slashing upward. He retreated a step and leaned back. Her sword whistled right in front of his face. He felt a breeze from it. Clever woman. He jabbed with the blunt end and caught her in the midriff. She grunted but kept her feet. He took another step back to give himself room.

The captain no longer had bodies to step over. She pressed her attack. Her sword moved so fast, it was a blur. Tom needed both ends of the halberd to parry the blows. Four Gods, she was fast. He didn't recognize the sword forms, either. She deflected the business end of his halberd into the wall. In the second it took him to pull free, she was inside his guard. Slashing at his armpit. The full plate didn't protect under his arms, which is why he'd worn mail and leather, too. Her blade quivered in the telltale way of steel striking mail. Her jaw tightened. She must not have expected that. She changed her strategy and went after the least-protected part of him. His legs. She landed a glancing blow on his left cuisse. Then a slash against his right greave. The armor held, but he couldn't chance a leg injury. Especially from the back edge of her sword, which appeared to be serrated. A maimer's blade, it was called. Took a special kind of viciousness to put that on your sword.

So he gave ground. One pace at a time. Gaining back a step here or there, but mostly losing it. He nearly hooked her sword hilt once. She twisted it free just in time and landed a riposte on his chestplate for his trouble. Then she pressed her attack again. He waited for a pause in the onslaught, but it never came. And this after she'd run for the length of the canyon in mail and leather. Tom would have been impressed if he weren't so focused on avoiding getting hamstrung. He yielded another step, and another. The captain claimed each one, fluid as a snake, her sword always threatening. Tom sensed rather than saw the end of the canyon. The captain's men had crept over their fallen companions – two of whom were already rousing – and now moved into a wedge formation behind her.

He was out of room, and out of time. But turning his back on swordsmen this close would expose him. So instead he lunged forward in a counterattack. Caught her blade with the halberd and followed on with the shaft. He was inside her guard. No way to strike, though, so he lowered his shoulder and rammed her. She turned her body at the last moment to make it a glancing blow. Still, it was enough to send her wheeling back into her men. Tom didn't wait to see if she kept her feet. He turned and ran. Straight out from the canyon's mouth. Conscious of how quickly and how many bootsteps followed. Out here they'd encircle him, and even plate armor wouldn't be enough.

A shout came from the cliffs above. Bows thrummed, and arrows exploded against the stone behind his feet.

"Take cover!" the captain ordered.

Tom glanced back and saw them all backed up against the cliff face to avoid the arrow fire. Hoofbeats echoed off the rocks as two horses came. Kat, riding for all she was worth, with a saddled horse behind her. The Groktar made as if to sally. A fresh volley of arrows gave them pause. Tom focused on the pommel and stirrup of the approaching horse. Kat slowed just enough. He threw himself into the empty saddle and spurred the mount forward.

The Groktar did give chase then, arrows or no, but were swallowed in a cloud of dust as Tom and Kat galloped around the bend.

CHAPTER FIFTY
Flight Plans

Kat knew the boys were late but didn't want to think about it just yet. Thinking about it would only lead to speculating about horrible things that might have befallen them. She and Tom had made it just fine, though it still felt like a close thing. Maybe the closest thing she'd had in a while. Watching the massive man in his seemingly impenetrable suit of shining armor running away from a pack of Groktar... well, that was startling. Some deep survival instinct screamed at her to saw the reins, turn around, and flee on her own. But she'd promised to bring Tom a mount. She'd spurred her horse on and prayed Tom would make it to his. All the while, trying not to look up and give away the boys' position.

Now she'd gotten Tom and gotten away, but Timmy and Abel still hadn't arrived. It should have taken the boys forty-six minutes to walk to the rendezvous point from the top of the cliffs. She and Tom had taken thirty-two minutes, and waited for another twenty-seven. There was no denying that they were late.

Four Gods, if anything happened to them...

She'd have no one to blame but herself, too. Who was it that brought them to the Red Rooster? Who was it that persuaded Darin to let them take part? She'd hoped it might give the boys some useful real-world experience outside the hayloft. They wouldn't be young forever, though admitting as much made her heart break a little. Men like Darin and Big Tom could teach them things. That's what she'd hoped, anyway. Instead she'd probably gotten them killed. Gods knew the Groktar had no mercy.

"They're late," Tom said, unprompted.

"Don't you think I know that?" Kat snapped. She felt a rush of shame after that, and tempered herself. "Sorry. It's just..." She trailed off.

Tom put a massive hand on her shoulder. "Don't worry."

"How can I not worry?"

"They're clever."

"They're still just boys."

"So was I, once."

Kat snorted. "I doubt that." She forced herself to look away from the trail and at him as he took off the plate armor and stowed it in the saddlebags, one piece at a time. "Where did you grow up, anyway?"

Tom gave her a flat-eyed glance.

"Forget I asked." Kat sometimes forgot Darin's warning about bringing up the past. "Just curious, is all."

"Little port village called Blackbay."

"Never heard of it."

"You spend a lot of time in the Scatters?"

The Scatters. Of course. The moment he said it, the puzzle piece snicked into place in Kat's mind. Maybe that was why he looked so different. Why he didn't talk as much. "No, suppose I don't."

"Then you wouldn't hear of it."

"Do you miss it?"

"No."

Kat got the sense that he didn't want to say more about it, which would otherwise be fine except she wanted the distraction. If the Groktar had somehow cornered Timmy and Abel... No, she wouldn't think about that. She couldn't.

A nightbird whistled from off to the north. In the middle of the afternoon, and in a climate far too warm for it. The sound made Kat want to collapse, she was so relieved. Tom whistled back before she could even summon her wits to do so.

"Been teaching them more than just tussling, haven't you?" she asked him.

Tom shrugged. "They learn quick."

That they did. Abel and Timmy came loping up a moment later, with big grins on their faces and shortbows still looped over their shoulders. Kat went to embrace them, only to be passed up as they ran past her to Tom.

"You were somethin', Tom!" said Timmy.

"We watched!" Abel said.

Timmy stared up at Big Tom. "Fought off a whole army of Groktar, didn't you?"

Kat grumbled something about the fact that when she'd seen him, he looked to be running away, but this was largely ignored as well.

"We saw one of them hit you, but it was like you didn't feel anything!" Timmy gushed.

"I felt it," Tom said.

"You never even flinched," Abel said. Four words this time. That was practically a long speech for him, and the lad was smiling. It struck Kat enough that she couldn't even begrudge Tom his newest fans. She found herself smiling, too. The job wasn't over yet, not by a bowshot, but they'd done their part.

Timmy turned around and seemed to notice her for the first time. "You were good, too, Miss Kat."

Kat ruffled his hair. "Watched me, did you?"

"I didn't know you could ride a horse."

"Didn't know I could–"

"And you stayed in the saddle, too!" Abel said.

Kat took a deep breath and decided not to point out that she'd been saddling and riding horses before either of them had shat their first swaddling clothes.

"Did we do it, then?" Timmy asked. "Did we get the wagon?"

"Looked that way," Tom said.

Timmy practically bounced with excitement. "What happens next?"

"We meet up with Darin and the cargo back at the Rooster," Kat said. Truth be told, this was the part of the plan that made her most nervous. Delaying the guards put them in some danger, certainly. But being anywhere near the stolen wine made them a target. Not just for the Groktar, but for anyone who crossed their path and saw the opportunity. Kat used to worry about it when she had barrels of rough ale in her wagon. To ride on top of twelve barrels of liquid silver was hard to imagine. "And we pray to the Four he knows what he's doing."

CHAPTER FIFTY-ONE
Seven Hells

Darin drove the wagonload of barrels down a narrow backcountry road near the border of Brycewold and Hulscot. The sun was out, finally, and felt warm on his face. The eastern part of this province contrasted with the imperial border in two very important ways. First of all, no crowds. That meant fewer prying eyes, fewer folks who might remember when he passed through and what he looked like.

The only people he saw from the road were shepherds tending huge flocks of sheep as they grazed on verdant hillsides here. He still marveled at how much of the queendom was given over for basic animal sustenance. It was a far cry from the Jewel Empire, where vineyards and orchards covered every patch of ground. Anywhere that had dirt enough to grow weeds, the empress claimed for her fruit production. It left very little for the common folk to survive on.

Second, the road was a single hard-packed dirt lane. Just wide enough to accommodate a wagon or two horses abreast. Inconvenient as hell when you were in a hurry, but Darin had time to spare. Slow backcountry roads like this one discouraged the sort of travelers Darin hoped to avoid. Brycewoldan patrols, for one thing, which were more prevalent near the border but made the occasional appearance in eastern byways. Darin's forged paperwork might pass muster with a patrol commander, or it might not. It really depended how well he or she could read, and whether or not they knew the look of the queen's seal.

With the first part of the job done, he and the others had scattered in three directions – Evie and Tom one way, Kat and her orphan boys in another. Darin hadn't liked the idea of bringing the boys along for this part of the mission, but Kat had persuaded him they could be useful without getting in harm's way. She'd proven herself right again. Now she'd be insisting they bring some of the boys on every mission.

All of that could be hashed out when they met up at the Red Rooster. For the moment, he had time to burn.

The route itself didn't offer the same straight efficiency of the queen's highway, but came damn close. Years' worth of wagon ruts suggested he wasn't the only one hauling goods on the out-of-sight highway. He followed these down a gentle ridge toward a narrow but swift-moving river. The water was running high for this time of year. Not the type of current he'd enjoy trying to cross with a heavy wagon, so he was glad for the narrow stone bridge that arched over it. It looked stout enough, and most of the wagon ruts suggested travelers took it regularly.

By unspoken rule, whoever set foot or hoof on the bridge first had the claim. He might as well chance it before some slow-moving peddler showed up traveling from the other direction. He flicked the reins and held his breath. The bridge didn't so much as shudder. Good. One less obstacle.

The bridge offered a spectacular view of the clear cold water. He trundled along for a moment, enjoying – as he sometimes did – the fact that he was still alive. Then three men armed with crossbows appeared on the bridge ahead, barring his way. At first glance, he thought they might be a Brycewoldan patrol, or some sort of village militia. Yet they carried no standard, and wore no recognizable uniform. That made them sell-swords. *Soldiers of fortune,* he corrected himself. Tom said the duke preferred that term. Though in this case, *highwaymen* might be a better word.

He didn't have to look to know that two or three more would bar the way he'd come. Damn. He should have known better than to expect such a nice bridge unguarded. He reined in, with the wagon right near the center of the bridge. "Afternoon. Can I help you gentlemen?"

The mercenary in the middle of the group answered him. "No, but we can help you."

"All right, how can you help me?"

"Looks like a heavy load."

"Which is why I'm grateful to have found such a sturdy bridge."

"What you got in the wagon there?"

"Nothing valuable," Darin said. "But I'd like to get it across this bridge."

"Safe passage, eh?"

"That would be most appreciated, thank you."

"Going to cost you."

Let the negotiations begin. "Don't have a lot of money, but like I said, I'd love to get home safe."

"Sure you would."

Darin sighed. "How much?"

The three mercenaries moved toward him, their crossbows raised. They were the heavier type, finely made. Their design was chillingly recognizable. Darin raised his hands slowly. Another figure moved out behind the mercenaries to stand in the middle of the bridge.

"How about twelve barrels of wine?" Harrison called.

Seven hells. Of all the goddamned times for him to show up. Darin forced a smile. "Thank the gods you're here, Harrison. I think I'm being robbed."

Harrison snickered. "You're being robbed, all right."

"You're over the deal line."

"The deal line ceased to exist when you decided some mouthy tart wasn't good enough for her husband," Harrison spat.

At least Annette's not here. Harrison might have a temper, but he operated with strategic caution. He wouldn't have his men kill Darin out of hand if it seemed like there could be repercussions. But when Annette whispered in his ear, all bets were off. She had a mean streak worse than anyone Darin had ever met. And for some reason, her hatred for Darin seemed personal. At least with Harrison, it was mostly professional.

"Surely we can reach some kind of arrangement." Darin spread out his arms and took a quick stock of his assets. Aside from the horses and the barrels, he had very little. A dagger in each boot, the forged papers in his jacket, and a purse with what remained of Zora's silver. None of which would matter if one of Harrison's men put a bolt into him.

"Here's the arrangement. We're taking everything," Harrison said. "The wine, the wagons, and our client's payment in full."

"Why would she pay you in full? You didn't steal the wine."

"I'm going to be the one to deliver it. That's all that matters."

Still his men moved closer. They were almost to twenty paces.

Darin sincerely doubted the War Maker had made the same modifications to Harrison's weapons as he had to theirs. No, these crossbows would be stone-cold accurate. At this range, even a child wouldn't miss. Judging by the scars and the heavy beards, these mercenaries left their childhoods behind a long time ago.

I need to buy time. "Do you know who she is?" Darin asked.

"She's the one going to make me rich."

"You really don't know, do you?" Darin hated to give hard-won information freely, but had little else to work with. "She's one of *them*, Harrison. A highborn."

"Good for her," Harrison said.

Fifteen paces. A trained animal would be able to make a killing shot this close. "Not just any noble," Darin said quickly. "A marquess. Aren't you curious as to why someone who can buy the wine outright would want it stolen instead? Doesn't make a lot of sense, does it?"

Harrison snapped his fingers; his men stopped advancing. They still kept their weapons trained on Darin, though.

"What's her game, then?"

Darin could have danced at winning a respite, brief as it was. Trouble was, he hadn't quite worked out the puzzle himself. "It's not about the wine. It never was." He couldn't be completely sure of that, but he did his best to project only confidence. "To the queendom, the wine is just a luxury. They buy it. They drink it. Sure, it costs a fortune but so what? The nobles have got more silver than they can throw away."

"You're just talking now. You don't know anything more than I do."

"The wine means something very different to the empress. Look at what she's done to build the market for it. Trained and armed a military force for transport. Claimed every scrap of halfway decent farmland to grow the fruit. She's staked the whole future of the empire on the wine, and the silver that it brings."

"That's her problem, ain't it? She's got her place, and we've got ours."

"For the moment. But I think that's going to change. The queendom is going to need men like us to make sure the common folk don't all end up in the dirt."

Harrison's face twisted into something between a scowl and a grimace. He didn't like what he was hearing. That didn't mean he believed it, but it was a start.

"This is a game to them. I don't think we should keep playing it," Darin said.

"And I don't think you should listen to a word he says," a woman said.

Shit.

Annette sauntered out from behind one of the bridge's columns and joined Harrison. "What have I told you about talking to him, my love?"

"He could be right," Harrison said quietly.

"He's *lying*. That's what he does." She glared at Darin. "He deceives people to get what he wants. And when he does, he tosses them aside like trash."

Darin bristled a bit at this accusation, but knew better than to rise to Annette's bait. She whispered something to Harrison, and his face darkened. He replied harshly. She rounded on him and let forth a stream of words that would embarrass a dockworker.

The men on the bridge still had their crossbows on Darin. If he reached for a weapon, that would only prompt them to shoot. Darin focused on the man in the middle, the one who'd spoken. "How much is he paying you? I'm sure I could offer more," he said softly.

The man didn't reply, but he also didn't pull the trigger. That seemed like a good sign.

"Let's see how much you might stand to gain." Darin tore open the purse strings and shoved a hand inside amid the silver. It sang to him as always, calling with its power. "Five pieces of eight to a man. Silver, of course." He hated to part with that much silver, but no amount was worth taking a bolt to the stomach.

No response. It was like the man was *deaf*.

Meanwhile, Harrison and Annette's disagreement had become a shouting match.

"So now you're taking his word over mine!" Annette said.

Harrison shook his head. "That's not what I said. I said we should get the information."

"If you believe anything he says, you're a fool."

"Don't call me that."

"Then don't act like one," she hissed.

Harrison glanced at Darin, then looked back at her. "We listen, first. If you don't like what he has to say, we do it your way."

"But–"

Harrison held up a hand to stop her next outburst. "It's my men and my call." He turned back to face Darin. Which is why he didn't see the dagger in Annette's hand. She spun and stabbed him in the chest with it. Two sharp jabs. Then a third. Harrison gasped in shock. He fell to his knees, the hilt sticking out of him. Blood bubbling up around it. His mouth worked, but no sound came forth.

"Now it isn't." Annette turned to the men on the bridge, who'd started to lower their weapons uncertainly. "What are you waiting for?" She pointed a bloody finger at Darin. "*Kill him!*"

The men looked at each other, then raised their crossbows. Darin closed his eyes and answered the call of the silver in his purse. Pulled the power into him. Time slowed to a crawl for everyone else but him. He saw the triggers pulled. Heard the deep *clack-thrums* of the crossbows loosing. The bolts glided at him through air that felt as thick as syrup. Three bolts, from three angles. No way they'd miss.

Unless.

He reached out with the power. It filled every inch of his being now. It was part of him. With a flick of his finger, he sent one bolt spinning out to the river. The next one, he flicked up into the sky. Things were moving faster now. The third bolt sped toward him. He flicked at it. Missed. Too quick. In a last desperate try, he swatted it to one side. The bolt hit the bench right beside him, shattering the wood. Then the world caught up to itself again. The bolt hummed and shook, its tip buried in the wood.

The men who'd fired looked at their crossbows in puzzlement.

"Kill him!" Annette screeched.

The men drew swords and charged at him. Darin whipped the reins as hard as he could. Both horses lurched forward. It bought him a moment to throw himself out of the wagon and over the side of the bridge.

Frigid water hit him like a wall. He clawed for the surface, but the current had him in its grip. He tumbled over once, twice. His lungs burned. He kicked and fought his way up. He finally broke the surface, gasped and sucked in air. The river pulled him down again. He caught a glimpse of the chaos on the bridge – Annette gesturing wildly as her thugs struggled to control the rearing horses. Then the water swallowed him again.

CHAPTER FIFTY-TWO
Counter Orders

The Red Rooster crew must have done something to offend the
gods in another life. That was the only possible explanation
Evie could think of for their run of bad luck. First there was the
Eskirk gala disaster, which had started out so promising only
to screw them in the end. The dreamwine job, too, seemed to
be going well. She'd guessed that Big Tom would be discreetly
tailing Darin on his drive to the rendezvous point, and she was
right. There was no talking the man out of something he'd set
his mind to do, so she joined up with him – Darin's instructions
about going to ground after the sensitive part of the operation
notwithstanding. So she and Tom both reined in to watch
Darin drive across the narrow bridge. They saw the men with
the crossbows.

Then Harrison moved into view.

"Uh oh," Tom said.

That about summed it up. The man had no sense of boundary
or propriety. Setting an ambush on a bridge like a common
thief. He and Darin had words, then men with crossbows
approached. Nasty pieces of work, those. Evie's father had hated
them, and said they were a dishonorable man's weapon. To
Evie, they were a powerful equalizer. As she was rather petite,
she'd found that men in particular sometimes had a difficulty
in taking her seriously. A crossbow cradled in the arm, casually
pointed in the area of a man's crotch, did wonders to improve

conversations. Unfortunately, this also meant she knew quite intimately what such a weapon could do at close range. And Darin had three pointed right at him.

"I should get down there," Tom said.

"Hang tight," Evie said.

The men on the bridge halted. It looked like Darin and Harrison were talking. Maybe that was good. Historically not so much, given their tendency to want to kill one another. Talking was a start, at least. Darin could talk anyone into almost anything. Whether that applied to Harrison remained more of a question, though. At least it was just him. On his own, the man could be reasonable. Impudent and cruel, perhaps, but still *reasonable*.

Then another figure stalked onto the bridge. Evie knew that frame, that particular rage-inducing swagger. She growled wordlessly.

"Is that who I think it is?" Tom asked.

"What is *she* doing here?"

"Wonder what they're talking about."

"Nothing good," Evie said. She could tell that just from how they squared off with each other, gesturing ever more vigorously. "We need to be ready."

"For what?"

Something happened on the bridge. Metal glinted in Annette's hand. Then she struck, and Harrison fell. She shouted at her men, and they turned as one to shoot Darin. Evie didn't know if she should scream or faint. In the end, she had time to do neither. Somehow Darin escaped, and a heartbeat later had thrown himself into the churning waters of the river.

"Did he just–" Tom started.

"Ride!" Evie spurred her mare down the ridge toward the riverbank. Darin surfaced for a moment, then tumbled over in the water as the current took hold. Evie caught the occasional glimpse of him as she and Tom charged downstream. The country was open here – mostly farmland – and she winced as her horse's hooves churned up the soft earth. Crops could be replanted, though. Darin could not. He'd never been a strong swimmer, truth be told, and he could be hurt. The current was fast, too. He managed to get hold of a dead tree that was half-submerged in the water. Evie turned toward it and prepared to jump free of the saddle. Before she got close enough, the water yanked him away. He probably hadn't seen her, either. He was still struggling, but more weakly. Making fewer splashes.

Hang on, Darin. Evie kicked her mount in the sides even harder, pushing for speed. She pulled even with Darin, then ahead. The horse jounced and swayed, galloping flat-out. She leaned low against her neck, squeezing with her legs, keeping her balance the way she'd learned as a little girl. The river curved in ahead. She glimpsed a rock outcropping jutting out in the water. It might do.

She pointed. "There!"

Tom surged past her and threw his reins across her saddle. He slid off the horse and hit the ground running flat-out, like a gleeman's trick. She pulled back on both sets of reins, arms stretched wide to either side, hoping not to trample him. He took three great strides across the rocks and planted a foot in the water. Here came Darin, pale-faced and splashing. Moving almost impossibly fast. Too far out in the middle. He seemed to right himself at the last moment and flailed for the rocks.

Tom chanced another step out into the current and lunged. He wrapped his big arms around Darin and plucked him out of the water like a bear catching salmon. Darin hung limp in his arms as Tom stomped back to shore.

Evie let out a heavy breath. Darin looked shaken, but his eyes fluttered open.

"Catch anything, Tom?" she called.

"Just one," Tom said, lifting Darin for her to see.

"Gods, it looks half-drowned. Throw it back, will you?"

Tom grinned. "Come on, Evie, can't we keep it?"

She sighed. "All right, but you're cleaning up after it." She dismounted and looped the two sets of reins over a nearby sapling.

Tom set Darin down on the riverbank, where he collapsed in a heap, coughing and sputtering. It looked like he'd swallowed half the river. He retched, and gripped the earth in both hands like he'd never let go.

His teeth chattered. "You shouldn't be here," he managed.

"We shouldn't?" Evie feigned puzzlement. "I could have sworn you said to follow closely and watch your back, which is what we've done."

"That's what I heard," Tom said.

"They got the wagon and horses." He looked at her, suddenly uncertain. "Harrison was there. Annette, she…"

"We saw," Evie said. She still didn't understand it. Annette and Harrison had been together for years. Thick as thieves. Always backing one another, not unlike her and Darin. She hated the woman as fire hated water, but she'd never have guessed Annette would betray him like that. Of course, what happened immediately after that was no surprise. Annette had been trying to kill Darin for years. "It doesn't matter now."

"Matters a little," Tom said. "We need to move."

Darin tried to stand, but only got as far as his knees. Tom hauled him up and held him steady. His legs had no strength. They half-carried him to where the horses were hitched. Evie untied her mount's reins and vaulted into the saddle. Tom didn't ask but heaved him into the saddle behind her. Darin's hands found her waist without any encouragement.

"See? He's not so bad," Evie said.

"Old habits," Darin muttered.

"We won't be able to ride far like this," Tom said.

She looked at Darin and saw that Tom was right. "I know a place not far from here."

"Can you get us in?"

"I believe so," she answered. *I just don't know what it'll cost me.*

CHAPTER FIFTY-THREE
Harlin Falls

Darin awoke in a dark, soft place that smelled of lilies. And roses. And dragon's eyes and lilac. A lovely bouquet of scents all mingled in his nose and teased his tired mind into wakefulness. The soft place in which he lay was unexpected. The last thing he remembered, Tom had plucked him out of the river and tossed him into a saddle behind Evie. He managed to get his hands around her, leaned into her back, and there the memories ended. This was a softness too pure and too uniform for camping. The air had a stillness to it. He was indoors. But not alone.

That realization made him force his eyes open, as little as he wanted to. He was in a large bed in a spacious, well-appointed room. It was completely unfamiliar, but there were little signs of wealth everywhere. The oil lamps, for one thing. All of them had wicks trimmed low, but there were *four*. Who had four oil lamps in one room? Rich people, that's who. Before he could stop himself, he let his senses reach out and they found cold metal everywhere. Gold plating on the sconces. Solid copper feet on a massive porcelain bathtub. There was silver, too, in fair quantities. Including a purse of cold spending metal in this very room. He knew those coins. Gods, the down payment. Somehow it had survived with him in the river.

When he'd jumped into the water, all he was thinking about was escaping from Harrison's men. Once the river had him, he'd thought that was it. He'd never have survived, were it not for Big Tom. And for Evie. After their rescue, he barely had time to speak a few words before the silver sickness took him. It was better and worse this time. Better because it seemed to hurt him less, but worse because of how close he'd come to enjoying the power.

Moments before, when the water kept pulling him down and his vision started to go black at the edges, his mind had gone to her. Evie. It wasn't because he thought he was dying, either. It was that he'd wasted the past few years of his life trying *not* to be with her. In that moment, his reasons had seemed foolish. Meaningless.

Now he found himself miraculously alive, and dry, and safe, in a room with her lying beside him. *I missed the sound of her breathing,* he realized. He caressed her side with the gentlest of touches so as not to wake her. She sighed. He brought his hand back with a twinge of regret, but she rolled over and her eyes were wide open.

"About time you woke up," she whispered.

"Where are we?"

"The keep at Harlin Falls. It's a barony in Fairhurst."

A barony. That explained the show of wealth. "How did you–"

"The baron knew my father."

Many barons had, but for one to receive Evie at his door and provide her with accommodations meant something. "How well?"

"Better than most." She glanced down, and plucked at some invisible thread in the linens. "We correspond occasionally."

They *corresponded* occasionally? Darin hadn't known Evie to keep in touch with anyone from her old life. Yet she never did anything without some purpose to it, so he felt like he should at least try to understand. "Evie–"

"He had offered to help me come back, if the opportunity presented itself. He would have spoken for me."

From that Darin gleaned two things. The first one, which didn't surprise him, was that Evie's goal was to make such a return to prominence. That's what drove her to be part of his crew and run her own little games on the side. The other thing was that she might have had help. By the way she spoke now, it seemed like that offer no longer stood. "But he won't now."

"*She* won't. The baron told his wife I was a distant acquaintance, a potentially valuable ally, and an ugly old woman." She cleared her throat. "Now that we've met in person, she knows that's not true."

"That you wouldn't be a powerful ally?"

She uttered a little gasp and jabbed him in the ribs with two fingers. He laughed despite the twitch of pain, and after a moment, she did too.

"Evie, I'm sorry," he said. "If I'd known this would cost you such an opportunity…"

"You'd have, what? Woken up and told me you'd sleep in the gutter?"

"I've slept in gutters before," he said, just a bit defensively.

"It's not your fault. I barely had my wits about me, too." She put a hand on Darin's cheek. It was so small and so incredibly soft, but there was strength beneath it. "I thought I'd lost you."

Her eyes said the rest. Darin didn't dare break away from them. His hand found the curve of her neck. He pulled her toward him. She let him do so. He could only screw this up by talking, so he kept quiet and closed his eyes. Her lips found his. He kissed her back, gently at first. When she didn't pull away, he kissed her harder. Pulled her more tightly against him. She twitched the linens aside and slid up against him, her body a fountain of warmth. He got both his arms around her. She put both hands on his chest and pushed him aside. That was a *no*. He had to respect it, as much as he didn't want to. He released her and laid back. Took a shaky breath or two. *She's right*, he told himself. *We shouldn't*. Not with the wine out there, and

Annette's men hunting them, and the balance to the Dame coming due. He hated that she was right. He was still arguing with himself about it when she climbed on top of him and kissed him again.

CHAPTER FIFTY-FOUR
Orphan Wagon

Kat didn't see a soul for the first three hours of driving her wagon east in Fairhurst. Not that she was particularly sneaky about her passage, or taking the kinds of forgotten backroads Darin would be trying on his way across Brycewold. The nameless hamlet just ahead, with smoke rising from its dozen chimneys, showed plenty of signs of life. There was movement in some of the windows as they trundled near in the bright orange wagon. She pulled back gently on the reins until the two mismatched horses slowed. They were, by her best guess, a retired racehorse and a plowhorse past her prime, but she hadn't enjoyed too many options. Imperial draft horses were simply too recognizable to take a chance keeping them. Luckily, she'd known a horse trader not far from the border who'd been all too happy to switch them out for whatever animals he had laying around. Literally. The first animal he'd tried to offer was a few days from death.

Kat had taken that opportunity to remind the trader that she not only knew how to spot a horse with the wasting disease, but had a number of friends in the area. Including the local constable, if memory served. The horses he'd offered after that brief conversation were somewhat better. The racehorse was a bit jumpy, and the plowhorse only knew one speed, but between them they could shoulder the weight of the wagon, the boys, and the barrels. These were stacked upright in the wagon in a tight rectangle with a piece of black-dyed canvas over them. Her job was the second most important one: getting all the equipment that implicated them in the wine heist home safely. Darin insisted on keeping it all for possible future use, no matter the risk. To be caught with a Groktar uniform, a wheelspike, and other bits of damning evidence would be hazardous, to say the least.

Even a country simpleton who'd heard the rumors and spotted the right combination of things in her wagon might put it all together. Hopefully no one would get close enough to see anything. The orange-painted sidewalls marked them as an orphan wagon. Kat hadn't seen one in a while, but such wagons used to ply the queendom backwaters to find homes for orphaned children.

Fittingly, Kat had instructed Abel and Timmy to ride on the canvas and look as unhealthy as possible. Both wore rag-sewn surcoats and were barefoot, having tucked their boots beneath the canvas to keep them out of view. Judging by the whispers and hoots of laughter, Kat strongly suspected they'd been trying to learn how to gamble with dice. The half-torn garments, simple as they were, continued to jump from one boy to the other.

"How long can we go bootless?" Timmy asked, as they trundled in toward the hamlet.

"Until we're back at the Rooster, and not a second longer."

"Aww," came the inevitable dual whines of protest.

"Someday you'll step on a swamp viper and thank me," Kat said. "Now, keep your heads down and try to look miserable."

As they rolled past the first of the thatched roof houses, she raised her voice. "Orphans! Orphans looking for homes!"

No response came from the shuttered houses.

"They're a bit scrawny, sure, but with three solid meals a day they'll be strong as bear cubs," she called. Judging by the wilted grain fields they'd passed, most of the villagers here probably didn't get two meals a day. It had been a hard, hot summer in this part of the queendom.

"Hale orphans, looking for homes!" she called.

The door of the fifth house cracked open. Abel and Timmy began coughing as instructed. Deep, wet coughs of someone with sickness in their lungs. The door snicked shut again. Kat hid her smile. They rolled on toward the last of the houses.

"Last call for orphans! Hungry boys looking to work!"

A curtain moved back into place at the last house, and then they were clear. The hunger comments nearly always worked. Times were tight, and few queendomers could afford taking on an extra mouth when the crops were dying in the fields.

They'd ridden past yet more barren fields and then continued on for half an hour when they came across the boy. The countryside had been rolling steadily by, and Kat was mid-daydream about what she'd do with her share of the silver.

"Miss Kat!" Timmy said suddenly. "Abel says there's a boy over there."

"Whoa now," Kat said, drawing up the horses. Were it not for Abel's young eyes, she'd have missed the boy for sure. He crouched in the shade of a half-dead conifer, his torn clothes blending almost perfectly with the bed of fallen needles. "Well, hello there."

The boy popped up, startled. Kat took him in at a glance. He had the look, all right. Wild eyes already looking for an escape route. Legs that trembled with nervous fear. Rags wrapped around his bare feet instead of proper shoes. And a gauntness to his core that told how long he'd gone without a good meal.

"It's all right," Kat said softly. "We won't hurt you."

The boy wavered, but still looked ready to bolt.

"My name's Kat. What's your name?"

"Bronny."

"Brawny, you say?" She lifted her eyebrows appreciatively. "Now there's a fitting name."

His lips twitched, though he didn't smile. "No, *Bronny*."

"My mistake, young fella. We were just about to stop for a bite. You hungry at all?"

"A little."

She dug an oil-wrapped package out of the burlap sack at her feet. "We've more than enough to share."

Her boys crowded up behind her, jostling one another for first pick. She had dried cherries and strips of hog meat in this package. The two scents blended together, one sweet, the other savory, in a strangely appealing aroma. Might even make for an interesting ale recipe.

Bronny tiptoed nearer while the boys got their shares. The aroma probably drew him. Spend enough days not eating and your sense of smell got especially strong. Kat still remembered what that was like. She offered him a scoop of meat and fruit with an open palm. "Go on, then."

He wavered a moment then darted forward to pluck it out of her hand. He retreated to his tree to eat it. The next bit she offered, he took and only retreated half as far. By the third helping, he was standing right beside the wagon. Kat passed a leather canteen of water back to the boys. Bronny eyed it with poorly hidden desire.

Abel shoved Timmy over to open up a spot on the canvas. "You can sit with us." Five words, bless his heart.

Bronny jumped right up and hunkered down beside them in the wagon. He accepted the canteen and drank it so fast, he choked. Abel slapped him on the back until he stopped coughing. His cheeks turned a furious pink, and he handed the canteen back.

"We're heading east today," Kat said. "Would you like to ride along for a while?"

Uncertainty warred with longing on Bronny's face. Then Timmy leaned over and whispered something – probably about the informal dice game – and the boy actually did smile.

"Okay," he said.

Just like that, she'd tamed another wild forgotten boy in this queendom. Saved him from a horrible fate, most likely, even if it wasn't permanent. Darin would undoubtedly throw a fit about adding another "stray" to the stables, but Kat wouldn't leave him behind. Not when she'd seen so many die before she could do anything about it. Besides, soon enough Darin would deliver the wine to Zora. Then they'd have all of the promised silver. There'd be more than enough to go around.

She took up the reins and began to urge the horses back into the road, but paused at the sound of hooves pounding toward them. Two horsemen came first. Behind them trundled a wagon pulled by two stout draft horses. Whatever they were hauling, it was heavy. She nudged her own wagon out of the road as far as it would go, since the group coming up clearly was in a hurry.

The horses and wagon thundered past with a great billowing cloud of dust. Through it, Kat managed a glimpse of the cargo – dark oak barrels branded with the seal of the Jewel Empire – and her heart sank. That could only be *the* wagon, only Darin didn't have it any longer. The well-armed riders accompanying it did not seem in the mood for questions. She kept her mouth shut and snapped her eyes forward until they were well ahead.

"What's wrong, Miss Kat?" Timmy asked.

"Something's not right." She snapped the reins twice to get the wagon moving.

Timmy flailed to steady himself as the wagon lurched back and forth. "Where are you taking us?"

"Back into trouble."

CHAPTER FIFTY-FIVE
Hollow Legs

Kat felt like an entire inch of road dust had coated her face. The wagon with the stolen wine had pushed on for leagues without relent. This made them easy to follow, as the dust was hard to miss. The weather had grown hot and the air thick, untouched by even the slightest breeze. The boys were complaining about the rough ride. Apparently, it had thrown the dicing game into shambles. And Kat's own horses looked to be at death's door when the wine wagon finally stopped for the night. The no-name village straddled the queen's highway, perhaps half a dozen buildings and three times that many thatched roof cottages. Dusk had nearly fallen, so the few locals still in sight hurried about their business. Predictably, the wine wagon and its armed guards took over the stableyard of the village's only inn, a stout two-story job with a weather-dimpled tin roof. There were four or five of them, as best she'd been able to glean on the way. Two outriders, and at least two more on the wagon itself. Possibly another horseman, though she couldn't be sure through all the dust.

Kat had halted the weary horses just outside the village so as not to draw attention. She emptied half her canteen into each animal's feed bag and watched the stables as they drank. The men with the wagon weren't Groktar. She knew that in her bones. For one thing, these soldiers left their animals harnessed to the wagon, even though it was clear they were settling in overnight. Maybe they hated animals or wanted a quick escape route. And then, unbelievably, they all walked in the door to the inn. Leaving the wagon and its precious barrels more or less unprotected outside. She couldn't exactly abscond with a heavy wagon and two strange horses as they were, but their casual attitude made her feel bold.

She climbed back aboard her own wagon and flicked the reins, urging the tired horses into motion again. There was nothing to do but keep a stately pace and pull into the open space near the wine wagon as if she were another traveler stopping for the night.

"This is madness, that's what it is," Kat muttered to herself.

"What's that, Miss Kat?" Timmy asked, popping his head up into view.

"Nothing." She eyed the barrels in the wine wagon, which were stacked neatly but not otherwise secured. The chain that normally held them fast was piled in a jumble in the corner.

Timmy already had his eyes on the building, and gasped. "Are we going to stay here?"

"Not exactly," Kat said.

"Aww."

Kat ignored the boy's whine and wracked her brain for an idea. What would Darin do in this situation? She lacked his talents, and she had no means to contact him or the others. That was assuming that everyone was all right. Darin wouldn't have given these brigands the wine without a fight. The thought chilled her. She shook her head. Nothing mattered, except here was the wine and an opportunity to do something about it. Step one, take stock of available assets. She had herself, the boys, two exhausted horses, several casks of Red Rooster ale, and various costumes from their exploits to the west. No help there.

Timmy, meanwhile, sat up and rubbed his eyes. He glanced over, saw the wine wagon, and his mouth fell open. "Is that–"

"Hush, you," Kat hissed. "Keep your eyes front." She took

a deep breath, nodded to herself, and stood. "I'm going in for a while. If I don't come right back, here's what I want you to do."

Soon after, Kat barged through the front door of the inn's common room in her best imitation of Evie. There was no bouncer by the door, but her entrance caught the attention of the barkeep, an elderly fellow who'd just served drinks to the wine brigands – that's what Kat had begun calling them in her mind, at least. They'd taken over the largest round table in the establishment, weapons plainly visible, and newly delivered tankards of ale already well on their way to being consumed. The place was dimly lit; perhaps one table in three held an oil lamp, and those in view had their wicks trimmed as low as possible. The air smelled faintly of smoke and desperation. It showed, too, in how quickly the barkeep hurried over to serve her.

"Pleasant evening!" he said, perhaps a bit too earnestly. He was an older fellow, stoop-shouldered and moving with a notable limp. "Are you drinking tonight, m'lady?"

"I certainly hope so," Kat answered, letting the *m'lady* pass without protest. "Got a little something for you. And your guests, perhaps." She heaved the cask up onto the bar, letting it thud down loudly. The noise drew the eyes of the brigands at their table; they were watching.

"What's that?"

"Red Rooster ale. Strongest brew you'll find in the queendom."

"Never heard of it, I'm afraid."

Kat put on a look of confusion. "Are you sure? Red Rooster, I said."

"I heard you." The barkeep wiped his forehead with a filthy rag. "Times are tight, though, and I'm hardly able to afford–"

"What's that you got?" called one of the brigands.

Kat met the barkeep's eyes. "Nothing up front, and we split the coppers?" she asked quietly.

"Done." The man looked back to his customers. "This here's Red Rooster ale, just come in. You've heard of it?"

The brigands consulted one another, and shook their heads.

Kat put on a scandalized expression. "Never even heard of Red Rooster ale!" She hooked a thumb in the direction of their table. "Reckon they're not from around here."

Wood scraped on wood behind her. Heavy footsteps approached.

"What's that you said?"

Kat turned just enough to get a side-glance at him. It was the red-haired fellow with the beard and mustache, the one who'd been torturing his mount with real spurs for the last few leagues. He was built like a brawler. Probably had five stone on her.

"I said, reckon you're not from around here." She turned back to the barkeep. "Best keep serving them the usual stuff."

The brawler leaned against the bar, just a shade inside her personal space. "What's special about Red Rooster ale?"

"It's stronger than you're accustomed to, I'll wager."

The brawler drained his half-filled mug in a few large gulps and slapped the empty vessel down on the bar, causing the barkeep to jump. "You don't know what I'm accustomed to."

Kat stared at him, aware that this meant looking up at a rather uncomfortable angle. Then she made an inviting gesture. "By all means, then. In fact, it's on me." She slid four coppers across the bar. The barkeep didn't miss a beat. He swept the coins into his apron pocket, hammered a tap into the cask, and filled two mugs.

Kat took her mug and raised it in casual salute to the bruiser. He took up his mug as well. By the time he drained it – with hardly a grimace, it must be said – he was surprised to find her mug already empty and on the bar. "About time," she said.

He looked at it, then back at her. "You couldn't do that again."

Kat shrugged. "Last place buys next."

To the brute's credit, he did side-eye her once, as if some deep-buried instinct whispered that maybe this was some kind of hustle. Then he untied a heavy purse at his belt and dumped several coins onto the counter. Some were copper, but most were gold. "Keep 'em coming," he told the barkeep.

Kat lifted her mug, saluted him again, and drained it in one long pull. Her opponent required two – he apparently felt the need to breathe while drinking, which gave her an edge – and her mug beat his to the bar a second time. He guffawed, more amused than offended at this point, and the commotion drew his companions to the bar. They were all four men, unshaven but otherwise bearing no resemblance to one another save the coating of road dust. Which, to be fair, wasn't half as thick as the mess Kat sported given that she'd traveled downwind most of the way. The brawler seemed to be their leader; with his encouragement they all plunked down coins on the bar and made it a group competition.

Kat lost the fourth round on purpose – winning every round would only make them suspicious. This brought a lot of cheering and chest-puffing on the part of the men. For her part, Kat plunked ten coppers on the soaking wet bar and demanded another go. The men were only too happy to oblige her.

At one point, just after she'd won the ninth round, the brawler gave her a serious look. "Where you putting all that ale, lady?"

"Right down the gullet, same as you," Kat answered.

"It's like you got a hollow leg or something." He shook another few coins out of his purse into one hand and tossed them carelessly on the bar.

It was just the two of them left by this point. The others had returned to their table, only to pass out. The barkeep swept up the coins, setting aside two of them into a little pile with a clandestine grin at Kat. He must not be used to this level of business. He filled their mugs quickly and slid them back across.

The room was not quite spinning yet, so Kat knew she could handle another draught. The brawler might not, though. He looked at his newly-filled mug as a swimmer does a circling dogfish.

"I'm feeling a little off," Kat said quickly. "Think this one might be your round."

His face resolved, and he picked up his mug. Kat did the same. They looked at one another and brought the mugs up. He tilted his head back and gulped. Kat did the same, but not as fast as she could have. He slammed his empty mug down with a flourish, two seconds before Kat finished. "S'mine!"

Kat set her mug down more gently. "You got me that time!"

"About ti–" he broke off mid-sentence. His brow furrowed. Then he tilted over and dropped like a stone to the damp floor, sending his stool tumbling.

Kat shook her head. *About time is right.* She turned to the barkeep, who stood with his mouth hanging open. "How'd we do?"

The barkeep recovered, swept the set-aside pile of coppers off his low table, and poured them into her hands. Thirty or forty of them. "Lady, you sure as hell can drink."

Kat tucked the coins into her purse. "One of the few things I'm good at."

The barkeep began prying his tap out of her keg, but she waved him off. "Keep it. Maybe your customers will like a little something different."

He smiled. "Very kind of you. Have to admit, I'm a bit curious." He found an empty mug, filled it halfway, and tried a pull. His eyes bulged, and he seemed to choke. Probably tried to drink it too fast.

"Best pace yourself." She stood, and the room did start to spin a little bit then. She took a breath and steadied herself before stepping carefully over the brawler on her way to the door. Full darkness and a sky brimming with stars greeted her outside. There was no moon to speak of.

Timmy's head popped up from the wagon. "That was a while."

"Not as long as it felt," Kat said. "You get things taken care of?"

"The barrels were heavy."

And worth their weight in silver. Kat recognized the casks that now waited in the wide square wagon behind the draft horses. She almost hated to see them go, but the stars started rotating to the left, so she focused her attention on climbing into the wagon seat. Even in her state, she could feel how heavy the wagon was with its new cargo. How little it shook when she put her weight on it. "Remember how you're always asking to drive the wagon?"

"You always say no," Timmy said.

"Tonight you get your chance."

He hopped up into the driver's seat before she'd even finished talking. "Wait till you see how good I am!"

Kat found her hat under the seat and dragged it down onto her head. "Wake me at sunrise."

CHAPTER FIFTY-SIX
Empty Hands

There were few things in life Darin enjoyed more than cresting the gentle ridge from where he could see the roof of the Red Rooster. Just as leaving for some distant locale to run a job gave him a stomach ache, coming home brought a sense of jubilation. Especially on those jobs where he'd nearly gone to meet the Four. This one sure qualified. Metallurgy might have saved him from Harrison and Annette, but it also nearly killed him in the river. Were it not for Tom and Evie's quiet disobedience of his instructions, he'd be a floating corpse right now.

Evie. The night he'd spent with her still felt like a dream. A vivid, perfect dream that he found himself reliving several times on the long ride back. Maybe that was why he rode a bit closer to Evie than usual, and why he kept looking at her. She'd even catch him doing it, and give him a little smile. As if she were remembering the same thing. Of course, that meant trouble, too. As much as Darin enjoyed it, he also hadn't forgotten the numerous good reasons that they hadn't stayed together. Two jealous types who spent their lives charming others out of things probably weren't meant to be a couple. One of them would have ended up dead for certain.

They were both a bit older now. More experienced. Knew each other better. Part of him said that mattered, while the other part said that people didn't change. He and Evie hadn't spoken about it yet. Big Tom's silent but persistent presence guaranteed that. It wasn't like they wanted to keep things secret from him – Darin privately suspected that the big man knew a lot more than he let on – but Evie had been raised in proper society where conversations about private topics had a time and a place. Both of which had nearly arrived when he first spotted the roof of the Rooster. Evie would be wanting the conversation. Wanting to know what things meant, or worse, where they were going.

Who was he kidding? She'd be telling him, not asking him. And that was probably why he felt in no rush to find out. If they'd succeeded on the job and brought back a fortune in dreamwine, things would have been different. She wouldn't have to associate with so many gentleman callers, whose very existence drove Darin to near madness. He wouldn't have to focus all his attention on finding and planning jobs. With the take from the wine, they could have just... been. Existed. Perhaps even together.

Of course, that was impossible now. A week ago, Darin, Evie, and Tom had crossed into Brycewold at a provincial checkpoint that was friendly to the gray shades of the law. For a small handful of gold coins, Darin learned that Harrison's crew of mother-killers hadn't entered Brycewold, at least on the same road.

Annette's crew, he corrected himself. He hadn't watched his old enemy bleed out, but he knew a killing blow when he saw one. Whoever's crew it was, they could be anywhere. Maybe they'd delivered to Zora already and collected the full payout. If they hadn't, though, it raised some difficult questions. Zora certainly expected *someone* to deliver the prize. If no shipment came, she'd go out looking for it. And the fact that she knew where to find the Red Rooster made Darin's back itch with discomfort.

In fact, it was a small relief to ride up to the stableyard and not find her there waiting.

The place was quiet, but in a good way. Darin could smell the hops blooming from Kat's garden. No matter what, it was good to be home. He and Tom dismounted, but Evie did not.

"Evie?" Darin asked.

"I'll be back later." She gave Darin a look that said *we'll talk then,* and cantered back out into the lane.

They watched her ride off. Darin looked at Tom, whose face betrayed no emotion. "I'm not sure if I should be relieved or offended."

Tom put a hand out for his reins. "I'll take her for you."

"You don't have to do that." Everyone took care of their own mount after a journey; that was the unspoken deal.

"I don't mind."

"Thanks."

He took both animals around to the stables, which left Darin to walk in the front door and check on business in the common room. The door was open, so the familiar smells of the place washed over him before he walked in. A hint of sour ale, a dash of smoke, and even the rare but delightful scent of freshly baked bread. Gods, but it was a relief to be home.

Seraphina stood by the hearth, stoking the fire and humming to herself. "So, you're alive after all."

"Sorry we didn't send word. Too much exposure."

"I had a feeling you'd see the–" She trailed off when she turned and saw him. "Lord and Lady, you reek of metallurgy."

"What?"

"You used it. I can smell it on you."

He considered denying it, but there was little point in that. "I had no choice."

"What happened?"

"Harrison." He told her about the ambush on the road, making his escape, and then almost drowning in the river.

"How did it feel to use your talents when you needed them?"

"Like giving in to a bad habit," he said.

"Pshaw!" She slapped his arm. "You enjoyed it, and you know it."

"Really didn't have time to enjoy it. I was too busy trying to stay alive."

"Do you still have the silver you drew upon?"

"Yes, but we need it to pay the Dame."

"That's too bad. Now that you're open to using your abilities, you need to start looking for your limits. How much power you can draw in, and how quickly you use it up."

"Hold on, now. That was a one-time thing. I never said I was going to start doing this regularly."

"Know what happens to the kid who sneaks in and plays with his father's sword whenever it suits him, without ever learning how to use it?"

"I wouldn't know. My father didn't get a sword."

"I'm aware of that. But you know what I'm trying to say."

That I'm dangerous if I don't learn. "Doesn't mean I agree."

"You have a talent, Darin. One that's useful, especially to someone in your line of work."

"That's exactly what worries me." It was too tempting to rely on metallurgy to do the things that took great skill and practice. The second he started to rely on it, that's when it would betray him. "It's too useful."

"And too dangerous for me to let you bumble around on your own."

"This is starting to sound like a conversation we've already had."

"Yeah, well, maybe this time you won't be so bullheaded about it."

"If I say I'll consider it, will you leave off?" He had a lot to do before Kat and the others got back. Starting with a bath. Maybe ending with a bath, too.

The door banged open. It startled Darin, but lacked the sheer brazenness of an Evie entrance. No, it was someone emulating Evie. He looked and noticed two things. First that Kat had made it back a full day earlier than expected, which was both impressive and a bit disconcerting. Second, she looked like she'd either lost a fight or caught the swamp sickness.

"I'm back," she announced, her voice sounding more gravelly than usual.

"You look…" Darin began, and then couldn't find the right word.

"Like you got run over by your own wagon," Seraphina offered.

Kat grunted. "Red Rooster ale will do that to you."

"Where are the boys?"

"In the stables. They wanted to see Tom first, no offense. Plus, they're telling him to get a weapon."

A sliver of worry invaded Darin's tired mind. "Why? Were you followed?"

"Don't think so, but I've got a wagon full of barrels out in the yard and I don't want them stolen."

Darin managed to hide his smile. "I'm not sure how much security is required for Red Rooster ale…"

"What about imperial dreamwine?"

Oh, right. That. Darin almost didn't have the heart to tell her. "I'm sorry, Kat. Harrison and Annette ambushed me on the way back. We lost the dreamwine."

"I noticed. Lucky for you, the boys and I picked it up on *our* way back."

What's she on about? Maybe her visible affliction had touched her mind as well. Darin didn't want to argue with her, and didn't dare let his hopes rise. So he walked outside himself for a look. Kat's wagon was in the yard like she said. The horses must already be in the stables. It did look like the barrels were piled higher than Darin remembered. He flipped back the burlap… and found himself staring at the crest of the Jewel Empire.

"Gods above," he whispered, and thrust the burlap back into place. Back in the common room, he found only Seraphina waiting. "Where'd she go?"

"Upstairs to sleep it off. Said she'd give you the full tale later," Seraphina said. "Did she really–"

"She did. I've no idea how, but she's saved us." Darin could scarcely believe his luck.

"Would you like a drink?"

"I'll pour it myself, thank you," he said, remembering her tendency to *accidentally* put sleeproot into things when she thought he needed rest.

"So untrusting, Darin." She *tsked*.

"Justifiably so, in this case. I feel bad drinking alone, though. Maybe Tom fancies a nip."

"He'll be seeing to Kat's horses for a while."

"Probably true. And Evie's already–"

"Convalescing on her own," she finished for him.

He laughed and shook his head. "How do you always *know*?"

"All of you have your patterns. Even if you didn't, I've got–"

"Talents of your own," Darin said. He could play the game, too. An odd thought struck him then. *We all have our patterns.* "So what's my pattern?"

"What do you mean?"

"You said we all have them. What's my pattern for when a job is over?"

"You?" Seraphina cackled. "You're all about subtlety. You break up the crew so as not to attract attention. You take the loot yourself, and don't trust anything but a wide country backroad to get home. Which is here, by the way. Whenever you're done with a job, this is always where you point your wagon."

She was right on every point. Dead on, in fact, which was more than a little disturbing. "How do you know all this?" She'd never come on a job, and though he wouldn't put it past her to do a bit of eavesdropping, this was more than you could guess from bits and pieces.

"I know *you*. The way you do things, boy, is governed by how you see the world."

"So I'm predictable, in other words," Darin said.

"Yes. But the good news is, you're only predictable to those who've known you a long time."

That should have been a relief, as the people who met that definition were on a very short list. And in that moment, one of them made a cruel, clever kind of sense.

CHAPTER FIFTY-SEVEN
Barging In

Tom had crossed this river a number of times, but never paid it particular mind. It was too wide and too fast to ford in most places. He remembered a bridge location or two, but Kat had them all marked on a parchment map of the Old Queendom. Gods, she'd been *everywhere*. Knew people everywhere, too. That's how she was able to arrange a boat on short notice.

The wide barge they were after had anchored for the night in a slow-moving eddy off the main current. Inaccessible from shore, but an easy target for a boat coming down with the current. Tom eased one of the oars into the water to make sure they'd slip right up to the stern.

"Be ready," Darin whispered, peering through the darkness from his perch in the bow.

Evie shifted her position next to him, hands moving to check her weapons. Kat touched the bolt loaded in her crossbow to make sure it was snug against the string. Tom hoped she wouldn't have to use it, though she claimed it wouldn't be a problem. He believed her, in the sense that she knew how to shoot. Whether she'd be able to stomach putting a bolt through a man was another story. Then again, it was her own crossbow.

She wouldn't need it as long as Tom did his job. Which depended on the information Darin had given him. There was little time to worry about this, though. The swift current brought them up against the barge. Darin used his bare hands to land them against the much larger craft. While he held it, Tom crept along the middle of the boat and vaulted over the rail.

He landed on the balls of his feet and froze, watching the deck. The lanterns strung along every ten paces or so cast weak pools of light. No sign that he'd been detected, but there would be at least a few guards about. He drew the banded flail from his belt. It was a stout but simple weapon, a short piece of wood attached by three links of chain to a longer shaft. Good for in-close fighting, and quiet if you knew what you were doing. He moved along the port side, keeping to the pools of darkness between lanterns. He found the first pair of guards just past the reardeck. Two swordsmen in mail and leather were making a slow circuit of the deck. They had their backs to him. He crept closer, moving on his toes.

The two guards – both of them men, both of them nearly as tall as he was – paused and conferred in low voices. Tom slid into the shadow behind a column of stacked crates. A good thing, too. The men did an about-face and started moving back the other way. Smart. Unpredictable routes made a patrol that much harder to foil. It was only dumb luck that brought these two right back past Tom's hiding place. He stepped out once they'd passed and walloped both of them in the back of the head with the flail. They went down like fainting goats. He dragged them into the shadows beside the crates, then rapped three times on the rail to signal the all-clear.

Leather creaked behind him.

Years of hard-won instinct made him roll down and to one side. Steel clanged against the hull where he'd stood a moment before. It looked like a throwing-dagger but he had no time to look. The moment he came to his feet, an assailant in mail and leather charged him. Too dark to see the weapon. He blocked the first slash by instinct. A metal weapon. One-handed. Might be a knife. What fool would attack someone his size with one blade? The realization came a second too late, with a lance of fire in his shoulder. A second weapon. Damn, he should have known. He whipped the flail around, but his adversary danced back.

They circled one another. Once Tom got a better look at his opponent, he realized two things. First, he wasn't facing a man, but a woman. That made her Areana. The enforcer. She wore leather and mail like she was born in it, and moved with a catlike grace. Second, she held fighting irons in each hand. Each of them about as long as Tom's forearm. The one in her right hand had a hook at the top to catch a weapon or yank a man off his feet. The one in her left hand was the pointed killing blade. Its tip glistened wetly.

His shoulder still burned, and the muscle felt like it was stiffening. He lashed out with the flail, but she leaned out of the way. Biding her time. She'd wait until he could barely swing the thing, and then finish the job. He'd no sooner thought that than she attacked. Blade first, then hook iron. She twisted it as he parried the second attack. They had another exchange just like it. Blade, hook, and twist. Each time he knocked her attacks aside and felt a little pull of resistance. She must be trying to catch the chain. With the right timing she could wrench the flail free of his grip. *Darin said she's a good fighter, but* damn.

They circled each other again. Tom spotted a moving shadow near the rail behind her. That meant Evie or Kat getting ready to board. Areana didn't have the angle yet, but if she heard... He couldn't take the chance. He launched into an attack. Swung hard and fast, trying to get around her guard. He landed a glancing blow on her side, crunching mail against the jerkin beneath. It had to hurt, but she gave no sign of it. Tough as old leather, this one. The ache in his shoulder became a searing pain. He gritted his teeth against it as Areana countered and tried to hook his flail again. This time, he let the chain dangle. She twisted the blade, caught it, and yanked it backward to disarm him. He didn't fight her. He let go of the flail. She stumbled back, off balance. Tried to fend him off with the other blade. He slapped it aside and slammed a mailed fist into her face. It snapped her head back and sent her sprawling to the deck. She landed in a heap and lay still.

Darin vaulted the rail, with Evie and Kat right behind him. "Quickly, now." He glanced down at Areana and paused. "Is that your flail?"

"She wanted to borrow it." Tom bent down to check Areana. She was still breathing, but she'd be out for a while. Still, no sense in leaving her armed. He collected all three weapons and hurried to follow Darin into the barge's interior.

When Darin spotted the Dame, she was pouring tea. It was such a Dame thing to do. Middle of the night, armed party boarding your private barge, and you decide to serve tea. Only two things ruined the facade. First, the fact that she'd removed the silk coverlets from a few of the birdcages. Her favorites, perhaps. The birds within chittered and flitted about, betraying the nerves of their owner. Second, the Dame wore a sleeping dress. Ornate and almost certainly tailored to fit her, it was nevertheless the simplest garment Darin had ever seen her wear. And he guessed that people in the queendom who'd seen the Dame's nightdress numbered less than ten.

"Evening, Darin," she said. "Fancy a cup?"

"Thank you, Dame, but I'm good," he said.

The Dame glanced up and spotted Evie. "You brought a friend, I see. Perhaps she's thirsty."

"She's not–"

"Actually, Darin," Evie cut in, "I can speak for myself. And yes, I'd love a cup, thank you."

Darin wanted to shout at her that it was a foolish risk to take anything the Dame offered in this situation. Instead, all he could do was look on while Evie accepted a delicate teacup. The Dame pretended not to notice the long dagger on each hip. Instead, the two women eyed each other over the rim, blew on the tea to cool it, and then both took a sip.

Evie nodded appreciatively. "Bergamot?"

"Indeed." The Dame smiled. "You must be Evie."

"Must I?"

"You're a woman of good breeding, as they say. Last time I checked, Darin had only one in his crew."

Evie took another sip, apparently enjoying the tea. Or Darin's discomfort. "Takes one to know one."

"So it does."

Big Tom's arrival offered Darin a brief respite from this inexplicable torture.

"Any other guards?" Darin asked him quietly.

"Two. They were on break."

Darin nodded. If they'd offered Tom any problems, he would have said so. "What about the oarsmen?" He'd never laid eyes on the men belowdecks who rowed the barge upstream, but he imagined there were at least ten or twelve. This gambit relied on them not being able-bodied fighting men.

"Chained to their oars," Tom said.

Something in his tone gave weight to those four words. He not only disapproved, but despised it. Probably something to do with the big man's own upbringing in the Scatters.

At least I was right about them not being fighters. Still, Darin reminded himself that the Dame was capable of much worse. If this went poorly, he'd be lucky to end up chained to one of her oars below.

The Dame gave Tom a cursory glance. She'd know who he was, certainly, and she didn't need to state the obvious. She did look back at him, though, and frowned at his belt, where he'd tucked Areana's fighting irons. That was it. A little frown, a brief dissatisfaction that her most loyal lieutenant might be dead.

That, more than anything, steeled Darin's resolve.

"At the risk of seeming ungracious, may I ask what brings you to my barge at this hour?" the Dame asked.

"Needed to talk to you," Darin said.

"There are couriers."

"This seemed like a good conversation to have in person."

"I hope you haven't come all this way to ask for more time to make good on what you owe."

"Not exactly. I'm here to let you know that we're square."

The Dame's eyebrows lifted. "Is there a large purse of coin that you're perhaps forgetting to hand over?"

"The Eskirk job was probably our finest work," Darin said. "Even half of what we carried out of there would have set us up for years. It was a good take."

"And a major investment on my part," said the Dame.

"I remember. We both had a lot riding on it. The heist itself went better than I could have hoped. Then everything went to hell on our way home. A silver witch caught me in the harbor, and a series of highwaymen shook down Evie and Tom on their way back."

"I believe I made my position clear when you told me this the first time."

"You did. And of course, I agreed to make good on what we owed. Which would be all but impossible, except another lucrative scheme came our way. Imperial dreamwine."

"For your sake, I hope this story ends with a big score," said the Dame.

"In a manner of speaking. We boosted the dreamwine. No one has ever done that before."

"Good." The Dame set down her teacup on a lace-covered table. "When can I expect payment?"

"Yeah, about that. Another crew intercepted me on the way home. Took all of the cargo. And nearly my head."

"So, you're broke again. That's what you came all the way here to say?" A dangerous undercurrent had entered the Dame's tone.

"The thing is, I couldn't help but realise how familiar it all seemed. We pulled off a daring heist, only to be robbed of everything on our way home. Once is bad luck. Twice begins to feel like a pattern."

"Maybe you're losing your touch."

"Or maybe someone's setting me up," Darin said. "Someone who knows me and how I think. It wouldn't be the first time someone seemed to know more than they should. Our new client, who calls herself Zora, knows a lot about us and our past. Things no one should know."

"What's your point?"

"My point, Dame, is that the only one other than myself who knows all those things… is you." *Other than Evie, of course, but she doesn't count.*

The Dame stared at him flat-eyed for a moment, her face unreadable. "That sounds like an accusation."

He held her gaze. "It *is* an accusation."

"Darin, do you have any concept of how much coin passes through my enterprise in any given month?"

He didn't just have a concept. He could have told her *to the coin* how much silver lay neatly stacked belowdecks, and in the trunks at the bow. "A lot, I'm guessing."

"More than you can possibly imagine. The amount you owe me is a teardrop in this river, compared to what I already have."

"I thought about that," Darin said. "Doesn't make sense for you to throw me to the wolves over your take on a couple of jobs."

"And then I explained to Darin that money isn't everything," Evie added, in a perfectly sweet voice.

The Dame gave her a cool look. "You'd know."

Evie's grip tightened on her teacup.

Darin thought it best to break in before the cup shattered and she tried to cut the Dame with the largest fragment. "So we decided that the only thing we have is the imperial dreamwine."

"The only thing you *had*, you mean," said the Dame. "Harrison and his crew have seen to that, haven't they?"

Got you. Darin paused to make sure he watched every detail in the Dame's face. "A fair point. But I never said it was Harrison."

The Dame pinched her lips together in a tiny movement most people would miss. "You always were such a clever boy."

Gods, we were right. Part of Darin still didn't believe it. Another part of him hated that it was true. "Why–" His voice started to break, and he took a breath. "Why did you even bring us into this, if you intended for us to fail?"

"Because I knew you had the best chance of succeeding," she said briskly. "Harrison is a useful dog, but he lacks a certain… finesse."

"Yeah, well, he's not going to be much use to you anymore. He's dead."

The Dame's brow furrowed. She opened her mouth to speak, then shut it again. She really didn't know.

"Annette killed him," Darin said.

"Foolish girl," muttered the Dame. "Why would she go and do that?"

"Because Harrison finally started to listen. Makes me think you didn't want men like him knowing what you're up to."

"That is unfortunate. It seems I'll soon spend my time finding *two* new crew leaders instead of one."

"Cost of doing business, or so I'm told. But don't go searching for my replacement just yet. I'm still breathing."

"For the moment." She must have seen something in his face then because she laughed. "Come on, Darin. You've got no leverage here. You lost the silver, and you lost the wine."

"We have you." Even saying that, Darin felt the weakness of his words. He didn't have the stones to cut her throat and throw her in the river, and that's what it would take. Besides, there was no guarantee that whoever replaced her wouldn't be worse.

The Dame smiled at him. "Again, for the moment." She knew him too well.

But she doesn't know everything. Like the fact that Kat had taken back the dreamwine. Still, he couldn't afford to have the Dame's agents after him as well. "Here's how it's going to go. We're square for everything, starting now. We keep anything we got from the dreamwine heist. We'll continue working for you, but with a few changes to our arrangement."

"Such as?"

"I get to bring Big Tom along when I come here."

Her eyes flickered to Tom, and this time they lingered on the fighting irons. "If you think that someone who's killed Areana will live long enough to–"

"He didn't kill her," Darin interrupted. He didn't need to add that Tom very well could have. "You will order Areana to return the courtesy. You'll also keep Annette and her crew on their side of the deal line. Last but not least, your take of our earnings is now one sixth."

The Dame stared at him for a long moment. If she agreed, they could all move past it. If not, then this might end in fire and blood. "One fifth," she said.

"One *sixth*," Darin said firmly. "But that can stay between us." After all, she had other crews to run. None of them needed to know if the Red Rooster crew got a better deal.

"Done."

Darin breathed for what felt like the first time. Even Tom seemed to relax.

Evie kept her eyes on the Dame. "Darin, how do we know she won't come after us the moment we leave this barge?"

"Oh, if I get even the faintest whiff of a threat in our territory, I'll start killing hostages," he said.

"You don't have any hostages," the Dame said.

"Didn't I tell you? We're taking your birds."

It was the first time he'd seen the Dame look surprised, and he truly enjoyed it.

CHAPTER FIFTY-EIGHT
Return to Eskirk

Evie hated the palace at Eskirk nearly as much as she hated coming here alone. Darin might normally have played the part of a gentleman chaperone, but there was too much chance someone would recognize him from the duel after the gala. She loved Kat and Tom like siblings, but one was too rough and the other simply too large to blend in among society's elite. That's exactly what one would encounter here, too. Eskirk was the true bastion of power in the queendom, which was both why she had to come here and why she might find it difficult to leave.

Fifteen years ago, before her family's ignominious fall, her mother might have been invited to visit. Sometimes Evie still daydreamed about what that would have been like, arriving in their black-lacquered carriage at Eskirk's front gate. Letting the pale white horses canter down the long, winding drive up to the front entrance, where a liveried doorman would greet them and ask their names. Walking at her mother's side up the elegant sweeping staircase to the massive wooden door. Hearing the Eskirk banners flapping in the wind while still more butlers took their riding jackets and showed them in for refreshments.

Half a year ago, she'd come in the back entrance as a temporary serving girl. She'd arrived on foot by the stables, and been searched twice by frowning guardsmen before she set foot on the property. Then she'd been handed servants' garb and an apron, and ordered to get dressed and find the steward to begin her shift. They expected her to work ten hours on her feet without rest, all for a single silver drachm. In the end, she did work for most of the event, though she found far more lucrative compensation glittering on the bodices of useless waifs with more money than sense.

Her visit to Eskirk today might involve less pageantry but it carried just as much risk. Maybe more. Despite what she'd told Darin, there was no guarantee that she'd gain an audience. She made him hand over a final piece of good parchment that she knew he'd been hoarding, and took special care in writing the letter. Only the gods knew how many hands this might pass through before the duchess read it. She kept it vague. She had information of significant value, and she was offering it for free. She signed the note with her full name. Her *true* name. She hadn't signed it in a long time, but her hand remembered.

Then there was nothing to do but wait. She couldn't force the duchess to grant her an audience.

She sat on a wooden bench in the shade of a little veranda outside the palace's main gate. The fact that the duchess had built such accommodations suggested that she took pleasure in making would-be callers wait outside. By early afternoon, the weather grew hot enough that she'd started to sweat into the silk of her third-best gown. She might have to try again tomorrow, which meant she'd have to find someone in Eskirk who could sell her a nice piece of parchment. She'd just stood to make her way down toward the town proper when a manservant came out of the palace to fetch her.

At last. She shouldered the bulky satchel with its fragile contents and followed him.

This did not mean that she'd get to see the duchess, of course. She reminded herself of that as the man led her through the great door and into the palace proper. It all depended on the next few moments, whether she was shown to an anteroom to meet some nameless functionary, or into the inner sanctum for the lady herself. For a brief moment, she had the horrible thought that they might bring her to meet the steward from the gala. He probably wouldn't recognize her, dressed as she was as a fine lady of the court, but you never knew. Some men memorized faces like Darin recalled silver coins.

So it was a great relief when the manservant led her into a sitting room that bustled with a half-dozen seamstresses and the unmistakable presence of the duchess herself.

She was a graceful woman, gray-haired but elegantly attired in a silk brocade blouse over tight breeches. Her patrician features still held the tautness of youth, and there was vigor to her movements. She paced back and forth, supervising the work on what appeared to be a large banner with her house sigil on a field of gold. The manservant announced Evie and withdrew, closing the doors as he did.

Evie dropped into a curtsy and made sure it was perfect. "Thank you for seeing me, your grace."

For a moment they looked at one another over the snick-snick of the scissors in six pairs of hands. Evie dropped her gaze.

"You sent an intriguing letter," said the duchess. She made a sideways glance at one of the seamstresses. "Straight lines, Giselle. Yes, just like that."

"Perhaps I've come at a bad time," Evie said, knowing quite well that she had not. The duchess had sent for her on purpose and at this very moment. Still, it was the polite thing to say.

The duchess dismissed it with a wave. "This is the least busy I've been all day."

Evie let her gaze fall to the banner. "That's a lovely color, your grace."

"I wanted silver, but I won't pay what the cloth merchants were asking." She put her back to the sewing and gave Evie her full attention. "So. You are Evie Garraway."

"Yes, your grace."

"I knew a family by that name. Quite successful, once upon a time."

"Once upon a time," Evie agreed.

"But no longer."

"No."

"Still, that's a name not easily forgotten."

Evie forgot herself for a moment, and snorted with grim amusement. "Tell that to my father's friends." She remembered who she was addressing then, and could have kicked herself for such foolishness.

The duchess offered a faint smile. "What happened?"

"He loved his card games a little too much," Evie said, summarizing the shock and embarrassment of a slow descent into poverty in a single, clean sentence.

The duchess shook her head. "Gambling houses. Some consider them a necessary evil, but they've broken more families than winsome maidservants."

"It happened. I'm not angry about it anymore."

"Oh, I don't believe that for a second."

Her remark took Evie aback. "I'm sorry?"

"You spent enough time in that life to know what it's like."

Evie fought against the instinct to squirm under the duchess's gaze. "Be that as it may, I came here for a different reason."

"Yes, yes. This vital *information* of yours. I can't wait to hear this."

"It's of a delicate nature." Evie glanced at the seamstresses, who at least had the grace to pretend not to be eavesdropping.

"I should hope so." She touched one of the girls on the shoulder. "Wider stitches, Tessa. My old eyes can barely see yours."

"Yes, your grace," the girl murmured.

The duchess turned back and gave Evie a full inspection for the first time. "You look like you could use a cup of tea. Come on, then."

Evie followed her into an adjacent room. The far door

whisked shut as they entered. There were two plush armchairs on either side of a gold-inlaid table. A teapot and two cups of exquisite porcelain waited there, too. Maybe the duchess was this well-prepared by chance. More likely, she wanted to take Evie's measure before inviting her in for a private conversation. How many people in the queendom would kill for a chair in a private room with the Duchess of Eskirk? More than Evie dared count, that was for certain.

The duchess gestured vaguely at a chair. Evie moved in front of it, but made sure the other woman had settled herself before taking a seat. One never sat while a lady of higher station was on her feet. Then she lowered herself slowly onto the cushion, fanning out her skirts with her hands just so. *A curtsy to the chair,* her mother had called it. Strange how old, hard-won habits came back so easily.

The tea smelled ready. "Shall I pour you a cup?"

"Not yet, child. I find it best to wait a few minutes after sitting." She sighed. "Never get old. It's the absolute worst."

Evie hid her smile behind her hand.

"You're amused," the duchess said.

"I'm sorry, your grace. It's just that you're a little… different than I imagined."

"Let me guess. You heard I was a merciless witch who orders executions as if they're bodily functions."

That's your reputation verbatim. "Not in those particular words," she said, with appropriate decorum.

"A reputation is a useful tool," said the duchess. "Being known as such helps me keep the other nobles in line."

"That's part of why I'm here, actually," Evie said. "A shipment of imperial dreamwine was recently stolen from the queen's highway."

The duchess kept her face as still as marble. "You don't say."

"It happened fifty leagues east of the imperial border, on the highway between–"

"Fairhurst and Brycewold," the duchess finished for her.

"How much should I read into the fact that you have these details?"

"As much as you need to, your grace."

The duchess scoffed. "I can't say I'm entirely surprised. The border duchies have been slipping for years."

"What if I told you that it was not entirely their fault? That someone had hired a crew to take the wine at that specific location?"

"I'd say that's an interesting theory. Or more accurately, an interesting accusation." She leaned forward to check the teapot. "Still not ready." She leaned back again, and put the full weight of her gaze on Evie. "I'd ask who underwrote the operation to steal the shipment, but the answer only matters if you can prove it."

"What would you consider sufficient proof?" Evie asked.

"Twelve barrels of imperial dreamwine."

Of course she'd say that. But Evie wasn't foolish enough to think she could drive a wagonload of wine barrels in here without attracting attention. Or to believe she'd be permitted to leave with it, if she'd done so. The duchess was not so wealthy that she could ignore a veritable fortune within her gates.

This was a delicate game, but she wouldn't have a lot of time in the duchess's company, so she made her best play. She took the heavy bundle out of her bag and unwrapped the cloth from around the dark glass of the finest bottle Darin had squirreled away in the larder. The cork came out with a satisfying *pop*. She poured two fingers into her own empty teacup, glad to have not used it for actual tea.

The Jewel Empire might claim that an imperial vintner was necessary to verify the provenance and custody chain of its precious wine. In truth, anyone who'd had it before knew that imperial dreamwine had a certain shimmer when poured. Judging by the duchess's quick intake of breath, she recognized it, too.

"May I offer you–"

"Please." The duchess shoved her teacup forward. "When you said you'd brought a gift, I had no idea…"

Evie poured her a more generous amount, equivalent to what a decent farrier might earn in half a year. The duchess lifted her cup and swirled around the silvery liquid. "Gods, so the rumors are true. Should I be concerned that a host of Groktar soldiers are about to show up at my gate?"

"I wouldn't be so careless, your grace," Evie said.

The duchess lifted her cup and tried a sip. Whatever she saw made her close her eyes, and lean back in her chair with a sigh. After a moment she tilted her head. "Aren't you going to try it?"

"It's a gift for you. All yours."

"Well, aren't you a polite little bird?" She took another sip, and the tension fell away from her shoulders. "Go on, girl. I don't want to drink alone."

Evie's hand shook a little as she lifted her teacup. The porcelain was thin as paper, and somehow worthy of the most expensive substance in the queendom. She brought it to her lips and took a delicate nip of it. The wine rolled across her tongue like a caress. The drawing room faded.

A great room with a roaring fire in the hearth. Evie was a little girl, perhaps twelve, and sitting on her mother's lap playing string-fingers with her. The fire was warm and cozy, and she'd never felt as safe as—

Quick as that, the vision faded, and she was facing the duchess again. She'd forgotten how powerful it felt. How real. Gods, it was no wonder people paid so handsomely for this.

She didn't wait to be invited to take another sip.

She lay in her childhood bed, tucked firmly into silken sheets that felt like clouds. Her mother brushed her hair, singing softly to her, while Father looked on from the doorway. They thought her asleep. They looked down at her and then at one another, and smiled in the intimate way of a couple deeply in love.

Back to the drawing room, and somehow her teacup was empty. So was her host's, but the woman made no move to refill them. Instead she fixed Evie with a level gaze and asked, "So, who was it?"

"I don't know her name," Evie said. She forced the nostalgia out of her mind; she needed to focus.

"So, it's a woman. A highborn, I'm guessing, or you wouldn't have come to me."

"She called herself Zora."

The duchess pressed her lips together in a disapproving sort of way.

She knows her. "I'm told it's more of a nickname," Evie said.

"Her real name is Lazora Fanelle."

"Fanelle?" The name tickled a memory in Evie's mind, from her childhood lessons on the highborn families of the Old Queendom. "There's a marquis by that name. In Brycewold, if I'm not mistaken."

"There *was* a marquis. Now there's a widow. Does she have the wine already in her possession?" the duchess asked.

"No, but she expects to soon."

"Why are you telling me this?"

"I thought someone should be aware, and the queen doesn't exactly return my letters." It came out harsher than she intended, but she met the other woman's gaze and held it.

The duchess laughed softly. "You're just like her."

Just like Zora? "You'll forgive me if I don't take that as a compliment," Evie said stiffly. She could be cold when she needed to, but Zora took delight in cruelty.

"No, not Zora. Your mother."

The words hit like a splash of frigid water. For a moment, Evie couldn't think of anything to say. "I was not aware that you knew her well," she managed at last.

"She didn't tell you?" The duchess huffed. "Now it's my turn to be offended. We were friends as girls, before your father stole her away from court." Her face fell. "I was sorry to hear of their difficulties. And a bit surprised that she didn't ask me for help."

Evie's heart sank into her stomach. The thought that her mother not only knew the Duchess of Eskirk but might have come to her for help and avoided their troubles, was almost more than she could bear. For so long, she'd assumed it was fate that sent her family down this road. The thought that it might have been pride somehow seemed worse. "Would you have given it?" she asked, her voice breaking a little.

"Probably not. Your father would only have gambled it away."

"Oh." So it wouldn't have changed anything. Knowing that took away some of the old heartache that tightened Evie's chest. She drew a shaky breath, then steadied herself. "Sometimes I wonder if there was anything I could have said, or done, to…"

"Nonsense. You were a little girl, and it wasn't your fault. People are who they are, and very little can change that. Like Zora, for example. I trust I don't need to tell you what happens once you hand over the wine."

Evie shook her head. Truth be told, that's what really bothered her about the arrangement. Every scenario that she played out in her head ended with Zora holding both the wine *and* the last payment. Usually with Darin, Kat, and Tom dead in a gutter somewhere. There wasn't much time, either. Kat and the boys would be arriving before long. Then things would start happening very fast. "She knows how to find us. And I can't think of a way not to give it to her."

The duchess pursed her lips. "Whose idea was it to take the wine so close to the border? Yours or hers?"

"Hers."

"What about the vintner?" the duchess asked.

"What about him?"

"Did Zora want him, too?"

Evie rolled her shoulders. "She always spoke of the wine. I don't think the vintner was part of it." A cold thought intruded, the possibility that Zora assumed "wine" meant "wine with vintner to certify it." *I hope she won't claim we failed on a technicality.*

"Then she can't intend to sell it," the duchess said. "I don't suppose she told you her plans?"

"Hardly. I had a thought for what she might intend, but it makes little sense."

"Share it anyway."

"What if she intends to give the wine back?"

"To the empire," the duchess said flatly.

"To the empress herself. But I don't claim to understand why she would."

"I can think of a few reasons, none of them good," the duchess said.

"Perhaps the queen could–"

The duchess snorted, interrupting her. "The queen hasn't gotten out of bed in half a year. Don't expect any help there."

Lord and Lady. It was no secret the queen's health had declined, but this sounded far worse. "That's unfortunate."

"It falls to us to look after the queendom until her majesty recovers."

"We would be... deeply appreciative if you could find some way to assist us." Evie plucked out the other item she'd brought, a single sheet of parchment with a wax seal. "It isn't much, but I'm prepared to offer this in return."

The duchess skimmed the parchment, and a hint of surprise flickered over her face. It was the first real show of emotion she'd given so far. Gods, but she played the game well. "It's not exactly the thing I normally go for."

"I understand. But it's all we've got."

"It will take some time to put words in the right ears."

Evie fought the frown that wanted to form on her face. Time was another thing she had very little of. "What would you have us do in the interim?"

"Make sure that the wine finds its way to somewhere safe. As far away from Zora as possible." She fixed Evie with a sharp look. "That being said, under no circumstances should stolen dreamwine come anywhere close to Eskirk lands."

"I understand, your grace."

She already knew what would have to be done. All she had to do was convince Darin.

CHAPTER FIFTY-NINE
Placations

Darin waited at the rendezvous point as twilight fell. He'd come alone, but not because he didn't trust the others. Tom was too recognizable, Kat too green – though she'd come a long damn way, that was for certain. Anyone who could single-handedly recover a stolen shipment from Annette's crew had a bright future in this world. Evie had been right on two counts. First, that this was the safest option for the dreamwine, and second that he'd hated the idea. He didn't trust the Dame not to interfere, hostages or no. Once word got out that an imperial wine shipment had been taken inside the queendom – and word *always* got out, as the constant references to the bathing merchant job had demonstrated – they'd be facing threats from every direction. The very existence of such contraband would draw opportunists from all corners of the realm.

Now, with darkness falling and no Groktar in sight, he had a moment to question the wisdom in sending word through intermediaries to request a meeting with the imperial soldiers. Tom had been right. This was foolishness. He was too exposed out here, and he should've known the guard captain wouldn't respond to his invitation.

Hoofbeats echoed through the woods. *Here we go.*

Three riders swept into view. Groktar. Thank the Four. Captain Guirao had apparently ignored the part about coming alone. Darin let them reach the clearing before he stepped out of the shadows. "Captain," he called.

Guirao reined in, but her two men kept going. They swept the full edge of the clearing – ignoring Darin as they passed – and rode back to her. All three dismounted. The captain spoke quietly with them, then came forward on her own.

Darin walked to meet her, his shoulders tense. This part of his plan made him the most nervous of all. "You didn't come alone," he said.

"Oh, you thought we should trust you?"

She had a point. Two men simply meant she was being cautious. Six or eight would have been far more worrisome.

Darin let it pass. "I hope your vintner was not hurt." The last time he'd seen the man, he was unconscious and tucked behind a boulder, but none of the rumors about the heist had mentioned him. The portly fellow might have been from the Jewel Empire and part of the winemaking enterprise, but Darin didn't want even more blood on his hands.

"Physically, he is well. The rest of that matter is between him and the empress."

Darin grimaced. "That sounds uncomfortable."

"Not nearly as uncomfortable as my discussion with her will probably go," she said.

She'll be executed, most likely, Darin realized. The empress would want to make an example.

"I might be able to help with that," Darin said. "How would you like your wagon back?"

"With the wine?"

"Yes."

The captain's face betrayed nothing. "In exchange for what?"

"Amnesty. From you and your men."

Otherwise they'd never be able to stop moving, stop running. The Jewel Empire still controlled the border, and as far as he could tell, gave little scrutiny to those riding into the queendom.

Guirao wore distrust like a mask. "If you're giving it back, why take it at all?"

"Because it hadn't been done, and I like a challenge," Darin said.

Her hand went to the sword at her belt. "You have some nerve thinking that you can arrange a meeting, boast to my face, and live to see the morning."

"I also have the dreamwine, which you'll never see again if you so much as touch me."

They stared at one another for a long moment. Maybe he was wrong, and she would take a petty revenge over a chance at redemption. But he dared not let his uncertainty show. The meeting balanced on a dagger's edge. Then she dropped her shoulders, and let go of her sword. "You'll give it back, and all you want is amnesty?"

"That's what I'm proposing, yes."

She mulled this for a moment, then shook her head. "I don't believe you. More importantly, I don't trust you."

"I'm close to being offended, captain."

"Good."

This wasn't going the way he needed it to, so he tried another angle. "You might not agree with me on this, but we're not that different, you and I."

"You're right," she said.

"I am?"

"You're right that I don't agree. One of us is a lifetime soldier whose career is in the rubbish pile. The other is the criminal responsible for putting it there."

He bit back a sigh. *Walked right into that one.* "I take it you've spent time in the empire. Ever get to the Nose?" That was the nickname for the southeast portion of the Jewel Empire, owing to the fact that the empire itself resembled the shape of a woman's face.

"What about it?"

Darin didn't like talking about his childhood, and avoided

it whenever he could. Most of those were not memories he cherished. He kept them locked up tight, but that vault would have to open a crack if he meant to bring her around. He switched to Vlaskan. "I grew up there, too. In a tiny work hamlet called Depretis."

Something tightened in her face when he said the name.

"You know it?" he asked.

"On the slopes of the Chalcedonian Plateau," she said in Vlaskan, with no trace of an accent. An imperial servant through and through.

"Yes," Darin said, back in the queen's tongue. He'd made his point.

"You were a vineyard laborer."

He nodded. "I was eight years old when they tapped us to work the vines. My brother was ten. We picked fruit twelve hours a day. Actually *wrapped our hands* around food, but were forbidden from eating." Just the memory of it made him clench his fists. He took a breath and forced his fingers open.

"That's a hard life," she said.

More than you know. He'd escaped and run as soon as he could, but not before losing his entire family to the unforgiving slopes of the empress's vineyards. "No harder than the life of one deemed suitable for Groktar training. Or so I've heard."

"You heard correctly." She lifted the sleeve of her left arm enough that he could see the scars. They were short, straight lines in parallel. Self-inflicted, judging by the angle. A hard life indeed, if that was her only escape.

"Then you understand," Darin said.

"So we might have had similar childhoods. That doesn't make us friends."

"For what it's worth, you and your men lived up to the Groktar reputation. I'm sorry about the heist," he said. He meant it, though perhaps not exactly in the way he made it sound.

"Your apology is not accepted."

"I'm offering it anyway," he said irritably. He didn't really expect forgiveness from a hardened Groktar commander, but this damn woman refused to give him an inch.

"Your giant injured three of my men," she said. "One of them quite seriously."

"But none of them were killed. You have to give us some credit for that." It wasn't easy to pull off jobs like this without putting bodies on the ground. That's why Darin always considered his crew a level above someone like Harrison, who razed and killed without a second thought.

"I will grant that you didn't take any lives, at least not directly. My men will heal. The Groktar reputation will not."

"I have an idea for that, actually," Darin said.

"I can't wait to hear it."

He ignored the jibe. "No one knows about our meeting here. When you return with the wine in your possession, it falls to you to explain how that happened."

"Is this the part where you want Groktar singing praises of your generosity?"

"Quite the opposite." No one would believe that, anyway. "The story I'd tell, if I were you, is that you and your men hunted down those responsible. Took back what was yours, and showed no mercy."

She stared at him.

"That's what you'd have done if you caught us, isn't it?" he pressed.

"With extreme prejudice."

"No one can deny that the dreamwine was taken. That rumor has already found its way out into the world. But this little fiction preserves the Groktar reputation of perseverance without mercy."

"For that to convince anyone, you'd have to be dead and gone."

"We will be." He'd faked his death on more than one occasion in the past. Sometimes it was the only way to get a debt forgiven, and even then, it didn't always work.

"It would have to be a convincing ruse," she said.

"No harder than masquerading as a Groktar commander."

"You made a dozen tiny mistakes. If I'd paid enough attention, you'd be rotting in a ditch somewhere."

That might still happen, he didn't say. "Even so. With no one around to dispute it, the final word on this incident will be yours."

She was tempted. It showed on her face. But the desire warred with uncertainty. "Why would you do all of this?" she asked at last.

"Because a life on the run, always looking over your shoulder, is not worth living." And because there was no safer place for imperial dreamwine than in her possession.

"Which is why you want the amnesty."

"For me and my associates, starting the moment you give your word."

The captain stared at him for a long moment. "You can have it for this transgression," she said. "Not future ones."

"Fair enough." Darin pulled a sheaf of parchment from his jacket pocket. There were seven, each one of them a hand-drawn map centered on the place where they stood. Each with a different location marked. He found the true one that marked the spot where the wagon of priceless dreamwine lay hidden. In the meantime, Guirao sent two of her men forward. They glared daggers at him through open visors. The bigger of the two snatched the parchment out of his hand and rode it back to the captain.

"Half a league south of here there's a dense stand of evergreens," Darin said. "You'll find a wagon there with all of your missing barrels."

"And if the wagon's not there?"

"Then I suppose the deal is off." Darin met her eyes. "But it'll be there."

"I hope I don't need to remind you to stay away from the empire and its soldiers," she said.

"I stay away from imperial soldiers as a matter of principle,"

Darin said. He wouldn't die at the hands of any Vlaskan. That was a promise he'd made to his brother, and one he intended to keep.

CHAPTER SIXTY
Sharp Ends

Darin sat alone at the smallest table in the Red Rooster's common room. The weather had begun to turn, and the chill night air drove in a crowd for the warm hearth and boisterous company. Men and women packed the other tables elbow to elbow around him. Behaving themselves, for the most part, owing to Tom's hulking presence near the door. Kat was slinging ale with both hands to keep them all content. She'd changed the ale recipe yet again, and now the brew had a slight onion aftertaste. It said something about the weather that the regulars were still drinking it.

Darin had told Zora to come tomorrow morning to take delivery. Naturally, he wasn't surprised to look up and find her standing in front of him. Her men trailed in after her, dark specters in chainmail with swords at their belts. She had twice as many this time, perhaps a full dozen. They took up positions around the room, hands on their sword hilts.

"Thought you were coming tomorrow," Darin said.

"I'm a busy woman."

And you thought I might be in the wind by tomorrow, Darin didn't add. "Order you a drink?"

"Considering what your girl served up at the outpost, I think I'll pass," Zora said. She took a purse from one of her men and plunked it down on the table. "The rest of your payment, as promised."

The coins were all there. Darin knew them as he would

a close friend. All silver this time, and so pure that its song was deafening. He remembered the thrill of reaching for that power on the bridge, and that made it all the more tempting. Still, there was one coin not present, and he didn't bother to hide his disappointment. "What about the goat?"

"Oh, this goat?" She dropped it down on the table.

He sensed the silver of it, but nothing more. No trace of the metallurgy that he'd put on it, in his fumbling attempts under Seraphina's supervision. Gods, it must have been child's play to flip that around. "Yes, that goat."

She kept it pinned beneath her index finger, and slid it away when he reached for it. "I think I'll hang onto it. I might need you again in the future."

Damn. That was always the trouble with an extortion deal. Now that he saw how it felt to be on the raw end of one, he almost regretted some of his previous dealings. "How do I know you'll eventually hand it over?"

"You don't."

Darin put on a smile that he didn't feel. "You know, I think I'll miss our business dealings."

"And I'm going to miss the smell of this shithole. Now, where's my dreamwine?"

"I'm not entirely sure," Darin said.

Zora's eyes narrowed. "What does that mean?"

Darin took a long pull of his ale and only grimaced a little. The onions were getting stronger with time. "Well, I assume that the Groktar are almost back to the imperial border, but the captain wasn't entirely forthcoming about their plans." He furrowed his brow. "She has some serious trust issues."

"You gave it *back*?"

"Yes. You know, I've heard that *giving back* imperial dreamwine is a great way to win favor with the empress. I'm expecting an invitation to the Jewel Palace at any moment."

"Given the last letter she received from Darin Fields, I wouldn't hold my breath if I were you."

A chill settled in Darin's stomach. "What did you say?"

Zora adopted a mocking tone. "Dear empress, your heartless workers killed my brother."

How could she know that? A letter he'd sent the empress as a child, and now Zora threw his own words back in his face.

"It sounds like he was a criminal, too," Zora said. "I'm curious. What sort of crime did he commit?"

"He stole a handful of grapes," Darin said dully. "He did that sometimes, mostly so that I'd have something to eat. Kept me alive, really. The orchard handlers finally caught him."

"What happened to him?"

"He died in the stockade."

Zora's lips quirked. "Well, that's the penalty for stealing in the empire."

Darin gripped the hilt of his dagger. He'd have gutted her then and there, if it wouldn't get everyone killed. He took a deep breath. And then another.

She reclaimed her purse of silver and leaned over his table. "It sounds like you're not going to be useful to me anymore. I have a strict policy on tools that outlive their usefulness."

"That sounds... well, exhausting," Darin said.

"Now would be a good time to tell your patrons to leave. Anyone still here in two minutes will regret it."

She gave no signal that he could see, but her men shifted simultaneously, coming up on the balls of their feet. Ready for a single order to do murder. In their dark mail and leathers, they wouldn't have trouble picking out friend from foe here.

"How many people are you prepared to kill in the name of your little barony?"

A flicker of uncertainty crossed Zora's face. It unsettled her that he knew, he could see it. "As many as it takes. Speaking of which, where's the girl?"

"What girl?"

"That slender little Garraway girl."

Darin pressed his lips together. *Yet another level to the Dame's betrayal.* Gods knew, Evie was careful with her name. "She's away at the moment."

"No matter. We'll find her."

"Oh, I'll tell you where she is," he said lightly. "She's dining with the Duchess of Eskirk. Her grace was *most* curious to hear more about our joint efforts on the dreamwine." He paused and tapped his chin, as if thoughtful. "I did promise to send word that all was well after we made our exchange. If I failed to do so, well... I imagine all sorts of interesting things might come up in their conversation."

"Such as what?"

"Oh, a baroness conspiring with a criminal organization to steal and then return a priceless trade commodity, all to win some points with a foreign leader." Darin leaned close and whispered, "Some might even call that treason."

"I sincerely doubt a peer would take the word of a trollop over mine," Zora said. "Even if the duchess believed such a fantasy, she'd never prove it."

"Would she really have to, though?"

Zora smirked. "You certainly make for an entertaining adversary."

"One of my many talents in life."

Zora leaned forward. "We both know how this is going to end. Because I admire your tenacity, I'll tell my men to be quick about it."

"Such generosity," Darin said, with mock sincerity.

She frowned, and then gestured almost lazily at Darin. "Take him."

The closest retainer came around the corner of the bar toward him. One of the inn's patrons happened to be getting up and stepped in his way. The next retainer was closing from the other side, already loosening his sword in its scabbard. Two more of the patrons began shouting at one another in front of a table, and leaped to their feet right in front of him. Hands on one another's collars, barring the retainer's path. Another bit of luck.

"I said, *take him*!" Zora snapped.

Her retainers jumped to obey, but the whole common room was moving. Mugs clattered down. Wooden chairs scraped against the floor. Patrons came to their feet and swarmed over the retainers, four or five to a man. Knives and daggers came out of boots, out of shirtsleeves. In less than twenty seconds, every single one of Zora's men had cold steel at his throat.

The room went still.

A fair-haired man with an overlarge mustache made his way through the patrons toward them, and put a hand on Zora's shoulder. "Guard-captain Salbas, m'lady. Her grace the Duchess of Eskirk requests your presence."

Zora shook off his hand. "Eskirk has no authority here."

"Are you willing to risk the lives of your retainers on that belief?" Darin asked.

She shrugged. "Do as you will. Retainers can be replaced."

It was almost fascinating to witness the change on the nearest retainer's face when she said that. It had been a mask of cold determination. A readiness to do whatever she ordered, even if it meant death. Now he frowned, and his shoulders sank a little. His hand, which moments ago had white knuckles where he gripped the hilt of his sword, now fell away from it.

"As it happens, her grace the Duchess of Eskirk owns the Red Rooster Inn," Darin said.

"What?"

Darin examined his fingernails as if unconcerned. "Turns out she liked what she heard about this place, and thus decided to acquire the establishment."

"Into which you've entered without invitation," Salbas added. "And into which you brought armed men prepared to do violence."

Darin spread out his hands. "I'd say that gives her more than just cause in demanding your presence for an explanation."

Zora clamped her mouth shut and said nothing, but glared daggers at him.

"On your feet, please, Lady Fanelle," said the guard-captain. He hauled her up by the arm in a decidedly ungentle manner.

Her retainers made no effort to intervene.

"A moment, guard-captain." Darin slid around the table and drew the sheathed dagger from Zora's belt. With his other hand, he palmed the Ganari goat from the table. "I don't want her to get any ideas."

"Appreciate that," the man said.

Darin glanced down at the man's rapier. "Though with a sword like that, I'm sure you'd be able to handle things just fine. It looks well-balanced."

"It is. Right this way, m'lady." He and his men escorted Zora and her retainers out of the door, and into the cold autumn night.

CHAPTER SIXTY-ONE
What Remains

Darin, Kat, Evie, and Big Tom lounged around a pair of mismatched tables in the Rooster's common room. It had taken Evie several days to tear herself away from the attentions of the Duchess of Eskirk, who'd apparently taken quite a shine to her. Seraphina was hanging around too, minding the bar while they took a minute for a quiet celebration.

"So let me get this straight," Kat said. "We don't have the wine. We don't have Zora. And now the Duchess of Eskirk owns this place?"

Darin brought over a tray of four mugs and handed them out. "That's just the cost of doing business."

"We're still alive, I guess," Tom said. "That's good for something."

"Officially speaking, we're quite dead," Darin said. "Those Groktar soldiers showed us little mercy."

"Right, I need to remember that," Tom said.

"Were they as good as you'd hoped? I forgot to ask."

Tom smiled. "Better. Haven't had that much fun in years."

Darin lifted his cup. "I'll drink to that."

The others drank, but he waited. He wanted to see their reactions.

Evie gasped. "Gods! This is dreamwine!"

"I may have switched out one of the barrels. Captain Guirao didn't notice."

She took another sip of it, more delicately this time. Her eyes sparkled with some distant memory. He had a guess but left her to enjoy it in peace.

Kat's shoulders fell; she exhaled slowly. "Tastes like… home. A warm drink by the fire, with the door barred and the boys asleep in their beds."

"What is it for you, Tom?" Darin asked.

He grinned in a boyish way. "Milk and honey. My ma used to make that for me when I was a boy, because I was always so hungry." His brow furrowed. "Haven't thought about that in a long time."

Darin looked at Evie. "What about you?" he asked, though he expected he knew. *The life she lost is not something you can easily forget.*

"You remember that night we spent in the woods in Fairhurst?" she asked.

"After rigging the horse races." That was the first job they all did together. Starter stuff, really. A new crew finding its footing together.

She nodded. "We stopped at that little copse of evergreens to camp for the night. The needles were brittle from the drought. We were all so parched, we could barely even talk. Do you recall what happened next?"

Like it was yesterday. "It started to rain. For the first time in weeks." She'd used a wide, heart-shaped leaf to pour the dew-sweet water into his mouth. Both of them laughing in sheer joy and relief. They'd still been together back then, too. Were they together now? He really wasn't sure. There was no question that night in the woods, though. Gods, what a time it had been.

"I felt like I'd found a family." Sadness flickered across her face, and then surprise. "I didn't think I'd be that happy again."

Darin loved her for that. She gave him the courage to try his own mug. Part of him already knew what the strange magic of imperial dreamwine would bring. It fell on his tongue, light and cool as a summer rain. He wasn't trying to taste the fruit, but he did. First the smooth skin of the grapes, still chalky from the dust-fine dirt of the vineyards. Then the biting-tart sweetness within them. He could hear his brother's voice, see those bright, furtive eyes that had watched over him. Feel the calloused skin of his hands, when he'd let the boy that Darin had been squeeze them until the hunger cramps went away. All of the sensations came and went in a heartbeat, leaving only the fading memory of a life cut too short, and the lingering heartache that the loss left behind.

Evie reached out and put her hand on his. She knew. That was her real talent, winnowing out the darkest part of an already-dark soul.

"So what did you swap this out for?" Kat asked.

"A barrel of Red Rooster's finest."

"They got the short end of that stick, I'll admit it. We'll have no trouble selling this."

"We can't call it what it is, though," Darin said. "If the captain got word of it, she'd be paying us a visit."

"I'll say it's a new batch of ale. And that I got lucky."

"No claiming credit for the job, either," Darin said.

Evie groaned. Tom frowned into his cup.

"What?" Kat asked. "We're going to need the work. Is the duchess even going to let us stay here for long? I'll have to find somewhere to stash the boys until we figure things out."

"This should hold us for a while." Darin dug the heavy purse out of his jacket and tossed it on the table. Soft metal clinked. A lot of soft metal.

Evie sucked in a sharp breath.

"Where did that come from?" Kat demanded.

"Our former client."

"She took it back. I saw it myself. Didn't she, Tom?"

"Thought so," Tom rumbled.

Darin shrugged. "What can I say? Before the guard-captain escorted her out, this purse found its way back into my hands."

And I figured I might as well get some practical use out of metallurgy, if it's going to be part of my future.

Seraphina winked at him from behind the bar. She knew, of course. She didn't love the types of things he'd asked her to teach him, but she was pleased that he was asking.

"I won't say you've totally redeemed yourself, but you're getting close," Kat said.

Evie rubbed his shoulder. "Yes, he is."

"I'm glad you feel that way, Evie. I was thinking, maybe you and I could take a little trip. Just the two of us."

"Ooh, somewhere nice this time?"

"Pure elegance, I'm told."

She gave him a little smile, but it was full of promise. "Aw, and I was beginning to think you took me for granted."

He laughed. "I'd never make that mistake. But I think you'll be pleased by where we're going. It's a castle large enough to host the finest gala in the queendom."

She frowned. "Eskirk?"

"Yes." He grinned, and held up the heavy purse of silver. "We're going to buy our inn back."

AUTHOR'S NOTE

Thank you for reading my book! I'm grateful that you gave it a chance. If you liked it, I hope you'll recommend *Silver Queendom* to a friend or leave a review at your favorite retailer site. Word of mouth is so powerful for up-and-coming authors like myself.

To learn more about me and hear about my upcoming books, please join my mailing list at:

http://dankoboldt.com/subscribe

Sign up and you'll get at least one free story to read. You can also find me on Twitter: @DanKoboldt.

Many people helped this book become a reality, but I'd like to thank a few in particular. My critique partner Dannie Morin is the reason the dialogue works. She also helped me realize that Darin and Evie deserved at least one night together. Mike Mammay gave an outstanding critique (as usual) and continues to advise me long after his career surpassed my own. My writing/support groups – Transpatial Tavern and The Clubhouse – helped me stay sane along the long journey to this moment.

I'm deeply grateful to my agent Paul Stevens, who read *Silver Queendom* several times and provided useful feedback at each turn. He also found it a home with the wonderful team at Angry Robot Books. The Robot Army welcomed me with open arms. I'd especially like to thank Eleanor Teasdale for believing in this book, and Gemma Creffield, Paul Simpson,

Travis Tynan, Rob Triggs, and Desola Coker for helping get it ready for the world. The gorgeous cover was designed by Alice Coleman.

Last but not least, I should thank my wife Christina for hours of proofreading and years of putting up with me in general.

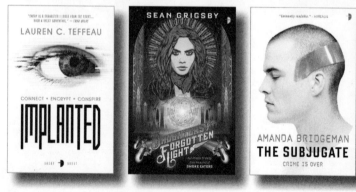